HORSEFEVER

HORSEFEVER

a novel by

Lee Hope

American Fiction Series

©2016 by Lee Hope
First Edition
Library of Congress Control Number: 2014950574
ISBN: 978-0-89823-332-2
e-ISBN: 978-0-89823-333-9
American Fiction Series

Cover design by Jamie Hohnadel
Cover painting by Richard Lethem
Interior design by Daniel Shudlick
Author photo by William Betcher

The publication of *Horsefever* is made possible by the generous support of
Minnesota State University Moorhead, The McKnight Foundation, the Daw-
son Family Endowment, and other contributors to New Rivers Press.

For copyright permission, please contact Frederick T. Courtright at 570-839-
7477 or permdude@eclips.net.

New Rivers Press is a nonprofit literary press associated with Minnesota State
University Moorhead.

Alan Davis, Director and Senior Editor
Nayt Rundquist, Managing Editor
Kevin Carollo, MVP Poetry Coordinator
Vincent Reusch, MVP Prose Coordinator
Thom Tammaro, Poetry Editor
Wayne Gudmundson, Consultant
Suzzanne Kelley, Consultant

Publishing interns:
Laura Grimm, Anna Landsverk, Desiree Miller, Mikaila Norman

Horsefever book team:
Molly Christenson, Zana Pommier, Jessica Steinke

♾ Printed in the USA on acid-free, archival-grade paper.

Horsefever is distributed nationally by Small Press Distribution.

New Rivers Press
c/o MSUM
1104 7th Avenue South
Moorhead, MN 56563
www.newriverspress.com

To Bill, my heart

CONTENTS

••••

••••

PART 1

NIKOLE AND CLIFF

SHE BENDS OVER HIM, MASSAGES his firm straight legs, and says, "You can do it, babe. You're the best when you want to be, which isn't often, but don't be afraid. You're just excited like me, and we can't help that. We've got the same temperament, both revved up, but we don't want to lose control, do we? Because then we won't win."

She's murmuring to Beau as she straps a galloping boot around each lower leg and fastens each Velcro strip even while he shifts and tosses his head and stomps. "You won't kick me, will you? Don't even think of it." Raising her voice a notch, Nikki winds and fastens the fourth boot, to protect his legs when he jumps. Then she steps back, hears the rustles of other horses in nearby stalls in this stark show barn. Beau's slicked black mane neatly braided, long black tail combed out, hooves buffed, studded iron shoes picked clean, bay coat curried and brushed, ShowSheen sprayed on, and between his legs, his sheath cleaned, penis drawn up inside it—geldings protective of their private parts from painful past experience.

Now all that's left, she thinks, is to compete, to win. She has evented Beau for two seasons at Intermediate, and he often places, when he doesn't get eliminated. A jokester, he bolts, bucks, balks, just for the fun of it. So he's sometimes dangerous, and the course south of South Woodstock is a challenging, hilly, two-and-a-half-mile run with a couple water jumps, which Beau hates. If she can only keep him in balance and get the proper rhythm and speed, she thinks, but he's a rusher, gets too hot, too turned on, too hyped. They feed off each other's energy, can't seem to stop, fear flitting like microscopic fireflies flashing off and on in her blood.

She draws in breath, and the sweet fragrance of fresh hay blends with the sweet-sour smell of manure and the particular heavy horsey scent that she has lived with every day these last many years. To her it's as if the entire world smells of horses—like willows and wildflowers and hair and dirt and sweat all mixed.

Beau's prancing, turning, turning, in his stall. She strokes his tensed, arched neck to calm him down, murmuring, "Baby, you're the best, and if I love you, you'll love me back. That's love, isn't it?" Stroking his firm flesh.

Then she thinks of Cliff, still closeted in the living quarters of their big horse rig, cordoned off in the owners' section across the lane. Her own husband won't come out to see her ride. Why shut her out when he knows if she places, she finally could move up to Advanced with Beau, her Thoroughbred bought four years ago off the track and hot-blooded, so no telling what he'll do, but that's the rush. She wants her husband to be there for her. A captive audience is better than no audience at all, isn't it?

"Beau, baby, I won't be long. Don't miss me too awfully much."

She lets herself out of the stall, glances back. Beau does not come to the half door and stick his head out to see her go. She hears his hooves whack wood, one solid rebellious thud, the whoosh of wood shavings across the stall floor.

She strides across the grassy strip, passes a few spectators in khakis or jeans and bright windbreakers, only forty degrees on an early spring morning in Vermont, even the dew is stiff. A half hour until she must tack up. She must keep her mind off winning, or she'll lose. She trots along a worn trail toward the competitors' trailers grouped behind yellow cord, ducks under it, passes many small horse trailers, then a few bigger rigs with living spaces, slant stalls, tack compartments, and comes to their six-stall rig that gleams, clean and new. When her husband drove off to buy it, she stood on their deck at home and called after him to get a used one, to spend less, but he didn't listen. It was one of his gifts to her, back when he hoped she'd only do dressage, riding circles in a ring, a stylized gymnastics. Dressage is too safe, too subtle, too many rules. She yearned to let loose, take jumps again, her old youthful desire flowing back, that craving for liftoff, suspension, flight, like two bodies in one, like she sometimes feels making love with Cliff, losing herself. And she has a self she wants to lose, contradictory, often at odds with itself, like now, wanting horses and wanting Cliff. Opposites.

So it drives her to frustration now that he hibernates in the cramped living compartment of their rig. A big bear of a man, inward turning, with his part intense German, part brooding Norwegian heritage. He's shut up doing the accounts for his properties, shutting her out the way he can, but she keeps going after him, as if to say, "Here I am, look at me," like she said growing up to her father who never looked for long. If she works hard enough, she thinks, she can get Cliff to do more than look, way more. Maybe get him to change his mind about her eventing. Although Cliff never changes his mind. Once he decides, that's it. But she'll try, try again.

❖ ❖ ❖

Cliff glances up as she takes a step in and leans against the metal trailer door. The second he sees his wife's flushed face, he senses her excitement, that rosy blush to her cheeks like she gets when she's having sex. Her face too pink, too flamboyant, too sweet, a radiant, small, fine-boned face, eyes too big, lips too full. The face of a whore, he thinks, but a high-class one, her small body clad in high, shining black custom boots with spurs attached and skin-tight beige britches. She tap-taps her crop against one boot.

"You wouldn't go to war without a weapon," one of her many riding coaches said. In her bright blue jersey with its golden racing stripe, and her protective vest, she doesn't look like somebody with a death wish. Cliff has married an addict who has to take ever bigger risks, not just ride on the flat but jump in cross-country, a phase where almost every rider has had broken bones, some riding with casts or cracked ribs, some lying in beds with bodies crippled or comatose, some dead.

"Won't you come watch?" she asks.

"You know the answer to that."

"Then why come here at all?"

Because he wants to be with her, he thinks, but says, "If there's an accident, somebody's got to truck what's left of you off to the hospital."

She shakes her head. "I can't think of accidents an hour before they call my number. I've got to go to the warm-up area."

He says nothing to this.

She sashays over to him, the click of her boot heels on the prefab floor. She lightly strokes his thin gray-blond hair back off his high forehead. He feels suddenly self-conscious, his hairline receded so much he's almost bald. Horses don't go bald, he thinks. Then she strokes down his neck, his thick arms, and her small hands close around his big hands curled almost shut. He doesn't speak. He doesn't believe in many words when a few will do. An old accounting trick.

She slides her hand off his. "So I'm going then."

"Go on ahead."

He bends his head down over his books, the latest construction numbers for that new development he's putting in on Emersen's old farm, two hundred acres, twenty substantial homes on five acres each, the rest green space, but a serious cost overrun. He seriously dislikes overruns, and his wife is running over him now, taking serious risks.

She clicks back to the metal door, opens it. He feels her standing there, waiting. "Aren't you going to wish me luck?" she asks.

He looks up at her again, says, "Break a leg."

She stares.

He smiles a little, so she'll think it's a joke, which, he tells himself, it is. He wants her to get scared, not hurt, just scared enough to quit.

She doesn't smile back. She says, "Don't miss me too awfully much," and goes out. The metal door snaps shut. He's alone in a box. He stands, starts pacing the small perimeter of his metal space, feeling claustrophobic, too big to be cooped up in this prefab, ultramodern cell—built-in, fold-up bed, fold-up table, upscale mini kitchen and bathroom, stainless appliances—all serving to close him into a space no bigger than the stall that Thoroughbred is in. Beau's still too much for her to handle, probably twirling around by now with that pent-up energy even though he's a gelding. If a stallion, he'd be a murderer. Maybe he is anyway, Cliff thinks. Horses are dumb beasts, a brain the size of a walnut, beasts of prey, one minute can nuzzle with you, the next kick in your skull, one minute trot nicely around with you on their back, the next minute buck you off, gallop away, leave you lying with a broken neck, and never feel a lick of guilt. Sociopaths. And his wife is in love with them.

But that's better than taking a human lover, Cliff tells himself. One reason he helps to support Nikki's horse habit. Better a horse between her legs. She's only forty years old, a decade younger than he, and she's trouble even when she's sweet, even when she devotes all her overflow to him. She's overcharged, overwrought, over-sexed. She's an addict. And he loves her for it.

◆◆◆

Nikki goes out by herself—her trainer stayed home sick, maybe just as well, Biffy always only saying what's wrong—so, alone, Nikki rides Beau out into the warm-up area. Beau was tacked up by an assistant, who said, "This horse is spoiled rotten." Now Nikki takes Beau over low practice jumps, slowly cantering past other riders, calling out a jump before she takes it, all the while visualizing the cross-country course that she has walked three times, but the horses aren't allowed to see in advance.

Last night, in their motel room—Cliff refuses to stay over in the tight trailer—she straddled a rickety chair and pretended she was galloping, half out of the saddle, and she shut her eyes and pictured taking each jump with rhythm and balance, although sometimes she couldn't help but see Beau rushing a fence, suddenly balking, tossing her over his head.

"You won't hurt me, will you? Not you," she says softly now, as the cross-country steward calls her name. She heads Beau toward the starting box. Along the course, bright spectators clump near the first three jumps in the valley before the obstacles disappear over the first hill. No seriously big questions or technical jumping efforts or tight turns on the course until the water jump. Meanwhile, a hundred yards or so to the left, by the finish line, a small group of owners, society ladies in pink or green Wellies and pale mountain horse parkas, smile slightly and speak softly behind suntanned hands. Nikki is not one of them, although she was brought up in that entitled set until her father went bankrupt, and they moved to a tiny rented house, and she had to sell her show pony and ride rented ones. Now her horse is a Thoroughbred that she couldn't resist. She's got an eye for racehorses that don't want to race but might want to jump. She pays for her own horses from her savings, won't take money from Cliff, who'd buy her an expensive plug to ride dressage in the ring when she wants a roughneck bred to run, for the cross-country is judged not on form but by time and jump faults. Forget dressage for now, she thinks, all that collection and etiquette that she was brought up with. Forget. Focus.

Soon Beau's prancing around the box. With ten seconds to go, she guides him into it and silently prays to God to let her win. But then she wonders if God cares about horse shows, so she says to herself, don't expect to jump perfectly, don't take the first jumps too fast, above all, don't look down.

The starter's counting down, ". . . three, two, one, have a good ride." And she's on course, Beau galloping flat out too fast, and she's leaning back to pull him in, which only makes him charge faster and rush the first obstacle, a brush jump, but he takes it straight on, skimming over it. Don't look down. His lift so light, and she's light-headed flying across the low field toward a table jump. He arches easily over it, and pounds around a bend, too fast again toward a bank, no time to try for perfect balance plus speed. Don't lean back. Leaping up onto the bank, a stride, then a drop jump downhill, and he's taking it, thank you, God, his stride balanced now as they glide through a patch of woods. A turn through another swatch of woods, an incline, then into an open field, up ahead a ditch with a log over the center of it, a Trakehner, both wide and deep, he skims over it, and damned he's good, if he'll only make it over the water jump ahead. He has balked at ponds and streams, don't think of that, don't clamp, don't panic, don't pull back—and he's on the bank and hopping over a fence down into shallow water and sloshing toward a fence in the center of the pond, a hitch in his stride, the tiniest. "Don't look down," she says aloud to him, but then she looks down, so he pivots on hind legs, swerves to the left, and she's out of her tack and almost over his head into swirling water over a half-foot deep. He halts, just like that, in front of the fence, her arms and legs wrapped around his neck. He could've easily tossed her off.

He never stands as still as this. He's looking down into the swirling pond. It's her fault, she thinks, sliding back onto the saddle. She looked down, so he did.

He's standing still, water up to his ankles. She's pressing with her legs, quickly swinging him around. One jumper penalty, but two more attempts. They canter, splashing, circle turn, and charge straight at the jump again, she doesn't look down but thinks of it and feels a kink in his neck and feels a shot of fear and thinks, Don't run out again, and he immediately pivots left, halts in the same spot. He read her mind. A second refusal, another penalty. No way will they

make the time limit now. But she circles and takes him at
the fence one last time, riding fast at it, asking for a bold
leap, whapping once with the bat, but thinks, Don't you dare
run out, don't you dare. So he swerves hard at the exact spot,
bucks once, and she loses her seat, slides off and plops into
water, her left foot caught in the stirrup as he trots, dragging
her by one leg, on her back, drenched, up onto solid ground,
where he halts. She swivels her foot out of the stirrup and
quickly stands, dripping brown water, but feels no pain so
swings back up on and sits erect, chin up, britches sopped,
boots soggy. Eliminated.

Dripping, she wipes her face and, with a fixed little smile,
walks him slowly off the course, past spectators and clumps of
pines and a bank jump, past scrub brush and pools of mud to
the finish line, to the EMS that checks out each rider who falls.

Then she passes the bright ladies sitting inside the red and
white striped owners' tent. The shame. It's almost always the
rider's fault. "Poor baby, forgive me," she says to Beau. But
horses can't forgive humans. And they never forget. So now
what? She fell. Will Cliff congratulate himself?

She dismounts, loosens the damp girth, and leads Beau
off to the barn and inside to his assigned stall where she slides
off his bridle, slides on the halter, crossties him in the aisle,
slides off saddle, saddle pad, unstraps galloping boots, hangs
tack on pegs. He doesn't need to be walked down or sponged
off since he's not heated up, not even breathing hard, didn't
take enough jumps. He's just standing there now like an old
plug, feeling perfectly calm, perfectly fine, rolling back his
upper lip showing the pink-yellow gums, like he's smirking,
like he's saying, The joke's on you, Nikki.

She looks him in his dark eye that is opaque, reflecting
nothing, not even her image, and she asks, "Can't you give
it a rest?"

Beau sticks out his nose and grabs her wet jersey sleeve
with his teeth, doesn't bite down, just holds it, another one of
his horsey jokes. He's got perfect mouth control, could bite a
single blade of grass, could bite a chunk out of her arm if he

wanted to, but he just stands holding a swatch of her sopped jersey in his long curved teeth. She taps his nose and he lets go. So much for that, another one of his games.

She unhooks the crossties and Beau pokes his nose into the hay bag. Munching away. Happy, fulfilled, complete in himself. Sometimes she wishes she could do whatever she wants and not give a damn. But it was her fault. She got eliminated so she's still sopping. She takes off her slippery helmet, nabs a dirty horse towel, pats herself down, and walks out, stained and damp, past a couple women contestants, their sleek dry hair pulled back in dry hair nets tucked under dry safety helmets, as they tap dry braided leather bats on dry custom English boots. They nod slightly at Nikki, then look away. I'll show you, she thinks, heading back to Cliff even though he won't know how upset she is. He'll only be glad she's alive, when it's not enough just to be alive. No, not nearly enough.

❖ ❖ ❖

She barges right in and immediately fills the space, even though she's small and thin, and seems thinner now that she's dripping wet, Cliff thinks, as she strips off her protective vest, and then, helmet in hand, she taps her crop against her slick wet boot, tappety-tap. The air crackles. Cliff feels her electricity seep into his skin.

"Eliminated!" she says. "Didn't even make it past the water jump. I fell, got soaked. I'm beside myself. Just thought I'd clue you in, in case you didn't notice."

Taking it out on me, Cliff thinks. Well, I can take it. Go ahead. "You're not hurt?" he asks.

She shakes her head. "The water cushioned my fall."

She sticks one heel then the next into the bootjack and pulls off boots that leak drops of brown water onto the linoleum. She strips off sopping socks, and says, "You might have brought us luck if you'd watched."

Blaming him, so he says, "Watching's overrated. Being a spectator is a bore."

"Beau wouldn't even truly compete. He rebelled." She stands to tug off her soaked britches, her bare legs speckled with bits of mud like a black rash.

"You get what you pay for," he says.

"Because Beau's a cheap track reject?"

"Because he's not trained right. He knows you can't handle him. He's got your number."

"And what's that?" she asks, stripping off her soggy jersey, tossing it into the heap. A brown pool spreads on the floor.

Cliff shrugs. Whatever he says now, he figures he'll get attacked. "You're too gentle. The horse thinks he can run right over you. It'll only escalate."

"How do you know?" she asks, standing, hands on hips.

There it is, he's the target now. He hunkers down in his seat. A former linebacker, he'll play defense.

She says, "I'll call Biffy for more lessons."

"Biffy doesn't know enough. Neither did any of your trainers. They couldn't get inside your head. That's where the problem is."

"So tell me, Cliff, exactly what do you recommend I do?"

A real doer. Can't stop doing to save her soul. But if she can't get better at this, she'll end up broken. Can't admit he fears that.

"Hire a topnotch trainer," he says. "Somebody tough, who will correct what you're doing wrong and get you to go all out. Or else, give it up."

"You're implying I don't go all out?"

"I've seen you ride. Either you're out of control or you hold back."

She shakes her head. "It's that obvious?"

"Maybe you lack the old killer instinct," he says, thinking of his old glory days going for the jugular on the college football field.

She strips off her wet undershirt, down to a wet sports bra and panties. And then she walks a few steps to stand over him. Even with him seated, she's only a little taller. If he stood up now, he thinks, she'd shrink to seem a little kid, which she definitely is not.

"I'm not giving up eventing, Cliff, and you know it."

She's as stubborn as he is, he thinks, when it comes to her obsession. So be preemptive. Run a blitz.

He says, "Then I'll buy you one."

"Buy me what?"

"A new trainer. Consider it our anniversary gift."

She sits down at that, on the one other chair, a little prefab, flimsy thing at the prefab table. Have to fold up the table to have enough space to fold down the bed.

"Our anniversary," she repeats.

"Our fifteenth. In two weeks." Thinking this is only the second marriage for each of them, so it's not that hard to keep score.

"Oh, yes . . . But you're against my eventing."

"While you were out there riding, I was in here thinking."

"You changed your mind?" Smiling a bit as if she's won.

"I just don't want to be the whipping boy for what you can't get."

"You think I'm frustrated?" she asks.

"*I* sure am."

She stares at him, cocks her head, maybe suddenly remembering they haven't had sex in one month. Which he sure as hell hasn't forgot. His eyes slide down her taut, speckled body, and she watches his slow gaze. She stands up, slips off her hair net, shakes out her long dark hair that swishes and falls over one eye, and she says, "I know what you're thinking."

He shrugs, meaning, hell yes.

"Oh, Cliff." And now she's sliding out of her mud-flecked sports bra and panties. He's eye level with breasts, outsized for her small frame. It's like her breasts have eyes looking into him. He feels a stirring at this soggy striptease.

Then she says, "I'll be right back." And she ducks into the tiny bathroom. One of her quick switches that catch him off guard, his own moods slow to shift. She comes out with a white towel and quickly wipes off her small, nude body, and towel-dries her hair. Then she comes to him and sits on his lap, straddling him like she'd sit a horse, turned on like she often gets after competing, so why not take advantage of it?

She's kissing him lightly on his cheeks, her lips close to his, a warm, light breeze on his lips. "I'll show you how to ride," she says. And she posts, hips sliding up down, forward back, her breasts like dough rising out of his hands as big as bowls. She's stroking him and saying, "If I love you, you'll love me back, won't you? Though we're so different, but we can't help that, so you won't hurt me, will you? No, you wouldn't do that."

What's she talking about, he wonders, about hurting her. It doesn't make sense, as he tenderly strokes her breasts with their dark eyes on him. He glances up and sees her other eyes drift off, and she's posting faster, and he realizes that she's not talking to him, not even really riding him. She's weaving slightly left, then right, and holds her hips up just a bit, in a half seat, like when she straddles a chair and pictures riding her horse over a jump. Right now, in this moment, Cliff could kill the beast.

Nevertheless, he gently lifts her off of him and stands, flips up the table, flops down the double bed, slowly lifts her up and lays her down on it. Then he quickly strips, and they're both nude on that hard mattress, and he's on top, and he says, "It's me, your husband. You know that?"

She grins like she's caught in the act, and then she's kissing him on the mouth at last, and, breathing into him, she says, "Cliff, you're the best."

Letting him know that she knows it's him, and she rolls on top, and she's riding again, and soon she's crying out, almost like she's falling, and he catches her with all his heart.

GABE

Mud season. Drives him nuts. Horses' hooves suck down in. He used to ride in mud until that slime-slicked day. Don't think of that. Gabe is lying on the couch in his and Carla's rented cracker box. He refuses to watch the TV, which sits across from him on a white plastic table. Sometimes he meditates and sometimes he reads those Eastern dudes, their How to Meditate books like How to Ride Dressage books. Both are light-seeking disciplines, for which reading doesn't accomplish squat. Light seeking . . . but when Gabe meditates, he often finds himself in a world dimmer than fog, like climbing into the mouths of caves, or diving deep underwater where light barely reaches, or walking outside on a faint moon-slivered night. Dark, can't tell a human from a tree from a shadow. Often he breathes in shadows and breathes them out. A Buddhist monk wrote that light and dark are inseparable and that shadows are also light. Gabe knows that murky world first-hand, like when he finds himself focusing only on what has happened *After the Fall*, as Carla calls the time after his accident. Before the Fall and After the Fall. One of their in-house jokes. They used to have more jokes Before.

In the two years After, Carla has switched from being a robust, lusty sex partner to acting like a mother superior, telling him what's right for him—time for your massage, your physical therapy, your pain killers, your bath, your walk.

Walk, hell. He wants to dance. Like Before, at the competitors' parties, when he was a single guy jiving it up, hip hop, be-bop, two-stepping with several women at once, five women riders to every man, a garden of estrogen. But after he married Carla, he only slipped once with Muffy Parker, who placed in the top ten for the high-performing list at the Rolex event. Not him, year after year a near miss, until just Before the Fall when he finally got the ride on the right mount, a Warmblood gelding owned by the president of a software company. Gabe would have qualified that time for sure, if it hadn't been for that rain-slicked cross-country course . . . Don't think of that. Don't go from shadows to blackout.

After the Muffy affair blew up, they had to leave Michigan. The horse world is a small world, reputations can quickly rise and fall. His fell. Then it rose in Illinois, until it fell again. What the hell. Except now he's a cripple with a nerve-damaged left leg, left arm, left face. Sometimes he socks his left side with his right fist and can't feel a damned thing. Can't walk without a limp. And him an almost high-performance listed athlete. His new sport has been to sit around the house and wallow in self-pity. Why not? But self-pity gets boring, so he meditates. The only trouble is that meditation is like clearing a jump. A few moments flying in air before you land, then the thrill is gone, got to do it over again.

Soon Carla will be home with her Midwestern cheer. She'll bustle about, give orders and uplifting tips, and make wisecracks. Maybe she'll bring the want ads again, some circled in red magic marker. Office jobs, indoors, yet he worked outdoors his whole life Before. Now he's as pale as a convict, let his silver-black hair grow long, ties it into a pony tail, got his ear pierced, wears a tiny gold hoop in it, should wear a ring in his nose like a pig and wallow in the mud of bitterness. He would, if it weren't for Carla. She's still got hope, but hope is yearning for what you can't get. Like the last want ad she brought home, for him to enroll in classes at a vocational school. He said, "Who's going to hire a one-armed carpenter or electrician? Besides, I've had almost two years of college." She said, "Go back to college then, become an intellectual. You lie around and read a lot anyway."

An intellectual. The bottom of the heap for a man who always had to act. But anything's okay for Carla, as long as it doesn't have to do with horses, and as long as he gets out of his funk. He calls it a funk. She calls it "a state of depression." Like it's a state of the union, a place you go to get depressed. Like this cracker box.

After the fall, almost that whole first year, he thought he was half a man, then one morning, he woke up with a hard on, and Carla rolled over and saw it through his sweatpants, and she was on him in seconds, and it functioned as it always had, if not better, because of the lay off. So now she knows the half of him that's dead does not include what's between his legs . . . and ever since, yeah, they've had some good sex, and she'll say, "Baby, you're a fine specimen," or "Baby, you're better than you think," or "Baby, you're all I need." Calling him baby, and she's become a Mama to him—take your vitamins, get a job, go outside, get some fresh air, get the red blood moving.

Doesn't she see that he's ecstatic to lie around inside and feel like shit? Some couch potatoes watch TV. He watches old eventing tapes in his head. Like his performance at the Jersey Fresh Three Star, came in fifth, can still see that bay clearing the corner jump, then the Trakehner, then the drop. The last thing he wants is his ever-loving wife hovering over him like his real mother who doted and nagged until she deserted him at age ten . . . She died drunk in a car accident, so Gabe blames her for it. Don't trust the motherly type. Mama, he started calling Carla, After. She takes it as a compliment.

Meanwhile, hell, welcome, self pity, my best friend, he thinks, while he breathes in self pity and breathes it out in the half-light of this cracker box, where he meditates on losing what he cherished most. If a god exists, he's a sadist. Any ex-Catholic knows that.

How did Carla get him to come to Vermont, shut in by hills, a valley of shadows? Maybe it's what happens after a thousand-pound horse somersaults and lands smack on top of your body and busts it up. Don't think of that.

He looks up from the vinyl floor, three rooms of that discolored prefab stuff, but in the kitchen, everything's sparkling bright like an advertisement for cleanser, Carla making their poor digs look shiny. Now he softens and thinks that without her love he'd be down and out. He owes her big time, but he also resents her for saving him. She's a busty Mother Superior of the flesh, one hundred sixty pounds, five-feet-ten inches of solid muscle, no fat, not to mention those awesome tits, and the ample ass—firm and round and fully packed. And her face, he'll admit, is still handsome at forty-five, high cheekbones, only a few wrinkles, no creases, no double chin. But what he resents most is her talk of a higher power, like he's an addict in AA, like when she said, "You need only open the door and invite Him in, and Jesus will be having dinner with you."

Jesus here for dinner? What would he and Carla and Jesus talk about at the battered Formica table? The two of them probably telling him to perk up, snap out of it, Jesus chowing down Carla's spicy hot Gang Bang Chili, or, better yet, her famous lasagna.

Gabe tries to visualize it, the way he used to visualize things when he rode, but he only gets more irritated with Carla for dragging in Jesus when she doesn't go to church and when Gabe's got Buddha and his wheel of suffering.

And then nine months ago, after they moved to Vermont, what did Carla actually drag in to save him? Not Jesus, but free weights. So Gabe actually started lifting again, with the one arm that still works. A practice that only emphasizes the difference between his two sides. The right now more bulked up, so the left looks more atrophied.

All this on account of a sport that has a bad reputation as a rich man's sport, though most competitive riders don't own their own horses, not at the higher levels. Yet outside of the horse world, you can get treated like a spoiled prig, like once at a party, a pot-bellied golfer found out Gabe evented and asked, "Is that a sport?" Gabe said, "You've got to be a triathlete because events have three phases. First, dressage like compulsory gymnastics in the ring. Second, cross-country where you gallop and jump over solid obstacles across the countryside. Third, the jumping phase over collapsible obstacles in the ring." The guy just looked at him and said, "But the horse does all the work." Gabe said, "In a sense, it's a finesse sport, like golf." The pudgy golfer said, "Golf is up to me, not up to some animal." Gabe said, "Then I'll take up golf. Get finesse without risking my life."

But after his fall, Gabe divorced horses and repudiated the horse world. Now he's a convert to the semi-dark, to meditating on his half-numb nerves, as if his spirit's half numb, in limbo, waiting for what?

And then, on this night during mud season, Carla bustles into the house, and she's all charged up and says that after she dismissed her third-grade class, one of the other teachers mentioned a neighbor, who owns a horse estate, is looking to hire a horse trainer. "So, Gabe, I've considered it, and maybe you should give the man a call. In fact, I've got his number right here." And she hands him a slip of paper.

Trying to save him again. "Sure, let's invite the guy over for dinner. We'll have him sit next to Jesus."

"Gabe, this could be the opportunity you've been waiting for. You just weren't aware of it."

This is what it's come to, now she's telling him what he wasn't aware of. There is no way in hell he'll make that call. He was never a trainer. He was a rider. Self taught, for the most part. Never went to those European clinics. Plus, he's forty-five years old, and crippled. He glances at the note. *Cliff Swensen. 802-878-6249.*

He tosses the note on the night table by the faded couch and says, "Mama, you swore you never wanted me involved with horses ever again."

"True . . ." she waits a beat. "But even horses are better than this." And she waves one big-boned hand over him on the couch, as if he's got leprosy, which maybe would be worse than being half dead. Maybe.

"Gabe, you're my first priority. You, and then my kids." She calls her students her kids because she couldn't have a child of her own, so she's driven to serve others, does volunteer tutoring, but no time for friends, she's too devoted to him.

"Saint Carla," he says.

"Oh, it's been tough, so it's for my good, too."

"As if good has anything to do with this."

"Why, Gabriel, baby, you know it does." And she shoots him one of her wide, warm smiles.

He makes a half-hearted attempt to half-smile back, but she misses it. She's already heading into the shiny kitchen to start making dinner. Her full, solid body almost fills the cramped space, a three-foot-long Formica counter, a half-sized fridge, an old, white electric stove with two burners, black coils that circle in on themselves like this whole place does.

And seeing Carla bent over that lousy stove, with her misplaced belief in him, he feels an undeniable urge to help pay off his medical bills that keep them in a place like this. But not with horses. No way.

After a little while, some tasty concoction simmers aromatically on the stove, and she comes back to the couch, kisses him on the forehead, picks up the note, goes into the bedroom for ten minutes or so, comes out again with the phone, and says, "Gabe, there's somebody who wants to speak to you." And with her hand covering the mouthpiece, she reverently whispers, "It's somebody who maybe can save your ass."

"Who?" Gabe cracks, reaching up with his good hand, "Jesus?"

CLIFF

AFTER TOURING THE THIRTY OPEN acres of fenced-in fields, Cliff parks the ATV by a boulder and, on foot, leads the little wiry guy up the back trail. Even though Gabe's got this off-kilter, lurching step, he seems to skim over the rocky path and keeps up with Cliff's long stride, neither of them breathing hard, the little man damaged somehow, but in shape.

Wordlessly, they hike uphill for a quarter mile or so. Not much further up, they'd get into foothills leading up into the Green Mountains, but they stop to look down over Cliff's rich valley land. Three hundred sixty acres, Northlands, a former Vermont dairy farm, dimly lit under a faint sun that's partly cloud-shrouded, but glimmering. Below, down a long forested hill, the river, swollen from melted snow, slices through the back acreage. The whole place is fecund even in the early spring, Cliff thinks, rocks sprouting up, they grow each year, but also the sprouts and buds have popped, and the fields seem almost already green, not quite, and the four horses, long necks bent, long tails swishing, graze far below in two pairs in two adjoining pastures. Cliff's is the big black part-Percheron, named Harley by a former owner. Harley has to be big to carry around Cliff's six-foot-four, 230 pounds. This fellow Gabe couldn't be more than five-eight, but he doesn't have to be big to do what he does. Yet Cliff wishes the dude didn't have a graying ponytail and wear an earring, and look like a middle-aged punk, not to mention his offsides smile, more like a smirk, tilted unrelentingly up at the right. His left side must have taken the hit in his accident, which his wife only mentioned, but which Cliff intends to learn all about for Nikki's sake. Usually, somebody has fucked up in an accident. Usually, accidents don't just happen on their own.

But now Cliff still stands at the ledge and gazes proudly out over his land, the smell of earth rising up, wafts of spring air flavored with dung used to fertilize the fallow pastures, and down below clusters of white birch and darker oak, budded branches swaying slightly in a faint wind, and there's the wide, light brown, sandy oval of the riding ring, and the small, dark brown squares of the asparagus bed and the herb garden, and past the long new post-and-beam barn, complete with cupola, looms the dark heap of manure that steams in the cold and rots from the inside out. Sometimes a plump, sleek groundhog perches on the top of the heap, sits on his haunches, eyes darting around like he owns the whole damned, dark, fermenting pile of shit.

"A good spot for horses," the dude says, gazing into the valley. Then he shuts up.

That's all he can say about Cliff's pride and joy? Each day Cliff slides his eyes over his property and savors it. Who said possessions can't make you feel good? And as he's looking, he feels the force of this place, a heat coursing through his veins, giving him strength.

And the long white farmhouse, barn attached, her dream house, Nikki called it, and it was her dream to own horses. Now she owns three, the fourth one Cliff's, the horses getting much of her love. We only have so much love to give, Cliff thinks, not like rocks that keep sprouting each spring, always more rocks. Yet he's got an affinity to rocks, They're how he got his nickname, playing college football, center linebacker, opponents hit up against his thick, stolid frame. "Felt like running into a fucking cliff," one player said. And the nickname stuck. Conrad "Fucking Cliff" Swensen.

"I like fields better than mountains," Gabe says, gazing up at the Green Mountains looming around them.

Almost like he knew Cliff liked rocks, so Gabe had to say the opposite. Cliff only bought a valley farm, he thinks, because Nikki needed pasture for her horses. He says, "Give me the mountains, the heights."

"One reason I left southern Illinois was because of the wind blowing across the flat fields," Gabe says. "The wind blew across and never stopped. I couldn't shake it. The wind chased after me wherever I went, even inside, if you know what I mean. An infernal wind, and all summer, it blew like hot jets. The wind got to the horses, too, spooking them. Wind like a curse."

Cliff wants to get Gabe off of the topic of the damned wind and onto training credentials, so he leads Gabe back down the path to the ATV, then drives bumpily across open back pastures toward the barn. Of course, Cliff already checked the guy's references that he got from his phone call with Gabe's wife. A woman named Muffy Parker in Illinois said that Gabe was "one of the best in the state at what he did." Cliff asked, "What's that?" She said, "He has a knack for seeing what goes on in a horse's body and mind. And in a human's too. He goes deep." Which, Cliff thought, is exactly what Nikki needs.

So this little man with the silver-streaked ponytail and the forceful, unbalanced gait and the long-winded rap is way beyond Nikki and Cliff, at least when it comes to horses.

Cliff parks the ATV, and they stride toward the new barn, where Nikki waits. Inside wainscoting, skylights, high-tech sprinkler system, six stalls. Nothing but the best for his wife, who had protested the expense and said that her cheap race-horses were used to simple room and board.

"Did you ever go to college?" Cliff asks the little dude.

"Two years. Got a scholarship to a small school on the plains of Illinois. They made me take introductions to things. I wanted to go deeper. So I dropped out. To go deep into horses."

"How deep?" Cliff asks, remembering what Muffy said.

"As deep as I could get. You ever go? To college, I mean."

As if Cliff's being interviewed. Cliff graduated summa cum laude from University of Vermont, majored in business. Numbers always came easily, and business principles, principles of any kind—logic, physics—all fine, all As. It was the slippery idea courses Cliff didn't go for, like religion and art, where Nikki shone. She would've been a painter or a potter maybe, if she hadn't been addicted to horses, even rode on the equestrian team in college. "I just have to use my body," she said. Yeah, right.

Cliff just says, "Got an MBA."

Then he starts walking, and they're almost to the mouth of the barn, when Cliff stops again and asks at last, "So how'd you have your accident?"

Gabe waves his right hand. His left, Cliff notices, dangles down at his side. That hand doesn't twitch, just hangs, like a vestigial appendage. Gabe must've been hiding it before.

"My horse slipped going over a jump. He somersaulted, landed on top of me . . . I got a concussion, a brain injury, right brain, so left side semi-paralysis."

Cliff knows he should feel some degree of sympathy, but he's coolly thinking, if this guy's brain-damaged, maybe I shouldn't hire him.

As if predicting Cliff's thoughts, Gabe says, "No problem with smarts. Speech spared. Just few nerve messages sent to my left arm and hand and face, and only partially to my left leg. If I was a horse, I'd have been put down."

A line so self-derogatory, it takes Cliff by surprise. But the guy just laughs, a short burst, and smiles, the right side of his lips twisting up. A cynic making a joke at his own expense, something that Cliff never does, and he can't help but like the guy for it.

And then Gabe says, "So I know what it takes to get broken."

"And what it takes to avoid it?"

"Got to have competence, agility, confidence, discipline, and the right vision."

Exactly what Nikki needs, Cliff thinks, but then Gabe adds, "Could be maybe why I don't want this job."

"So why are you here?"

"To please my wife. You know how hard that is."

Cliff has to smile along with the guy at that. It's gotten harder lately with Nikki, that ten-year age spread between them meaning more than it used to, her growing more reckless just when he's settling down.

"Think maybe you can please my wife, too?" Cliff asks.

Gabe half grins again. "It's up to her to please me."

Arrogant, Cliff thinks. Maybe one of those horsemen that women used to like, back before he got flattened.

Then they're in the barn and Gabe and Nikki meet. Nikki's on edge, all bristly energy as she quickly gives Gabe the barn tour, six roomy fourteen-by-fourteen-foot stalls, heated tack room, hot and cold running water, all the amenities. But like with the mountains, Gabe doesn't seem impressed. Just asks to see the horses. So Nikki gets a halter and goes outside to bring in Beau, both men following. Druid, her ancient, retired, college show horse, ambles arthritically up to the gate of the east pasture.

Gabe glances at Druid and says, "He's what, twenty or more?"

"Twenty-seven," Nikki says.

Then she's pointing to the far end of Druid's pasture, to where Gracie trots up and down, a whacky, two-year-old filly that Nikki recently bought off the track when her daughter left for college, although now Nikki's calling Gracie "her future star."

A racehorse that refused to race. Threw herself over backwards instead. A miserable wretch, in Cliff's opinion. Bites the hand that feeds her. Nikki's got a scar to prove it.

"A good one," Gabe says, eyeing long-legged Gracie, cantering now, tossing a couple big bucks.

Who is he to make the bad seem good? Cliff wonders, but Nikki's nodding yes.

And then she waves to the next paddock, where Harley stands, placidly grazing, but Nikki says, "Harley's a pasture bully, an alpha horse, has to defend his turf, so I have to keep him and Gracie separate."

As if it's all Harley's fault. He's a hulk, prone to occasional hoof abscesses so can't be ridden regularly, but he's stalwart and loyal. Cliff's about to defend his horse, but then Nikki goes into Harley's pasture, to catch Beau, Harley's pal, and through the fence, Gracie bolts, which triggers Beau to bolt, too. So much for equine gratitude. Both of them saved from the meat factory yet galloping along each side of the fence and racing flat out, when neither of them would race for shit on the track. At the far fence, Gracie swerves toward a pole, set up on blocks in her paddock, and clears it by several feet. Gracie, although untrained, likes to fly riderless over fences, as if she were born with wings like Pegasus. Did Pegasus have one horn in the center of his forehead? A unicorn? Cliff gets his mythology mixed up. All those decadent Greek gods causing havoc on earth. Cliff doesn't believe in one god let alone a whole herd of them.

Finally, Nikki has clipped a coiled lunge line onto Beau's halter and leads him into the ring, where she unrolls the long line and lets Beau trot out to the end. She's going to show off Beau's walk, trot, and canter gaits with no rider weighing him down. She stands in the center of the ring, the position of power, and says, "Trot!" Flicks her long lunge whip in the air, the whip only for show, but Beau immediately takes off at a gallop, dragging her feet off the center spot, and she's yelling, "Trot, trot!" Meanwhile, Gabe's standing there with this lopsided grin while the heavily muscled gelding drags Nikki half across the ring, her calling, "Whoa, whoa," Beau having a hell of a good time doing the opposite of what she wants.

At last, Beau decides on his own to halt, swivels his rump to her, another sign of disrespect, and stands totally still, as if to say, Come on over here, and I'll lift my hind legs and kick the shit out of you.

It's all show, Cliff thinks, because Beau could have charged her, run her down. He's just tormenting her for fun. Cliff can't help but like Beau's spirit, his grit.

Gabe calls, "He's got the hindquarters and the speed to make a good jumper, but his attitude sucks."

Nikki looks at Gabe and calls, "I know that!" She's breathing hard, clearly irritated, hands on hips, and walks over to Gabe, leading Beau on a shortened line, and asks, "So what would you do about it?"

"Ground work, fitness training, repetition, but mostly you changing your attitude so he'll change his. You're afraid of him. And he knows it."

Cliff's nodding at that.

"Fear is contagious," Gabe says.

"Sure as hell is," Cliff says. "Fear's got to be expunged."

Expunged. Gabe gives Cliff a look. Like he didn't think Cliff could use words like that. Cliff with a graduate degree. Gabe, the college dropout, the part arrogant, part self-deprecating one-time athlete. No cowboy type, not with his ponytail and earring and his numbed half. Not at all what Cliff had expected.

Nikki's tap-tapping the lunge whip against the sand, shoving the tip of the long whip deep in. "You can't order me to get rid of my fear any more than horses can get rid of theirs."

"Sure I could. If I wanted to," Gabe says, and he's smiling that halved smile again, like it's an ongoing joke.

Nothing appealing about that lip-curling grin, Cliff thinks, and with the guy's face all creased from the sun, he's looks fifty but could be less, maybe closer to Nikki's age.

She's smirking back at Gabe, like sure, she's going to get fear-free today. And she asks, "And just how would you do that?"

"Training's mostly repetition," Gabe says. "Gotta love it."

Nikki hates repeating things, Cliff knows for a fact. She does it but gets bored fast, yet now she's nodding, like yes, this is wisdom.

"And training's knowing when to move on," Gabe says, "so let's see now if Beau knows how to do that."

Gabe steps toward the end of the ring where the irrepressible Beau still waits for another chance to goof off, and without the lunge whip or a crop, Gabe steps toward the big bay's haunches and slowly waves his right arm. Beau gives him a one-eyed look, like what's this guy doing? But Gabe steps closer, to within a few feet, flaps his good hand, and Beau takes off galloping again around the outside of the ring, so Gabe steps into the center, the eye of the storm, and every time Beau slows, Gabe lurches toward him, sometimes waving his right arm, so the horse gallops again. Then Gabe steps back to the center until Beau tires and slows, when Gabe lurches forward and flaps, so Beau speeds up, until he slows. And so it goes for maybe a half hour until Beau's snorting for breath, wearing down. Then he simply suddenly halts and turns to look at Gabe with both eyes. Submission.

Gabe turns away from the heaving horse, and Beau takes a step after him, and Gabe walks off toward the gate and Beau follows. When Gabe gets to the gate, he stops, and Beau halts a few feet behind. He's hooked on Gabe, with no line.

An old cowboy trick, Cliff thinks, but Nikki's got her hands clasped as Gabe steps out of the gate, loops it shut, and says, "You could be doing that yourself. The gelding's just testing."

Then Nikki's talking about her plans to compete, saying that she must jump clean at Intermediate to qualify for Advanced, but, of course, she realizes, without a major shift, she hasn't a chance.

It's as if, without even consulting Cliff, she is trying to hire this sprite.

"This horse needs a confident rider," Gabe says. "You've got to trust."

At the word trust, Cliff asks, "You have a wife? Any kids?"

Gabe says, with a flicker of a twist to his upper lip, "No kids, but Carla would've made a helluva good mother. Too good."

Nikki has been a good mother, Cliff thinks, although inclined to excess, so much so, in fact, that she has spoiled Lisa, like she has spoiled her horses. But not her husband, not anymore.

Gabe limps over to the fence again and calls out to the big chestnut mare who immediately spooks, bolts away, yet

Gabe's nodding at that bitch, whom Nikki renamed Gracie, and she said, "This mare will bring grace into my life." As if Nikki hasn't found grace yet, as if she is still seeking it.

◆◆◆

Soon they're sitting on white Adirondack chairs on the deck, overlooking two separate pastures where the horses graze in two separate pairs on short, pale, spring grass sprouting out of mud. They will rotate the horses to two of the far pastures, Cliff thinks, once that grass is thick and rich, and they will save some pastures to grow grass for hay. During their first years here, he hired a farmer to cut hay and rope it into bales with a baler. Then he and Nikki would drive their own tractor and wagon into their fields and haul up the bales themselves, Cliff swinging bales by the twine up to Nikki who'd stack them in the wagon, their two tanned, strong bodies sweating and working together in the sun. He never had to tell her the pleasure he took in their shared physical labor.

Now the three of them sit drinking Copper Ale, a local brew, while Nikki has been telling Gabe about how Beau balks at water jumps, about her fall and getting eliminated at the last show. Then she says, "It was my fault."

"Yeah," Gabe says. "But that's no reason to feel guilty about it. Guilt gets you into trouble."

"Guilt keeps us in line," Cliff puts in.

"Horses don't feel guilt," Gabe says. "They do what they do and that's the end of it."

"And I envy them for that," Nikki says, smiling at this Gabe, with his chiseled features, ascetic, almost priestly, if not for the askew, hard-nailed mouth.

Gabe flashes a tilting smile at her and says, "I could rid you of your guilt, too. But that would cost you more."

As if he could make a dent in Nikki's Protestant guilt that she schleps around like a cloud. Cliff eliminated his that he got growing up Missouri Synod Lutheran, but Nikki gives in to hers.

"No guilt and no fear," Gabe adds, half smiling. "You'd have my personal guarantee."

Suddenly Cliff realizes that this guy is not just joking. He would train Nikki, not just her horse. Gabe could perhaps purge her of some of the very qualities that drive Cliff nuts. What about her obstinacy, he wants to ask. How much to get rid of that? And how about her self-destructive recklessness? Or would Gabe encourage her risk-taking side? Cliff wonders why he's hiring someone who could possibly lead to his wife's downfall. But otherwise, she'll continue to compete without the expertise, far more dangerous.

He slowly slides his checkbook out of his denim shirt pocket and starts talking salary. He has already spoken about a trainer's standard rate with a neighbor, Neil Fergusen, so Cliff mentions that amount. But Gabe says, "I'm not sure yet if I'll do it." Figuring the guy's bargaining, Cliff adds a couple thousand, but Gabe says that money has nothing to do with why he'd take this job, if he does. "And it's not just about winning," Gabe adds. "Not just about beating those bastards."

Cliff doesn't ask who the bastards are. He knows. It's how he used to play football, center linebacker in charge of defense, sole purpose to devastate the person across from him, his body a trained weapon, never out of control, every moment a test of your being, if you're hurt, don't tell, bring him down or he'll bring you down, train and train for a burst, for a fraction of a second at the time of impact. Collide and destroy.

"It's more than winning," Cliff agrees, thinking this guy really was a triathlete.

"But winning's what I want," Nikki says, nodding like yes, she'll win, that's it, she's already convinced, when she isn't even sure this guy will train her yet. It's at this moment, as Cliff's watching her smile beatifically at the little offsides man and act like a petite fanatic dying to be purged, to be martyred for a horse, that Cliff's instinct says he could be making a big mistake in being generous.

And then Nikki asks, "Gabe, what would make you take the job?"

He looks out into the fields, to where the mare grazes, and says, "That bitch."

An untrained mare that can't compete for several years, Cliff thinks. What's this, a lifelong commitment?

But then Gabe gets up and says, "I'll think about it," and he walks off to his pickup, his limp more pronounced. Maybe he's tired, or maybe Cliff is just looking for what's off. Maybe that conflicted, damaged guy won't be back.

As soon as Gabe drives away in his beat-up Chevy pickup, Cliff decides to remind his wife that this sprite would be his gift, and says, "Happy Anniversary, babe."

Nikki, all revved up, starts pacing around him like he's the center of her circle, and asks, "But do you think he'll take me on?"

Take her on? "Maybe," Cliff says, thinking, maybe not.

"Then we'd be saved!"

Who does she mean by *we*? Her and him, Cliff wonders, or her and Beau? And why use the word *saved*? But he won't let her see that he doesn't see. He simply takes her arm in his and leads her off toward her dream house, which he once hoped would be enough.

CARLA

CARLA OPENS THE OVEN DOOR, checks her lasagna, sees it's bubbling, turns down the heat. When Gabe gets home, she's got her apple crisp all set to go in. Two of his favorite dishes, to celebrate, though he's late. She's almost ready to call Cliff Swensen and ask where her husband is.

But she waits. Cliff Swensen sounded dubious when she first called about the trainer's job. She gave him a sales pitch and said horses had been her husband's life, and he was an "Olympic-caliber equestrian," who would train through "thought control and discipline," and these last few years, he has "lived like a monk, meditates twice a day and abstains from just about everything." Cliff was shrewd enough to ask why Gabe wasn't competing anymore. She said, "He had a bad fall, got a little limp and can't compete, but he's willing to devote his energy to training others. It's his way of giving back." Cliff said, "You make him sound like an altruist." She had to laugh at that since Gabe has been too down to think of anyone but himself. But she said in her best schoolteacher's voice, "Give my husband a chance." And Cliff Swensen said, "Have him give me a call, and we'll meet." A man who makes his mind up fast, trusts his instincts, like she trusts hers. Even when she loses her temper—a "hot head," Gabe calls her— she still instinctively knows she's right.

Yet after that call, she felt an unaccustomed rush of self doubt. Two years ago, after the fall, Gabe seemed broken in body and mind. When first home from the hospital, he used a bedpan, and she'd roll him from side to side, sponge him off, and empty his debris. She got to know him from the inside out. He rebelled against her knowing, calling her his "partner in despair." Saying she was "too damned merciful." She resented him for resenting her, though he couldn't help it, and sometimes he'd thank her, like the time he asked, "What would I do without you?" She said, "You'd go under." "So let me go," he said. "Over my dead body," she said. "It's *my* body that's dead," he said. But no one could stop her from healing her man, not even him. Only trouble is, he still hasn't healed.

She even took a semester leave of absence from her third-grade kids. Reading is her specialty, opening up new worlds of words to little ones, who believe what's in print, and what she says.

But with Gabe, nothing she said or did had the effect that his meditating did, though he'd say things like, "We're all born to suffer." She'd say, "Not me." Yet she suffered along with him, for that's what marriage can be. And, too, sometimes when he sat alone in their bedroom, or out under the crabapple tree in a half lotus position and did his breathing, she admired him, wrestling with his demons.

Yet he's still depressed, and she wants her old husband back, an outdoorsman who tempered his death wish with a joy de vivre, a lover who dished out compliments, "Carla, you're the steady one." "Carla, endurance is your main virtue, second only to your love of me." After his fall, his sweet-talk mostly vanished. Of course, it vanished with other women as well. One benefit.

And now, at last, as the sun sets, she hears the clank of Gabe's pickup. She smoothes down her flyaway, bleached blonde hair, slides out her triple-cheese lasagna, and slides in her apple crisp. She doesn't allow Gabe to cook because he forgets that his left side can't feel much, so he often scorches himself, a burnt child who does not dread the fire.

His pickup makes a coughing racket. Then silence. She

hopes they'll have something to celebrate, for he could have messed it up, a man of radical ups and downs, or at least he was before his fall. Ever since, he's been in that trance.

She goes to the front door and swings it wide as he limps up the cement steps. He's wearing his old blue mountain jacket with two vents in the back. He looks like a horseman again. But beneath the jacket is his long-sleeved denim shirt—always long-sleeved to cover that left arm, as if she hasn't memorized each atrophied inch. She opens her arms, gives him a big bear hug, feels the tension in his body, and asks, "Baby, how did it go?"

He hugs her, says, "Don't know yet." Pulls back.

She lets him go, and he comes in, gets a Heineken out of the small fridge. She tells him dinner's ready, so he sits at the little kitchen table, and she carries out the hot casserole, scoops out bright lasagna onto the yellow imitation fiestaware plates, and says, "Your favorite."

He thanks her, absently, and she sits as he takes a few distracted bites, and she asks, "So did you take the job or not?"

"That little woman needs work."

"What kind of work?"

"She needs more self-control. Doesn't collect herself enough. I'd have to retrain her."

"How?"

"It's technical."

"Isn't everything? Gabe, you were a detail guy with horses. You obsessed on the littlest thing." Like he did with lovemaking too, she thinks. Before the fall, he was a master of detail. After the fall, she thought their sex was all over with, until one morning, in bed, his part rose up, but he lay there and left the technicalities up to her. Half a man is better than no man at all, but it depends on which half you get.

Now she says, "You can handle it. You're a really good handler. I speak from experience." She smiles but he's looking off, over her head, an old glow in his dark, heavy-lidded eyes, one eye still as glass, except it can see. She asks, "So what about the horses?"

"Beau's a ten-year-old gelding, in his prime, good shoulder angle, maybe not scopey enough but good enough for Advanced and possibly three-star. He's agile and has a big heart."

"A big heart counts for a lot."

"And, Mama, you've got one." He gives her his half smile, lips curled up on the right, but then his gaze drifts off of her again, and he says, "But it's the mare who I fixed on. Almost seventeen hands, full of it, only two years old, bones still too soft to compete. But a real beauty. And she jumped by herself, like an angel. She floated on air."

In a rush, Carla knows he has fallen in love at first sight, and she asks herself, can I let him love another again, even if she's a horse?

"She's got the devil in her," he says, "but I'd control her mean streak. Shape it to my purposes."

"You can shape the devil, Gabe?"

"Hell yess. So, Mama, should I make her into all she can be?"

"Sounds like a big job, even for you."

"Then why'd you set this up?"

She only says, "Just promise me you won't jump her yourself."

"I couldn't even if I would."

"Well then, it's up to you."

"Damned right, it is," he says, suddenly like the old Gabe. Willful, determined, not stuck in a coma or a trance.

Then he stands up and says, "Your lasagna was great." And carries his cleared-off plate into the kitchenette.

Extra mozzarella, ricotta, Parmesan, and milk fat, that's her secret. A Midwestern farm girl, she grew up on butter, cream, and cheese. Got big strong bones, not shattered bones with pins in, like his. And she feels for him again and stands and lifts the heavy casserole and carries it the few steps to the linoleum countertop.

"I'll need some time to myself," Gabe says, limps into the bedroom and shuts the door.

She thinks of him meditating on what to do, sitting still and straight on the bed, his limp leg out straight, the good one tucked under, in half a lotus position. He'll wait for inspiration to strike. Of course, you can be inspired to do wrong.

She checks the oven, slides out her apple crisp, browned on top, and she only hopes his love of horses will draw him out of his broken self and resurrect the old cocky, jokey Gabe she first met at a party after an event. She went with a girlfriend who rode. Carla wouldn't go near horses herself. Gabe was dancing with a bunch of women, and he had this sexy sway to his hips, an athletic grace. She watched him and he watched her back, and later by the appetizer table, he came up to her when she was spreading a cracker with some Brie, and he said, "Good cheese." What a pathetic opening line, she thought, but they talked, and after a while, he said he liked women taller than him. She'd been five-ten since eighth grade, too tall for most guys, and the biggest boys asked out the tiniest girls, but now here was a sportsman, who only came up to her chin yet gazed up with his dark, intense eyes and his slow wide grin, and right then she fell for him.

After an hour or so, Gabe limps out of the bedroom and says, "I called Cliff, and I said, 'If I take the job, I'd have to have total control.' He didn't say anything to that. So I said what one of my trainers once told me, 'It's about discipline, not domination.' Cliff said, 'That's more like it.' So I said, 'I'll take it on. The two horses. And your wife.' Then we talked salary, and that was that."

Carla feels a rumbling in her gut, but says, "Baby, maybe now I'll get you back."

He flashes his new half scratched-off grin, his old one was full of teeth and gums, and he says, "Don't worry, Mama, I won't forget who got me into this."

A compliment or a threat? She lets it slip. "Ready for some apple crisp?"

"Hell yes." He sits at the table again, and she sets down a heaping, steamy bowl of it, with that special crispy sugar crust he loves, and tart Granny Smith apples, sweet-sour. He digs in, the spoon clutched in his good hand, his bad hand hidden from her under the table top, even though she knows each and every hope he's got cupped in that numb, loose fist, its fingers curled like a claw.

Gabe and Cliff

GABE WATCHES CRITICALLY YET HOPEFULLY, as he has watched each day for the last six weeks, while Beau and Nikki have practiced his exercises, Beau sometimes still playing around, Nikki sometimes still tense, still sometimes failing Beau's tests when his tricky temperament ricochets off hers. But, hell, they're getting more in sync, so think positive, Gabe tells himself. Since taking this job, he has been training himself by repeating inner messages like I am calm, I am impervious . . . like he used to believe back before his fall, when he got close to perfection, teetered at the very edge of excellence, but you make one slip, you lose, the end.

He keeps those thoughts private. He must infuse a fearless self into this woman, for she has suppleness and agility, yet she often loses focus. She's mostly courageous, even reckless, but once in a while, unpredictably, she's tense, shot through with fear. Dangerous for her, if not for the horse.

That's why he has made her go back to the basics for three weeks, then did three weeks of Preliminary level intervals on his master schedule. "The seventh day is a day of rest," Gabe said, when he first nailed his six-day schedule to the barn door, hammered it in hard. She said he reminded her of Martin Luther nailing up his treatise against the Catholic Church. Gabe, an arch ex-Catholic, said, "This is as religious as it gets."

But her conversion is taking longer than he planned.

"Center your balance and breathe," he often tells her. "Follow the horse." And some days she does, but other days she grits her teeth, all conscious determination, uptight like some spoiled, rich, upscale bitch who believes she can get whatever she wants by willing it to come true. There's more to her than that, Gabe thinks. Sooner or later, he'll get down to her center, where that fear springs from.

But now, out in the high field this morning, he's impatient, fed up. He sets the rails higher, at three-feet-six. He's got to get her to consistently take Beau over those rails and do it right. "Follow your body, your instinct," he calls while she circles Beau, preparing to approach the line of jumps.

At his words, she only tightens up more, so Beau gives another little buck. Then she gallops him at the jumps. Six strides to a crossrail, three more strides to a vertical, four strides to an oxer—a spread jump with two rails, one higher than the other.

Takes more courage if you've got fear than if you're fearless, Gabe thinks, but the horse doesn't care about that distinction. A creature of prey. Her fear only inflates his. She's peering down at the ground like that's where she's going.

"Look up," he calls. "Eyes toward the next jump."

She looks up, her lips set tight—tight beige britches, tight black t-shirt, everything tight—Beau hops over the crossrail, the horse not big, but has a good eye, the aura of confidence Gabe looks for, and the balance and rhythm to win at Advanced. And Nikki has the athleticism to win as well, her body lean and defined, even though her conformation is somewhat off. She's too petite for a top equestrian, and too top heavy, which throws her off balance sometimes, her tits an encumbrance like now, approaching the oxer. She's tilting back a bit, so Beau swerves, runs out of the line of jumps so she almost loses her seat.

He'll have to whip her into shape. She's almost forty, almost past her prime.

"Keep calm!" he calls. "Act fearless." Though fear's a survival instinct.

She trots Beau over to Gabe, halts, looks down, and asks, "Are you telling me to be a hypocrite?"

She's not mad at me, Gabe thinks, but at herself.

"Start out as a hypocrite," he says. "Pretend you're at peace, you're totally calm. Then practice. Sooner or later it'll come true."

"What kind of truth is that?"

"Got to dream."

"I do," she says, sitting stiffly on the surprisingly quiet horse.

"And got to stick to our schedule."

"I'm sick of schedules. I've had schedules my whole life."

"Tell yourself you love them. Then you will."

"I won't."

"Don't say won't or don't."

"You're a friggin' disciplinarian," she says, with all the pent-up frustration of the last six weeks.

Yet her frustration is nothing compared with his. "Try it again. Full force. All out. No fear!"

"I can't get my fear to disappear like magic."

"Say, 'Welcome fear, my old friend.'" A line from one of his meditation books.

"I welcome what I want to avoid?"

"You breathe it in."

She shakes her head no but then squeezes her legs, and Beau charges at the line of jumps. She's in sync with her horse and in a correct half-seat, and Beau smoothly clears the cross-rail, the vertical, the oxer, and the rest of the grid. She circles to take the jumps again, clears the crossrail, the vertical, and Gabe calls out, "You got it!" But at that, she leans slightly too far forward, so as Beau lifts to clear the oxer, he taps the front rail out of its cups, and when he hits the earth, gives a couple more of his trademark bucks.

"That's it!" Gabe calls loudly. "Dismount."

She walks Beau over, swings off, and, one hand on her hip, peers at him. "What's next?"

And Gabe says, "We've got to purge your mind."

◆ ◆ ◆

Behind the post-and-beam barn, on a hillock under the willow tree overlooking the four fenced-in pastures, he and Nikki sit side by side, backs straight, her legs crossed in lotus position, his in a half lotus. The willow tendrils sway slightly, stirred by a warm midsummer breeze. As a kid, he used to strip willow branches of their leaves to shape whips for his pony, a stubborn, stunted pinto that felt no pain from a delicate willow switch. Gabe had to learn to strategize, keep his mind ahead of the horse, manipulate the little furry beast.

Now he tells Nikki to shut her eyes, relax, take a deep breath in and out, "a cleansing breath," and to follow her breath, to focus as air slides from her belly, up and out. "And if thoughts pass through, watch them, don't judge, no matter how bad they are. Your mantra could be, 'Breathe in fear, breathe out calm.'"

He shuts his eyes, hears her deep breaths. He breathes along, slides in and out of focus yet keeps trying to burrow into that dark, dim spot where he goes when he meditates . . . he has flipped Buddha upside down with all that enlightenment, Gabe thinks, for he doesn't believe in the pictures of happy, chubby-cheeked, big-bellied guys sitting smack in the center of mandalas. No, we are of the nature to suffer, we are of the nature to die, Buddha said. He was a wanderer like Gabe has been, like he had to leave Illinois, and before that Michigan, and before that Wisconsin . . . had to reinvent himself over and over again, once because of the curse of trainers—that time-dishonored tradition for trainers to seduce riders or vice versa. A tradition he adhered to once, but never again, not after Carla found out, so the horsewoman's husband did. After that, his marriage was a kind of low-grade penance until his fall. No matter, he's got higher values now. He's going to be as celibate as a goddamn godless priest.

For the horse comes first. But now his mind's wandering again, so he concentrates on his breath, and after almost a half hour he finally finds that deep spot inside, his own silent black hole where shadows take on human shape and whisper words he can't quite hear, a dangerous hunting ground where if you take one misstep, you slip and fall and it's all over with.

He hears her breathing next to him, deeply in and out, as he told her to, and he sneaks a peek at her face, dreamy and relaxed, as if she's susceptible, so he starts softly talking to her, telling her to think positive, to relax, disengage, distance. He wants to tell her to be estranged, but he only softtalks for a while about letting go and feeling centered, and then he softly says to visualize herself on a horse, to picture the horse on a course, and to picture the various jumps, and he names oxers, Trakehners, corner jumps, triple rails, and the splash, and says, "Soft hands . . . soft thighs . . . soft eyes," his voice a soothing drawl. "Imagine yourself in the start box, feel it . . . the countdown, one minute . . . thirty seconds . . . and you're off," he goes softly on. "You're light as air . . . you don't walk on ground . . . your horse is smoothly floating over the fence . . . you're light as clouds drifting, coasting up, you're a sky walker rising though blue . . . you don't dwell on earth . . . you're a feathered flying who-knows-what, you've got bird bones, you're lifting off, hanging in air . . . lifting higher . . . into space . . . you're high, you're hot, you're rising up . . ." Droning on in his most soothing tone, even while he wants to take her down into his private space.

He opens his eyes and hers are already blinking into the fading daylight. He wants to share one of his secrets, but she's not ready yet. He wants to say, Got to ride into the dark where you see nothing but yourself and the horse, you're in a cloud, the two of you as one, a beast with two heads, everything else but shadows. Ride into the storm not into the light. Ride as if you're ready to die for it.

But she's sucking in her breath. Her eyes all bright from meditating, her face flushed, relaxed, she softly says, "Do you know what my mantra was? 'Lord, have mercy, have mercy on us.'"

As if the Lord's got anything to do with horses.

◆◆◆

In the next few weeks, he and Nikki meditate each morn-

ing before they train, and he dips into his inner shadow
box while she seems to float around in some pale haze. Yet,
to his surprise, after each session, she works better with
Beau. Gabe tells her to focus, to feel the horse, to ride
deeper in, to find Beau's center of balance. Yet all the while,
Gabe knows that she can't find Beau's center if she hasn't
found her own. Gabe found his during his accident, had
his nose and mouth rubbed in dirt. Dirt up his nostrils,
in his mouth, breathed in dirt as damp as snot, swallowed
dirt before he passed out. Dirt's got a peculiar chocolaty,
wormy taste. Dirt's where he came from. From dirt to dirt.
He knows what he's made of. Hasn't told anyone, not even
Carla. Sure as hell not Nikki.

Now this morning, her warm-up completed, Nikki trots
Beau to a new, higher grid of jumps that Gabe set up, a couple oxers, a few verticals. This time she barely touches Beau's
flank with her crop when he's off at a big trot, and Gabe's calling, "Don't think of the don'ts. Breathe, focus, let him find his
legs. How does that *feel?*"

Although he can't teach feel, he almost hears her drawing in breaths even over the hoofbeats, and she's sweeping
toward the first vertical when Beau gets that slight hitch and
gives that little telltale pre-buck grunt, but she just calmly
sits deeper, and Beau skims over the row of jumps, his back
rounded in a fine bascule, an arc, ears forward, legs tucked. At
the end, he circles cantering, no circus stunts.

That's the spirit, Gabe thinks.

For the next half hour, Beau flies over the jumps in
rhythm and balance, and only at the very last fence at the very
end of the practice, when the animal must sense, from Nikki's
body shifting or tensing, that it's almost over with, does Beau,
full of his own horsepower, slide to a stop just in front of the
last rail, toss his head, prance a dance step. A refusal. The
jokester sabotaged her yet again. This horse is too smart for
his own good. Good thing most horses aren't, Gabe thinks,
probably why they've survived from prehistoric times because
what they know best is how to run away from trouble. Which

humans don't. Humans not only run straight into trouble, they manufacture it. He ought to know.

Nikki brings Beau down to a walk and they come over to Gabe, and she dismounts. Her face is tight, eyes squinted almost shut, so he says, "Soft eyes."

But her eyes don't go soft, they still look hard.

"Remember, we almost got there," he says.

"But I didn't. I won't."

"Don't you ever use no more negatives like 'didn't' and 'won't' with me," he says. "Tell yourself you'll get there yet, then you will."

"Get where?"

"To where you've got to go. Hell, woman, don't you know that yet?"

"You just said don't," she says.

And then they're smiling at each other in a burst, a flash of recognition, then it's gone.

He refuses to let the light in. He feels only this inner push to turn her into what he used to be, to shape her into his surrogate.

He only says, "There's no other sport like this. Two bodies as one."

"Ever since I was a girl, I felt that," she says and starts leading Beau toward the barn, and Gabe keeps step. "I had my own pony that I rode bareback, but when I was six, my sister, thirteen years older, my father's favorite, died in a freak riding accident, and my mother, grief-stricken, left us. My father made me sell my pony, and not long after that, his business went bankrupt, so we lost everything. But I still secretly mucked stalls at a nearby farm in order to exercise their ponies, and sometimes when I rode, even though my sister was so much older and I never really knew her, I felt her sitting behind me, riding double, urging me on, even though you can die from it."

Gabe says, "So you know what it is to lose everything."

"Yes, although I was only a small child. So I didn't know what it really meant."

He says, "I know."

"What?"

But he won't answer that.

◆◆◆

Ten days before their first event, it rains, an early morning downpour, rattles of thunder, lightning streaks, a hot, slouchy wind wafting in from the west, but he knows what he's got to do in the rain, which natters at him, sets even his numb nerves on edge. He doesn't want to do it, knowing it might all come back.

But he puts on his slicker and drives to Northlands and meets Nikki in the barn and tells her they must go out on the trails today. She says, "Beau will act up."

"That's the point."

She says, "He hates rain as much as water jumps."

Gabe wants to snap, you'll do what I tell you to and fucking like it. Like his father used to say to him. Instead, he says, "I evented a horse who freaked out in storms and on mud. It turned out bad for all concerned. Real bad. So tack up."

She looks at him curiously as if he'll say more. He only says that they'll go down to the river and teach Beau to take water jumps in the rain, so after today, no storm or sleet or water of whatever kind will ever scare him again.

Gabe doesn't say that he hasn't ridden since his fall, not to mention in a storm. You've got to get right back on the horse that tossed you off, or you'll be friggin' forever scared.

One-handed, he saddles up Druid, an old gentleman who will jump whatever his arthritic legs will still carry him over. Gabe wants to ride the still whacky Gracie, who would have gone to the killers if Nikki hadn't bought her right off the meat wagon at the track. Gabe has only done groundwork with Gracie, and Nikki has only ridden the mare in the ring, where even in that safe encircled space, the mare still freaks. She's too green for the trail where she would surely bolt. But Gabe knows he can train her because he knows where her soul rests, in a primeval bog, and Gracie knows that he knows that. She's the horse he should ride to purge himself of his fall because she so resembles the horse he rode that day—graceful, hyper, crazed.

Frustrated, he tacks up old Druid, and mounts from a mounting block, and straps his left leg to the left saddle flap with two lengths of leather. His leg doesn't seem to belong to him. It seems like a piece of tack.

He should keep his feet free in the stirrups in order to slide off if the horse falls, but he sets off on old Druid. Even strapped on, Gabe slip slides a little, and Druid senses that but just ambles along. Some horses sense their rider's vulnerability and give them a break. Though Gabe only feels more frustrated to be catered to by an arthritic has-been.

The rain spatters down on the horse's rain-repellent hair and spatters against Gabe's helmet and into his eyes like it did that day, and he feels a slow, hot infestation of fear as he knew he would when he took this job. They take the path past the paddock and up the hill, through the field by the foothills. Even the high field is mud-slopped, and Gabe wonders why he's slogging along through high grass, rain pummeling down, sopped branches shaking showers onto them. But he forces Druid ahead, the old horse looking down to see where to place his hooves in fields usually fertile, though gray now with mud, where you can sink in, like a woman can suck you in, tantalizing you to come deeper, so you've got to watch your step.

The humidity weighs on Gabe, drenching hot even as they enter into the dripping back woods and start downhill at a walk on soggy, sometimes overgrown, root-ridden trails, cleared by Cliff or his hired man. Sometimes the thick branches shelter them from the rain, but usually rain pelts through onto him. He wants it to rain harder yet, to slice down like it did then. He needs to jump in rain. He hasn't since his fall. That's what's wrong with him.

The horses slog downhill through deeper, gray clay mud to the gravel river road that runs alongside the shallow, stirred-up river, to a place where a fallen log lies lodged between rocks, nature's own water jump. The opposite bank looms high, mud-slicked.

Nikki can't get Beau over his fear of water, not to mention to climb a slimy bank where a horse knows it could slip. How to get a horse to overcome its instincts? At the riverbank, Gabe urges Druid ahead of Beau, down into the stream-fed, fast-running water, for then Beau, herd bound, should follow.

Druid sloshes into the river, Gabe telling himself, "Go ahead, fall, what have I got to lose? Ride into it." Yet the fear flows through him like it never did before his fall, fear of falling in front of her, fear that babbles like the river with a voice of its own.

But Druid hops over the soaked black log and scrambles up the mud-slicked bank, Gabe still on, lopsidedly. Then Beau's following, hopping lightly over the log, leaping up the muddy bank after Druid.

Got to do it over and over again until the horse has it ingrained. Gabe turns Druid back down the bank, splashing into the river, popping over the log, up onto the slimy lower bank, Beau following, and they cross the river over and over, back and forth in the slicing rain, until both sopping horses could sprout gills and fins.

On the way back to the barn, Gabe slumps in the saddle, and his right side aches from keeping his left in place, yet he doesn't feel purged. Couldn't restore himself to a fearless daredevil by riding off balance on an old plug over a low, moldy log. He'd have to ride that same strung out, hyper, three-star Thoroughbred over the same damned three-part water jump in the same damned hard-slicing rain and sucking mud. No way can he do that, so the fear ferments.

But now the rain stops, just like that. The clouds have already sifted off somewhere, and a faint, hazy sun bears down. Nikki and Beau trot up next to him, and he says, "You did it." She's nodding, smiling wide, saying yes. She's got the glow that he can no longer get, a high that lets you take any risk. He thinks, Goddamn, I'm transforming this woman into someone else, for her sake.

And back at the barn, while she's hosing down the heated-up horses, cross-tied in the aisle, their coats soaked from river water and sweat, Gabe says what he'd only thought before, "Nikki, you've got to ride into the cloud." She turns to look at him, her face blank, water from the hose still flowing onto Beau. Gabe wants to tell her how in water the horse senses that it's heading back where it came from, from clay, from mud, from gray primitive ooze.

He says, "In the event next weekend, you gotta ride to where you can't see anything but yourself and the horse, only the two of you, everything else is but shadows. Ride into the dark, not into the light. Ride as if you're ready to die for it."

She shakes her head. "What?"

She's still not ready, not yet. He shrugs.

Then she looks down, the hose still spewing water onto Beau's legs, splashing onto her britches, already sopped from the rain and the river. She twists the nozzle to low, aims it at her face, and lets the cool spurt trickle down her cheeks, her neck, drops beading on her smooth, tanned skin. She runs one wet hand through her dark hair, her head tilted back, and water drools onto her t-shirt that clings, and she's all droplets and dripping clothes pasted onto her, and onto her breasts, flattened under her sports bra.

He looks away and hears himself say, "You'll get a ribbon next week if you let go and collect yourself, both at once."

She shakes her head. Not buying it. He hates not being believed. Even when he bullshits, he means it. Who's the damned trainer here?

She turns her back to him, unhooks Beau and lets him go into his stall. Gabe watches her too-small ass in the tight, damp workout britches.

"You look elegant on a horse," he says. "But you look awfully small off of one."

She's out of Beau's stall and turns her back to Beau's head that's poking out over the half door. Beau's eyeing her hair as if it's hay.

She flips back her long hair. "Maybe that's why I ride. To look elegant." Teasing him now.

"If that's why, don't put me through this."

And then Beau swiftly grabs a swatch of her long dark hair in his teeth and tugs, just a bit, but Nikki's trapped, her head tilted back, and she's saying, "Beau, let go!" He just chomps a little as if on strands of hay.

Gabe says loudly, "No!" Beau immediately drops the swatch, telltale dark strands dangling from his mouth. Having a good time like Gabe used to do before. Gabe's got to smile.

Now freed, Nikki smiles back, a kickass smile, a wide, white-toothed, gummy affair. "Gabe, you saved me."

She chuckles at that, yet it's exactly what he intends to do. Save her, yeah, goddamn redeem her, from herself.

"You better believe that," he says and reaches out his good hand to slap her five, and she slaps back, a sharp, profound smack, like they're sealing some pact. But then, she glances out the open barn door, suddenly says she's got to go, and she's walking off, out of the barn and across the wide lawn. His eyes follow her little equestrian's ass, encased in spandex, and she's swishing it, and then he sees who she's shaking her booty for, her husband, leaning against the fence. Cliff, the landowner, spying on them, one work boot propped on the bottom fence rung, one elbow cocked on the top rung, chin in hand, looking morose, as if they're doing something wrong.

Gabe feels like calling out, Hey, you ought to be damned thankful. I'm shaping up your wife, for God's sake. I'm turning her into someone else. Isn't that what you hired me for?

◆ ◆ ◆

Cliff came outside just in time to see them slapping five. They haven't even won anything yet, but they're already celebrating. It's this damned enthusiasm that Cliff can't stand, this ebullience, when meanwhile the jumps grow ever higher, more dangerous. This sport's a foolish excess, an exaggerated risk for a sensual high . . . and yet . . . didn't he feel that high when he hit up against opposing linemen, a perfect tackle, the sweet spot, a bliss that he has felt otherwise only in sex when it's lusty and furious, like his and Nikki's still is, sporadically.

And now Nikki's striding straight over to him and saying, "Honey, that's the best yet." Meaning risking her life, and she's telling him how maybe she can place at her next horse trial in two weeks, maybe even get a low enough score to win, if she "religiously" practices and follows Gabe's schedule "to the letter." And she says, "Gabe believes in discipline." She, who always rebelled, like when Cliff ordered her to stop eventing and said, "I want you alive not dead." And she said, "Really? That's sweet," as if he didn't mean it.

She's striding past him now into the house, so he follows her into the kitchen. Since it's almost six p.m., she's taking a flank steak out of the fridge and unrolling it, then whipping up her soy and lemon marinade, scoring the slab of meat with one of her dull knives, soaking the meat in the brown mix in a white dish. Only then does she turn to Cliff, who has felt compelled, for some reason—maybe because of her rain-soaked, clinging clothes that reveal her every curve and protuberance—to hang around, and she must sense his eyes on her and steps up, gives him a big damp hug, and says, "What a big man you are. Cliff, honey, after dinner, why don't we go upstairs to bed?"

Like riding's foreplay. He says, "The main reason a woman rides is to press a warm beast between her thighs."

She smiles, sets one hand on one hip, and says, "Then let me press you, sweetie," in her sweetest voice.

Why resist? He asks, "Why after dinner?"

"We should eat first, or we'll get into a bad mood. You know, discipline."

"Gabe's influence again."

"It's the psychology of it. Gabe says you've got to welcome your fear. It's will versus instinct. It's finding the center of your balance. It's being centered."

"Sounds like he's your analyst. Where's the horse in all this?"

"Oh, he's under me. Under my control."

It's not Nikki's fault that this trainer is acting like an obsessed therapist for the horsey set. Cliff's got only himself to blame for hiring the guy, and he hates blame, especially blaming himself, so he drops it.

Then she says, "Sweetie, my first trial since we hired Gabe is a vital test, so you've simply got to come this time and watch me ride."

He thinks again of her and her trainer slapping five, sharing victory before they've won, the guy cheering her on to take even greater risks, and he says, "Maybe I will."

She claps her hands. Doesn't slap him five. "See, Cliff, I knew you'd come around."

Around to what? But he doesn't ask.

Dinner is going to take a while, so he goes upstairs to his office, sits at his desk, and writes out checks for plumbers, carpenters, electricians, architects, and subcontractors. Then he takes a break to gaze out the window over his fields, as he often does, and up to the foothills and the woods higher up, where in bird and deer season, he goes to hunt, his unloaded rifle locked now in the metal case next to a file cabinet behind his desk.

And he looks down into the valley, where his wife thrives, while he craves the heights. She's a meadow girl, a lover of sopping wet dew in early morning fields, of mud, sand, and clay, of footing that has a give. And she has a give, sometimes too sensitive, yet there's a marble core you can hit up against. From the first moment, he felt her challenge mixed with her sexuality. After they'd been married a few years, he said, "You came as advertised." She said, "That's one of the best compliments you've ever given me." He doesn't give many, he knows that, yet he still desires her often, like today with her rain-sculpted breasts.

But by the time they sit down at the Shaker table to eat, she has changed into a dry t-shirt and jeans, and she's talking about their family life, a change of topic that's not the least bit erotic. She's reminding him that Matt is flying into Logan from Seattle on Friday and that Lisa will be coming as well, so Cliff should be back home from the office early because it's Matt's thirtieth.

As if he'd forget his own son's birthday. And Nikki is saying that since Matt's new promotion, maybe he'll be happier, and things will be easier between her and him.

Cliff says nothing to this. During the summers, back when Matt lived with them, he ignored Nikki as much as possible. No denying his son's antipathy that only got more entrenched the more Nikki tried to charm. The more Nikki chatted, the more silent Matt got. The more she hovered, the more he shut down. Once Matt said to Cliff in private, "Tell Nikki to back off." Can't blame Matt for that. Yet Matt's distancing from Nikki was nothing compared with Cliff's to Matt's mother, Cliff's ex-wife, a proper lady, conservative, sedate. Cliff wanted action. Someone full of it. Now he's got what he wished for.

And he made a private vow to never divorce again, no matter how desperate.

"It will be a lovely family reunion," Nikki says, her old optimistic family spirit kicking in.

Dream on, he thinks. She hasn't seen Lisa since the beginning of summer when her daughter got a college internship in Boston. As a little girl, Lisa, deserted by her real father, craved her mother's affection, always wanting more, a bottomless pit. Not like Cliff himself, who, when he hits his intimacy limit, needs space. Nikki used to make jokes about how sometimes in the middle of the night, he'd wake and sit bolt up, fists clenched, asking, "What is it, who's there?" She said he had to protect himself even from his dreams. He said, "Hell yes." Proud of it. A carryover ever since he served in the Persian Gulf War, a lieutenant in the reserves, only in the desert three weeks. Saw mostly sand and bombed-out tanks. But he learned a discipline more strict than what Nikki's learning now. He knows how to protect himself.

Nikki's daughter protects herself, but by mouthing off. Yet, in spite of Lisa's teenage bitchiness, when she left for college, Nikki mourned, so she bought the mare off the track. When Lisa came home for her first college break, Nikki showed her daughter the new mare and asked what to name it. And, Lisa said, "Just don't name it Lisa." She already knew that she had been replaced. But Cliff did not know that he had been too, not back then.

NIKOLE

NIKKI PEEKS IN THE OVEN. Inside, six tiny quail, featherless, headless, stuffed and roasted to tender perfection. On the stove simmers one of her red wine sauces that disguises the stringent taste of wild fowl. She hands Lisa a knife, a cutting board, and a bowl of veggies.

Lisa starts hacking away and asks, "So what's for dinner? More little birds Cliff slaughtered?"

Ah, the good old blended family life, Nikki thinks. Jealousy and strife, but there's love mixed in the recipe. She turns off the oven, slides out the roasting pan. The little birds sit stewing in their own juices. She calls from the kitchen, "Cliff, dinner is almost ready!"

"Don't do that, Mother."

"Don't do what?"

"Don't dote."

Nikki claps her hands. "That's it! I have to dote completely if I want to win."

"Dote on Cliff?"

"On Beau."

They both chuckle at that miscue—they've had a lot of miscues over the years—but then Lisa wisecracks, "Beau gets all your attention anyway." And she hacks up more onions and mushrooms and tosses the bits into the burbling, blood-red sauce.

"Lisa, when I was your age, I competed on my college equestrian team, and since I couldn't afford riding much in high school, I felt like I'd been set free. I felt a desire to win that I've started feeling again. Can you blame me?"

"Sure I can."

Since she hit her teens, Lisa blames Nikki for almost everything. Lisa once said she wanted a normal mother, a logical lawyer maybe, not a part-time real estate agent and part-time horse fanatic. "Why don't you get a real job? Not with horses. They're just pretend." Nikki had saved up enough to fund Lisa's college, but Lisa knew how to get at her mother. Especially now that Lisa lives on campus and can come home, drop a few verbal bombs, then escape back to the groves of academe.

Nikki went to college on a grant. Her father never earned back the money he'd lost. And she had never seen her mother since she ran off, so Nikki learned mothering without a trainer. And she often let her daughter off easy, for Nikki had been a "bad girl" herself, or so her father sometimes said, when she resisted his orders. "Why can't you be a good girl like your sister?" he once asked. Good girls end up dead, she almost replied.

"I mean, it depends on why you want to win," Lisa says now.

Nikki sets each bird on the serving plate. The decapitated quail look as if they're nesting among the greens trimming the platter. She wishes they could fly away. She says, "Lisa, you're just jealous."

Lisa tosses her long, dark hair. "Not of horses, not me. But Cliff is."

"You're quite the authority on jealousy." When Lisa was six, after years of it being just the two of them, Nikki asked how Lisa felt about having a stepfather. Lisa said, "I don't want to share you with anyone." And after Nikki and Lisa moved in with Cliff, Lisa wrote Cliff a note and slid it under his bedroom door, 'Fuck you, Cliff.' Nikki hadn't known that Lisa even knew the F word, let alone how to spell it. Cliff told Lisa she was grounded for the weekend, and Lisa, never grounded before, banged her head against the wall of her room and screeched, while Nikki, heartsick, waited outside Lisa's door with Cliff and presented a united front, which Lisa still resents.

Now Nikki quickly carries out the platter to Cliff at the head of the table and catches herself almost doing a little dance, almost doting on him again, and when she sits, she waves her arms toward him as if to draw him out, to make him say something. Not a blessing, for he doesn't believe in prayer, but at least a birthday greeting for his son sitting to his right, so it seems like a normal family life.

They all sit silently around the cherry Shaker table, which a Vermont craftsman made, and which Lisa also has criticized. Lisa likes tables made of iron and glass. Lisa likes loft apartments in big cities, not horse farms "in the middle of nowhere." Matt lives in a big city, too, Seattle, with its torrents of rain and tortuous traffic jams, although he got his undergrad degree at his father's alma mater. Matt, not tall or big-framed like his dad, but with the same big hands and feet.

Cliff just sits and eats. He doesn't talk and eat both at once. And now Lisa starts in on religion. Nikki's father said not to discuss politics or religion at dinner. Nikki once made the mistake of telling Lisa that, so at meals Lisa consistently brings up one or the other.

Lisa's asking now why she was baptized as an infant. "Since I can't remember it, what's the point? What good is a new life if you're too young to have had an old one?"

"It was to protect your innocence," Nikki says.

"Innocence is like virginity," Lisa says. "You lose it."

No one says anything to that, so Lisa starts in on how her mother used to take her to a different church each Sunday, and they'd go out afterwards for brunch to critique the service. "No wonder I'm a skeptic, after my mother's revolving door of faith. And now she's a Unitarian and they can believe anything."

Cliff laughs at that. Once when an altar boy, he fell asleep at the altar during a service. And Matt laughs, so Nikki laughs at herself, although during her church tours, she was seeking something that she sensed lurked just out of reach.

Regardless, the laugh's on Mom. Family unity at last.

Except after that, Cliff falls silent again, his face a mask. When in a bad mood, Cliff says, "The world sucks." When in a good mood, he says, "Life's a trade off." He makes Lisa look like a warm, fuzzy optimist.

And Lisa goes on with her riff. "The historical Jesus was a Jewish mystic and a rebel against the establishment. He didn't have a doctrine. He preached love, not punishment."

Nikki thinks how Lisa, without realizing it, is proselytizing for Jesus, who forgave the lowest of the low, even if they didn't deserve it.

"Cliff, do you agree?" Lisa asks, leaning closer to him, in his face, as she often has been.

"Nyeah," Cliff says. A New England word that could mean no or yes.

Cliff's a public nihilist, a closet pantheist. He worships nature, Nikki thinks, especially the land that belongs to him, the land he knows and loves.

Matt switches topics from Jesus to the Patriots, and he and Cliff talk of the latest trade of an aging star for a rookie to shape up their line.

But then Cliff interjects, "Nikki's no rookie. She's getting shaped up by a professional trainer. She's headed for Advanced."

"Advanced what?" Matt asks.

Cliff doesn't answer, so Nikki says, "A higher level than what I was on."

Lisa cracks, "A higher plane of consciousness? Are horses your religion now, Mom? Wonder what God would say to that."

Cliff laughs again at that, and so do both kids. Nikki gets up and starts to clear the table of two plates with skeletons soaked in red sauce. Lisa peers down at the remnants on her plate and says, "Poor dumb bird," obviously not feeling like a hypocrite after just devouring it. Again casting bait out at Cliff.

Again, Cliff stays silent, doesn't bite.

So Lisa adds, "Cliff, don't tell me you've become a fellow believer in horseflesh."

Cliff shoves back his chair and stands so quickly that the dishes on the table rattle. He says, "I need a break." And heads into the living room, his heavy tread creaking up the stairs. He's going off to calm down, Nikki knows, for the children's sake. All these years, he has never raised his voice to them. This time she lets him go.

She says, "We'll take a little while to digest dinner before Matt's birthday dessert." Orange soufflé, one of her old gourmet treats, his favorite.

"Sure, Mom, be polite no matter what," Lisa says.

Matt stands and heads into the mudroom and out onto the deck.

Nikki leaves the dishes with Lisa and follows Matt into the night. He sits slouched in an Adirondack chair and stares up as if memorizing the constellations for when he returns to the Northwest, where sky is often obscured by rain and fog. Here in Vermont, the stars often glow crisp and clear, which Nikki often appreciates. Not now.

She sits down next to her stepson on the spare white chair. Matt doesn't speak. She and Matt have never had it out. Whatever "it" is. Matt didn't attend their marriage ceremony, neither did Lisa. Nikki and Cliff eloped, married by a liberal, Unitarian minister in a small church not far from Killington, a ski resort. They didn't invite their kids, who didn't want them together. "Happiness is as fleeting as orgasm," Cliff said, "so grab it while you can."

Matt's still staring up at the sky. She's used to being ignored by him. It only makes her want to talk more as it does with Cliff. Doesn't get her anywhere, but it's better than sitting so still in this star-studded silence.

"Do you want to talk about your Dad?" she asks.

He shakes his head. They both sit staring up at the sky. She can't even find the big dipper, not to mention the little one.

"So how's your new job with the Seahawks?" She asks, to fill in the gap.

He says, "I keep track of those who keep score."

A scorekeeper, like his father who periodically erupts, only about once or twice a year, and only with her, not with the kids. Although sometimes he lists her wrongs over the past months. "In February, you said that . . ." and "Last spring, you didn't . . ."

"So you like scorekeeping?" Nikki asks.

"I like that there are clear rules, so if there's a challenge on the field, the right call can be verified."

"It's like judging eventing," she says.

"I'm dealing with humans, not animals."

"Sometimes animals are more . . . loving."

He slides down lower in the Adirondack chair, so his head tilts up more, like a stargazer instead of an ethical scorekeeper, his only view the dark sky with those spatterings of light. "More loving than my Dad, you mean?"

"Oh no, not more than Cliff."

Thinking how Cliff hides his love, and how Matt once said Nikki got too hyped, and his Dad too morose. "Together, you're one manic depressive," he'd said.

And how Lisa used to say, "Hey, Cliff, lighten up," or "Hey, Mom, tone it down." Yet Nikki couldn't stop seeking what lay hidden in Cliff, and he didn't stop letting her seek.

"It's a matter of letting it out," she says.

"Nikki, ease up. Back off." Matt sounding like her trainer now.

He just keeps staring up at nameless bright spots in the black as if they have some significance. Yet she's going to love Cliff's son in spite of all obstacles. And the delicate orangey scent of her soufflé drifts through the open window out onto the deck and tempts her to go back inside to reassemble this blended family that she is fated to have, like some preordained accident.

She stands. "Matt, are you coming in for your birthday dessert?"

To her surprise, he stands and slowly walks back in with her. These small gestures of his are all she can hope for.

Matt sits down in his old place, and Nikki calls up to Cliff, whose footsteps sound heavy down the stairs. He dutifully re-takes his seat, and Lisa comes in from the kitchen where she was actually cleaning up, and then Nikki goes to the oven and carries out to her merged family the warm soufflé, smelling of orange blossoms and spice. She sets the dessert in front of Matt, but as she bends over him, he quickly draws back, sits straight. He must want her not to be this close, must want her not to exist, must want her to be a star shooting far away through the night, eventually to fall and extinguish itself.

CLIFF AND GABE

HE DOESN'T WANT TO BROIL in this midsummer, smarmy heat at this horse-smothered estate, sleek horses and riders everywhere he looks, three huge outdoor rings and one indoor with stadium seating, plus six barns and several miles of cross-country course. It all makes Cliff's own farm seem like an amateur operation. He'd really rather be somewhere else.

But Cliff thought his being at her first Intermediate U.S. Equestrian Federation sanctioned event would somehow keep his wife safe. And now he's waiting for her turn on course. She's due in nine minutes, riders at three-minute intervals, each eventer a potential victim lurching toward premature death. Cliff tunes out the horses like he tuned out dressage on day one. Didn't even drive up for it. Nikki said it was invented by the military to prepare horses for battle in war, but to him, it seems tame—collected and extended walk trot canter movements in a ring—like watching paint dry. Which is why Nikki craves cross-country, for that rush like Cliff got playing football, also got a concussion, broken foot, hand, fingers, ribs. Secretly, he sees why his forty-year-old wife is making her Intermediate debut. It's her middle-aged coming out party.

So he actually made the mistake of driving up last night. Might as well have separate beds the nights before she competes. She practiced her pelvic moves on a straight-backed chair. Another virtual reality horse show.

Yet, of all three phases in this trial, Cliff will admit, only to himself, that cross-country is his favorite, precisely because it's so damned dangerous—bust a leg, get flattened, break your neck.

He even brought his camera along, a 600 mm lens for close-ups. Has the thick, long, thing pointed toward the earth. Got a shot of a fall when one rider "left her tack." A jump judge said the horse "missed its spot." An ambulance carted the rider off. In high-risk sports like downhill skiing or hang gliding, there's only your own body to control.

Now the annoying female deity's voice blasts through the loudspeaker that number thirty-eight, Nikole Swensen, is on course. Adrenaline shoots through him, and he thinks, damn if he doesn't want her to win. Nikki's usually the contradictory one—up one minute, down the next, while his moods settle in for weeks, sometimes months. "Cliff, why are you so down?" She used to ask. He'd say he didn't know. She'd say, "Well then, let me cheer you up." And sometimes, he'd feel mellow for a while, but then she'd get too upbeat, too clingy, so he'd retreat. His calm sets her on edge. She's gullible, overly affectionate, unpredictable. How the hell can Gabe train her?

In spite of all that, Cliff dutifully stands by the finish, where he can see across several open acres, the last four jumps. One is a water jump. In its center sits a big, fat, fake yellow duck—probably six feet wide, four feet tall. Like some giant yellow bath toy, it seems to float in the shallow, man-made pond. What will horsepeople think up next?

And then he spots, stalking through the small outdoorsy, preppy crowd by the finish, a tall attractive woman who seems to be heading straight for him. She's almost six feet, dressed in a long flowered skirt and white blouse and carrying a picnic basket and a folded lawn chair. A bleached blonde with frizzy curls. An outsider for sure, but she steps right up to him, sets down her basket, unfolds her chair, reaches out a long hand, and says, "You must be Cliff. Gabe described you as a big bear. I'm Carla."

And Cliff's shaking a hard, strong hand and looking into steady, unflinching eyes that know what they want. She must be about three inches taller than her husband.

Then Carla's talking about how she skipped the dressage. "Boring," she says. "Top hats and tails, and the horses doing those collected and extended gaits. They all look the same. How can I judge?"

"Couldn't agree more."

"And if you can't judge it, what good is it?"

Cliff falls silent at that.

"And the way they have to take off their hats and bow their heads to that judge in her box. I don't bow to anyone."

"I bet you don't," he says, deadpan.

Carla casts him a sidelong, appraising glance and says, "And as for cross-country, it's a minefield out there."

"It sure is."

"So we agree on that much."

"On minefields, yes."

"Well, that's a start." She reaches into her picnic basket, takes out a thermos and two plastic glasses, unscrews the thermos lid, pours some pink thick fluid into each glass and says, "Strawberry daiquiris, here, try one."

Daiquiris at noon in the sun? He remembers the viscous drink from his high school days, but he takes a glass, as Carla says, "I only came along for moral support."

Cliff's not sure what morality has to do with this, so he says nothing again. Saying nothing has got him far in life.

Suddenly the loudspeaker deity announces that Nikole Swensen, number thirty-eight, has cleared the Dippity Dip.

"Eight minutes until your wife gets to us," Carla says. "But this is only the beginning."

"Of what?"

"Of them moving up. Once they qualify for two-star events, they'll want three, then four, and once they get a red ribbon in Advanced, they'll want a blue. There's no end to it. They're hooked."

Again, he makes no comment.

"So what do you think?" she asks, not letting him be.

"I think you have a point."

"You're right. But you don't have to be so polite. We're going to be together a lot. We're both horse widowers."

As if their mates are already dead.

"So let's go to the competitors' party tonight," Carla says. "I like to make my presence known."

No problem for her there, Cliff thinks. Even sitting on the collapsible chair at his feet, Carla seems formidable, but also appealing in her wide-brimmed straw sun hat and immaculate white blouse that only partly disguises a sizeable bust. He wonders how little old Gabe handles her.

"Ribbons," she says, sipping her daiquiri. "Why do they want ribbons so much? Even blue ones are just strips of cheap colored cloth. Better would be prize money, but it's not money Gabe's after."

"What is he after?"

"Oh . . . fame and glory. Or else death and destruction. Don't get me going. I tend to exaggerate."

"It's better to understate."

"Yeah, I bet you hold things in."

He swallows some of his daiquiri.

And Carla says, "But they both need to do this, Cliff, so you and I have to rise to the occasion, you know, in order to keep on top of it. That's what I'm telling myself. And I bet you are, too."

Now she's telling him what he's telling himself? She's obtrusive, too direct, although she could be right.

He realizes that in the last minutes a few riders have crossed the finish, and he hasn't noticed, he was so distracted by this down-to-earth woman who seems to know her own mind. If only Nikki always did, but then he might not still be intrigued.

"She'll be coming any minute now," Carla says, sadly.

◆◆◆

Gabe half jogs, half limps, on a shortcut as he tracks Nikki through pines and birches toward the last hilltop to the water jump. He has walked this course many times with her, and memorized it, so for this entire run, even when they're out of sight, he has felt like he's riding double with her, seeing the jumps from between the horse's pricked ears . . . spectators only splashes of bright color, grass sliding into green strips, white rails flashing up . . . he and Nikki counting strides in the combinations . . . almost losing control in the Labyrinth. Balance yourself, he thinks, and now they're tearing across a flat stretch to make up lost time before they sweep over the Carpenter's Table and gallop across a small bridge down an incline. Let go, he thinks. Focus. They leap over the Tiger's Trap, and a quarter acre to the Coffin, number thirteen, but Beau keeps his feet under himself, and they're over it, then uphill and down into a stand of oaks, and out of sight to a Trakehner, a log over a ditch. Beau hates ditches in shadows, jumping into the dark . . .

Gabe has to leave them to shuffle fast up another path to the last hilltop to keep watch over water, and soon Beau comes flying down the slope to the drop into the pond. In the center a duck, a splash obstacle, a serious question, their former downfall. But Gabe's feeling he's one again with the horse, with her, they're riding double, he's soft talking into her ear, both leaning back too far, so as Beau splashes down into the man-made pond, they slip in the tack, the big yellow duck ahead, her elbows flapping. Beau's big chance to balk or buck. Eyes up, Gabe thinks, and Nikki lifts her head, and right then Beau slows, takes an extra stride, gives them a break, so they can right themselves, before Beau's flying up over the duck and hanging in air . . . Then he's sloshing through and out of water like he was trained to do, and he gallops downhill toward the brush, coming up fast, sailing over it, and around a bend between oaks and pines toward the Dippety Dip, got to make up time, as Gabe limps further along the hilltop in time to see Beau surge out of the oaks and gallop flat out down a half acre of a flat treeless stretch toward the finish,

Gabe thinking, We're as one again, we're sailing over the line, and we click our watches off, Nikki and I, at the same second. We made it, yes, we went goddamned clear.

And he's slapping his good thigh just when she's slapping Beau's neck. Gabe hurries down a shortcut, a bumpy path, scuttling as fast as he can with his tilting lope, and he gets to where she's dismounted when, damnit, out of the side of his eye, if he doesn't see Cliff striding toward them from way over by the finish. Right when she and Gabe are both patting Beau's neck, both stroking and gently slapping Beau, both saying things like, "You're the best." "You've got what it takes."

Gabe looks at Nikki and says, "Good ride."

"I can't believe we got through clean."

That's where she is. Just wants to make it clean when he wants way more than that. But he can't say this because now the omnipresent Cliff steps up and congratulates only her, all because he writes the checks. Cliff doesn't see that Beau got her through that course, and Nikki's all aglow like she's responsible. Gabe wants to say, "Nikki, Beau, and me, we did it together." But why bother when Nikki's thanking God. And now Carla has to appear, and she's giving Nikki the once over, for they haven't met. That shrewd gaze a woman has sizing up another woman. Nikki only comes up to Carla's shoulder so Nikki seems delicate, even childlike, compared with Carla's rounded, womanly self.

Nikki's got her eyes cast down, seems a little self-conscious with her helmet off, her dark hair flattened under a hairnet, sort of like the nets waitresses wear. Same hairnets . . . different worlds.

"I'm Gabe's wife," Carla says. "Congrats on taking his advice, because he's a real expert." Giving him all the credit.

Nikki says, "I'm glad to finally meet you, but we'll have to talk later, because now I must be with my horse." The sturdy gelding all lathered up from the late July heat.

"Carla, see you back at the trailer," Gabe says and walks off with Nikki and Beau.

From behind, Carla says, "I'll be waiting for you, babe," like a loving threat.

On the way to the barn, Gabe says, "Carla's all invested in my being a trainer. In fact, it was her idea."

"And it was Cliff's idea for me to hire one."

"So now we're stuck with each other," Gabe says, with a wry grin. "And stuck with being in their debt." Yet in the past he'd gotten paid by multiple owners to event their horses and hadn't owed anything to anyone.

He and Nikki lead Beau toward the barn to their assigned stall and untack him before their groom arrives, Bunny Henderson, who also mucks stalls at Northlands in order to pick up free rides like Nikki said she did after her father went bankrupt.

In the murky light, Nikki strokes Beau all down his neck and withers and says, "Oh, baby, you're my hero." Sweet-talking, her voice real soft. "You're my love," while she's bending down to massage each leg.

Gabe softly says, "You're what I've been waiting for." And he waits.

Nikki glances up at him from her crouch, like he maybe said that to her.

But he keeps his eyes on the horse. Don't get into what could bring you down, he tells himself. Cross that line, no going back.

Then Bunny comes up to Beau, and she's giving congratulations and talking about going clear in the jumping phase on day three. She's not a bad girl, medium height, medium brown hair, medium plain face. Bunny manages the barn. Nikki manages the barn accounts, under Cliff's oversight. Cliff, the Overseer, Gabe thinks.

Gabe steps into the aisle with Nikki and asks, "So what do you think of Beau's performance?"

"Well, he was . . . unpredictable."

She's the one who's unpredictable. Gabe feels his old impatience spurt up but forces himself to keep positive, and says, "You're both turbo charged."

"At the ditch, number ten, he almost ran out," she admits.

"I saw that. Why do you think he swerved?"

"I was on his mouth."

"Right. You didn't let him have his head. That's why you got that little buck after he landed. Lucky he didn't buck you off."

She nods.

"And why do you think he almost balked and almost chested the Table at number twelve?"

"My elbows were flapping."

"Beau got you over that jump. And why did you almost come out of your tack in the water before the duck?"

She shakes her head.

"Over the drop into the water, you got left behind."

"I was left behind," she repeats in a solemn tone like it's some kind of existential state. Gabe knows what it means to be left behind, and he knows if he hadn't been riding double behind her today like some kind of friggin' guardian angel, she'd have at least twenty penalty points.

"But we got Beau through the water, his old nemesis," Gabe says. "So now all we've got to do is go clear tomorrow, and we're on our way up."

"*We?*"

"Yeah, we're riding in tandem. Didn't you feel that?" And he's smiling, as much as he can, but she cocks her head as if she didn't sense him breathing into her brain.

"Like I felt as a girl," she says, "with my sister."

"Nikki . . . I'm not dead."

"No . . . she says absently, as if he's lost her to a past ghost when he wants her to be present now, in this instant.

CARLA AND NIKOLE

THAT NIGHT, CARLA FINDS HERSELF at the competitors' party inside the clubhouse because of a light summer drizzle. Nikole stands out, wafting through the casually-dressed crowd in black jeans and a black top that shows cleavage, looking like she just popped out of a victory cake. This little woman is just the type to appeal to men, with her little uptilted nose, bud of a mouth, tiny body, and small thin bones—not like Carla's big-boned frame, thanks to good farm genes. Except she's barren. But she's got Gabe.

He's talking with Nikole and a couple of lady owners about straight fetlocks and an overstride. The influential ones hire top riders, like Gabe once was, to ride their hundred-thousand-dollar-plus event horses. Nikole is one of the few owner-riders who bought her horses for cheap off the racetrack, yet the ladies gather around Nikole and Gabe, leaving Carla off to the side.

Gabe's saying, "Horses are more than a sport, they're a way of life." Carla has heard this line however many times. And then Gabe's talking about how if Beau goes clear tomorrow, he'll place in the top ten, his first ribbon in an Intermediate competition.

"Placing at Intermediate is good enough for me," Nikole says.

"It's good enough for now," Gabe corrects. "Then we'll go higher."

"Because of you, Gabe," Nikole says and lifts her glass to toast him. The ladies toast him as well, but then, as if he really doesn't count, they glide off in a cluster, a pastel bouquet. They never did notice Carla still standing there, though Carla knows she's hard to miss.

She holds her spine straight. She's got no money but she's educated, put herself through the local teachers' college by working as a waitress, wore a starched yellow uniform and a hairnet, sponged off Formica table tops for truck drivers, the jukebox wailing Waylon or Wynona or Willie, and on occasion she swayed her hips to the beat. Shake it, yeah, move it on out. Now she's forty-five, but still ripe.

A small band is warming up, a drummer and a guy on an electric guitar, who's adjusting an amp, her foot tapping to the beat, though gone are the days when Gabe danced. He had rhythm in his feet, his bones, his skin.

Cliff comes out of his corner and is rounding up his wife, but Nikole says to Gabe and Carla, "Let's go back to my trailer for a nightcap."

Carla never liked people who call a drink a "nightcap." Plus, Nikole has a clipped speech like she was bred into this horse world. Yet didn't Gabe report that Nikole's father lost all his money, so as a girl, she had to work as a stable hand in order to ride like he did? Gabe clearly respects her more for having been rich, then poor, then rich. To Carla, it sounds like a schizoid relationship to money. Better to accept your lot in life. As Carla's mother used to say, "Make the best of what you got, and don't ever give it up."

Soon the four of them sit on flimsy foldout chairs behind Nikole and Cliff's big fancy rig with six stalls when Nikole has got only one horse that can compete now, Gabe said. But the rig was a gift from Cliff. Cliff's shut up inside himself but buys only the best. An all or nothing kind of man.

They sit into the night with citronella candles flickering, turning their faces light then dark, light then dark. Gabe's talking about how Beau should go clear tomorrow, and Nikole's smiling an itty-bitty smile. Then Gabe says that Nikole rode cross-country the best she could, given she'd never competed at this level before. Nikole's smiling a bit more at that. And Gabe says that it takes more courage to ride if you've got fear than if you don't. Now she's beaming, lapping up praise like she's starving for it. The quiet Cliff, for all his fancy gifts, probably forgets the power of praise, and he just sits still, watching over them.

Gabe, on the other hand, is overdoing it. Carla knows how to shake him up, chat about his pock-marked past in the Midwest—his ill-fated liaison that he confessed, or his fall that he refuses to discuss—but Gabe would be furious. Plus this arrangement was all her idea in the first place. Yet another good deed leading to perdition, perhaps. So she just sits by the rig on a shaky folding chair, Gabe tilting back on his, it might cave in—would serve him right—while he says that Nikole's got a good eye for horses bought off the track, for talent, confirmation, and gaits.

If Nikole hadn't ridden when she was a kid, she wouldn't be competing. A lot depends on the family you're born into, Carla thinks. Hers was poor with a strict Protestant work ethic, so sports seemed self-indulgent.

Maybe that's why she fell for Gabe, his self-discipline was mixed with a sense of play. Now he's saying, "It's the natural movement of the horse I want to enhance." Gabe's good at saying lines like that, although he means them.

That's also how he got her to fall for him. It's your natural movement, Carla, you've got what it takes . . . Carla, it's not only your big tits I love, it's your big heart . . .

She's a believer, except when she doubts. Why, the messes she's got that man out of. It seems as if she was predestined to marry a man whom she needs to save. A man who's leaning toward Nikole Swensen and saying, "We'll have to intensify our training schedule."

Nikole's nodding like she thinks training, not talent, can get her to win.

Carla shoves back her chair and stands over them all. "Well, Gabe, it's after midnight. Guess we better be getting to bed."

"You go on ahead, Carla. I'll be along shortly. We've got to strategize for tomorrow here."

"But, Gabe, you look awfully tired with those dark circles under your eyes after all you've done today."

"Mama, I'm not tired yet." Smiling his lopsided smile.

She's still not used to it. Big Mama. Sweet Mama. *Mama mia.* Mama any way you look at it.

She glances over at Cliff, but the big man sits as stiff as if rigor mortis has set in. Why doesn't he say something?

She's got to go alone. Not that she's jealous. Ever since Gabe's fall, women don't look at him the same way, now that they're not sure, and can't ask, if he can still function in bed. And Carla's not about to reveal that he's still in gear when he's in the mood, which is off and on.

She lifts her chin, thrusts her shoulders back, and simply says, "Gabe, I'll see you in our trailer soon."

Nikole says good night, and Cliff does not. Carla slowly steps off toward their tiny camper built into the well of Gabe's pickup, a camper barely big enough for him and her to fit. Nikole and Cliff, even though they have modern sleeping quarters in their big fancy rig, will sleep in a hotel like some owners do. But Carla's used to tight quarters and to cradling Gabe in her strong arms, and sometimes he nestles into her bare breasts, like the child she never had.

◆ ◆ ◆

The three of them sit until the music and voices from the competitors' tent fade like at dusk when the chattering of birds dwindled into the dark. They've been talking horse talk that Cliff refuses to speak, Nikki thinks, until now at last, he's standing up to go. Even half shrouded by night, he still looms large.

"It's late," he says. Doesn't ask what she'll do.

"I've got to check on Beau for the night," she says.

Cliff waits silently.

"A horse who events cross-country can colic afterwards," Nikki adds. "You know, its intestines can twist after all that it puts out."

He turns and lopes off, and it seems to her this man is made of shadows and silences as he merges with the dark and vanishes into the compartment of their rig, and the door snaps shut with that tinny click. Even though they've got a motel room, she knows he'll stay there until she comes in. He'll strip off his clothes, leave them all neatly folded in the top built-in bureau drawer. He's obsessively neat from his military training, served two months in a war he was against. Never shot a soul, he said. Was that regret in his voice, she wonders, heading into the barn with Gabe.

Beau's sleeping standing up like horses usually do, protecting against predators. He's instantly awake. She and Gabe go inside the stall, check Beau's pulse, and run hands down his legs. After that, he swivels his hindquarters, gently knocking Nikki off balance.

"Still up to his tricks," Gabe says.

And you? She wonders. What are your tricks?

They step out of the stall and she stops, so he does. All down the long barn aisle, at each stall, saddle racks wait empty now, while inside darkened trailers, freshly polished saddles—Black Country, Stubben, Devoucoux—sit like huge, shiny mushrooms glowing in the night.

In the empty, dim barn aisle, the heavy, sudsy horsey perfume of saddle soap, leather oils, and cream conditioners, like nectar, still fills the air.

She inhales as deeply as she can. Then she turns to Gabe and says, "I don't know you."

"I'm the guy who got you to ride the way you rode today."

"I mean, beyond that."

"You're not the type to look beyond."

Oh, but she is. Even as a girl, she was often looking beyond to an invisible God, whom she felt watching her but never heard His voice, although she kept listening, kept thinking she'd hear words, tips, advice, such as a trainer gives, about how to get good.

"What are you, my analyst?" she asks. "That's what Cliff called you."

"Cliff thinks he's running the show."

She's suddenly irritated at his criticizing Cliff, and says, "He hired you."

"I was too good to resist." Gabe's smiling his loopy grin again, as if he's poking fun at her, and that makes her want to poke back.

"Gabe, did you know that you're my fifteenth wedding anniversary present?"

"The hell I am!"

"A new trainer is what Cliff said he'd get me, and he did."

Gabe hesitates. She watches him while he ponders that. "So I'm bought and paid for, is that it? Wrapped up with a bow?"

"I didn't mean it like that."

He thinks again. "Well, maybe I'm a gift from on high." And he half grins. "That's what my Catholic mother thought when I was born. That's why she named me Gabriel, after the angel who flew in and announced to the Virgin Mary that she was pregnant. An immaculate conception. Yeah, right. Gabriel probably knocked her up. I bet you didn't know I'm an angel's namesake."

Nikki shakes her head, takes another look at him, his eyes light brown but hard and clear, translucent like water. Beau's dark brown eyes are opaque. Soft eyes.

"But now I'm a fallen angel," Gabe says, still smiling his cockeyed grin, trying to make a joke of it. "My horse fell, so I did, had my wings sheared off. There, do you know me better?"

She's not sure what to make of this, with his grin half on, half off. She shakes her head no.

"Well, that'll have to do for now because you've got to get your beauty rest for the jumping phase tomorrow. Got to dream that you'll go clear."

"And if I go clear, then what?"

"Then we move on until we qualify for FEI competitions, where we'll truly make our mark. Beau's got the sense to tell the cross-country fences, where he jumps flat, from in the ring, where the rails fall so he's got to pop high and round. Some horses have a natural sense for that. Of course, you've got to trust him to do his job." And then Gabe is going on again about how many strides to take between fences, just like he'll do in the morning when they'll walk the jumping course in the ring to figure out their line of attack.

He's more obsessed than I am, she thinks. "Horses are a religion to you," she says.

He looks directly at her and says, "You got to be willing to die for it."

She thinks of her sister and old photographs of how elegantly the lithe, blonde Tricia sat a horse. Then one day she had vanished. Her father came to Nikki and said that Tricia was gone. Nikki asked where, and he said Tricia's horse balked at a jump, and she somersaulted forward and broke her neck. Nikki asked, "What?" Her father said, "Your sister is dead." And again Nikki asked, "What?" For she didn't believe it. And her father would not allow Nikki to go to the funeral, so often afterwards Nikki felt her sister riding with her and wondered if her spirit hid in the horse barn, or in Tricia's old room, still decorated with ribbons and plaques. Nikki had no proof Tricia was truly dead. Only an absence.

"Are you?" Gabe asks.

She doesn't answer.

"Because if you're not willing to take the risk, I'm not putting in six days a week training you. I've got no patience for dilettantes."

She wishes Cliff hadn't gone to bed. Yet she is also glad that he did. She looks away, down the barn aisle, hears the rustling of horses in dim small spaces, feels their pent-up energy, beasts meant to roam during day or night, and she says, "I better go."

"Wait, hold it right there!" Gabe says, stepping up next to her and taking both her hands in his. It's odd feeling his two opposite hands, the right one warm and firm and tight, the left hand with no grip, a shell overlaying her hand. He says, "Since my fall, you and Beau are what I've been waiting for without knowing it. We've got to have discipline, dedicate ourselves. Be like monks, take vows."

Almost like marriage vows, she thinks. Let him who is against this speak up now. But Cliff isn't present.

"We're one of a kind," Gabe says. "So promise me."

They're standing eye to eye, Gabe only a few inches taller, so it's different from tilting her head back to see up into Cliff's eyes. Gabe's waiting, and she feels revved up. Then she hears thuds, maybe horse's hooves from the stalls, or is it the one-two beat of a human step? *Never do bad when the horses watch*, an old stable hand once said. She listens . . . hears only the snorting and stomping of animals, yet her hands slide out of Gabe's, and she quickly steps down the long aisle to the wide mouth of the barn . . . sees no two-legged shadow in the night.

Gabe comes up behind, steps close. "Nikki, you just balked."

"Maybe I'm untrainable."

"Like hell you are."

But she heads out into the night, loping fast toward her husband, who maybe sleeps, or maybe lies awake wondering if she's doing what she just almost did.

◆◆◆

She steps into the sleeping quarters of her big rig, eases shut the steel door, a faint metallic click. Her eyes gradually adjust to the shadowy light, a small wall sconce Cliff left turned on, like a nightlight for a child—sweet, although she regrets the gesture, for it means he thought she'd be out extra late. She eyes his bulk under a white sheet on the bare, hard bed. He's on his right side, his wide back to her. He usually sleeps on his left side facing her.

"Cliff," she whispers, so as not to wake him up, if he really is asleep. Doesn't he want to go to their hotel? He has always refused to spend the night in the rig, too closed-in.

"Cliff?"

Only the hum of the miniature fridge in the compact, built-in, stainless kitchenette. And his breath, heavy, regular. Could he be faking heavy breathing just to avoid her now? She feels guilty. Sins of omission. She wants to confess to a vow that she hasn't made yet. She's on the cusp of wholly dedicating herself to a world that he's against.

"Cliff?" A harder whisper now.

Only that heavy breath, as if officially asleep. Or maybe he's got soft eyes like horses have and can see almost all around, like God's eyes, and can see her now. She straightens, nervously smoothes her hair.

She slides off her britches, drops her black top, and, leaving on her bra and panties—for she wants him to wake and go to the hotel where he likes it—she slides into bed next to his bulk. Immovable.

She taps him lightly on the shoulder blades with her fingertips. Only the steady rise and fall of his chest, his back.

"Cliff?" Ever so softly.

Only that breath in and out, as if he's meditating, which he never does. Cliff, a man of immovable justice, would say a mantra like, Fuck her, fuck this BS.

Yet she wants him to wake, to hear his few hard words, to feel how hard he is. She snuggles lightly next to him and lightly taps his shoulder blades again, but he keeps breathing with depth. So she tap-taps, tap-taps again, as she'd tap a horse lightly with a crop to get it to move forward, and then finally, Cliff wakes or was awake all along. He rolls over and takes her in his heavy arms, his big hands gentle but incisive, a surgeon's hands, that dexterity, both hands moving deftly now, so different from Gabe's one-handed grip, and she doesn't pull away from Cliff's tender grasp.

◆◆◆

The next day, right after the jumping phase—all that training for less than three intense minutes in the ring—she's heading back to the barn with Gabe, and they're jubilating. She rode Beau out to get a ribbon. He only ticked rails twice, otherwise popped over jumps, plus one time fault, so they're in the top five. She's buoyant, floating above it all, feeling like a girl again winning a red ribbon in her first show. She was only eight, and when her father didn't attend, she dreamt of running off to become a circus star and perform Roman Riding, standing with one foot on the back of each of two galloping horses, leaping through death-defying hoops of fire—whatever it took to make her father come look.

Now Gabe's skipping along even with his limp and saying he was watching her every move. She laughs loudly at that, feeling a joy she hasn't felt in that farmhouse thick with moods and thoughts, and all for what? Why that heaviness when no one has died? Why that silence when she wants to talk? Why does Cliff move slowly when she bounds ahead? Why does he seem collected when she feels reckless? Why must he hide his tenderness when she's clinging with hers? And why does she feel this lightness floating next to Gabe and Beau, her feet not touching the ground, a miracle to walk on air? Even though they didn't win a blue, Gabe's saying that they'll get one soon. And she believes him, for she believes they're blessed, believes God might just be present, or some holy spirit is. And she's smiling, she's light-footing it, she's an athlete, she's golden, and it's not about ribbons, it's transcendence.

CLIFF

TWO MONTHS AND TWO HORSE trials later, Cliff stands alone on his deck and eyes the manure pile behind the barn and thinks how each horse produces fifty pounds of manure each day. Fifty pounds times four horses equals two hundred pounds per day of shit. No wonder the groundhogs that burrow into the pile are glossy and fat. When Cliff's in a good mood and sees the patriarch, the biggest and sleekest of the underground rodents, sitting and preening himself on that mound of dung, he thinks, Yeah, Mr. Groundhog, go for it. But when he's feeling down, like now, and sees the fatso-glorified rat poised on top of a pile of shit, he thinks, "Hell, that's life."

If it weren't for Nikki's obsession, he'd sell all her shit-producing beasts, even Harley, his half work horse. In the old days, draft horses worked from dawn to dusk, but now these one-ton powerful beasts stand around and munch on grass and hay, all that untapped energy building, excess strength chugging through their veins, through their thick limbs, enough energy to split their skins.

Maybe that's why Harley gets sucked in by Gracie when she's in heat. Harley got gelded late so he still has some residual male instincts. Sometimes she teases him through the fence, pressing her hindquarters up against the rails, lifting her tail. But when Harley falls for it and comes close, she kicks. Frustrated, he charges up and down the fence line. The two of them must be kept separate because when she's not in heat, she's even worse. She'll attack.

As dusk creeps in, a damp chill pervades the air, cold for early fall, yet Cliff, though wearing only khakis and a short-sleeved shirt, stays out on the deck. He craves the cold. He even likes a good, crisp windchill. Reminds him of hunting season in a few months. Should do some target practice down in the gravel pit. Got to respect the winter, keep moving, and wear layers, hats, insulated boots, and gloves. This early chill is bad for horsepeople who must ride on almost frozen soil. Like Nikki, who complains that it's tough on Beau's legs to jump on ground as hard as cement. Ever since that first trial six weeks ago, something has set her on fire within. She could melt snow, she's so hot, burning with desire for a dumb beast.

And in two days, she'll be leaving with Gabe for their fourth trial. If they go clean again, they'll be qualified for Advanced events in late fall, and she'll be gone with her trainer even lon-ger then. Not what Cliff had in mind when he bought her that little lopsided man. Gabe's half numb, and the other half is obsessed. Yet that half is totally focused, which Cliff respects, but he also doubts. The little guy sometimes sits cross-legged under Cliff's willow tree like he's got a monopoly on calm, but really Gabe's jumpy underneath. Cliff can sense the little guy's restlessness, like back in his football days, when Cliff used to sense his opponent's weak spot. He'd lie for guys who hit him hard, once waited a whole season to get one opponent back . . . just before half time, hit the guy so hard it blew out the kid's knee. The weaker of two forces yields. If Cliff had let down his guard, the kid would have killed him and loved it. The middle linebacker led by ruthless command. From snap to whistle no-body wanted to break the legs of a ball carrier more than he did. Collide and destroy. The essence of collision—train for months for a fraction of a second, the moment of impact. Lately, Cliff sometimes finds himself thinking of that moment again.

◆◆◆

That night, he's sitting with Nikki at the cherry Shaker table by the picture window overlooking the paddock. Dusk's dying now, horses shut in their stalls, the paddocks and lush fields fading so fast that at any moment he'll have to imagine all the rich, darkened land, which belongs to him. He knows every twist of the terrain, where sandy soil pans out and clay begins, where the ground is hard and where it's soft, where grass grows thick and where it's sparse. Horses make you notice the texture of the earth. They're good for that much at least.

He and Nikki are eating dinner, her chicken cordon bleu, one of his favorites. Mealtimes are the times they tend to talk, and she asks, yet again, if he won't change his mind and come watch her ride at the Massachusetts trial this weekend.

Cliff ponders why she keeps harassing him. He watched at that first trial, then at the next two he went but stayed in the rig. As she takes higher jumps, his body's stressed. He stands so military stiff that afterwards his back aches. This time, she knows he's got a major real estate deal that he's closing on, so no way can he take off for the three days, plus one more to arrive early, plus two more for trailering up and back.

"Do you really think Beau can win at Advanced?" he asks.

"He's only ten, so Gabe thinks we can place and get me mileage while Gracie comes along. Gabe says Beau makes it on guts, but she's the natural-born jumper. I've only jumped her in the ring, but Gabe says she's making real progress."

Gabe this, Gabe that again. Cliff remembers the other day when he left late for the office and saw Gabe standing out in the center of the ring, while Nikki rode the great big bitch over low jumps, clearing them by several feet. She's got lift, no denying it. Gabe also has been lunging the three-year-old, doing so-called "ground work" on ground that belongs to Cliff. Gabe is training the mare so that years from now she'll compete at Advanced and advance the level of torture for Cliff, who has endangered his wife by hiring that perfectionist.

"Gracie is truly talented," Nikki says.

As if talent makes up for her having a mean streak that makes her unpredictable as hell.

"Of course, the only one who can control her is Gabe," she adds.

"At least during the winter," Cliff says, "there are no shows, so we'll live a normal life."

She looks down at her plate. "Well . . . yes . . . except Gabe says that this winter we should move Beau and Gracie over to Meadowlark Stables with its heated indoor ring. You know, to keep practicing, to keep them in shape for the spring, because we've got to think ahead, Gabe says."

Give a horsewoman free rein, this is what you get. Where's the bottom line?

"This is all adding up," Cliff says. "Stalls cost a lot at an indoor ring, plus vet bills for all four horses. Plus feed. Plus farrier costs every six weeks. Plus show fees and boarding. Plus the trailer. Plus insurance, plus . . ."

"I'm paying for all that," she cuts in, proud to have invested her savings, though she's lost some in the present market and could run out.

"Not to mention the trainer's generous salary," Cliff adds.

"I'll withdraw more and pay for him, too," she says.

Another one of her double binds. He'd have to take back his gift.

He shakes his head no, and they eat awhile in a thick silence, her baby potatoes overcooked, her chicken breasts dried out, her red wine sauce too syrupy thick. She never cooks like that.

"You've got a responsibility to your family," he says, "not to get hurt."

"I'm working hard not to."

"You won't win a first."

"It's an art, Gabe said. Takes years and years to perfect."

"Takes a lifetime."

"Well . . . yes . . . more or less."

More or less than a lifetime? Cliff shuts up again.

"Cliff, are you all right?"

"Best I've been in a while," he says, with a twist to his lip. Pretty soon he'll be smiling like that trainer does, crooked, cynical half smirks. Gabe has driven her to a fever pitch. If it were about sex, Cliff could forbid it.

She's looking down at her chicken breast, takes a bite, chews longer than usual on the rubbery chicken, her jaws making half circles. He's chewing harder too. Then she looks up and stares at him. Maybe she doesn't like the way he chews either. Or maybe she thinks his long jaw with its cleft shows character. Or maybe not.

"Cliff, are you telling me not to compete?"

He shifts in his chair. "I'm closing on the campground deal this Friday. Forty condos. So you're on your own."

They chew in silence. He tries to spear a few baby red potatoes that roll around on his plate and soak up the syrupy sauce and melted cheese. Got to be hell for his cholesterol, and his heartbeat's shot up. His chest aches.

"Well," she says, "I'll miss you."

He almost springs up, flips over the table. Miss him? Horseshit. She'll be focused totally and solely on the fourth trial. He knows that as surely as he knows, he knows for a fact, that he can't give his wife what her horse and trainer can.

♦ ♦ ♦

The next morning, before leaving for his office, Cliff goes upstairs to his den to get his briefcase, and he decides that a call to Carla should be at the top of his agenda today. She and he have hung out together at previous shows. She tries to provide moral support, saying things like, "When Gabe gave it up, he got so down he wasn't himself. So we've got to cheer them on." As if Cliff could be a cheerleader for what he fears. And one time she said, "Better horses than some other vice."

She's savvy, practical, down-to-earth, weighs alternatives then sticks to what she decides, stubborn, but so is he. And now things are heating up, so he needs backup, right when Carla said that she couldn't go to the next trial. He'll have to do some persuasion. Won't tell Nikki that. Won't expose himself. *Don't show your flank*, his father used to say when Cliff expressed his emotions as a kid. *You wouldn't say that.* Even when he felt good, his father said, *Watch out, or your bubble will burst.*

He calls and tells Carla that he can't go to the trial. She says it'll be hard to get time off. Cliff says, "One of us should be there, in case of emergency." She waits a beat, then says, "I'll call in sick. Wouldn't want them to feel neglected."

Cliff feels damned neglected, remembering when Nikki used to be all over him, like when they first met at a reception at the Quechee Club. Nikki, a top broker with a competing agency. Dressed in classy black, she darted about, trailing a hint of the scent of heat. She left with a pocketful of men's business cards, but she chose his. At the time, he felt fortunate.

Yet when she moved in with Lisa, only four years old, an instant family in his condo, he felt claustrophobic. Nikki sensed it, did a sort of soft shoe shuffle. Come on baby, let's play, let's dance. Sometimes he couldn't play to save his soul, so she dragged him to that woman therapist who asked why he felt sad and fell silent, and when he said he didn't know, the therapist said, "You need to do more together." So Cliff bought the farm and had the barn built and bought Harley, for Nikki had Druid. They took long slow trail rides together through the woods, where in certain slant lights, her delicate skin shone with a beauty that seemed innocent, and he'd halt his horse, and so would she, and they'd lie under trees and have leafy sex. But other days, when she'd cling to him and ask for compliments, he'd go hike alone in sweet silence. But then his horse started getting hoof abscesses, so Cliff couldn't always hack Harley on rocky paths, and Nikki started riding more often by herself.

"I mean, I give Gabe lots of attention, when he's around," Carla's saying. "But men are little boys who want a woman to be at their beck and call, and that's what you're missing with your wife, right?"

Nikki's too quixotic and Carla's too tough to be at any man's beck and call, Cliff thinks. Carla always says what she means. Cliff tries to mean what he says or else not to speak, so sometimes others underestimate him, which has helped him close some lucrative deals. He's no glad-hander, no back-slapper.

Carla's going on about how Gabe's acting lately, like he's on top of the world, but he was down and out after his fall. "Almost had his life smushed out. He won't ever talk of it, but that's how you die, you know, alone. If you don't believe in something beyond yourself."

Small comfort to Cliff who refuses to believe in an afterlife, in God, or in sin. Not after all those childhood threats of hellfire at Bible school camps and after watching films of Martin Luther's life in the basement of the Missouri Synod Lutheran church. He felt that it was only him and God across a void. Now all that's left is the void.

"Gabe's body was shattered, so was his spirit," Carla says. "Now he's revived. It took your wife's horses to bring him back, but she's the weak link. She thinks she has overcome her fear, Gabe says. But I know once fear sets in, it hibernates, and sooner or later, it creeps out again. I told Gabe that. He doesn't agree. But, Cliff, you never know when your wife might slip. Like a horse can slip. All of a sudden, when you're least expecting it. Know what I mean?"

"Got to go," Cliff says. He doesn't say he's late to meet Charlie Richardson and the present owners to tour a two-hundred-fifty-acre campground with forty rotted cabins and two deteriorated 50s style restaurants off Route 112. After they close this Friday, he'll send in his demolition crew, then construct luxury condos and a few upscale shops, but keep a hundred acres of open space. "Cliff, you protect the country-side," Nikki used to say, as if he's a green activist. She even got him to donate another hundred acres he owned for a nature preserve. He has shaped the neighboring countryside, used to feel like a goddamn god, he thinks. On the first day he created the earth, and on the seventh day he took a rest, and on the eighth day he created a condo development.

"So you've got to believe," Carla says, surprisingly still on the phone, "in your own powers of persuasion."

Persuasion. Cliff thinks of his hunting rifle. The Persuader, he nicknamed it. But he won't mention that. Just says he's got to go, he's late for an important appointment. And he hangs up.

◆◆◆

Nikki's first night away, he can't call her, it would seem like he's checking up. But finally late, after ten p.m., she calls and says they arrived safely in caravan with her driving the rig, and Gabe following in his pickup with Carla. Then Nikki quickly adds she's spending the night in the living quarters of the rig while Gabe and Carla are sharing the camper in the bed of his pickup.

Good old Carla, Cliff thinks. At the same time he feels burrowed in, crouched, ready to spring. But he says nothing.

During the next days, Cliff's polite when Nikki calls each night, although after each call, he feels worse. Like the night before dressage when she said, "Oh, Cliff dear, I'd miss you so, if this weren't so all-consuming." Translated, she didn't miss him. But he said nothing to that. Then she added, "But I miss you now, hearing your voice." Even though he'd hardly said a word. It was her doublespeak, warm, misleading, probably unintentional.

Then when she called after dressage on day one, she said she placed twentieth, in the top third of the pack, and she added, "Beau did his half passes especially well, so I'm focusing on the positive." Cliff said, "Too bad you only got twentieth." Offering sympathy, sincere enough. But she said, "Oh, but twentieth is good enough because I'll make it up tomorrow on cross-country. That's what Gabe said."

And after day two, cross-country, when she called, she said, "Beau came in just under the time, so we moved up to twelfth. He's terribly improved, and I love him for it, not that I didn't love him as he was. It's just that now I love him more." As if, Cliff thinks, creatures must "terribly improve," in order to be loved more. Then she said, "We're not in the top ten

yet, but we did our best, which is what it's all about, isn't it?"
She sounded elated but deflated, both at once. "But if we go
clear in the jumping phase, we could maybe still get a ribbon,
and, Cliff, if you were only here to see it, my joy would be
complete." He asked hopefully, "Your joy is incomplete?" She
said, "Yes, but it's still joy, even if it is diluted."

Ah, diluted joy. Cliff knows it well.

Meanwhile though, his trusty buddy Carla is keeping
him informed, calling him at the end of day two with her report. "The three of us go out each night, and your wife never
gets tired. She can't sit still to save her soul. I've always been
comfortable in my own skin, but she seems to want to split
right out of hers."

Cliff thinks, Yeah, Nikki's ready to burst apart, or burst
forth, as if her small body is a chrysalis, and she'll soon emerge
in another form, when he wants her to stay as she was, a loving mother and wife, and a professional in his field, not in
this foreign world.

"But don't worry, Cliff, we can handle her."

"Sure," he says, figuring he'll come up with a way. He can
usually handle Nikki. She just hasn't been aware of it.

GABE

WHILE HE AND NIKKI ARE celebrating going clear in the show jumping phase and qualifying at last, slapping five, joking, and laughing, Carla suddenly strides into the barn with that forward pitch to her gait, steps up, looks at Gabe, congratulates him, then right away says, "But we have to pack fast because I've got to get to that after-school meeting. You know how I was brought up to be punctual."

"We've got to celebrate first," he says. "We got a fifth."

She turns to Nikki, helmet off, sweaty hair matted down, while Carla's is neat and dry, and she says, "I'm so proud of Gabe after all he's been through. As a kid, his parents divorced, so he lived with a single mother who bossed him around until at age fifteen, he moved out and lived in the YMCA. Worked as a stable hand to pick up rides and worked his way through two years of college. But, of course, all of that is nothing compared with his suffering after his fall."

He shoots Carla a look. "The past has got nothing to do with this."

But Nikki says, "Tell me more about the fall." She never asked about it until Carla had to bring it up.

Carla says, "Oh, it's up to Gabe to do that . . . but after it, he got so down, sunk so low . . . who'd guess he'd be so up now. He's come into himself again, and I'm proud of him."

She's still not congratulating Nikki, so Gabe says, "Nikki's getting better all the time."

"Because of your teaching," Carla says.

Nikki kicks up shavings with the toe of her boot. "I should call Cliff to let him know how well *you* did, Gabe."

"Good idea," Carla says. "Keep Cliff involved. He's the devoted type."

As if I'm not, Gabe thinks. He should get a blue ribbon for loyalty. Since his fall, he's been a friggin' priest, chaste, devoted to something beyond himself.

The victory spell broken, Nikki quickly steps out of the barn to make her daily call to her husband, like a religious rite.

"Why bring up my fall?" Gabe asks his wife.

"I just wanted her to know that you've had your share of suffering, so you don't need any more."

"What's suffering got to do with winning?"

"You still don't know?" she asks, but then she gives Gabe's good arm a pat. "Now you get that tack packed, and I'll see you at the trailer ASAP." She flashes him a sweet smile. "I've got obligations, too, you know," and she heads on out.

He's left with Beau, who did his best, though Gracie would've got a blue today, if she'd been trained. With her big sloping shoulder and big girth, her angles beyond decent, she can cover ground. She hasn't been worked out this entire week that they've been gone, so she'll have stored up her bitchiness. That three-year-old sails over low rails like a dream, it's when she lands that she's a bucking maniac. She's like a woman who's good in bed, but out of it, can drive you nuts. Like Carla, though before his fall, their sex often got like they'd rehearsed it too many times, like a horse gets ring sour, going around and around again.

Nikki's back, saying, "I told Cliff about the ribbon, and he said it was getting more dangerous, and I said I didn't want to hear that, so he hung up. I sense one of his explosions coming on. He'll say yelling is the only way he can get me to listen, but that will only make me want to event more."

"So event more," Gabe says.

She seems to consider that, and Gabe visualizes them competing year-round, and he feels that lightness sift back in, as if he's on horseback, caught midair, jumping again, rising to . . .

"I've got to call him back," Nikki says. "I can't stand it when he hangs up on me. He knows that."

"You're training him to hang up on you."

But she's already heading out again, punching Cliff's number into her phone.

He wonders what Cliff will do when he finds out that in order to get really competitive, they should winter Beau down south and compete on the Florida circuit. Not even Nikki's ready to hear that.

And now she's pacing about outside, talking to her "devoted" husband, as Carla called him. Gabe will have to wait . . . like he's waiting for that mare to mature, praising Gracie, nattering at her, stroking her, lunging her, doing whatever it takes to get her to do what he wants.

He looks down the long aisle, out the open door, and watches Nikki pacing on the grass out of earshot, cell phone pressed to her ear. She's all aflutter, little hand batting air as she talks, hands like little wings, like she's a bright butterfly caught in the filament of Cliff's web, her wingbeats silent, beautiful, but futile . . . Got to stop pictures like that from skittering through his mind.

He turns away, goes to their stall and starts packing tack into the two trunks—saddle pads, spare crops, wraps, boots, lineament, grooming supplies, first aid kit, stud kit, sweat sheets, coolers, fly masks. The only time he's neat and organized is with horses and their tack. At home, he tosses his clothes around, leaves dishes and food lying out. Carla cleans it up but makes wisecracks, like "I could find you anywhere by tracking the crumbs you leave behind."

He sure as hell hopes she can't, because he has to go places she doesn't want him to go, yet he doesn't want to hurt her, not after all she's done for him. Big Mama got him into this, and she deserves his respect.

One-armed, he drags the steamer truck up to the rig and heaves it up into the tack compartment. Nikki's saddles hang inside on two saddle racks. The eventing saddle, which she just used, gently cups, custom molded to fit her undersized ass. He visualizes her tight butt lifting out of the saddle to take a jump, to fly, to win, and his good fingers slowly stroke the shiny, smooth leather seat until it's as warm as if she had just sat in it.

Nikole

She and Cliff are sitting in the dusk on matching Adirondack chairs out on the deck, bug repellent smeared on their hands and faces, citronella candles flickering, and she inhales the medicinal, lemony scent. A chill to the air, a few premature hints of fall in late August, some leaves already turned light enough to see at night, bits of bright refuse in the flickering, dark woods.

"So tell me more about the show," Cliff says, their first time to really talk since she got back hours ago.

Nikki tells herself not to report the unabashed joy, so she simply says, "It felt good to win."

"Almost win," he points out.

"We qualified for Advanced, and we placed ahead of horses who cost much more and had more experience."

"Well . . . fifth is better than sixth."

"The horse that got first has won many three-star events."

"So the odds were in your favor."

"How do you figure that?"

"You've all trained for years, so it's time for the one who usually won to lose, and for the one who usually lost to win."

Sounds like he's saying he wanted her to win, when he doesn't even want her to compete. She wonders about her husband. She lets out her emotions and he holds his in. She doesn't know which is best.

They sit silently and the citronella candle flickers in the starless night. She glances over, and he's looking straight at her, so at last she asks, "Cliff, why are you so upset?"

She expects him to say he's not, but he waits, then says, "Twenty days out of the last ninety, you've been on the road. Plus ten hours a day spent with two horses, seven days a week, unless it rains. That's 720 hours this summer alone."

"You added it up?"

"I'm a math whiz. Remember?"

As if he's making a joke of it, but she's sure he keeps secret accounts of her failings. Like with his first wife, before he moved out, he wrote down her good and bad points in two separate columns. The bad list was twice as long.

"In fact," Cliff adds, "it's about time for me to have a little talk with your trainer. Maybe give him some time off."

Nikki stares at him. She doesn't know if he means it. She says, "I can handle Gabe."

"He thinks he's running the show."

She thinks of alpha horses, like Harley and Gracie, and how they must be kept separate, or they'll fight it out for dominance. "When winter comes," she says, "the shows will stop."

"Yeah? We'll see." Cliff takes off his glasses and wipes them on the sleeve of his denim shirt, a tell for when he's really upset. His exposed eyes, too pale, watery. Unmasked, he looks vulnerable, appealing, and she suddenly thinks, What does all this add up to, his keeping score of the number of her hours spent away? It means he's missing her, but he can't say it.

He's watching her, with his exposed eyes, as if waiting for her to say something.

And she blurts out, "Oh, Cliff, if only we could share like we used to!"

And she reaches out and touches his hand on the broad, oblong armrest of the Adirondack chair, but his thick fist stays curled. It doesn't unclench to take her hand, as if his hand is as numb as Gabe's bad one.

◆◆◆

That night she cannot sleep, wondering what must be brewing in Cliff, lying next to her and snoring in a deep, vibrating baritone, and she tries to pray to a personal God, or to a God in nature, or wherever God is, to protect her marriage. To Cliff, if God exists, it's in his land, not in a church, like the Unitarian one where she goes sometimes, where God depends on your interpretation. She tries to pray to this free-floating God, but feels only a free-floating anxiety, as if everything is impermanent like after her sister's death and her mother's desertion, and her father's bankruptcy. Like when her big red-brick house, her lavender room, her white pony, all vanished, and her father fell silent and depressed, and they lived in a tiny rented church home. If she asked about death, her father told her not to think of such things and to follow a middle path. A demand which only added to her chronic restlessness. "You're always in motion," her father complained. "Can't you ever be still?" Only when she secretly rode other people's horses did she feel still and centered inside, but that peace was transitory, like her sister's life. And it seems now, as Nikki lies in this renovated farmhouse with its antiques and embossed tin ceilings and wide plank floors, as if it's all fragile and transitory. But that's one reason that she loves Cliff, because he believes this land is lasting, solid, so he holds her to the earth, while she risks it all . . . drifts up.

◆◆◆

The next morning after their talk, Cliff seems more morose, not less. They sit at breakfast at the cherry table, and both stare out the picture window overlooking the pasture and silently eat their cheese and herb omelets, sipping coffee, when Cliff suddenly, gruffly, says, "I've been thinking about what you said about sharing more, and I thought, why not? So I've got an idea."

Then he waits until she asks, "What?"

"How about going trail riding together like we used to?"

Sharing the horses? She's speechless. And she remembers

a few years ago, him astride Harley, her on Druid, trotting through high grasses and wildflowers, the smell of sweet blossoms, pungent weeds and horseflesh, the grasses parting in their wake. "Isn't this great?" she'd call ahead to Cliff, for he always led, Harley with the longer stride. "Isn't this fun?" But Cliff only rode on ahead, not too far, slow motion, caught up in one of his spells, giving in to the motion, the rock and sway. "Cliff, isn't this the best?" But he didn't turn back, so sometimes she'd trot up next to him and catch a glimpse of his hard, bony face at peace, almost beatific, like in a sweet death. Yet other times, they'd race through fields, alongside the woods, their horses careening too close together. The thrill of that. Though an old neighbor saw them once and said, "Your horses are too herd bound. It's an accident waiting to happen."

"Harley needs to get back into shape," Cliff says now. "And it's my day off. So let's go for a ride."

She's still taken aback. "But Beau needs a rest, and Druid's lame again. I'd have to ride Gracie."

"I saw you jumping her the other day. She seemed fine."

Nikki flashes on jumping Gracie in the ring over a line of low rails, trotting over each low jump after stepping over cavelletis, when out of the side of her eye, she glimpsed Cliff at the fence. She was so focused on the mare, she didn't notice when he left, Gracie easily clearing the rails, set low to protect her still-young bones, though some Thoroughbreds race at this age. For once, Gracie didn't buck, so Nikki called to Gabe, "She's the best she's ever been." Gabe said, "Because she knows I've got my eye on her." But Nikki was the one riding, not him. Sometimes Gabe seems to lose that distinction. And after the session, Gabe said, "Don't ride her without me there." As if she has no control over the mare, as if it was a dare.

Now she says, "Cliff, the trail's different than the ring. Nothing's holding her back."

"You don't want to go? Okay, fine." Shoving back his chair and standing, as if to leave.

She quickly says, "But I've got to try her alone sometime."

"You won't be alone."

"I didn't mean it that way."

But they both know what she meant—she'd feel alone, riding without Gabe.

Cliff heads out toward the barn, and Nikki notices only then that he's already got his old black riding britches on, his legs so big around that it would take two hands to encircle one thigh, and he's walking out with his linebacker's gait, charged up.

As if he knew she'd go.

◆◆◆

In the barn, the stalls are all already mucked, the horses already fed their morning grain, the Hendersen girls already come and gone by eight. Nikki and Cliff tack up, Harley standing like some plug, which is deception, Nikki knows. Harley's a fiery powerhouse of a beast, his bones twice as thick as Gracie's. Cliff grooms him to a high show sheen, as if he's going to compete.

Gracie's already quivering with nerves, her skin jumps when Nikki slides the pad and saddle on, the mare not calm like in the ring, but she hasn't been worked out in over a week, so Nikki tells herself, it's got nothing to do with Gabe not being here. It's only a matter of keeping Gracie at a walk or trot, not letting her go all out and get heated up, not getting overcharged, not feeling fear if Gracie does. Then Nikki notices, she's got the Not's again. Not a good sign.

Before long, they're heading out, up the side path, past the fenced-in fields, and up the long slope, Gracie shying away from the lily pond at the bottom of the hill where some little turtle makes a soft, reptilian splash. Then they slow-trot along the mile-long path, which Cliff had cleared with a backhoe for lines of jumps that border the woods that lead up into the foothills. Cliff and Harley in the lead, Nikki hoping to God no stray deer bound out of the underbrush, or no quail get flushed out of the high grass and scare the shit out of Gracie, who's already side stepping, prancing, curling her body, while Harley surges straight ahead with his longer stride, pounding earth, dirt puffing up from his wide saucer hooves. Harley's full of it.

Nikki calls, "Slow down!"

Cliff slows Harley to a brisk walk, for surely Cliff knows that the rider in front should wait for the ones behind, knows that herd bound horses stress out if they feel left. Now Gracie trots faster to catch up, Nikki deep breathing, trying hard to think positive, yet feeling the old familiar telltale prickling in her veins—fear has an itch. You want to scratch it, but that will only make it worse. What's the worst that can happen? She'll get bucked off, but she won't die like her sister did.

They ride silently at a walk, with Harley soon drawing ahead again, into the thick woods, then down the steep narrow forest path that leads them to the river road, where, to the right, the river flows, its shallow rippling water perfectly clear, mirroring red-yellow-brown pebbles beneath, the river always running like Gracie wants to run, pulling against the bit as they trot single file along the flat expanse of gravel road. Harley trots farther in front again, and Nikki wants to call, "Isn't this the best?" but calls instead to Cliff's back, "Slow down!"

His wide shoulders draw tight in irritation. He always liked to charge ahead, though not this far, but he slows Harley, so Gracie catches up to her big boyfriend, who, when she's not in heat, she attacks.

Don't move the way fear moves, Nikki tells herself. Gracie was under control in the ring, now she isn't. A bait and switch. Nikki's nerves firing up as they come to the fork in the river road. The right fork leads along the river to the dam and the small waterfall near the back of Cliff's office, a renovated church. Years ago, in moonlight, they once skinny-dipped, swam up to the lip of the dam, the very edge of the spilling falls, and embraced, tempting fate.

Cliff and Harley take the left fork, away from the river, leading up the old, rutted logging road into the pines and oak, toward the high west field, lovely but desolate. Why go up there now? Nikki calls ahead, "Everything all right?"

"Couldn't be better," Cliff calls back.

She must keep her fear hidden, even though Gracie's vibrating between Nikki's thighs.

Harley clatters up over rocks, trotting faster the closer he gets to the high field, a big wide open space he remembers from past rides. Horses don't forget. Almost at the top of the root-ridden path, they pass the ruins of an old farmhouse. Only scattered, rotted boards and a broken-down stone foundation and a tiny family plot with a few graves dating back to the revolutionary war, the plot closed in by a tilting, black iron fence. Once, when Lisa was younger, Nikki had hiked up here with her daughter who had to be carried when tired, and saw the worn, lichen-covered limestone markers, their dates almost worn off. The light sifted down through the oaks and dappled the stones, and it was lovely. Nikki set Lisa down and, only four, Lisa darted through the broken iron gate. Only the top of her head, her shiny black hair, poked up over the high grass that bent and waved as if in a giant breath as she scampered across the graves, and Nikki called, "Don't run on the dead!" Lisa pivoted and raced right back, calling, "Don't run on the dead or they'll wake up!"

Now Harley trots on past and up the root-ridden path, but Gracie turns her head to look at the yellowed graves. Her eye rolls back, white-rimmed, as if the ghosts of the dead have woken after all, and she spooks, breaks into a canter to catch up to Harley, who has drawn ahead once more. Gracie's picking up speed, Nikki's calling again, "Slow down!" Her voice maybe drowned out by the muffled, rattling whoosh of a gravel truck passing below on the river road.

"Whatever you do, don't canter!" she calls to Cliff, already almost up to the top of the hill.

He doesn't answer. Didn't he hear?

Nikki feels the hot rush, the itch, Gracie tossing her head, whacked, prancing, dying to break free, and cantering, she catches up to them at the top of the incline, where the dense pines part into the upper west field, a few acres of open high grass, sunlit and waving in a breeze. Harley shakes his oversized head at the sight of all that empty free space, and he bolts. In that instant, Nikki's sure she sees Cliff's big arms move forward, and his hands open to let the reins slide through his thick fingers. He gives Harley his head, and Harley gallops an all-out, earth-shaking, draft horse pound of a gallop, so Gracie yanks the bit into her teeth and takes off after him at a jet-fueled run, Nikki yelling, "Whoa, whoa!" Gracie bolting full force to catch up, then bucking at the gallop, several side-twisting bucks, Nikki losing her stirrups, sliding in the saddle, another crooked buck and another, and Nikki's flying so high up she has time to think, Don't land on my back or face. Midair she twists to the right, hits the sun-baked earth.

She's broken something but feels no pain, feels only through the ground the pounding of Gracie's distancing hooves. Gracie's racing off without looking back, leaving Nikki alone.

She touches her head, safety helmet still on, but at a slant, as Cliff's distant baritone calls, "Whoa!" Trying to halt Harley at last. While Nikki sits up to see, Where is Cliff, where is Gracie? Her head whirls, and she sees only lightning bolts shooting through shadows, and she lies back down, lies flat, yellow streaks inside her eyes, and before long, a dark shape emerges, a half shadowy face.

"Nikki, are you all right? I'm here, are you all right?" She starts to sit again, reaches up toward him, but he fades, turns dark . . .

She wakes to feel Cliff's lips on hers. *Why kiss me now, didn't I see your hands let the reins go?* His breath hot between her lips, he turns his head, inhales, turns back, breathes into her mouth, and she thinks, *He must be giving me mouth to mouth, he must think I'm dying, or dead.*

"Get off of me," she says, in a rote voice that can't be hers. "Take the horses home and come get me in the Rover," she commands in that flat tone.

Cliff jerks back, stares down at her and asks, "You're sure you're all right?"

"I got knocked out. Now I'm awake," she says firmly. "Take the horses home and come back for me in the Rover," she repeats, like she'd talk to a hired hand, like Cliff talks to Gabe.

"Don't move," Cliff orders. "Stay right here!" Which only makes her want to jump up, run off. Then he's loping off through the high grass.

She lifts her head to see the horses grazing nearby. Can only see half of their heads and strips of lower legs through the lightening streaking in her eyes.

She can only half see. Why didn't she tell Cliff that?

She's not thinking right but soon hears the horses trotting off and lifts her head again to see a slice of a dark man on part of a dark horse and a splintered, golden, four-legged shadow in tow. Gracie, trotting along behind on a line, still does not look back, not a drop of guilt. The fractured shadows disappear into the dark of trees struck by the lightning bolts in her eyes. They're all three gone like a shadow in evening.

"Don't leave me alone!" she calls, and tries to stand to go after them, but, head spinning, her right knee sears pain, seems to split. She sinks down and lies again on her back in high grass, slices of pine, shimmering sky, silver cloud whirling, overhead. When she hit the ground so hard, she knew she had to be broken. Why didn't she feel pain till now? Why didn't she tell Cliff to call an ambulance? Whose fault is this?

She is alone, and she silently prays not to be. She lies still for a while on the hard-baked ground in the high, yellowed grass, and the furtive chirps of invisible birds strike up a chorus in the surrounding trees, still whirling, and she wonders, why did he kiss me on the lips at a time like this? What will Gabe say? It's the rider's fault. Her head's spinning round, as if she'll pass out again, and lightning streaks through the high, dappled grass that's swaying when it should stand still, and she hears a rustling, as if a creature's stalking her, but sees only rippling grass with its bushy tips and sprays of goldenrod. Yet she feels a presence hovering, she's sure of it, as if the spirits of the dead from the graveyard below have risen up to whirl in the high field, where the sunlit grasses bend and wave, iridescent, backlit. Dizzy, she shuts her eyes and instantly feels as if she's inside a giant kaleidoscope where shifting shafts of light and dark whirl and merge and split until she feels the hovering closer, more intense, and warm breath on her face and lips, and she feels a burst, an exquisite high . . . and opens her eyes . . .

Only the waving bleached field, not a single living creature. She is alone again.

♦ ♦ ♦

In the emergency ward, Cliff stays with her while she waits for the surgeon to come and tell her the results of the x-rays of her ribs and knee and the CAT scan on her brain. She's coasting on painkillers, and she jokes about ghosts. "You don't believe in ghosts, do you, Cliff? But I felt them up in the field after you left." He's shaking his head as if she's lost it, and doped up, she says, "It was like I was kissed by a spirit. Are you jealous? But I thought it was you, and I felt high, I did."

Cliff says, "As long as it was me, that's all right."

But it wasn't only Cliff, she thinks.

By the time the surgeon comes, her knee has swollen to twice its size. The surgeon, a little guy, emaciated, in scrubs, peers down at her, prone on her hospital bed and announces that according to the CAT scan, she has no brain damage.

She says, "That's what I thought, because I can think," She's smiling at him, making light of it.

The small man crosses his arms across his chest and says, "There are more head injuries from horseback riding than from motorcycle riding."

As if she had to ride at the edge, so this is what she gets. This is her punishment.

Then the surgeon coolly announces that while her concussion was mild, the x-rays of her knee show that her patella is misplaced, could be a hairline crack, tendons twisted, and, therefore, she will need a knee replacement.

She looks directly up at him. "Sorry, can't do that. I've got a three-star event coming up. Then I have to ride all winter to keep the horses in shape. No time for an operation. No time at all."

Cliff says under his breath, "Maybe it's the drugs she's on."

The surgeon says, "You had a near-death experience. What have you learned?"

"Oh . . . I felt something up there alone in the high grass . . . a presence."

The surgeon smiles, lips too pink and thin. "Patients often imagine such things at times of severe trauma. Light in a tunnel, and so on. It's electrical discharges from the brain."

She doesn't mention the light whirling in the dark, just says, "I felt a presence hovering for many moments."

"Such moments pass," the surgeon says. "Then what?"

She can't answer that, and Cliff's nodding now as if this surgeon gets the award for best bedside manner for atheists. Cliff doesn't believe in spirits or ghosts, holy or otherwise, or in God, she thinks, wishing she could conjure up that presence now, but it was invisible and elusive, and she is drugged. The two men discuss her medical care as if she's not there . . . yet, Cliff drove the Rover back for her into the field, lifted her up in his strong arms, gently laid her on the back seat, the leather cold. Still seeing lightning bolts, she said, "Don't take me to the local hospital, take me to Burlington." Still giving him orders . . . in shock, and maybe he was, too, or else why take orders from his broken wife instead of calling an ambulance? Why wait?

Now she asks the small surgeon, "How soon can I ride with a displaced kneecap?"

"Not until after surgery and after months of rehab. That is, if you ride again, which I advise against."

She will ride whenever she wants, she thinks. She will compete in her first Advanced competition with her displaced knee, and she will have no fear.

Then the surgeon precisely says, "If you do not have the knee replaced, you will walk with a limp, then with a cane, and finally, you'll be in a wheelchair."

Then he orders her to stay the night, but she refuses and says she must get out of this place immediately. The doctor argues for a bit but cannot force her to stay and he knos it. He leaves. Nikki limps to the closet, takes out her clothes, drops her Johnny, and nude in front of Cliff, suddenly shy, quickly puts on her bra and her soiled shirt, yet even with painkillers, can't pull on her tight britches, so she asks Cliff for his long parka.

Cliff says, "If you know what's good for you, you won't leave."

She says, "Then I don't know what's good for me."

In his long parka that comes to her knees, and her hospital slippers, she walks down the gray corridor leaning on Cliff, who signs out at the nurses' station. She does not limp, she tells herself. as Cliff, coatless, follows her into the elevator, and as the elevator coasts down, she's floating, suspended in air, like when she jumps, and while it's probably painkillers letting her drift, she tells herself that she is absolutely fine.

Grounded again, out of the elevator in the crowded lobby, she slips out behind Cliff, then orders him to bring around the car as if he's her valet.

"You can be as stubborn as I am," he says.

"Thank you, dear," she says, with a little drug-infected grin.

He shakes his head. "Nikki, this is so like you."

She wonders which "you" he means, but he lopes off to get the car, and she tells herself that when they get home, she'll rest up, and tomorrow, she will ride again, but Beau, not Gracie, not yet.

In the Rover, all the way to Northlands, Cliff talks of her operation and how they'll find the best orthopedic knee specialist, and so on. He's acting awfully considerate while she wonders if he's feeling guilty and wants to ask, "Why did you let Harley run?"

For she saw his arms slide forward, his fingers open on the reins. But he's saying he'll take time off to help her through rehab, and he's acting so altogether loving that she stays silent and stares out the window at the whizzing, dizzying landscape, hazy mountains, shrouded foothills, and valleys so bright green they hurt her eyes.

When they pull up to the Northlands, Cliff hops right out, opens her door, and helps her out, a real gentleman. But she slips out of his grasp and steps on up to the house alone, her knee shooting pain even through the codeine haze. She straightens her back and walks more or less in balance to the deck, though while climbing the steps she almost trips and falls but catches herself, gets into the house, and limps through the living room to the couch before she collapses. Cliff comes and stands over her. "The surgeon said you'll have to stay off that leg as much as possible."

She looks up at him. "Cliff, you don't really think I'll stop because of a fall?"

No, she thinks, it only spurs her on. She was spared, but her sister wasn't, so she has to make up for being alive.

"Nikki, you're drugged. You don't know the pain you're in."

"And you do?"

"I'm a pro at feeling pain."

The pain is hovering, invisible, below the surface, like the presence hovered up in the field. Now, lying down, she's suddenly sleepy and turns her head away from him to face the back of the black leather couch, but she says, "I'm going to compete, and you can't stop me no matter what you do."

Saying it like an accusation. As if he's responsible for her fall. "You're riding for a fall," her father used to say to her as a girl when she talked back. As if he wished she'd have the fall her sister had.

"I'm not stopping you, fate is," Cliff says. She feels his rough, warm hand on her forehead, gently smoothing her hair, but she saw those same hands open to let the reins slide through. Why did he let Harley go? Why didn't he pull back?

She's coasting off. She doesn't ask.

GABE

THE MORNING AFTER THEY RETURNED from the event, Nikki calls and says, "I've got a bit of bad news. I rode Gracie and . . . I fell . . . got shaken up a bit. I'll be fine, but I wish you'd wait to come train until tomorrow after Cliff leaves for work."

"Why's that?" Gabe asks, instinctively suspicious.

"Oh . . . I don't think he'd approve of my riding so soon."

"Why not?"

"He thinks it's worse than it is. You know how Cliff is."

"Yeah, Cliff makes me look like an optimist."

"So I'm asking you, Gabe, to cooperate."

"What happened? Did Beau get hurt?"

"In fact, I wasn't riding Beau . . . I was riding Gracie."

"In the ring?"

"Well, not quite . . . on the trail."

"Damnit, I told you not to ride that mare on the trail alone. Why'd you take such a chance before Advanced?" Thinking now he'll have to purge her fresh fear. How could she do this to him?

"Actually, Gabe, I rode with Cliff."

"What the fuck?"

"Cliff thought it would be a way for us to get closer."

"You're lucky you didn't get hurt so bad that you can't compete. Was it Cliff's idea for you to take Gracie out?"

"Leave Cliff out of this," she says, and she hangs up.

He punches her number on his cell, gets her message, leaves his, telling her to call back. But he knows she won't. She's doing to him what she does with Cliff, avoiding conflict.

Gabe limps straight on out of his rented house and sits under the crabapple tree on the scrap of lawn. The tree's a scrunched up, scrawny thing with a few tiny, withered apples fallen onto the yellow grass beneath. He sits for some time in its sparse shade and tries to calm down, but his mind spins. Good thing Carla's off at work, or she'd be coming out and asking what he was doing here so long. She'd try to stop this spin he's in as he deep breathes and his mind circles around about why Cliff wanted Nikki to take the mare out on the trail, when it's Cliff who preaches how dangerous riding is.

◆◆◆

When Gabe gets to Northlands the next morning at eight thirty, Nikki's not in the barn. Cliff's Rover is gone, so Gabe goes to the house, limps the three steps up onto the deck, rings the bell, and waits quite a while before Nikki opens up. She's not in riding gear but in faded jeans, a UVM sweatshirt and sneakers. Yet no trace of an accident, her face unmarked, her body seemingly intact. She gives him a little bud of a smile, and he asks how she is.

"Great. Just great."

"So why did Cliff—"

"If you even mention Cliff, I'm going inside." She's already half turned toward the house, poised to dash back in.

"All right, all right. Just tell me about the accident."

"Oh . . . you know, one of those freak things," she says, with a pert little smile.

"Nikki, how exactly did you get bucked off?" Still keeping his surface cool, like, Hey, accidents happen all the time, so what the hell?

"Well . . . we rode along the tree line and then down through the back woods to the river road, and Harley kept surging ahead, and Gracie kept trying to catch up, and then we turned up the path past the deserted house and the family plot, and when we got up to the high west field and all that open space . . . Gracie bolted and bucked, and I got tossed off, but I had time to twist in the air, so I landed on my side. Just lucky, I guess."

Nikki talking in a matter-of-fact tone. Both of them acting so damned cool and calm.

He's shaking his head. She's got a self-destructive streak. More headstrong than he'd realized. She's so little that she sometimes seems innocent, which Cliff takes advantage of.

"But, Gabe, something strange happened up there while I was lying in the high grass. Cliff had taken the horses back to get the Rover, and I was alone and everything was whirling around in a breeze, and I felt this whirlpool, this . . . presence. I did. I felt it as clearly as if it had a body, but, of course, it didn't, but it was hovering by me, and it was comforting, like the Holy Spirit, or spirits of the dead. If you know what I mean."

Gabe has never had a ghostly visitation in his entire life, not even when he was down and out. He waves his good hand, dismissing spirits of all varieties and breeds, and asks, "Why did Gracie bolt?"

She nods, as if she knew he'd ask. "It was my fault. I couldn't hold her back."

He shakes his head. He wants to blame it all on the almighty Cliff. But he says, "You've got to get right back on the horse that threw you. Ride into your fears."

She nods, not meeting his eyes, like she might not do what she knows she must.

He says, "I'll tack her up while you change."

"Oh . . . I think I'll just wear what I have on."

"You're sure you're not hurt?"

"A little stiff," she says, with that damn brave smile riders get after a fall. "But that's part of it."

Hell yes, he thinks, it is. He's ridden with way more wrong with him than this, until after his last accident.

They head down the deck steps toward the barn, but she lags behind, so he slows, but she slows again—not her usual light, quick step—so he slows more, but then she does, until they're walking very slowly, single file, her following when she usually darts ahead, as if she's hiding something. She's afraid. He'll cure her of that.

Once in the barn, she asks him to tack up Gracie, and she goes on outside to wait by the paddock, which she never does, as if she's avoiding him. One-armed, he tacks up Gracie, leads her out to the ring. Then Nikki asks for a boost up like a frail old lady who can't mount herself.

He holds out his good hand, cupped. She sets her left foot in his hand, swings up, presses her legs on, and Gracie trots off, while Gabe's eyeing the mare, not taking his eye off. For Gracie needs to believe he's God, or she won't give in.

Nikki's body sits totally stiff. Gabe tells her to relax, but she only stiffens more, not posting, sitting the trot, bouncing, Gracie surging ahead with her extended, free floating stride, Nikki sliding in the tack, but she calls, "See, look! I can do it!"

She's all off balance. He calls, "You won't stay on like that."

"Stop saying *won't*. Think positive."

Meanwhile Gracie's doing a pent-up trot and Nikki's tilting too far back, but she calls, "See. I told you!" Bouncing in the saddle like a novice. Then Gracie canters. Nikki, sliding more in the saddle, tilts to the left, still doesn't fall and calls, "See! Look at me!" Clearly, she's damaged.

He steps in front of the mare to block her path. Horses won't run you down if they can avoid it. He waves Gracie into a corner of the ring where she halts. He grabs the reins, ties them to a fence post, yanks them tight, then reaches up for Nikki, who's still tilting left, and, one-armed, helps her swing down. She lands on both feet, but her right knee buckles. Gracie peers down at her, the mare's long lower lip hanging loose, showing her bottom teeth, nodding her head, as if she's thinking, yeah, take a look at that poor, deluded human.

"Nikki, what the hell?"

She turns her back, walks off, tilting left. At last he sees it—a definite hitch to her gait. Her injury must be real bad to make her lean so much. "Goddamnit, Nikki, you're lame!"

She lurches on. "No, see, I can walk just fine now. Gracie healed me." As if that hyper mare is a miracle cure. Nikki shuffles on. He limps after her out of the paddock, catches up, and they're limping side-by-side in sync, step-drag, step-drag, though he's off on the left, and she's off on the right. Then he asks, "What's going on?"

She stops, turns, and looks past him at the mare, still hitched to the fence post. "The surgeon said I fractured my patella. I need a knee replacement."

Gabe stands perfectly still. They'll be out all season, no three stars, no wintering down in paradise.

"But, Gabe, I can still compete, if I play it right."

"*Play* it right?"

"I just have to adjust to the pain."

He used to think that he could make his body do whatever he wanted it to. Every horse that ever tossed him, no matter how broken he was—once a broken collarbone, once all his ribs, once an arm, once an ankle—no matter. After every injury, except for that last fall, he got right back on and rode through his pain. But now he knows there's permanent pain that you can never adjust to, that takes over who you are.

He says, "If you fall again on that knee, you could end up like me, only half here."

"Gabe, half of you is more than most men have."

He's struck silent.

Then she says, "I just have to practice more, be more disciplined, more focused. I'm going to visualize winning, and visualizing makes it real, right?" Giving him back his own lines. She's got the same drive he does, the same calling. He understands, Cliff doesn't.

They're halfway to the house, in the frail shadow of the weeping willow tree, branches stripped, though the season is still snowless, when he blurts out, "This is what Cliff wanted."

She limps away fast, across the lawn to the deck. He lurches after her up the steps, and says, "Cliff set you up."

She turns back to face Gabe then. "If I tell Cliff you said that, he'll fire you."

Fire him? This is his life.

She opens the front door and Gabe stands right there and says, "Get that damn operation over with!"

She disappears yet again into her house, and Cliff's. Shuts the door. Shuts him out.

Gabe stands fixed in place. Been fucking fired before, but not like this. He knew from his interview when he first saw her ride, from the elegant way she sat a horse, from her rhythm and balance, and from the quality of her Thoroughbreds, that he would never again in his crippled life have another chance like this. And now today when he saw her riding through her pain, showing a grit he'd thought her too fragile to possess, he knows she is a true horsewoman, so he absolutely cannot give her up.

NIKOLE

It isn't until the next morning that Cliff mentions Gabe. Cliff tromps downstairs and stalks through the living room, where she's lying on the leather couch. He's dressed for the office in a sports coat, khakis, and hiking boots. But instead of passing through as she wants him to, he sits on the mission oak rocker, where he doesn't rock but plants his feet firmly on the floor, and says, seemingly nonchalant, "By now you must've broken the news to Gabe."

"He came by yesterday morning and watched me ride."

"How'd he take it?"

As if Cliff takes pleasure in her pain, but no. He's not that perverse, and she says, "Gabe said I'm lame, and he wants me to have the operation, too. So, Cliff, he agrees with you."

"He does, huh?"

"He said to get the damn thing over with."

"And you told him all about the unfortunate accident."

"I said Gracie bolted and bucked me off, so it was my fault."

Cliff sits in the rocker, still doesn't rock, his big hands clutching the arms as if to keep it steady at all costs, his thick fingers turning mottled. And she almost asks him then, why did you let the reins slide through your hands?

But Cliff says, "Surprised he's not trying to talk you into still riding at the next event. That man will be the death of you."

She almost laughs out loud, thinking the opposite, but holds it in. "Cliff, you were an athlete. Did you ever get hurt and go right back on the field to play?"

"Football's a team sport. And more violent. You've got to think, 'I'm going down, so I'm going to take you down.'"

She wonders if he has taken her down, but that can't be, no matter what Gabe says.

"So there's no reason for your trainer to be coming over until after your rehab. If ever." Cliff's sitting all tense, his hands still clutching the stationary rocker. "It'll only make things worse." He's peering at her. "Do I have your word?"

Cliff wants her to make a vow, like after he'd twice proposed marriage, and she'd hesitated, so the third time, on the sidewalk in downtown Burlington, he yelled, "Are you going to shit or get off the pot?" At last, she'd said yes. And now she says, "I promise, for now."

"For now?"

"I'll tell him to work out Beau and Gracie at the Meadowlark during the winter months. But, Cliff, I'm not firing him."

Cliff stands up so fast the rocker flips up and back, up and back, and he walks on out, the rocker still flipping a bit, as if he's still sitting in it.

The front door clicks shut. If she didn't have this limp, she'd run after him, try to explain why she can't give Gabe up, that he knows her fears like no other trainer has. But Lisa said, "Don't go after Cliff when he's mad." Yet Nikki wants to apologize, like when her father got mad and wouldn't speak to her, so she wrote notes saying sorry for staying out too late, or sorry for talking back, or sorry for being bad. But sometimes she'd say things like, "Someday I'll do something truly bad, then you'll see." Then her father sent her to her room, and she'd lie and wait for his heavy steps, for him to stretch her across his lap, pull down her panties and spank her bottom with the spatula that her mother used to flip pancakes.

But now when she stands to go after Cliff, pellets of hot pain shoot up from knee to crotch. She sinks back down. She can't compete. Cliff has won. Though surely Cliff would never hurt her on purpose. Gabe put that suspicion into her head. It was an accident. Or God's will, if God wills pain like this.

◆◆◆

The three-week wait for the operation is like waiting for her punishment. During a visit to the orthopedic surgeon, the young doctor said she must have a high pain tolerance to still be walking. She said, "I learned that as a girl." The surgeon said, "Well, you'll need it." Then she said she wanted a spinal, to be awake, but the surgeon said she had to be put to sleep. After they left his office, she said to Cliff, "Surgeons are perverse." Cliff said, "Ah, Nikki, we all are." She told herself that he didn't mean it.

For surely Cliff is not perverse. He has never laid a hand on her in anger, although he socked holes into a few walls and kicked holes into their bed.

Early in their marriage, she took a photograph of two gaping black holes in their box springs, had the photo framed, and titled it "Married Life." Cliff actually laughed at her little joke, as they often used to laugh back in the days when she also took photographs of rocky cliffs and hung them up about the house. Back when they'd go out dancing at night, or on hikes, or camping trips with the kids, back when they lived a seemingly normal family life that vanished after their children left, and Nikki and Cliff found themselves left with only each other to love.

Then she bought her young mare. But now both show horses have been trailered off to the Meadowlark. She forces herself not to dwell on the starred three-days that she will miss, as she will her horses. But the longer she waits for her operation, the more she pictures her husband's big hands gliding forward, the thick fingers opening a fraction of an inch to let the reins slide through. Why hasn't she asked Cliff why his hands did that?

After an argument, Gabe agreed to stay away until she

was healed. "In order to keep the peace," she said. But Gabe still sends daily e-mails or makes cell phone calls "to update her on the horses' progress," and also "to give her tips on how to feel centered." He can be uplifting with his light laugh, and during the last call, he said, "Now you know how I felt after my fall, being only part of what you can be. After this, you'll feel even more driven, except you will get your full body back, so you've got to win for both of us."

Only once during his spiritual rah-rah routines did he ask for all the details of her fall, especially how Cliff rode that day. Gabe must sense she'd left out Cliff's role, yet she will not tell because Gabe will never understand a man like Cliff with his heavy tread, his heavy heart, his daily admonitions of what she should do and should not. If she held out each hand to weigh their souls, the hand holding Cliff's would sink, but the one with Gabe's would rise, light as air, although air has no shape of its own.

◆◆◆

When Cliff drives her to the hospital for her operation, she keeps noticing his over-sized hands clamped on the steering wheel, their backs laced with blue veins, the skin rough as a stable hand's, and how his thick fingers uncurl a little, maybe an eighth of an inch, to let the wheel slide through his grasp. Finally she asks, "Cliff, why did you suggest we go trail riding that day?"

His fingers tighten their grip. "For old times' sake. You know, like back when we'd trail ride together, and do *other things*."

They ambled their horses through woods and sometimes dismounted to mount each other, and it was lush and rich, but now Cliff steps on the gas, the Green Mountains swishing by in a gray blur, his hands clamping tighter on the black wheel, white-knuckling it.

"Cliff, when we got to the high west field, and Harley started to bolt, I saw your hands open. You let the reins slide through."

Her own hands closing tightly in her lap, his eyes steady on the road ahead.

"Yes," he says, "I did."

That's so like him, she thinks, to be honest even to his own detriment.

"Cliff, why did you let Harley run?"

He glances over at her. "Because he wanted to."

Then he looks back at the road, drives on.

As if he had nothing to do with it.

They both fall silent.

◆◆◆

An hour later, Cliff sits with her in the waiting room, gray walls, gray furniture, and she waits and thinks of escaping and remembers Gabe asking, "Do you want to be like me, half there?" Yet she asks the receptionist to see the surgeon. Cliff asks why doesn't she simply get it over with. She says she's still not sure if she wants to go through with it. Cliff says nothing, goes over into the gray corner, and sits on a gray chair.

Soon the surgeon comes out in his scrubs, and Nikki asks yet again about the odds for her full recovery.

The surgeon betrays no emotion, just says, "Let me do what I know how to do."

"You don't understand. I have to be able to event again."

The surgeon gives her a cold clinical stare. A gray God passing judgment on a risk taker who deserves punishment.

She steps over to Cliff and says, "I'm walking out of here."

"You know, Nikki," Cliff says under his breath, "you can really be a pain in the ass."

She thinks, If I die in this operation, those will be my husband's last words to me.

But then she looks up at his face, tight and strict, yet his brow furrowed in what must be true concern for her, and she says, "You're right. I can be."

Then she turns and leaves him behind as she limps into the pre-op room. Even though a nurse waits inside, Nikki feels alone in the pale room, but she lies down on the sterile white bed. The nurse hooks up the IV and leaves. As the anesthesia gradually feeds into her veins, Nikki feels a hovering again, an invisible nearness, a faint, flickering presence . . . if she only could grasp onto this tease as she slides into the dark.

◆◆◆

Short strands of white and red wool yarn dangle only a few feet from her face, yarn unraveling from the bottom edge of the thick macramé tapestry on her living room wall, a tapestry of a white unicorn posed in a field of red blossoms. She never noticed before the unicorn's hooves coming undone.

But now, flat on her back on the narrow hospital cot in her living room, she can't avoid seeing the lower rows of strands dangling just out of reach. She needs a hammer to pry out the nail in the corner, then stuff the fraying yarn behind the tapestry, then nail the corner back in place.

She doesn't see how much longer she can bear seeing this magical creature unraveling. Or how much longer she can bear not being able to walk unaided, or to shower alone, or to climb steps without pain that leaves her breathless, so she can't say her mantras, can't search for a presence. A presence that came in a field, then vanished when she opened her eyes. That's the trouble with spirits, she thinks, they're fleeting, they don't last. You can't force God to come to you, like you can't force a horse.

Supposedly she is on the mend, although she feels more pain-riddled than before, her knee swollen and scarred. She has no inclination to get up. She has lain on a foldout hospital cot for two days and is supposed to wait to walk on the walker one more day until the traveling nurse can get out to their farm. Nikki tried a few exercises in bed—rollovers, leg lifts—felt pain, took meds, and now lies and stares up at a unicorn that each day seems to unravel more.

"For God's sake, answer truthfully, are those horses worth this?" Lisa had asked at Nikki's bedside back at the hospital.

Lisa is no athlete, a self-made city chick. "Truthfully," Nikki said, "yes." Lisa shook her head and scolded, "Mother, you've got a self-destructive streak. You're an adrenaline junky." Nikki, leg swathed in bandages, a post-op IV dripping morphine into her veins, just laughed at her daughter acting like a tough-love mother, until Lisa said, "Those horses don't care if you live or die." Nikki didn't confess that it wasn't the horse's fault. For when she first woke after her operation, Cliff was sitting at her bedside, both hands folded over both of hers, as if to hang onto her even through death, and he said, "Welcome back to the living." As if he truly meant it. And she felt a surge of relief, then love.

Now she lies alone on the portable hospital bed in her living room and misses Cliff, who's away closing on another deal that he predicted would last into late afternoon. Yet she also misses Gabe. He would bring with him the sweet animal scent of horses, the fresh aroma of the outdoors, where, to ride cross-country, you should know the shape of the weather, the consistency of the soil, the rise and fall of hills, the solidity of riverbeds.

She glances away, up at the delinquent red and white strands of tapestry, and she dozes off . . . then wakes to hear a truck pulling up the crushed, granite drive. Checks her watch, only two o'clock. Out the bay window in the living room, she sees the battered blue bed of Gabe's pickup. In moments, his light knock at the front door, a quick rat-a-tat, like a bird's beak. She doesn't answer. She wishes she had makeup on. And more than that, she wishes Cliff had given her another bath, although it takes an hour to sit on the geriatric, plastic- and-chrome shower seat while he shampoos her hair, suds her body, nude but no desire in it, repulsed, as she is by her own weakness. Why doesn't Cliff seem repulsed, his hidden tenderness revealing itself in the slow, gentle sudsing, and in silence.

She does not call for Gabe to come in, even as she hears the front door flip open and he calls her name. A melodious tenor, not like Cliff's gruff baritone. She still doesn't answer. Gabe must know Cliff is gone because the Rover is. But Cliff could come home early. Then she hears Gabe's step and counts fifteen quick, off-kilter strides until he's through the kitchen, through the living room and kneels by her bed. Must be the painkillers that make her feel like she's floating high, or is it seeing him again, his silvery pony tail fastened with a flashy red band, his long mouth at a slant, his eyes too wide for his narrow face, eyes with such a dark light that she can't look into them.

"Nikki, you look ravaged."

She pats down her unruly hair, smoothes down her sweatshirt.

"But don't worry. You'll be riding soon."

"Not if I can't walk."

"Hey, where's my gutsy horsewoman?"

She doesn't feel gutsy, lying prone in her sweats and looking pale and wan with no makeup. "I've lost the whole season. All we were working towards."

He leans over her. "Snap out of it."

As if it were as easy at that.

"After my fall, I almost drowned in self pity," he says. "It took me down deep into places where you have never been. So get up, get going."

Get the red blood moving, her father used to say to her as a girl when she'd lie in bed in her lavender room and daydream after her mother left, a mother she only vaguely remembers. As she barely remembers her sister. For her father told no family stories although sometimes he called Tricia a star, which Nikki was not.

"Come on. I'll help you up," Gabe says, sliding the new, unused, rickety aluminum walker from the foot to the head of the bed. One-handed, he gently takes one of her hands at a time, sets them on the upper rail of the walker, folds her fingers around the rim, and says, "Tell yourself, you can do this."

Cliff predicted Gabe would start her training too soon. But she's got two good hands to his one, so she sits and pulls herself to a stand, clutching the infernal walker. It feels good to be upright. It feels marvelous.

Gabe says, "Now take a step."

He doesn't help.

"Center yourself, go ahead."

She tightens her grip, centers her weight, takes a step, then another, pain surging where her real knee was, Gabe saying, "That's it, keep going. No pain, no gain." She takes another step and slowly shuffle steps across the long living room. "Good," he says, "but your approach is too slow." As if she's riding.

She smiles a little, circles, picks up her pace, the pain hovering, Gabe saying, "Keep a light touch. Elbows in. Soft hands." They're both smiling now. She tucks in her elbows, step steps. ". . . three, four, five . . ." He's counting strides.

And they both laugh, and she walker-steps back, and he's applauding. "You're the best. Now repeat, till your legs have it down." Like horses' legs repeat a new move over and over again in order to get it automatically.

She shuffles up and back, up and back, across the wide plank floors, past the cacti in the window, past the unraveling unicorn over the couch, until exhausted, she eases herself slowly down onto the hospital cot and lies back. Gabe's saying, "You've got what it takes. You're on your way to the top." He's sliding over the mission oak rocker, and sitting, tilting close. She looks up into his soft, shadowy eyes as he rocks back and forward, and says, "In two months, it'll be mud season, and you'll be practicing again. We'll start back at Preliminary, then Intermediate, then by fall we'll be riding Advanced. And when the weather gets too cold, I've got a new plan that will make up for lost time. We'll go down south to Florida and compete on the winter circuit, in paradise."

Paradise, when she's lying here unable to walk? "There you go," she says, "dreaming again."

"It's not dreaming to want to win."

"No, it's not. But now we're both saying 'not.'"

He smiles halfway. "If not for you, Nikki, I'd be crippled inside like when we first met, but now I'm not and don't forget it."

Yet it's Cliff who has been nursing her through this. "Cliff could be back any minute."

Gabe rocks forward, back, the chair flipping hard and quick.

"I don't want any conflict," she says, "not when I'm like this."

"Don't you blame him?"

"Gabe, he blames you."

"Eventing's not what almost killed you. It's—"

"You've really got to go."

Gabe's rocking faster, clickety clack, while Cliff held that chair steady in place. "Okay, okay, but promise you'll picture us down in paradise."

She says, "Yes," although paradise is the furthest place from her mind.

Gabe still rocks too fast. "That's my Nikki," he says, as if putting his brand on her.

She looks up out the bay window, where the Rover will be pulling up any minute. "Gabe, I'm awfully tired."

At last, he stands. "I'll be by tomorrow, and we'll set up a six-day schedule for you. We'll keep doing more intervals until we've got you visualizing jumps and flying high right here in your own living room."

Then he goes on out.

Through the big bay window, overlooking the near east pasture and the drive, she sees him climbing, with an offsides hop, into the cab of his ramshackle pickup. Then he's backing it up, starting to head out, when she hears the Range Rover's whirry roar, the crunch of stones, and sees the black Rover pulling up as the blue pickup heads out, hardly enough room for them to pass on the narrow drive at the edge of the steep hill leading down to the lily pond. Cliff's Rover spits stones and slides to a stop right next to Gabe's truck, so the truck stops. Cliff gets out and takes three long strides around to the driver's side of the pickup, and his mouth is moving. Gabe must be saying something back because Cliff shifts his stance, spreads his legs, but then Gabe's pickup just slowly glides off, leaving Cliff standing, hands on hips, watching Gabe go until long after the pickup vanishes. Still Cliff stands watching the empty space.

She lies inside and waits for her punishment.

At last, Cliff heads toward the house. The front door slaps shut. His familiar step thumps to her bed—that heaviness for a man so quick on his feet. He stands over her and doesn't say a word. It would be better if he did.

"Cliff, what were you thinking out there?"

He cocks his head, as if trying to recollect. "I thought what if I'd stayed in the Rover as your trainer backed up, and the Rover swerved against his pickup, so it teetered on the edge of the ravine. And the Rover slammed against that piece of junk, a good solid impact that sent it rolling down the ravine into the lily pond with him in it. And it sunk thirty feet into the muck, down to where the snapping turtles hibernate, maybe woke them up from a long winter's sleep. That would've been a shame, right?"

She keeps her face perfectly still. "Gabe just stopped by to make sure I'm all right."

Cliff still stares down at her. "What did he have to say? Give you any riding tips?"

"Not when I'm out of commission."

"You're never out of commission, not the intrepid Nikki. You're going to event again, aren't you?"

She gathers herself. "All that accident did was prove I can have a bad fall and still live."

"Yeah? Well, you got lucky, which doesn't mean you will again," he says in a low tone, almost as if it's a threat. But no, he must be looking out for her, that must be it.

She looks away from him, up to the red and white bits of yarn from the macramé dangling only a few feet from her face. Why had she never noticed this unraveling when she walked upright? She desperately wants order right now in her house.

He's turning to leave.

"Cliff, could you do one thing for me? Could you go out to the barn, get a hammer and nails from your tool kit, and come fold these raggedy strands up under this tapestry and nail the corner down?"

He turns back to her.

"I can't bear to see all this unraveling."

He shakes his head. "Got to tend to the horses. Do barn chores that haven't got done."

"It'd only take a few minutes."

He looks up at the unicorn, his pale gaze unreadable. "I'm late. Got too much to do." And he stalks out of the living room.

"Cliff," she calls after him, "just do this one thing for me!" But he doesn't stop, like he didn't in the high field. He slams on outside.

She looks up and now it's as if those strands of yarn have grown longer. She'll have to nail down this tapestry herself. She's not yet strong enough to climb down the deck steps with a walker to get out to the barn for a hammer, but she could get a rock from the rock garden bordering the deck. Pluck a rock like it was a flower. She grabs her walker, stands, and slowly shuffles across the living room. Soft hands, elbows in—good thing Gabe trained her for this—she gets to the front door and, one-armed, swings it open and shuffle steps onto the rough deck boards, but the rubber tips of her walker catch, she slips, the walker flipping out of her grip. She collapses on her left side, protecting the right, but pain whooshes through her right knee. She lies stiff, out of breath.

The winter sun shines weakly down on her. She deep breathes in and out for a while, then thinks she must get that rock. She drags herself on her belly across the deck, breathes deeply and reaches over the edge down into the rock garden. Her fingers poke into damp dirt, probe, then close over a rock, big enough to fill her palm. She clutches it, belly crawls back to her walker, uprights it, leans on her strong arms and left leg to draw herself up. She tells herself she is fearless, and slowly shuffles back, the rock braced between the walker and her left hand, pain vibrating from her new fake knee, yet she doesn't give a damn if she dislodged the implant because she got that rock, the rock like the hammer which Cliff refused to get. She must tack each aberrant strand firmly in place, she thinks, pain surging inside her bad knee as she shuffles across the living room to her narrow bed, where she sits, twists, lifts the rock and taps the nail back and forth until it's loose. Then she sticks it between her teeth, tucks each strand of yarn up behind the tapestry, tugs them flat, then pounds the nail in until the tapestry is stretched tight, and at last the white unicorn stands smooth, stiff, and elegant again in the blood-red landscape.

PART 2

CLIFF

MUD SEASON. THE WINTER HAS slid by, and Cliff's already missing the cold, sitting in his upstairs office and gazing out his window at his acreage, a brown mush now in early spring, like it was a year ago when he hired his wife's friggin' trainer, who soon will slide back in with the mud, and her two show horses. Beau and Gracie haven't been at Northlands since last November, the first hunting season Cliff has missed in his adult life. Even though in October, he'd done target practice down in the gravel pit, he couldn't go hunting after Nikki's unfortunate accident and leave her alone for days. So he didn't go out into the woods to shoot a buck, didn't gut it, or rope the corpse to the top of his Rover, or drive it home, or tie a noose around the buck's neck, or hang it to cure from the oak out front. Didn't cut it down, or hack the carcass into hunks, or carry them inside for Nikki to chop into steaks and wrap in aluminum foil to store down cellar in the deep freeze.

Last fall, he just cared for her and sometimes pictured those bucks, twelve point racks floating through the woods, Cliff camouflaged, hidden for hours like his father taught him to wait, like Cliff taught his son to sit motionless in a thicket before the kill, his mind a blank, sensors pricked. The closest Cliff gets to praying.

But last winter, he also couldn't stay cooped up all day with his wife. In the mornings, he'd work in his big den with windows overlooking the snowy acreage, the dense packed woods, and the river, a stiff white stripe. In the afternoons, before dark closed in, he'd go down to the mudroom, strap on cross-country skis, and slide out on top of deep snow that cloaked the paths he had bushwhacked himself, or else glide on cross-hatched, packed-down snowmobile trails. He'd coast across the white crust under glistening, arched, iced branches and along the snow-loaded river, dark cavities speckling it, the faint whoosh of water running beneath the crust. A quiet, frozen loveliness, a deathlike, shining peace. And sometimes, he'd savor fresh, falling snow. He'd ski out into it and sometimes tilt his head, open his mouth, and catch delicate, tasteless flakes on his tongue. And sometimes he'd ski up into the foothills, for he still lusts for the twisting rush of a good downhill cross-country run, like his wife loves the risk of cross-country riding, so she had that fall. He thought she'd learn from that, but no . . .

Once he skied across the pasture up to the snowed-over path along the tree line, bushwhacked all the way to the downhill path that leads to the river road, and slid alongside the snow-topped river to the fork up into the woods. Then up through bare birch, oak, and snow-tipped pines to the high west field where he slid across the wide, flat white space to the spot by a pine grove where she once lay. Whitened now, blanked out, all trace of her erased, and he wondered, why didn't he pull his horse back? But he refused to think about that. He turned and skied silently back down his rough trail, past the buried cemetery. Only the curved tips of yellowed gravestones poking up through the white, and he slid on thoughtlessly through the barren woods down to the river road then up the forest path to his property, across and back down to the stark, white farmhouse, where she waited inside.

Although, typical Nikki, she just didn't wait. All winter long, for hours each day, he'd hear from downstairs the clatter and whoosh of her exercise bike and her treadmill, the faint thump of her free weights, the even fainter slap of her body doing exercises . . . she couldn't hold back, almost always in movement. A twenty-degree bend for her knee grew to forty degrees then to ninety. While he bushwhacked and blazed trails alone outdoors, she tortured herself indoors to be ready to ride in the spring. Yet all winter long, neither of them mentioned riding, her trainer, or her fall. It was as if they could only talk about the cold, or about what they'd eat that day, or sometimes she'd ask about his business deals. But he never asked about her horse business.

All winter long, the only one to bring up the accident was Lisa, who once when visiting, cornered him alone in his study and asked how it happened. Cliff said the mare was a vicious bitch. And Lisa, being Lisa, had to say, "Maybe it wasn't all the mare's fault." Cliff said, "Accidents are acts of God." And Lisa, being Lisa, said, "Cliff, you don't believe in God." He admitted, to himself, the truth of his disbelief. He said, "Accidents are simple, but unfortunate events that usually happen on their own, so no one's to blame." Lisa replied, "Bullshit." Cliff shut up then. Let Lisa try to make ominous sense out of what seems to be fate.

Now, during mud season, Cliff wants snow back, wants winter when nature is mostly quiescent, not the harsh passions of spring with its rutting and birthing. Looking out the window from his study, he sees a sea of brown, and behind the barn, the brown dung heap still steaming in the cool, early spring. As soon as the ground firms up, he'll hire somebody to spread the manure over the fields to make it rich. Now the mud just simply sits and waits to suck you down into it, like horses can suck you in.

During the winter, Cliff had managed the barn. Hired a guy to snowplow, a woman to clean, and the Henderson girls, whom he rarely saw, to muck and feed Harley and Druid, while the fancy horses, Beau and the Bitch, still were boarded at the Meadowlark. The farm had all functioned efficiently under his control, but now that it's spring, and Nikki can walk without a cane, she insists on taking it over again. She seems to have forgotten what he's done for her all winter long.

Like the day when she had to nail in that wall hanging and fell on the deck and was in pain, so he drove her in for x-rays. The fake knee wasn't cracked or displaced, and he felt goddamn glad of that, yes, he did, even though the whole way home, she went on about how her surgeon had made her walk again, as if the surgeon were God. And she called her prosthetic knee her "miracle knee." She has to believe in miracles even when it was medical science, and Cliff, that cured her. Any damned fool could see that.

And what about shortly after her operation, days she seems to have forgotten, when she couldn't even bathe herself, those long sponge baths he gave her while she sat on that butt-ugly, aluminum rehab bench in the tub, her knee swollen, red-slashed . . . the soft crush of the sponge as he slid it across her back, water trickling down onto her firm ass. He dipped the sponge in sudsy water, filled it until sopping, dripping full, then slowly, gently squeezed it down her front, watched the suds bubble on her breasts, watched the bubbles pop, before he slowly, gently, wiped the soap off. All the while, she sat saying how she could hardly wait to bathe herself. Beneath the perfumed soap, he could smell her frustration.

Sometimes, not often, he remembers when shortly after Nikki came home from the operation, he caught Gabe backing out the drive in his disgusting pile of junk pickup. *Ram the fucker down into the ridge,* a voice said. *Collide and destroy.*

◆◆◆

In early April—occasional snow still falling but quickly melting into muck—Nikki makes a deal with Cliff to ride again. She promises to start out riding Druid, twenty-five years old, too arthritic to act up, perfectly happy to just amble round and round the ring. She wants to get herself in shape for the "season," she said, shooting Cliff this rebellious look. So he is made aware of what he has tried hard to ignore all winter long—except for when he sends the monthly checks, hers for the board, his for her anniversary gift—that Gabe has been exercising Beau and the damned mare indoors. Keeping Nikki's steeds in shape.

One morning, when she comes in from riding poor old Druid, Cliff asks, "Haven't you learned?"

She cocks her head, peers sideways at him through a dark wall of hair, and asks, "Learned what?"

He heads on out into the mudroom, sits on the bench, straps on his skis, only to realize that it's spring, so the thin snow's too mushy. He refuses to go back into the house where they'd have to talk, so he just sits in the mudroom awhile, until she passes by on her way to the barn. Neither speaks. Why talk about what she has not learned?

Then one night in mid April—the snow at last finished with its silent meltdown—Nikki cooks one of her gourmet dinners, his favorite, venison, almost the last of his steaks stored from the season before, down cellar in the deep freeze. Next hunting season he'll have to kill twice as much in order to refill the empty space.

She has simmered his thawed steaks in her rich red wine sauce. She even lights candles, puts on a CD, jazz blues, Sonny Rollins on the sax, notes so long and sweet they slide through his ears, into his blood, down between his legs.

They're sitting at the cherry table by the picture window and gazing out at the soggy, brown-spotted pastures and the brown dung heap, half-hidden behind the barn. Harley and Druid linger out in the near pasture in the cold, deep mud, both still with their heavy winter coats, like prehistoric shaggy beasts. "Let them be natural," Nikki had said.

And now, staring out the picture window, she says, "Cliff, this week Beau and Gracie are coming home from the Meadowlark."

Gabe will be back on Cliff's land. That little guy's been here in spirit anyway, Cliff thinks. Gabe hasn't come by, but Nikki said he has called and sent e-mails. Nikki claimed Gabe was helping her to meditate, to visualize what she couldn't do yet, to picture jumping, feel each liftoff, each landing.

That's probably true, so now Cliff will be paying that pseudo-guru to trespass again and will have to look at that lip-curled, cynical grin, as if whatever Gabe says, he means something else, which is only one reason Cliff can no longer trust the tough guy with a limp more like a dance step. Cliff plans to fire the fucker the first chance he gets.

Now at the candlelit dinner, while the saxophone wails sensuously, Cliff hears himself say, "Nikki, maybe your fall was a sign."

She peers at him long and hard.

"A sign, you know, to give it up. Eventing and all its . . . accoutrements."

"*Accoutrements?*" she asks, and now she's looking away, resting her chin in her right hand, dark hair falling over one eye again, as if to prevent her from seeing him, like in the high field that day when she lay on her back and gazed off over his head.

"You want me to give up my passion since I was five years old?" she asks, and she turns her attention to the meat on her plate, his venison that she braised for hours in onions, red wine, herbs, olive oil, to tenderize it, to please him. She forks a piece into her mouth, chews and chews, as if it's rubbery.

He cuts a chunk, swallows his piece whole. "I won't be going to any more of your shows."

She stares down at the slab of red meat on her plate, does not beg him to come like before. He almost asks, don't you want me there? But he shuts up. Think before you speak, his father often said. If you're hurt or angry, don't mention that. Don't show your flank.

Cliff notices that he has swallowed all of his venison. Doesn't know when. Nikki stands and clears the table as usual, her limp barely detectable, if it's there at all. Perhaps he's imagining that she's offsides. He sits and bows his head, as if saying grace after the fact. But he has no God to pray to like she does, meditating each day all winter long. She once said her mantra is a prayer and asked him to meditate with her. He said he already knew what was inside his head. She'd been trying to convert him, but to what? He remembers, before her fall, seeing her sitting under the willow tree on the near hill, Gabe sitting next to her, both in the same lotus position, both motionlessly meditating on the same god. Horse worshippers. Heresy.

Now he hears her light step coming in from the kitchen. His head's still bowed. She must think he's depressed, for he feels her fingers threading through his thin, silver hair, lightly touching the bald spot in the smack dab center of the top of his head, like some monk with a tonsure. He lifts his head to look up at her, and she's peering down at him, her dark hair like blinkers covering both sides of her eyes. Her small hand keeps stroking his thin hair, stroking it like she strokes horsehair, but he wraps his arms around her small waist, buries his head into her pelvis. And now her hands grip his arms, trying to lift him up, so he stands, takes her small hand, and leads her through the long living room—past the spot where her hospital cot once stood—and up the silent stairs, down the hall to their bedroom.

They each undress, and he hasn't seen her nude since he showered her. He's struck by how white her small, compact body is, white, except for the dark-eyed nipples, the dark patch between her legs, and the blood red scar on her knee. Then she's lying flat on her back on the bed, like she lay flat in the field that day, looking past him again. He can't bear that, and he climbs on top, and sticks it deep in, then deeper. He sighs and so does she, yet the whole time, she is wordless, even when she comes, and all the while, he's careful to avoid her hurt knee. Wouldn't want to open up that scar and all that it's holding in.

Afterwards, he says, "That was the best it's been in a very long time."

And she says, "God help us."

As if God has anything to do with sex.

◆◆◆

Beau and Gracie return, shiny, fit, and full of shit. Gracie has grown another half a hand, Nikki claims, and, of course, along with the beasts comes Gabe. He looks fit and full of shit as well, dressed in black jeans, high black rubber boots, and a navy blue mountain horse jacket. Looks like he's some upscale horse owner, except for his ponytail and his lurching limp, which seems even more exaggerated now that Nikki has lost hers. Gabe flashes Cliff that familiar, ironic twisted grin. His intense, dark gaze incandescent, fixated, like a crazed seer. Cliff wants to cast out this false prophet the first chance he gets, but how?

The spring days slide past, and all throughout mud season and deep into June, from dawn to dusk, Nikki stays outdoors with the horses and with Gabe, who's got her riding longer and harder than before. "To make up for lost time," she said. Ironic that the accident Cliff had thought would make her stop instead has turned her into more of a fanatic.

Sometimes, he comes home early from the office, stands at the fence, and watches them. Gabe, in the center of the ring, calling out commands. "Leg on." "Elbow out." "Keep your mind ahead of the horse." Gabe standing, good arm lifted up, like he's giving an equine benediction, or a horsey sermon on the mount.

And Gabe often says, "Try it again."

He says that over and over again. And she'll take the jump again and again, and each time Cliff can't tell the difference. But Gabe will say, "Eyes up," or, "Soft eyes," or, "Pick up the pace," or, "Ride forward through the turn," or, "Balance the canter," or once in a while, he will say, "Good." Then Nikki will smile like a small child, white teeth flashing.

Once in a while, Cliff will wave Gabe over to the fence. "How's it going today?" Cliff asks this time when Gabe steps up.

"Better. But sometimes she doesn't listen."

"I know what you mean."

"Sometimes she's a prima donna, too sure of herself. Other times, she's too anxious. She still thinks too much."

"Better than not thinking enough."

Gabe grins halfway at that. "Defending your wife?"

"I'm a big believer in family values. And you?"

"I believe in horses. They lead you into yourself."

"Yeah? What do you find? Do you see the light?"

Gabe shakes his head. "Cliff, if you want to talk ideas, I can do that, but not with the horse waiting here. Horses don't like ideas. They just act. So you got to keep an eye on them all the time. Can't think of much else. Or else . . . you can have an accident. Know what I mean?"

Cliff shoots the dude a warning look.

But now Gabe's staring at Nikki as she takes Beau over a brush jump he set up, a bunch of sticks attached onto the top of a rail. Looks artificial as hell.

But the horse, not into ideas of what's artificial or real, takes the jump with plenty to spare. Shows it respect.

"Sit deeper into him," Gabe calls.

Deeper in, Cliff thinks. How much deeper can she go? He says, "Nikki's jumping again because of your influence."

"She's got what it takes. I only tapped into it."

"Nikki wasn't jumping such high fences before you started *tapping* into her."

"But she wanted to. She had athleticism. A natural talent. An inborn sense of balance. She just had to develop it, to go deeper into herself."

Suddenly Nikki, as if she knows they're talking about her, trots Beau over, both lathery, sweaty hot, smelling leathery.

Well?" she asks. "What did you think of that?"

"Shows an inborn sense of balance," Cliff says too slowly. "A natural talent. Now go deeper. Tap into it."

Gabe keeps his eyes on the horse and says, "Pick up the pace. Try it again."

Nikki nods at Gabe, as if Cliff's not there, and swings her sweaty horse around, his dark hindquarters rippling, and trots Beau out to the center of the ring again, to retake the brush jump, and Beau gallops toward it but rushes the rail—even Cliff sees that—Beau, speeding up, swinging his tail, takes the jump, but on landing, lets loose a couple little light-hearted bucks, full of his old tricks. He's a light-footed trickster like the light-stepping, offsides sprite, almost skipping now back out to the center to the ring in his delight to be back in the center of things.

Cliff takes giant steps back toward the house, goes on in, snaps shut the screen door with a flick of his thick wrist, feels the hardwood floor tremble under his stomping feet.

GABE

SEVERAL MONTHS LATER, DRIVING THE four-hour ride back to Vermont from the Stuart Horse Trials in upstate New York, Gabe's in his pickup with Carla while Nikki drives the rig in front. The back door of her trailer has its top half open, so all he can see ahead is a horse's ass.

The further north and the closer to home they get, the more the Green Mountains loom. They seem like Cliff's own personal mountains, and Gabe remembers Cliff's one big boot propped up on a rock during that job interview at Northlands, Cliff saying he liked peaks better than valleys. Well, this is my peak now, Gabe silently tells Cliff, with your wife.

For Gabe has not felt, since his own fucked-up fall, as upbeat hopeful as he feels now. In the last months of this season, he has finally been getting Nikki to drop the nots, can'ts, and won'ts and to visualize his dream. Yet it's taken all this long summer and five events to get back to the point where they were before her so-called accident, until now at last, she's finally won a ribbon at Advanced. But instead of celebrating with his student, Gabe's again shut in the cab with his wife, who has tagged along to every show this season. Carla's flowery perfume—magnolia maybe, mixed with dandelion—fills the cab and his lungs, while he's thinking how during Nikki's rehab all winter long, he trained Gracie and

Beau at the Meadowlark. Did mostly ground work. Hired a girl to exercise them, but occasionally he had to ride himself. Always off balance, he sewed weights into the pant leg on his atrophied side to fool the horse into thinking he had muscle where it's mostly skin and bone. Strapped his weighted leg to the saddle and willed himself to think his numb side could feel, and the worst part was, sometimes his left leg seemed to send little shots of pain in through the gap, but mostly, he felt half dead. So when he'd meditate, he'd dip down again into shadow thoughts—like wondering why Nikki would be normal after her fall when he was permanently twisted after his.

He has not allowed himself to replay his own fall. He will never allow himself to visualize that. Only Carla knows the inside story, he thinks, glancing over at her in the passenger's seat. Her head is tilted against the window glass, her lipsticked lips parted but silent, as he drives along behind Cliff's big, gleaming rig, the top half-door open, Beau's black tail streaming out in the wind like a flag of mourning.

During the spring and summer, he massaged Nikki's atrophied leg and her bruised ego. Made her do endless intervals and made her meditate. But even though he got her to visualize winning again, she still doesn't have his *Fuck you, death* attitude. It must be Cliff who's holding her back, boycotting her shows, saying he doesn't want to see her fall again, so she keeps calling him on her cell phone to let him know she's alive. Cliff's diverting her, fanning her fears. At Northlands, Cliff occasionally watches them train, stands and stares, big arms looped over the top rail of the fence. An extra-large, humpbacked whale of a man, pretends calm, but aggressive as hell. And Carla's getting buddy-buddy with Cliff, often on her cell with him, her mouth working double time, maybe trying to make up for Cliff's mouth not moving much.

But Gabe has won this round, and after winning the ribbon this afternoon, he and Nikki were all fired up, her stroking Beau, sweet-talking him again like old times. Gabe's going to win through this little woman because she finally knows how to levitate.

Now Carla wakes up, lifts her head off the side window, rubs her eyes. Gabe tries to keep his eyes on the road and the horse's hind end.

"Where are we?" she asks.

Up a horse's ass, Gabe wants to say, but he dutifully says, "Crossed into Vermont about thirty minutes ago." He's staring straight ahead, focused, intent. Beau's tail still billowing in the wind. Should be tucked in.

Without looking, he feels her gaze. "Gabe, what were you thinking?"

She's got to know what he thinks even when she sleeps. Doesn't she know that after each trial, he replays each jump in his head?

"Nikole won't get it back," Carla says.

Beau got Nikki over a few of the tricky, more difficult fences, the "serious questions." Beau's a jackrabbit with a built-in spring, but the fear deep in her has resurfaced since her fall. Although she never again mentioned her sister's death, Nikki takes death-defying leaps one day, only to hold back the next.

"I mean, sure, she went clear," Carla says, "but a few times just barely. It's the horse who deserves the credit, not her. Gabe, honey, you know what I think?"

He shrugs. He can't read her mind like she reads his sometimes.

"It's time for us to move on," she says.

"Oh yeah? Why?"

"Well, you know, we've always stayed in one place too long, until trouble hit, and, well . . . I've got the sense that it's coming again."

Now, when he's just won, when he's got Nikki at the edge of what she could be? Now, at this moment, Carla says to give it all up?

"Gabe, we should head south, you know, someplace warm where you can ride year round. Just you and me."

He keeps his eyes on the road ahead, on that horse's tail. The tail lifts, arches, and a dark clot of dung plops down into the trailer, plops again, and again, and he thinks, Carla's

shrewd, got to give her that. She must know from past competitions about the southern circuit during the winters, although she never went. He tries to picture this round, cream-
fed farm girl in Florida by the beach, but when he glances
over at her, she looks like a solid, middle-aged woman who
thinks she knows what's right, so she's meddling in his horse
business. And then he visualizes . . . a little woman with bones
light as a bird's, voice airy, chattering, and she lifts up and he's
in flight with her, in tandem straddling an animal, defying
gravity, slow motion hang gliding in air . . . if only for a few
moments . . . feeling like you'll never again set foot or hoof on
this fucked-up earth . . .

"Gabe, watch where you're going, for God's sake!"

He swerves back into the lane and follows along behind
that great big, shiny, overpriced rig and thinks he still hasn't
had it out with Cliff about Nikki's fall, which she won't discuss. But now Nikki is poised again at the very edge of paradise, so Gabe's got to think ahead of Cliff, like you think
ahead of a horse, to foresee its next move.

"So what do you think?" Carla jolts him back. "About us
going south?"

He knows he should tell her now of his plan to do the
Florida winter circuit and invite her to go along, but he says,
"I think . . . first, Beau's got to place at a few more events
up north."

"You can't leave her, can you?"

"I was talking about her horse."

"I know what I see."

"I've got to focus, Mama, on the road."

"Your eyes are on the road, but your focus is on Nikole
Swensen. I've been going to these shows for years, and I've
seen it all. She's not consistent. She's talented, sure, but she's
too little, for starters. If it weren't for her long legs and short
waist, she wouldn't have the balance she's got."

Long legs, short waist. A perfect body, Gabe thinks, for
an equestrian.

"Not to mention," Carla goes on, "that she's accident prone.

She had one fall before Cliff hired you and now she's had another one. One more and she'll be a wreck."

It's some of what he has feared himself, and he tells her to drop it. To his surprise, Carla settles back in the passenger's seat and crosses her arms against her chest, like she's won that round. Let her think that.

In a while, they turn off at Quechee and pass its gorge, tourists bending over the guardrail and peering over the edge of the crevice. Normal folks who get to the very edge, but won't ever take the leap.

At last, a half hour later, Nikki drives on toward North lands, but he turns off to drop Carla off at their house, so she can change clothes and take her old Honda to go teach. She works hard at work that she cares about, but not as much as he does his. As she slowly climbs out of the pickup, she smiles with dark red lips. "Gabe, we've got so much to look forward to."

"Yeah," he says.

"I mean us two, together," she adds.

Here's Carla, the woman who rescued him after his fall, his best human friend, still wanting to share her life with him. Yet as she strides off with that confident gait, her flowery perfume still fills the cab, a fragrance too sweet with a whiff of pungent herb mixed in, and as he drives off, he rolls down his window and sucks in fresh air.

❖ ❖ ❖

Soon he's headed up the long, curved, crushed-granite drive leading to the long white farmhouse and two-story white barn with its useless cupola, and behind them, Cliff's rich rolling valley acres. Riverfront land is sought after, desired. It's this horse property that seduced Nikki, not Cliff, Gabe tells himself as he parks between Cliff's Rover and the rig, with its four-doored cabin, crew seat in back, and six slant stalls, all for one horse. Another of Cliff's gifts to his wife. As is Gabe himself.

At age sixteen, Gabe, the son of never-married parents, moved into a cell at the YMCA. The humidity from the pool a floor below turned his green carpet brown, and his bare feet sunk into the mold. Yet he was grateful to get away from a mother who nagged at him to give up horses and work indoors on a local assembly line. "I'm not an indoor kind of guy," he told her. She said, "Indoors is where you get ahead."

He climbs out of his pickup, heads straight toward the barn, where Nikki must be, to finally rehash the event, but in that moment, Cliff steps out of the sleeping compartment in the freshly returned rig and leaves the heavy door open. What was he doing in there?

Gabe nods at Cliff, who nods, then stares. The big guy is always eying him, watching for some mistake.

"She got a fifth," Gabe says.

"So I heard," Cliff says, and he turns back toward the trailer as if to go back in.

Gabe walks on ahead, but he feels off balance now, tilting more, his limp worse when he's on edge, as if his numbed nerves can feel after all.

He goes into the barn, and Nikki heads toward him from Beau's stall and flashes him a still-enthused smile and says, "I'm still high from our win."

Gabe says, "Yeah, and isn't that great," even as he hears the trailer door outside clank shut, a metallic whack.

Nikki turns toward the sound, her senses pricked.

"How's Cliff taking it?" Gabe asks.

She keeps looking over his shoulder, so Gabe looks back, and Cliff's standing at the threshold, half in the barn shadow, half in daylight.

Cliff says, "Cliff's taking it better than can be expected. But Cliff doesn't like being talked about in the third person, especially when he's present."

"Gabe, Cliff has got something for you," Nikki says, to smooth things over, and she waves Cliff on in.

But Cliff stands where he is and says, "Cliff thinks he and Gabe will talk in private."

Cliff maybe wants to have it out now, too. Probably never expected his little wife would get so far all over again.

"I'm staying," Nikki says.

"Gabe agrees with Cliff," Gabe says.

Nikki lifts her hands and says, "Far be it from me to interrupt."

She's a walking, talking interruption, Gabe thinks, as she stalks on out of the dim barn into the sun, and her small body lights up as she flits off, no limp now, light-footed as she escapes.

Gabe turns to Cliff, still at the mouth of the barn, and asks, "So are you and Nikki going to celebrate her comeback?"

"Every day's a celebration here at Northlands." Cliff's delivery dry, tongue-in-cheek.

"She's back to where she was before," Gabe says.

Cliff looks smack into Gabe's eyes, Cliff's that shade of barely blue you see right through, and he asks, "Are you back to where you were before?"

Gabe straightens up. "What do you mean by that?"

But Cliff just dips his hand into his shirt pocket and pulls out a folded blue check. "Was going to give you this."

Gabe stares at it. The check hangs suspended in Cliff's big hand.

Cliff flicks the check. "It's yours. Take it. A bonus. For my wife's comeback that she and I will be celebrating tonight here at Northlands."

Cliff's fingers open, but Gabe's good hand does not reach out, and the check falls, floats, and swishes in a light breeze down onto the dirt where it alights next to a stone. Cliff nudges the stone with the tip of his Bean boot and rolls the stone on top of the check. The breeze flutters its edges a bit. The stone a paperweight.

Gabe keeps staring at the fluttery check. Does Cliff expect him to kneel down to get what he's got coming? "I deserve a bonus because she brought home a ribbon."

"Too bad it wasn't a blue. But you know what blue ribbons remind me of? Blue balls. Blue balls and blue ribbons,"

Cliff talking louder, on a roll. "Blue balls, you know, a condition some guys get. A pain like getting kicked in the groin, if a guy gets turned on and can't fuck."

"I thought we were talking about checks."

They both look down at the check, still stuck under that rock.

"Bet you'd work for nothing," Cliff says, "if you could afford to."

Gabe lets him have it. "Your wife deserves to go further."

"How so?"

What Gabe means is Florida, the winter circuit. But Cliff's not ready for that. "To go further with what she loves," Gabe says.

And he feels the big man's body tense.

"You want your wife to be happy? Then let her go."

Cliff steps back.

Gabe tries one last time. "It's unity she wants. Being as one."

"Being as one," Cliff repeats, like it's some kind of perverted liturgy.

"At one with the horse," Gabe says. "It's way more than ribbons." Thinking perfection, perfection.

"You're putting her life at risk again."

"It's not eventing that almost killed Nikki," Gabe says.

Cliff eyes furl up so tight, his pupils seem to disappear, a narrow-eyed, Scandinavian, blue-eyed mean. His ancestors Vikings, brutal beasts. Then he shakes his head, looks down.

"Look, maybe you're just trying to protect her," Gabe says. "But you can't."

Cliff taps the stone with the toe of his work boot, shoves the stone off the check. In the breeze, the check flaps on the ground like a bird just trying its wings, before it flits up, drifts off, Cliff eyeing Gabe like he expects him to run after it. Gabe watches the small blue paper sway up, down, then land in a rhododendron bush where it snags on a leaf and looks like litter.

"You've got a black belt in meditation," Cliff says, "but you're still an SOB."

"It's not supposed to make you a better person."

"Yeah. So be happy you've still got a job."

Cliff can't fire him, Gabe thinks. Nikki would never forgive it.

"But I've got you sized up," Cliff says real casually. "Sooner or later, you'll screw up." Then he turns and ambles on toward his big white farmhouse and goes on up the steps, across the deck, and inside, where Nikki waits.

Gabe feels like calling her to come out, but it won't help, like when he was a little kid and his pony ran off, and Gabe searched the fields and kept calling her name but couldn't find her. Later, his father found her down in the swamp, sunk up to her chest in mud like quicksand, so he said he'd had to shoot her. Gabe said, "You could've got a tractor and dragged her out." But his father said she was too far gone. And now Gabe's up against another man like that.

Gabe goes into Gracie's stall, for she's been neglected while they were gone. She's got dried dirt in her coat from rolling in mud, so he clips a lead line onto her halter, leads her outside, and hooks the big chestnut to the line at the hosing area to the right of the barn door. She tosses her beautiful, finely sculpted head, a trace of Arabian in it, wild-eyed but elegant.

He'll give her a bath, hose her down in full view of the house. Sooner or later, Nikki will see, wonder what's going on and come out.

He turns the nozzle on full blast, a mistake, hosing down Gracie too hard and fast, she dances about, rears halfway up. Why did he do that? "No," Gabe says, tugging on the line. Gracie prances a circle round him, so Gabe's got to turn round, the slick green hose winding round his legs. Meanwhile, who knows who is watching from inside through the picture window, so Gabe can't turn off the hose now.

He steps out of the coil, lowers the blast from Gracie's chest to her forelegs, but Gracie, still threatened, rears again, higher, dragging Gabe, one-armed, a few feet. Gabe, humiliated by unseen eyes on him, squirts her all over her one-ton body and she rears again. Goddamn, now it's war, got to finish what you start, both knowing it, her rolling eyes showing the whites, Gabe squirting a stream at her hindquarters. She rears high, her front hooves miss his face by inches, so that the nozzle slips and shoots a blast squarely into her face, and she rears and yanks the damned line out of the barn wall, hook and all. He drops the hose, grabs one-handed for the flying line, catches it, but she's fast-stepping backwards down the drive, digging in her hind legs, yanking Gabe, his heels dug into gravel, her dragging him down the driveway. *What the hell was I thinking?* Gabe asks himself, sliding along. Can't force a thousand-pound beast, but now he can't give up, even being pulled right past the deck, past the picture window, where Cliff must be watching Gabe getting dragged along like a damned amateur.

Gabe lets the line go, it flips, and Gracie dashes off, pops a side-winding buck, only to quickly stop fifty yards away, munching grass over by the manure heap, Cliff probably watching the whole time, Gabe ready to shoot the two-timing bitch, but no. He deep breathes, tries to collect himself, then ambles toward her across the lawn, toward the dung, him acting real cool like this happens all the time, like he didn't fuck up. He hardly ever does, not with horses, he thinks. He very slowly, casually, ambles over to Gracie, who ricochets, lickety split gallops about thirty yards, suddenly halts, and grazes again. A goddamn tease, tantalizing him, lets him only so close, no closer, then takes off. "Who do you think you are, you two-timing bitch? Miss High and Mighty. The hell with that, I'll show you who you listen to," he says softly, so as not to scare her off.

But just as he gets close enough to snag the line still attached to her halter, she bolts, slides to a stop just far enough away, so he must saunter after her, and she does this over and over, and each time, she lets him closer. He's saying, furiously soft-voiced, "You motherfucker, two-timing whore, you let me get this halter on, or you're going to the killers, you're dog meat."

But she spurts off, so he must stalk her again, and so she leads him on for a half hour or more, teasing, cavorting. Once

Gabe glances sidelong at the picture window and catches a glimpse of the dark bulk of Cliff's body there, silvery hair reflecting the sun, and behind him a fainter, smaller shape, or Cliff's shadow perhaps. Gabe must persist, until finally, Gracie, even with her walnut-sized brain, tires of her new game, stands still, and lets Gabe approach and simply slide the halter on. He quietly curses, "You bow-splinted sack of bones, you ribby, swamp-eyed, bushy-tailed plug, you jacked-up, crazed cock tease, you think I love you, bitch?"

❖❖❖

It's after dusk when Gabe finally gets back to his rented one-bedroom cape. He stopped to meditate in his pickup by the side of the road, but kept seeing himself limping back toward the barn with the mare—he'd forgot that he even limped—and seeing Cliff's dark shape close to the glass. Gabe had never lost his cool with a horse before. Better to lose it with humans. He'll have to make it up to Gracie.

Now he goes on inside, and Carla's got the table set for their dinner with her mother's old dishes with red rosebuds around the rims, dishes no man would buy. The fishy smell of tuna casserole is wafting out of the oven, although it's way too hot in late summer to bake with no air conditioning. But Carla has to suffer again. She has suffered enough, but then so has he.

Before long, she sits, sweating, across from him at the white Formica table, and they're eating the soupy casserole, which he says is better than anything he could get in any restaurant, and she's asking how was his day. Still making an effort at being kind, like she always has, if he cooperates.

"My day sucked."

"Tell me all about it."

"Don't feel like it."

"Gabe, honey, you haven't been yourself lately. I mean, I've never seen you so distant. Tell me. I can help."

"You can't."

"Well, I know you got mad at that mare today and sprayed a hose at her and had a tug of war. Because when you were late, I called Cliff's cell. We talk quite often, you know, two horse widowers. Cliff was not impressed with your little show. In fact, he was hinting at maybe firing you."

Gabe wants to ask exactly what Cliff said, but he holds back.

Carla goes on, "Oh, I know what you think, that Nikole will save you. But she's not who you think she is. She's obsessed, impractical, a dreamer. Cliff brings her down to earth. He's devoted to his family and he's rich. That should be a recipe for marital bliss."

"Cliff doesn't determine what she's worth. She pays for her own horses and their upkeep."

"So she could move them to another barn, is that it? Maybe winter down south? That's what you want, isn't it? See, I know you better than you know yourself. I'm telling you, Gabe, if you get Nikole near the top, she'll drop you for one of them hotshot Olympic trainers in a flash. Not that you're not as good as they are. You're better. I know that."

"You don't know Nikki."

"She's Cliff's. Her and his land. They're who he is. That's how that man thinks."

Unfortunately, Carla's often right. He takes a long look at her across the Formica table. Hair brassy yellow under the overhead light, only a few wrinkles at the corners of her sharp blue eyes.

She says, "Cliff will never let her go."

"You can't keep somebody against their will."

"Oh, but, Gabe, baby . . ." And she slides her arms, bare in the short-sleeved dress, across the table and leans, her tits pressing into the Formica, and says, "I've kept you all these years, didn't I? Even with, you know, your 'slip up.'" And she's smiling at him, her teeth still white, although slightly crooked.

He thinks, Goddamnit, maybe she keeps me *because* of my so-called slip-ups.

And now she says, "Baby, I've tried to forgive because it's not all your fault."

Her forgiveness eats away at him. That's the trouble with marriage, your mate knows too much. It gives her a hold over him. All of which must show in his face because she adds, "You know I'd give my life for you, if it came to that."

"I've got no intention of either of us dying anytime soon," he says, wishing she didn't love him this much. It's suffocating, right now at least. "I'll be on the road more this fall at three-days, like maybe even the Fair Hill International."

"But, Gabe, I can't leave my students again without losing my job." She slides her arms back, folds them across those familiar breasts, which he once appreciated, even sucked at them. She shoves back her chair, stands, and clears off some dishes. "Gabe, that rich lady's in another class. She's leading you on."

Then Carla heads into the kitchen. Maybe Nikki is like Gracie, rearing up, taunting him . . . letting him get only so close before she bolts . . . but no, Nikki has dedication. She's an athlete, a true horsewoman. She wants to keep moving up as much as he does. She'll go down south with him in order to get to the top. Nikki shares his dreams. He is convinced of that.

NIKOLE

AT THE LAST EVENT, GABE'S words ricocheted inside her head, "Welcome, fear, my old friend," until finally, she felt fearless and placed second. Beau was bold and hot, at his peak, and so was she, sizzling with desire to win. All summer long, she worked toward eliminating the fear from her last fall, she and Beau practicing increasingly intense exercise intervals—how many strides between jumps, which line to take—until Beau did it automatically. "Fear is an inborn instinct, especially strong in creatures of prey," Gabe said. "You can outsmart that instinct in horses, but humans outsmart themselves. And, Nikki, you think too much. You work against yourself. Trust the animal. Don't make it depend on you."

During practice sessions, she still messes up once in a while, especially when Cliff watches from the fence, and then Beau balks or knocks a rail out of its cup. If only Cliff didn't watch. Yet even when he doesn't, she sometimes feels unseen eyes on her, the omniscient gaze of her sister perhaps, so Nikki feels as if she's riding not for herself or for Gabe, but to prove her sister's death was not in vain to a father who is also dead, and then Nikki thinks, yes, Gabe's right, she thinks too much, which any hot, decent horse rebels against.

◆◆◆

On one late summer day, as she and Gabe sit after meditating together yet again under the willow tree, the long, thin branches trembling and closing them in behind a gently stirring green veil, Gabe softly says that she still hasn't gone far enough, she needs to penetrate to those deep places inside, to a new level of awareness where none of the trappings of society would seem real. "It's lonely to shut out normal life," he says, "but if you let me, I'll lead you into a shadow world where light and dark mix, and one's not better than the other, and we're no better than animals."

He's an equine preacher, she thinks.

And then he says, "I feel closer to horses than to humans because horses are the same as they've always been, primitive but trainable."

She smiles. "That's how I am."

He smiles back, but says, "In order to be truly trained, you need to go down south to paradise, where the weather is always warm, and the sun almost always shines, so we can compete year round."

He's a true believer, she thinks, while she still feels balanced on the brink of where one world ends and another begins. Or maybe this is paradise, the teetering phase before you take a jump, when you gather yourself to rise, believing you can fly . . .

"So will you go, Nikki? It's the right path. I know you want it."

Her first instinct is to say yes, to live only for the horse, the sport, the risk. But Gabe adds, "Then your entire past will be small and insignificant." His dark eyes lit with a familiar fervor.

She says, "I can't leave my past behind."

"I did, so you can."

"But, Gabe, you haven't."

"Sure I have. You just don't see that yet. Goddamnit, Nikki, you're trouble."

"I'm a hard keeper," she says, and they both smile at that. A hard keeper is a horse that no matter how much you feed it, can't gain weight.

But Gabe's smile is only half a smile before it's gone. She senses how frustrated he must be to wait almost two years for her to be only maybe half as good as he once was. Yet sometimes, it all comes together in a perfect jump—time slows, and she's slow-motion floating up, one with an animal, each more than it was alone, and then it's as if Gabe's in the saddle with her, like her sister was, sharing that quick fix of ecstasy.

◆◆◆

During the last weeks, as it draws closer to her first international, starred, three-day event, she has again started quoting Gabe to Cliff. Can't help it, her days filled with Gabe's talk about impulsion, counting strides, performance grain, wormers, flounder, colic. Cliff seems to tune her out, until one night she says, "Gabe said I have to let the horse go, yet I also have to make it obey."

"Does Gabe make you obey?"

"That's not what I meant."

Cliff shakes his head and mutters, "Horse talk."

"Horse talk is like language any trainer uses training any athlete."

"It's a foreign language to me. Once when I tried to give Gabe a check, he started talking about oneness and being. What's that got to do with a bonus?"

Typical of the two of them, she thinks, Cliff, the down-to earth businessman, trying to cut a deal. Gabe, the dreamer, speaking of oneness. Sometimes she misses Cliff's stolid presence. Sometimes she misses Gabe's ebullience. Then Cliff says, "Anyway, once this season's over, you'll have more time for your family." Translated, that means she'd have more time for him. Cliff speaks a foreign language, too. She has to speak what's on her mind in order to know how she feels, but Cliff seems to know what's in his heart without words.

Yet lately, he has been like a volcano warming up, little spurts erupting. So she does not mention going down south this winter to compete. She will wait to see if she places at the Fair Hill International. If she does, then surely Cliff will understand that she deserves to move up. She's trying her damndest to think positive.

◆◆◆

The morning of the day before she leaves for Maryland, they're in bed, Cliff and her lying side by side. Usually, she gets up at five-thirty to ride with the dawn before the early September heat, while Cliff stays up late at night and doesn't rise until seven. This morning though, she still lies next to him, for she feels Cliff's frustration, and she strips off her loose, thin nightie, and in the dim light of a gray morning, she slides closer and lightly strokes his bicep, his body rigid, and she wonders if he's also stiff below the waist, for she has been frustrated as well. During the last weeks, the few times when they did have sex, he lay flat on his back and waited for her to initiate it, and once when she asked if something was wrong, he said that he didn't get excited anymore from just looking at her, that she should do something to turn him on. But when she asked what, he only shrugged.

Now in bed, not even glancing at her bare breasts, he asks, "After this big show in Maryland, then what?"

"Well . . . then maybe we'll travel to another one farther south. It stays warmer longer."

She wants to say Fair Hill is the end of the season up here, wants to mention Florida, wants to say if it hadn't been for her fall, maybe she'd be winning blues by now and could take the winter off. But she only says, "It depends on how we do."

"You'll use the Meadowlark indoor ring again this winter. Can't let those beasts get out of shape."

"I'll just have to see."

"We'll see about what you have to see." He lies flat on his back, arms down at his sides, his dark blue boxer shorts almost matching the navy blue sheets, and he says, "This winter, things will get better."

Why can't he just say he wants her here with him, without horses, without Gabe?

What would she say if he said he needs her? But he says, "You said Beau can only go so far, then you'll switch to Gracie."

She pulls the covers up over her breasts. "Gabe says one day she could make the Olympics short list."

"Gracie almost killed you."

"She's come a long way since."

"Gabe says that, too?"

"It wasn't Gracie's fault."

It's the closest they've come to talking about who's at fault for her fall. He lies flat, his body stiff, corpse-like. Why doesn't he defend himself?

"Cliff, I love you, as much as you'll allow me to."

"How much is that?"

She can't answer him.

He asks, "And how much do I love you?"

"Oh . . . as much as you're able."

He sighs, long and deep from the belly, it seems, like you belly breathe when you meditate, from the center.

She rolls down the patchwork quilt and dark blue sheets, reaches down and runs her fingers, ever so lightly, down his bare barrel chest, and slowly massages his flat abs. She can see his quick, instinctive response beneath the blue shorts, then her hand lightly slips down inside. He lies perfectly still, and she slides her hand slowly up and down, lingering at the tip, practiced at this, and she's aroused because he is. After awhile, she climbs on top, and they join together, and he brings to it all the pent-in, loving force that almost never shows itself in words.

But even while they have sex, she wonders what he'll do if she places at the next event and wants to go south to compete? She remembers Gabe said, "If you stay with Cliff, you'll have another accident."

But now Cliff holds her tight and rams it in, as she likes it, and her wondering ceases.

Afterwards, she kisses Cliff's bare shoulders, thick neck,

bristly cheek, smooth lips, and his eyelids, already shut, as if he's asleep.

CLIFF

THAT AFTERNOON, IN CLIFF'S OFFICE conference room, he chairs a meeting on his Killington condo complex and adjoining shops. Bankers, brokers, and lawyers all cluster around his Vermont custom-made cherry conference table in front of the floor-to-ceiling picture window, which overlooks the waterfall, the river swirling with fallen leaves, the riverbank swarming with leaf peepers. He longs for when the tourists vanish and hunting season begins. Then his cell phone rings, Carla's number flashing on the screen.

He asks for a break and heads into his inner office, where the high-gloss cherry floor and built-in, custom-crafted, Birdseye Maple cabinets usually please his eye. Not now. Carla went to all the horse trials this summer, and after each, called to "rehash" them. *Rehashing* is Carla's word for venting. In her reports, she never gives Nikki credit for anything. Carla is jealous, although she won't admit it.

Now Carla's voice, gravely, with a faint southern Illinois accent, says that she can't get time off to go along to the next event, so they'll be "horse widowers" again. Cliff blocks that term out. He's a pro at throwing blocks. Got to follow family tradition. *Don't expose your flank.* Any horse knows that.

Carla's going on about how Gabe and Nikki will be taking more risks, and what does Cliff make of that?

"Not much."

"Maybe you should. See, I've been through this sort of thing before."

"What sort of thing?" he asks, wishing he hadn't.

"Oh you know, ethical issues."

Give me a break, Cliff thinks, and says nothing. Saying nothing has gotten him far in life.

And Carla says, "I mean, what if they lose their . . . family perspective?"

Family perspective. That's a good one. Cliff makes a note of it. Maybe he'll use it himself in family arguments, which are happening more and more frequently.

"So, Cliff, maybe we should take a closer look at things. For example, they've been exchanging e-mails, although they see each other every day. I don't happen to have his password, not that I'd use it, but in my view, it's getting more intense."

"I've got a conference waiting for me."

She forges ahead, "I mean, I'd feel different if Gabe hadn't done what he did in the past, not that I can go into that. Suffice it to say, I took steps and got that all fixed."

Cliff tells himself that if she's implying her husband had a fling, it must've been before Gabe was injured, so it's in the past. Of course, trainers fuck their riders. Doctors fuck their patients. Professors fuck their students. Lawyers fuck their clients. It's all part of fucking life. He's had plenty of chances himself. Women are attracted to him because he doesn't talk much, so they put words in his mouth that they want to hear. Make it too easy for women, they'll think you're a sap. His father taught him that, before his mother left for another man. After Cliff left his first wife, he vowed to Nikki, "I'll never leave you, but if you betray me, it'll get ugly fast."

"In any case," Carla persists, "to be fair to all of us, we should probe into this."

"Fairness has nothing to do with it," Cliff says.

"Oh, but it *should.*"

Her and her talk of should. He says goodbye and clicks

off, but for some reason the first thing he thinks is what about those e-mails? He knows Nikki's password.

He returns to the once-vital meeting and somehow gets through all the bickering over percentages, square feet, interest rates—everyone looking out for his or her own self-interest. Self-interest is what motivates us. Capitalism is built on that, and on greed and fear. Everyone craving a bigger share, afraid they might lose out. Life sucks, Cliff thinks, but he manages to sign off on the contracts, then leaves his office, and hurries out to his Rover.

He floors it back toward Northlands. Paid cash, no mortgage. Now ten years later it's worth three times as much, Nikki's name on the deed with his. One of his talents, knowing what to invest in, except for, maybe, investing in his wife. Why does she have to be so haphazard, so unpredictable? Why can't she be more like his first wife, stubbornly boring but unrelentingly safe?

He turns off Route 21 to take the short cut across a narrow dirt road along the bluff, over ridges and ruts, the SUV's shocks kicking in, sixty thousand bucks for this souped-up truck. He steps on it, going over fifty across bumpy terrain, picks up speed, rushing toward property willed to Nikki. And if she plays it straight, it will stay like that. Why can't she revert to who she was?

He presses down on the gas pedal even as the road curves along glittering granite bluffs. To his left, about forty yards below, the river runs brassy brown and flat. He's careening around curves, swaying close to the base of the bluff. The Rover hits a bump and swerves, sideswipes rock, gets knocked off track. He's suddenly totally focused, turning into the skid, the Rover heading toward the steep, tree-ridden river bank with him pumping the brake, scraping gears, hands clutching the wheel, he jabs it left, the SUV tilts, about to flip. *What the fuck.* He'll die thinking that. But he rights the thing. It finally halts, almost at the edge.

He sits, goddamn hot, body still braced for a collision, feeling the fury that follows fear. Goddamn road, goddamn SUV, goddamn wife.

He pounds his fist on the dash, then sits smoldering, trying to get a grip.

After a little while, he gets out, slams the door, checks the SUV, on the passenger side, only one long, neat scratch, silver on black, easily fixed, an innocuous scar.

He feels his body relax, go slack. He's sorry about that. He doesn't want calm. He wants the anger back. The smoldering inner heat. He grew up with it. He's used to it. He wants the tension back, too. The thrill was worth it—so quick, a blip, a ditch–can switch life to death. In this instant, he sees why Nikki jumps horses, the hot streak of adrenaline filling your veins, your heart, your head, making you feel life is most vital and intense, just when you're risking losing it.

◆◆◆

He parks by the willow, sees Nikki riding Beau in circles out in the back field, taking him over a few jumps, Gabe standing in the center of the ring. From here, they're little specks, so small could squash them underfoot. He heads up the deck and steps into the house, surprised that on seeing them, he's wrought up again, as if something he has been holding in is finally busting out.

He heads straight for Nikki's first-floor office, looking for what? Pawing through folders in her small file cabinet that's in chaos, the opposite of his neat ones. He finds her divorce decree from when she was twenty-three. Brokerage statements of her investments, several hundred thousand that more than doubled before she moved her money out of stocks into money market accounts and switched to part-time to devote herself to her young daughter, to his son, and to her husband. Back in the good old pre-eventing phase.

Back when she filled the house with her constant movement, extra small but full-bodied, flitting off to work in short black dresses or flowing black slacks, her long, dark hair swept up and pinned on top of her head, tendrils dangling, a tease even then. She carried a thin black folder with all the pertinent statistics. A professional, she found out what people wanted and gave it to them. Like she did with me, he thinks, rifling through her thin files, nothing else personal except a couple corny Hallmark cards from him with his handwritten notes . . . "You're always on my mind" . . . "The love of my life" . . . "The woman I've been waiting for." Romantic B.S. Though he meant it. And she'd given him cards on which she wrote sweet nothings about undying love. Now he rips his own excesses into small shreds, wads them up, and tosses the papery mess into her trashcan.

Then he remembers her e-mails. Nikki told him her password about two years ago, probably thinks he forgot. *Solace.* What a laugh. He seeks solace now, can't get it from a god who fucked up, the world a tragic accident. Where's the intelligent design in a world that sucks, where your wife could be fucking around? The happy people are all on Prozac or Zoloft . . . his doctor said he should go on that stuff. Sure, hell, take a pill, be comatose, get impotent. Where does that get you in bed with a wife who craves sex? He sometimes wishes he'd got a woman who didn't.

Solace. He types in her password and her e-mail opens up. Under Sent, he finds, among horse show stuff, Gabriel@ yahoo.com. Gabriel. Not Gabe. Gabriel, some angel . . . the annunciation, right? What has this Gabriel been annunciating to Nikki?

In her Sent file, three Gabriels. A trinity. Cliff opens the last one first. *Dear G. It's three a.m. Can't sleep. Keep wondering can I discipline myself enough to do it right? N.*

Nikki always hated words like discipline, responsibility, consequences. He used to love her wild side, his ever-loving party girl. The opposite of his first wife, too sweet, too serviceable. She bored him limp.

Though he got Matt out of that deal. Yet Matt didn't inherit his mother's sweet, nurturing temperament, instead got Cliff's stubborn, sullen moods. Give me a nurturer now, Cliff thinks, somebody to wipe my brow, cater to my every need, answer my beck and call.

He clicks open e-mail number two. *Dear G. I was just lying in bed with the windows open and a gentle summer breeze slipping in, and I was visualizing taking the right approach and using my whole body in balance and rhythm and not coming in too hard and fast. Hope it works. N.*

Coming hard and fast. Bullshit. She can't be that oblivious to not "visualize" what Gabe would picture—her lying nude in bed with a breeze caressing her bare skin as she visualized riding with her slim, muscular legs spread—which is how Cliff pictures her now.

And for a few seconds, Cliff can't blame the guy, then he immediately does again. Blame others, not yourself. His father taught Cliff that.

His clicks on Gabriel e-mail number one. *Dear G. Thought about what you said today about moving as one. Not getting ahead of the movement. Not getting behind. Sitting deep. It all makes perfect sense. N.*

What the hell is this, some kind of equine code? Sending sexy memos that could be about riding a horse in case her husband ever remembers to seek *Solace?*

He checks her Inbox, but nothing saved from Gabriel. She must have deleted them. Maybe Gabriel couldn't write in code. Or maybe it's not a code. Maybe these messages simply mean what they say.

He prints out all three messages to Gabriel. With a jaded pleasure, deletes the originals. Shuts down her computer, goes upstairs to his study, files the emails in a tax folder in a locked cabinet, stomps downstairs into the kitchen, sits at the Shaker table, stares out the big casement window, and tries to picture a horse-crazed, sexy wife, who is also innocent.

◆◆◆

At dusk, Cliff sits in the same spot. He's drinking a single malt scotch in the gathering dark and feels that hot, side-winding anger kicking his guts like he could give birth to it. For the last couple hours, he's been staring out at his land. On the hill by his house, the weeping willow flits its long branches in the wind, as if waving him on to do more than he's done. And in his open meadows, the high grasses bend and undulate, except for in the pastures that those horses have chomped down. If he got rid of those horses, there'd be no more trampled, denuded fields, no more dung heap spreading out from behind the barn. Horses stain the landscape, the sweet-sour smell of their manure blowing through the open window into his home and filling it with horseshit.

At last, Nikki appears, simply ambling on up from the barn toward the house, then up onto the deck, and into the kitchen, trailing with her the scent of sweat, late-blooming wildflowers, and the pungent odor of horseflesh.

"Had a great practice," she says.

"Congrats."

She gets a white wine from the fridge, pours herself a glass, and asks, "Care to sit with me on the deck?"

"Why not?" And he follows her out.

They sit side by side, just in time to see Gabe limp out of the barn and climb up into his junked-up truck. He flicks Nikki a wave, but doesn't acknowledge Cliff's presence. The little twit acting like he owns the place. Cliff needs to get a strategy, like in football, to call the right plays that wreak the most havoc . . . that thick, viscous pleasure, the thrill of impact.

Gabe's pickup chugging away—a wise man gets out when the getting's good, but Gabe's not wise enough to get out for good.

Cliff gazes out at the pastures again, emptied of horses for the night, and she's talking in that soft voice she has sometimes about how well Beau did, even though they're tapering before the next event. She's exhausted, she says, then she stretches, and a whiff of horseflesh from her wafts back at him on a gust of wind.

Then Cliff notices rapid movement to his left from the manure pile, partly hidden from view behind the barn, except from the angle from where Cliff sits. The groundhog has emerged out of the depths of his burrow in the pile of dark dung mixed with pale wood shavings from the stalls. That pile has got real substance. About six feet high, spread wider at the base, and now at the summit of the brown heap, the groundhog sits on his haunches, his sleek, brown coat glistening, black paws bent in front of his chest, twitching his head this way and that, feeling on top of his shitty world. Cliff envies him.

Then Cliff looks over at Nikki and asks, "You have anything to tell me?"

Her chin juts up like she's been slapped a head-flipping whack. And he feels what's latent in him churning again.

She turns to him, her gaze surprisingly direct. "There *is* something . . ."

He waits, not allowing himself to feel.

"Cliff, if we do well at Fair Hill, then the best way to make up for the . . . time I've lost . . . you know . . . from my fall . . . is to compete this winter where it's warmer, like down south in Florida. Of course, I want to discuss this with you before I make definite plans because we both have a voice in it." And then she's going on about how he'll understand because he was once a dedicated athlete himself, so he knows how much it means to compete in peak form in championships, and that's what Florida could be like. "One peak after the next."

Then she waits. He runs one hand through his thinning hair, smoothes it back, smoothes it back.

"And Cliff, you could take time off and come down south with me, or fly down each weekend, or for the shows, if I go, that is, or you could telecommute and work long distance."

She knows he closes deals in person on the force of his personality, not to mention real estate's in trouble lately with foreclosures going up and prices down.

But she says, "Visualize my competing year round and moving up on the international circuit."

She says *international circuit* almost in a tone of awe. Like it's fucking religious.

He gazes hard into her small face, skin too smooth, nose

too delicate, lovely, even now. But does she really believe he'll toss over his professional life to play audience to her, her horse, and her damned trainer?

He only says, "Beau deserves the winter off."

"But he's dying to jump."

"Dying. Yeah, right."

Cliff stands up, stalks into the house, through the mudroom, the kitchen, the long living room, and up the steps built to never creak—that goddamned good workmanship worthless now when everything seems at stake. He goes into his study, unlocks the file cabinet, slides out the three folded Gabriel e-mails, tucks them into his denim shirt pocket, and tromps back down the steps out to the deck, where she still sits ogling his fucking fertile fields.

He plops down on the Adirondack chair and quietly asks, "So what's going on with Gabriel?"

At the name Gabriel, she glances at Cliff, then her eyes shift up, not focusing on him, but on something shifting inside herself. "You ought to know. You hired him."

"And now I'm firing him."

"Why now, when I've been riding as I never have, in rhythm and balance, as one?"

At these very lines from her e-mails, Cliff pulls out the three sheets from his shirt pocket, slowly unfolds them, and even more slowly hands them across to her in the matching Adirondack chair. She takes the pages, skims through. "Cliff, it's horse talk." In her softest voice.

Not what he expected. No signs of guilt. No accusations about his spying. No fake outrage.

She refolds the e-mails, stands, and starts off into the house with them clutched in her hand. He's right after her. They're his only evidence. But of what? This is absurd, he tells himself, still trying hard to keep the lid on.

"Give them back," he says, catching up.

"Cliff, they're mine."

"Like your trainer is?"

"Yes."

Who does she think she's talking to? Her employee? He grabs at the papers, but she dodges back as if he's trying to hit her, for Christ's sake, and then she's dashing into the house, the papers clutched in one waving hand, and he's calling, "Come back!" But she speeds up, so he takes off after her just in time to see her dart into the downstairs bathroom. The lock clicks.

She's yelling through the hollow door, "Don't you dare come in, don't you dare!"

She's daring him?

He bangs on the door, yells, "Open up, open the goddamn, fucking door!"

"Don't you dare come in!"

So he's suddenly kicking it, kicking for all he's worth, craving impact, a hot pain in his foot, and wood splinters. He reaches in through the jagged hole, finds the knob, turns it, and the fucking, fractured door slides open. She's stepping back from him, which only makes him more furious.

She's clutching the papers to her breasts, stepping back, and he's heading toward her then, his fists raised. She's cornered by the shower. She bends down, crouches on the blue bathmat, arms crossed on her knees. She peers up at him for a few moments, and his tight fists suddenly feel odd stuck high in the air like that, as she cowers in the corner by the very tub where he sponge bathed her during her rehab, soap bubbles trickling down her bare breasts, muscled thighs, mangled, swollen knee.

She's deep breathing like when she rides, collecting herself, he knows that, and he waits, and in a few moments, she stands up perfectly straight, posture correct, the equestrian again. She's breathing slowly in and out, and she looks up at him, her gaze direct, and says, "Go ahead."

His fists drop to his sides, his fingers unfurl, and his hands hang there. Whose hands are those, brick hard, rock big?

She's standing straight, erect. He's slumped now. Her small hands clenched into what could be fists if they weren't so fine-boned.

He wants to reach out and stroke her cheek, but her small body stands stiff with resistance.

"Nikki," he whispers.

She stands straighter, raises her small fists. She looks ridiculous. No hope for reconciling now. Who the hell is guilty here? Cliff didn't lay a hand on her. He only wanted to.

He turns, heads out, steps over the shredded, splintered boards on the bathroom floor.

They'll have to use the upstairs bathroom for a while, he thinks, until he repairs the hole in this door, measures and saws fresh boards, nails them over the damaged panel, spackles, sands, paints a primer, spackles, sands, paints a first coat, spackles, sands again, then a second coat, until the door is pure white and almost as good as new, and only then, maybe, can he shit in peace in his own house again.

CARLA

She has fed Gabe his breakfast—two of her homemade plain donuts and fresh black coffee with cream and two teaspoons of sugar. Carla was raised to take her coffee black, not to make a fuss. Although she intends to make one now.

He has been in the shower a half hour to prepare his body for the trip to the Jersey Fresh. She sits in the easy chair, watches a blank TV, and tries to shut her husband in a box. Like she shut her brother in a box after their parents died because Kyle hustled over to their little farmhouse and lugged out every last stick of oak furniture, so by the time Carla got there, all that was left was clutter and knickknacks. Her mother used to lead her around that dark house with its sloping floors, point to the oak table with its four leaves, and to the hutch, and to the four poster bed, and say, "Carla, when I die, you're getting that and that and that."

The box her brother is in is still sealed shut. The trouble with sealing Gabe off is that he repents, or at least apologizes, and says sweet nothings, and she falls for it, or he thinks she does. Not anymore.

She sits and waits. She's wearing her shiny pink robe with the low scoop neck that shows off her deep cleavage. Give him a sight to remember her by.

When he finally emerges from the tiny bathroom—men

are the prima donnas, take more time primping than women any day—he's jiffy clean, long, narrow face freshly shaved, ponytail tied tightly back, and wearing jeans that she washed for him, along with an inevitable long-sleeved shirt, as if he can disguise what he's ashamed of.

He's all primed for another horsey adventure without his wife. She asked her principal for the days off, but two other teachers were out sick, so she can't leave her kids. Now she turns to her super clean husband and asks, "Where will you be spending the nights?"

"You know, in the rig at the show campground."

"And Ms. Nikole?"

"She's got reservations at a B&B a few miles away."

His usual riff. He'll be with that horse day and night. She wishes she could be treated as well, given rubdowns, brushed, petted, idolized.

"So you're not staying at the B&B?" He promised after his one and only slip to let her know if he is ever again tempted.

"Mama, you've got B&Bs on your mind."

Not a direct no or yes. "So you'll be back in one week?"

"Sooner, if Beau's disqualified."

"You can get disqualified in all kinds of ways if you're not careful," she says with a flip of a smile.

He just stands at the edge of the kitchenette, the counters clean and sparkling, her homemade plain donuts heaped on a plate. Why make a dozen when he's leaving? Err on the side of generosity is her motto, or it used to be.

He waits, his big, old, frayed black duffle bag in his good hand, a bag big enough to stuff half his clothes inside. Could be all packed up and moving out and she wouldn't know it. He's probably trying to come up with some compliment before he leaves like he used to way back when he used both sides of himself and was on the road so much that she couldn't always go along. After his fall, he stuck around home a whole lot more. What seems a tragedy can be a blessing in disguise.

Now he says, "Carla, you know I appreciate all you've done for me."

"More than you know."

"More than I deserve."

"That's for sure." She tries to smile but feels her upper lip flatten the way it does. She wishes it wouldn't thin out and reveal her upper teeth like that. Makes her look tough even when she's not.

And all the while he's still standing there.

"Well . . . hang in there, Big Mama," he says, sets down the duffle by his feet, takes the one step to her, and wraps his good, muscular arm around her waist. His arm stays planted but does not do what his arms and hands used to do, slide on up to her breasts, definitely bigger than Nikole's, although Nikole's are bigger in proportion to her little body. But it's more than Nikole Swensen's body that Gabe wants. He wants her soul. Carla senses this with all her female instincts. She can almost smell his want, for now, in his embrace, he does not smell like he did years ago when she first welcomed him into her apartment in Racine, Wisconsin. His hair flyaway then, no pony tail, his body skinny even for a lean man, though both halves worked, back when he was a first-rate athlete. He'd come home from riding in an event all hyper and full of lust, and he'd nestle in her breasts. How she loved the fresh air flavor to his skin, like river water, fresh air, and sun—the great outdoors' own cologne. But now, if she kissed his lips, although he just showered, he'd seem to taste of barn and tack, as if that sticky equine stench is embedded in his pores.

It's awkward with him still standing, his arm around her waist. She strokes his pony tail that feels tight and dry under her fingertips, not like human hair, more like thick rope.

"Well," he says, "I guess that's it." And he lets her go, steps back, and picks up his duffle, as if he's going to just leave her like that in the smack dab center of her small, yellow kitchen. But then he hesitates and turns to her. "Mama, you better hear this from me. If we place at the Jersey Fresh or in Maryland, Nikki and I plan to head down south with Beau and do the winter circuit in Florida. It's paradise for horses down there . . . of course, you're welcome to come along, but I know you've got your kids, and I'll be back in the spring."

Carla stares at him. His face is too long, with a sensitivity that he usually has trouble covering up, but right now his expression is blank. Innocent. Like his partially paralyzed left side always looks. Like his conscience has tuned out. He knows she can't afford to give up her union job, not to mention all her little children, to follow him, not if he's coming back next spring.

She says, "Cliff will never let Nikole go down south."

"Cliff will want her to be the best she can be, which I know is what you want for me, that's why you got me back into all this."

"Gabe, you're going over the edge."

"I'm taking the next logical step."

She shakes her head, no, and no again.

He says, "You can spend your winter vacation down there, and you know I'll miss you, you're my conscience."

"You've got one?"

"Thanks to you." He half smiles. "And I've got a hell of a wife."

What's a hell of a wife? She wants to ask. But he's heading straight outside, the puckered, torn screen flapping as the door snaps shut. She hustles right out after him, her long, pink robe swishing in a bright, snappy breeze. He's already climbing into his sorry excuse for a truck. He thinks he can pop this Florida bit on her, then just drive off?

By the time she gets to the driver's window, the motor is making its usual racket. She raps on the glass, and he rolls the window down, only halfway, like she could climb through that narrow opening.

She grabs onto the window's edge, gives him her all-knowing stare. "You're not going down south all winter, and neither is Nikole."

Gabe looks straight at her. "Don't tell me what to do. I've had enough of this Mama stuff."

He guns the motor. Her hand's still clutching the pane. He rolls the window up. She yanks her fingers out.

That does it. She marches around, stands right in front of

his wreck of a truck, and spreads out her thick arms as if to hold it back.

He slides out of the cab, and she feels yes, he's giving in, like he's still an invalid. "If Nikole knew what I know," she says, "you'd be out of a job."

He limps up close, gets in her face. "Don't you ever, ever stand in my way again!"

Then he swivels round, limps back to his rusted truck, climbs up in.

Like hell I won't, she thinks, standing right where she is, not budging, her strong legs spread, arms held out to brace against the hood of his rusted old heap, no air conditioning, sweat up a storm inside this battered den of his twisted desires. And he desires Nikole. Carla has seen it in his gaze, in the half lowering of the lids of his big, hooded eyes, in the cock of his head, in his teasing, familiar tone. Carla knows what goes on inside his pants before he does.

She stands with her arms outspread in front of his godforsaken pickup. He guns the motor, inches forward. She thumps her fists on the battered hood.

He thrusts it into full speed reverse, backs up about twenty feet, swerves left and passes her full speed ahead, the truck rattling off over the small yard through her garden, flattening her hydrangeas, her Rhodies, her rhubarb, and then his worthless jalopy is bobbling over the crumbling curb and onto the dirt road, and he's off, bouncing over ruts.

God forbid that he crashes before she's had her chance to make him suffer. When she found out about his last affair, she visited that society woman's house, asked to meet with the husband, explained the sordid situation, told him to fire Gabe, and that was that.

That one was easy. This one is Gabe's last chance. It's desperation that makes him so passionate. Carla would feel sorry for him, if she could, but she can't. It comes to her what to do. Got to meet with Cliff again.

◆◆◆

This time, she called ahead and set up an appointment for three p.m., so Cliff can't cut it short like he did her last phone call. At a quarter to three, she's stationed on the riverbank in front of Cliff's office in a renovated church. Its two-story, arched windows that used to be stained glass, have been replaced with clear glass to let the outside in. The religious way is to keep the outside out, so you look inside yourself, but a river view costs a lot, so you have to show it off.

By now, she has calmed herself somewhat. Like her mother said, "Carla you're a good girl, until somebody crosses you, then there's all hell to pay."

To kill time, Carla waits outside and looks across the river at the glass factory, which has gone upscale, even added a restaurant, baby boomers and yuppie tourists jamming in to eat gourmet food, to buy hand-blown glasses, pottery, and such. Upstairs, there's seconds on sale—glass vases, dishes, and lamps that are slightly askew or with strange bubbles, impurities like our souls have, like her husband's soul does, Carla thinks, and her own. And our bodies have impurities too, especially his.

She feels a sudden rush of sympathy for his broken body, like when he came home from the hospital after his fall and started limping around, step-hop, step-hop. She bought rugs with pads beneath in case he fell. And she kept him on a strict schedule—time to take a bath, time to go to bed, time to eat. He turned into an indoor man who smelled of talc and lineament, sterile, domesticated at last, although so depressed that she'd try to lift his spirits, saying, "Gabe, we have each other, that's what counts." Or, "Gabe, we're in this till death do us part." He only got more down. So one day, she said, "Gabe, let's start over again. We'll move east to the Green Mountain State where your dad was born."

Vermont seemed like a second Eden to her two years ago when she and Gabe first arrived, but a second Eden's not enough for him. Now he's talking of paradise. Well, paradise is a tricky place, one tiny temptation, one bite, and you fall right out of it. Paradise is a one-night stand.

On the dot of three, she steps into the foyer, no stained glass, or narthex, or dark wood, or cross, any trace of God stripped out. Cliff meets her at the inner door and shows her into his sterile, pared-back inner office, like he speaks pared back, and he sits next to his big, sleek desk, not behind it, on a black leather couch. She catches a glimpse of herself in the large plate glass window that makes her look older than she is, cheeks sagging, mouth set in a pout, when she was raised to be consistently upbeat. She smiles a bit and sits on the other end of Cliff's leather sectional sofa that lets out a sigh as her dress slides up over her knees. She tugs the hem down and says, "It's gone on to the next phase."

Cliff immediately gets up and steps across to the big glass window and looks out, no eye contact. She's almost relieved. His gaze can be a gray-blue shock. Back turned, he asks, "So what's your strategy?"

"Cliff, either you and I work together, or God help us."

"We're not a good match, God and I."

"Well then, it's time for you and me to exercise our free will over those who have been exercising their free will over us."

Cliff turns and gives her his slate stare, like hitting something hard, like being flattened. Carla sits up straight. "Good posture," her mother said, "can make you seem like a lady even if you aren't." Nikole is posture perfect when she rides. She'd lose her perfect posture flat on her back on a mattress in a B&B.

"Before Gabe left," Carla says, "he told me they're going to compete on the Florida circuit this winter."

"Nikki said it's the only way to make up for the time she lost." Cliff's voice totally calm, as if it makes perfect sense.

So he already knew. Takes some of the punch out of it. But she says, "Gabe will never make it big. He gets close, really close, but then something goes wrong, like when he had his last fall. He let his horse . . . well . . . sometimes Gabe gets in over his head. That's why I'm here."

"You're here to help. Is that it?" Cliff asks, staring down at her with that hard gaze.

"Cliff, we can't go to that next show, but there are peo-ple trained to watch. And you can afford to hire somebody like that."

He turns his back to her again, looks out his floor-to-ceiling window at the glass factory across the river. She feels bad for him. He must feel humiliated, considering whether to hire somebody to spy on somebody else he hired, a man who might be seducing his wife. Carla gets up and steps over next to him, and he looks around at her, his gray eyes half closed, looking in, and she sees the sorrow in his lost inward glance and wants to fold him in her arms, but knows she can't, so only thinks, These men, they're the children I never had.

Cliff turns away, steps over to his big, dark wooden desk, sits down behind it, opens a drawer, takes out a checkbook, rips off a check, signs it, holds out the blank signed check, and says, "Use it according to your free will." Is that a twitch to his lip? Is he smiling a little bit? Not like Gabe's fixed smirk. This one is sincerely cynical.

She tries to smile back, because she got what she wanted, didn't she? This check doesn't make her his employee.

"But whatever you find out," Cliff says, "keep me out of it."

She wants to ask, Can't you face up to the facts? But asks instead, "Are you going to fire him?"

"Is that what you want?"

"Only if he's got it coming."

"You want to be fair," Cliff says.

"Of course. Don't you?"

He shrugs. "What's fair?"

Fine. She'll have to manage things on her own. She's used to that. She takes the check, pops it into her hand-em-broidered handbag that she bought at a county fair north of Woodstock, and says she'll be in touch.

And she steps on out of that stripped back place, away from the man stripped of his pride. She's doing this for Cliff, as well as for herself.

GABE

Rain's pecking at the red-and-white owners' tent, a nattering rat-a-tat on canvas. If its insistent beat keeps up, the ground will be soaked for cross-country in the morning. Through the rain-smeared wall of plastic windows, Gabe watches the blurred flags duck and flick in the night wind. A claustrophobic competitors' party after day one. Nikki and Beau came in twelfth, surprisingly good since they're usually middle of the pack in dressage. Beau was in top form—obedient, supple, on the bit, executing a graceful extended trot, an expressive medium canter, and fine half passes. But not with enough collection yet to compete against some of the more impressive Warmbloods. Even so, when they posted the scores, one girl, standing by Gabe, said, "How did that Thoroughbred score so well when he's not scopey enough?"

Jealousies mingle under the tent, competitors, owners, and students circling or sitting at white-linen-covered foldout tables. Some well-groomed ladies brush by Gabe with a faint nod, many not quite sure who he is, some know but ignore him, maybe heard about his last fall and blame him for its aftermath. He wants to yell at these sleek ladies and understated men that he had a reputation once, that he was almost long-listed for the Olympics, that accidents show you can't control life, that we're all of the nature to suffer, to die.

He nabs a few hors d'oeuvres off a platter at the buffet table, while volunteers ladle homemade chicken and ribs out of casseroles, Sterno flames beneath. The equestrian set carries heaped plates to the white tables under the lightly billowing, rain-dimpled tent. He feels like he's in a huge helium balloon, like his one balloon trip, a birthday gift from Carla—the soft rush of jets beneath, floating slowly enough to savor the drift, like an ultra-slow-motion jump, sailing up and away from people like this.

People who claim to be riding only against their own best scores, to get their personal best. What B.S. It's being the best of the best. It's giving all you've got. It's transcendence. That's what Gabe seeks. But it's hard to focus on perfection with rain peck-pecking like this. The footing tomorrow for cross-country will be as treacherous as the rain-slicked day when he had his fall.

He brings himself back to focus on the huge tent trembling in the night wind, the wall of drenched plastic windows smeared with trickling rivulets making the space inside even more closed in, while Nikki circulates, works the crowd, the riders all tanned, in shape, real athletes.

What money can buy, Gabe thinks, as Nikki hovers and flits from rider to student to owner and to the next, propelled by her constant restlessness and her sporadic urge to please, although she's not trying to please him now, leaving him alone at this table meant for six in the corner of this big top, a circus of horsepeople.

She darts past, says she'll be back in a minute, then she's off again to mingle while he lingers at the edge of a small group of big-name advanced riders—Tommy Forst, Kelly Curtain, Mindy Colpits—surrounded by students and acolytes, a clique where he never really belonged. A couple riders, Babsy Knoll and Reggie Reynolds, over in the corner, competed in the World Equestrian Games and were short-listed for the Olympics and are riding several mounts, some young ones to give them mileage. They're riders like he used to be, training mounts for the old-moneyed owners, carefully groomed women with their tucked-in hair and tucked-in speech, who think these hired athletes exist only to service them. Not like Nikki, whose father went bankrupt, so Nikki knows how transitory it all is—big horses, big rigs, big farms. She doesn't cling to land and possessions like Cliff does. At least that's how Gabe has her sized up, and he hopes to hell that she'll place in the top five and prove to herself that she's good enough to compete down south, because once in paradise, Nikki will become all she is. She's not there yet. She's at the edge of where one world ends and another begins.

He's strategizing, thinking ahead of this woman, in another class from him, but not old money, and at last, she flits back to where he sits. He's had more champagne by now, so he's bloody high. She looks down at him. He's used to seeing her from underneath, her mounted on a horse and him earthbound. He's used to talking up at her, giving her commands, but now in dim tent light, her dark eyes shine, and it's as if he's looking into dark water and sees his own reflection, misshapen.

She looks past him, beyond the shelter of the bright tent, through the flapped-open plastic doors to the awning fluttering in the wind, rain still streaking down. On her face, this sappy, yearning gaze she gets sometimes when she talks of Cliff. "Looking for someone?" Gabe asks. She shakes her head, no, glances back down at him. He says, "If this rain keeps up, there will be more withdrawals tomorrow, so less competition. Even with studs in his shoes, we'll have to decide if it's safe to ride."

Ordinarily, she'd compete no matter what the weather, but that's what he did on that rain-sopped day, the land a slippery bog. Don't think of it. He must keep this show separate from his last one. The rain hammers at him, hostile rain pocking the tent roof like footsteps overhead, like somebody's walking on canvas, a rain-soaked spy.

"Let's go," he says. "Got to get our beauty rest for tomorrow."

He takes her arm as if they're a pair, and they walk out of the tent together, out from under the dripping awning into the downpour. No rain gear, so they're immediately drenched, rain prickling their clothes, their skin. She tilts her face up and rain slides down her cheeks like tears.

◆◆◆

In the morning, the rain has ceased, but mist gathers into low clouds that fill the dips among small hills, the ground pocked with puddles and muck, yet the horses have set off on schedule, at two-minute intervals. The loudspeaker, though, soon announces additional withdrawals, as Gabe predicted. He figures only about half the entries will complete clean and fewer than that inside the time, for some riders will take the longer, easier, safer options over jumps, not what he chose to do on his last ride when he chose the shortest, fastest path, but the deadliest.

About a half hour before Nikki's start-time, low-lying clouds darken and a light rain sifts down, so the footing, already a scummy mess, turns to muddy slush. And then, only twenty minutes before her start, the loudspeaker blasts news of a fall at jump number seven, the Loons.

Gabe calls Nikki out of the warm-up area, where, due to the damned mud, she has been taking jumps slowly. She dismounts, and they stand under a dripping overhang of the barn nearest to the start box, him in an ankle-length brown slicker and rain hat, her in a weatherproof cross-country jacket, Beau in his natural water-repellent horse hair, almost impervious to heat or cold, a coat that's protected horses since prehistoric times. It's the footing that could do Beau in. "Maybe you should scratch," Gabe says. "Your call."

Nikki shuts her eyes, bows her head, like she's praying. To what? God's no intelligence hovering up there or inside. It's not God who's been helping her, it's been Gabe. A true horseman competes no matter what the elements. He waits.

She lifts her head. "You said ride into the dark, so here goes." She swings back up into the saddle, flips him a wave, and immediately trots Beau off, spattering mud in the slicing rain as he circles the start box. Gabe thinks, Hell, let her risk it all, do what she's driven to do, and he aches to be out there himself again at the very edge where nothing else exists, only him and the horse.

The starter's counting down, then says, "Have a good ride." And Beau takes off, kicking up mud clots, galloping up a hill toward a brush jump, easily clearing it, Nikki in good two-point, seat out of tack, and at the top of the hill, they rise over the Commonhouse Logs, then disappear into a grove of oaks.

Gabe knows he'll never make it through the muck to the back course in time to watch most jumps, so he lurches up the dirt road toward the hill by the finish and hears the announcer blast out that number twenty-three just "left his tack" and has retired and that number twenty-five, Nikole Swensen, just cleared the Loons. Gabe again feels he's on the horse, even though he can't see it, for he has walked the course three times and knows it by heart. He visualizes them slogging through the muddy Labyrinth, then doing a sinking gallop to slosh through a rain-swollen Miller's Pond and the Glades, then heading toward the Roundabout, then Natty's Bridge. In his mind, he hustles and weaves with them, even as he lurches toward the crest of the back hill and passes Dapper's Ditch, a shallow pit with a rail over it, four jumps from the finish. The ditch seems deeper than the ditch where he crashed, his fall shimmering at the edge of his consciousness.

He passes that serious question and at last gets to the top of the hill and stands by the Little Red Schoolhouse, and he sees a hundred yards or so downhill, a brush jump, then a half acre to the finish as the rain slices down, slicking his slicker, picking at his nerves. He looks down at the red, wooden, miniature one-room schoolhouse with its painted, fake windows and doors, and he thinks, Why the hell do they invent absurd jumps like that? And in this moment, he doubts the whole damned equine enterprise with its jumbo hundreds-of-thousand-dollar horses, super-sized rigs, and excessive estates. It's a rich man's sport, a fancy farce, where riders can afford horses on a higher level than the riders are, where the Association cut out the old Steeplechase with forgiving brush jumps and instead privileged cross-country with faster speeds over exacting, nit-picky show jumps. The whole horse world seems like a deadheaded dream.

Rain pelts his exposed neck, dribbles off his hat brim, smears his vision, like that last day, and against his will, he finally visualizes, blurred as through a waterfall, the gray Dutch Warmblood gelding he rode, galloping along the long, narrow field, spectators lining it, their faces pink swatches, the grass blurred green stripes as he galloped the horse up to a hedge, the beat of hooves, takeoff, a whoosh, a swish, that dead silent floating, then the hit, hoof to earth, then hoof beats, and him already craving the next uplift . . . about fifty yards ahead, the blurred Snake, a six-foot, bright green, fake reptile wrapped round two jump posts . . . rain driving down, splattering into puddles. His mud-spotted dapple gray already had slid once on a smear, but didn't fall, mud spattering him and his mount as they galloped up a slick incline leading to the Snake and over it and on to the next complex of fences, offering a lower but slower route, or a faster but higher option. He spurred his horse on straight, taking the direct route. The animal lifted, but somehow slipped, caught a foreleg on the rail and flipped, somersaulted, and fell on top of Gabe, the impact crushing his bones, the horse heaving itself up, maybe trying to protect his rider. Gabe didn't see the gelding then, saw only mud, black rain . . .

But now over the rise, Beau comes galloping for all he's worth. Gabe checks his stopwatch, Beau's still under the required time, his brown coat mud-spattered as he smoothly closes in on the Red Schoolhouse sitting in a swamp. Look up, Gabe thinks, and just then Nikki looks up, switches her crop, and Beau sails over the miniature red school and thunders downhill toward the brush jump and the finish, but he's galloping too fast on this slippery, blackened surface. Gabe wants to race downhill, yell at her, Hold back, swerve off, withdraw.

But she's galloping flat out like he trained her to, tearing across the slough of a field toward the ditch, flying up over it . . . landing, yes, and she races Beau a hundred muddy yards to skim over the brush and then another fifty yards of slick muck and crosses the finish. Yet in that instant—the very moment that she's safe—Gabe slams his good hand hard against his good leg, feels the pain and curses God and his own crippled fate. Why is he a spectator, stuck on the ground, while she defies gravity and falls upwards?

Meanwhile, Nikki's slapping Beau's neck and trying to pull him back, the hardy bay still cantering like he was born to run in muck. Gabe's slip-sliding down the drenched hill, his boots sinking in. By the time he limps to the finish, Nikki has already swung down and is waiting. Thoroughly revved, she's babbling on about the footing and the Splash and the Loons and how Beau almost balked and was running ahead of her and slid several times and almost fell. "But we made it through!" Water streaming down her face, her clothes rain-soaked, the horse heaving, mud-splattered, the three of them standing in a deluge, ankle deep in muck, but Beau still sturdy as hell, while the fine gray Warmblood Gabe rode that rain-soaked day shattered its right foreleg, its fetlock bent at a right angle, so the gelding had to be put down. Like Gabe should have been.

Nikki's beaming, rain-soaked, breathing hard, in ecstasy, after risking her life. She's an addict, too. He has created her in imitation of himself, but there must be something in his face, some doubt, because she says, "Gabe, don't worry. We'll go clear in the ring tomorrow, and we'll place."

Thinking positive, goddamnit. He's sick and tired of thinking positive. It's not what animals are about. Animals are mostly instinct. Dark urges, bright lusts. But he doesn't say that, for Nikki is ready, primed, at the brink. Just as he can tell the moment when a horse has stopped resisting, so he can tell that this woman finally has taken the leap of faith.

NIKOLE

THE NEXT DAY, HEADING HOME from the Fair Hill after the show-jumping, they've been on the road all afternoon into the dusk, first Nikki driving the rig, then Gabe, both too hyped up to nap, yet both too tired to drive straight through. She checks her horseman's travel guide, calls a recommended B&B with stables, and makes reservations for two rooms for one night. It doesn't seem right for Gabe to have to sleep in the empty trailer out in a parking lot, and besides, she's feeling generous, even excessive.

She's still high after going clear jumping in the ring and placing second, her first red ribbon in an international event. Yet the farther from the showground they get and the closer to Vermont, the more often she tries to phone Cliff, who doesn't pick up. So the more Nikki sinks into a sort of funk, feeling happy and melancholy both at once, as she often does, wishing she didn't, wishing there'd be one clean, crisp, clear feeling, without another contradicting it, wishing there'd be one clear decision to make about the Florida Circuit even while she focuses on getting home to her husband.

Gabe's taking his turn driving Cliff's rig. He looks small behind the wheel. Cliff fills the driver's seat. She picks up the map. Gabe says something, but she's focusing on which routes not to take. He asks why she won't put that map down and talk to him.

"Because I don't want to get lost."

"Yeah, that'd be a shame. We might even end up down in Florida." His tenor laugh lifts, not like Cliff's low guttural laugh that stays down inside of him, on the rare occasions that Cliff laughs anymore.

She turns on an Eva Cassidy CD, fast forwards to "Somewhere Over the Rainbow," the voice pitch perfect yet haunting even while Eva sings that if birds can fly . . . why can't I? Gabe taps the beat with his right fingers on the wheel while driving one-handed. Nikki pinned the red ribbon to the passenger's visor over the dash, where it flips and trembles in jets of air conditioning. Indian summer has slid in after the rain, so it's strangely warm for the end of October, the hard sun slanting in through glass onto her skin as they go forty-five miles per hour in the slow lane so as not to unsettle Beau. It would all seem celebratory if not for her husband.

When she called Cliff after the medal ceremony, his voice sounded deeper down in his chest, where she couldn't get at it. She said she'd won a ribbon, a red. He said, "I suppose congratulations are in order yet again," in what seemed a sorrowful tone. So she upped the ante and said she felt "ecstatic . . . you know, a natural high." He said, "Highs don't come naturally to me." No, she thought, they didn't. Had she ever seen him ecstatic? "So the next stop is Florida?" he asked. "The next stop is home," she said, "after tonight." She added she'd be staying at the Breezy Meadows B&B, alone in a single room. Cliff said nothing to that. So she hurriedly said, "But, of course, I've been staying alone in single rooms each night I've been gone." He said, "They've got lots of single rooms in Florida. Doubles, too. Even got oceanfront suites down there, or so I hear." She sighed, "Cliff, come with me." He said, "Yeah, right." She said they'd talk it over when she got back, and meanwhile he should try to "focus on the good." At that, Cliff hung up on her.

Her ribbon trembles from the visor, blocking part of her view of the road ahead.

Dusk edging into night, they're only halfway to Vermont. As night falls, they arrive at the B&B and check in. After they've fed and walked Beau and shut him in the stall in the small barn for the night, Nikki takes one of his saddles out of the tack compartment, and the leather conditioner, a sponge and cloth, and a fold-up saddle rack—she finds it therapeutic to polish tack—and she carries the gear, while Gabe carries the duffles, to their room doors, opposite each other on the first floor. Gabe goes into his, and she into hers, each to shower and change alone for dinner.

She sets the saddle on the rack and opens up her windows to air out the old-fashioned place—four-poster bed, patchwork quilt, hand crocheted pillows—too pristine, too innocent. She lowers the yellowed, rickety Venetian blinds, quickly showers in the small shower stall, slips into a fresh black top and black jeans, and then she calls Cliff again, who again doesn't pick up. She leaves a message with the name of the B&B and her room number, so he'll know she's got nothing to hide. Then she goes to meet Gabe in the B&B's cozy restaurant, where they savor thick, buttery sirloin steaks and a good bottle of cabernet, and they talk horses. After dinner, Gabe orders cognac, to celebrate, he says, and in moments, they tilt snifters of thick golden fluid, and she toasts, "To not losing."

"How about toasting to winning?" Gabe asks.

"We haven't won a first yet."

"We almost have."

So they smile and drink "to what almost is."

And then Gabe nicknames her Tricky Nikki. "Because you almost know what you'll do, so I never know for sure."

She laughs at that, harder than she'd expect, for after almost winning, she feels especially tricky tonight.

"Know my new nickname for Carla?" Gabe asks. "The Advocate. Wants to be my advocate even when I don't need one."

"You're tough on her."

"Yeah, well, she's a tough advocate."

"So is Cliff."

They both nod, don't click glasses, take long sips of cognac, and Gabe says, "But, Nikki, like I said before, down in Florida, our pasts will be small and insignificant."

Can't eradicate the past. She says she must get some sleep, and she tells the waitress to put the check on her room number, and then they head down the long first-floor hall to their separate rooms right across from each other, and say goodnight.

She goes into her musty, sterile room, and behind the billowing, transparent white curtains, the venetian blinds softly rattle as warm air sifts in through the open window. She's slightly off balance, she rarely drinks this much, and she strips and slips on a filmy white nightgown, originally bought to please Cliff, back when they still made love a few times a week, and he'd take his sweet time with her until they both ached from pleasure. She lies back on the high, soft bed and tries to visualize Cliff here now, sharing in this win, as much as he can, which isn't much, yet she lies and pictures his small sly smile before sex, and his thick, still-powerful body, the gray-blond hair thick on his arms and legs, though his chest bare, and she slowly slides her hand down between her legs, but hears a faint creak in the hall. Footsteps perhaps. She gets up, goes to the door, puts her ear against it, and listens, momentarily wondering if it could be Cliff. Only five hours to get here with no horse trailer slowing him down. "Who's there?"

"Open up," Gabe says.

She feels let down, yet also relieved, and opens the door. In moments, Gabe is sitting on the single wing-backed chair and saying he couldn't sleep. Although her gown's not transparent, she feels self-conscious, so she steps to her duffle and takes out an extra-large UVM t-shirt, one of Cliff's she sometimes sleeps in, and slides that on over the nightie. Gabe starts right in about Florida. Neither man can stop harping on it. Gabe's going on about "galloping on soft white sand beaches by the open sea, waves cruising in under a sun that doesn't stop, where it's always hot . . ." Sweet-talking, trying to seduce her with sun, she thinks, when she loves snow. She grew up in Minnesota, then moved to Vermont. Snow is in her blood, cold runs through her veins, as it runs through Cliff's.

As Gabe's rambling on about riding past waves into "the silent gap where desire and thinking stop."

She slides the saddle and its rack next to the bed, gets the polishing cloth, the sponge, and the Lestoil conditioner, and sits in the lotus position on the edge of the bed. Sprays rich yellow Lestoil onto the brown leather and starts rubbing, rubbing it in, while Gabe's talking of paradise, in this tone as if paradise exists, which she still doesn't believe, even though the closest she's come to it is the deliciousness she has felt with Beau and Gabe, not with Cliff, not for years. Gabe's still sitting on the wingback chair as she's rubbing and working up a sweat, no air conditioner in this B&B. And Gabe's talking about registering for events down south and finding a boarding stable, and how it's already late, and the competition's intense, so it's exhilarating down there, not to mention the gorgeous weather. "It's perfect," he says, "and perfection's what we're after, and you're getting closer to it." As he speaks, the half of his face that shows his feelings livens up, all energized, and he's half handsome, she thinks, that chiseled nose, the hollowed-out cheeks. He must have been a terribly sexy man, before his face froze half slack, half blank. Yet he's still more animated than most men, and she's rubbing the leather harder, putting her whole body into polishing tack until the scar on her knee aches in this lotus position, until she's sweating so much she has to slip off the damp t-shirt and take a break. She leans back against the pillows, and feels the nightie slide up her bare thighs as the light from the table lamp glares in her eyes. Gabe stops talking and is staring hard with the intense gaze he uses to judge a horse.

She sits up, tugs down the gown, and again starts rubbing the soft damp cloth round and round, polishing the leather to a high gloss shine. Gabe starts in on Florida again, saying how they've got to get away from the rock hard, frozen winter soil in Vermont valleys. All the while she's rubbing the saddle— seat, pommel, flaps, leathers—rubbing faster until her hand aches, and the saddle shines as if sun's gleaming down onto it, and she's sweating even in her nightie. Gabe stops talking again, as if waiting for her to do something . . . But suddenly she feels other eyes on her, and the slats on the blinds rustle on the open window of her first-floor room. She feels vibrations from outside, like footsteps, perhaps Cliff's, quickly slides off the bed, rushes to the Venetian blinds quivering ever so slightly in a slight breeze. Two lower slats are missing, and a couple other lower slats are bent and form an opening to see through. Was that gap there before? She bends to peer through the hole, the top of her nightie gaping open to reveal her breasts. She yanks up the thin flimsy fabric, wonders if anyone is out there and what to say to Cliff, if it's him, what story to explain that yes, her trainer is in her bedroom, yes, she's in a white nightie, but she is innocent.

Even though she doesn't feel innocent.

"What are you looking at?" Gabe asks.

She still bends, peering out through the gap, seeing only the tended gardens and the parking lot, a few cars, a couple small horse trailers, and their big rig. No movement. It's dark except for a sliver of moon and the beams where the parking lot lights shine down—in the lot, a dark blue Camry sedan that looks official—but surely her imagination's running ahead of her like Beau sometimes runs ahead. She turns back yet quickly picks up Cliff's damp t-shirt and hurriedly pulls it on as if she's been nude.

"You're pale," Gabe says. "See a ghost?"

She slumps down onto the bed. "I just thought I heard something, but no one was there."

"Nikki, for Christ's sake, picture him gone. Vanished."

"Gabe, could you please leave? I'm awfully tired. I need to sleep."

He slowly stands, very slowly, but goes to the door like a gentleman, and she thinks, for a moment, that he will leave without a guilt trip. Like the guilt instilled in her as a child, born into sin, in need of forgiveness, which she won't get, not from Cliff. She sinks down into the bed, but then Gabe turns to look at her again, and she's conscious that she's lying curled, her skin shiny with sweat, and the saddle by the bed is shiny, too, and what if somebody's looking through the blinds right now, watching her coiled on the bed with this man watching her? On the white walls, the blinds cast shadows of dark lines. She shuts her eyes, bows her head and prays that no one is out there in the dark.

"What are you thinking?" Gabe asks.

"I'm praying, ssshhh."

"Nikki, you're waiting for the Holy Ghost to come and drop the answer on your plate. Well, guess what? He's not coming. Not to us."

But she believes in the Holy Ghost, a billowing, transparent presence, a hoverer in high grass, for the few moments when it's present.

She doesn't say a word, and Gabe goes softly out the door. It clicks shut, but she knows he's not done with her yet, and neither is Cliff.

◆◆◆

The next day, heading north as she drives her rig closer to home, Gabe's asking how Cliff still has this hold over her.

She thinks a moment. "He cares more than he says."

"What about your fall in the field?" Gabe asks. "Why did you never tell me the details? Has Cliff made any threats?"

She wants to confess how she partly dreads going home because of the broken-in bathroom door, splintered boards, raised fists. She felt like some small animal, crouched in the corner, before she stood up to Cliff and he left her alone. That night, she locked herself in their bedroom alone, sat in the lotus position on their bed and vowed to meditate until she saw what had happened from Cliff's eyes. After an hour or so of seeing nothing at all, she felt a fear that was not hers, as if his fear had invaded her, a heavy, steady weight, not the flickering erratic sparks she often got. She felt his inner heaviness, and thought it must be hard being him.

She waited until dawn, then went downstairs to where he lay awake on the leather couch, and she saw across the threshold into the kitchen, to where the bathroom door, unhinged, rested against the wall, a jagged three-foot hole in the door's lower half, like the hole in their box springs years ago. But she couldn't photograph and frame this and turn it into a private joke.

This time, she stood over him and said, "I've been sitting up doing my breathing." He said, "Breathing is easy. We all do it, until we stop." She had to take a few deep breaths before she said, "Cliff, I meditated until I could see things from your point of view." He didn't look up, just said, "So what is it? You tell me." She said, "You think all you did was kick in a bathroom door because I'm going to Florida." He said, "Sounds okay so far." She waited a beat, then said, "You weren't going to hurt me. You thought you were losing me. So you did what you did." She didn't mention the word fear. Let him save face. He thought a long moment, looked up into her eyes, and said, "Nikki, you just saved us a lot of grief." Then he took her in his arms and held her, and she clung tightly to him, and she remembered her father saying on her first wedding day, "You're getting married for the affection you didn't get growing up."

Now in the rig with Gabe, she says, "Not real threats, no."

"Cliff's perverse. It'll only escalate."

"He's no more dangerous than eventing."

"He's out to control you."

"And you're not?" She steers into the fast lane, the congestion of New Jersey having long ago given way to the dense fall foliage of Western Massachusetts, and now to the partially fallen foliage in Vermont.

"Nikki, I want what you want."

Sure he does, she thinks. Gabe's glossy and bright while Cliff's muted and dark. Although she wonders again about that secluded side of Gabe, a fall that he never speaks of.

As she turns off 89 onto 21 into Quechee, she passes leaf peepers out in force, city dwellers celebrating the death throes of fall, their vehicles clogging the narrow roads. She glances at the blur of trees, some already stripped bare, others spotted with leaves clinging to life, like she's still clinging to her husband, she thinks, drawn back to what Cliff has *not* given her. And to what she has not given him. To what they once had. To what is missing now.

After she passes through Woodstock toward South Woodstock and heads close to the dirt road turnoff to Gabe's house to drop him off, he says, "I'm going to Northlands with you."

"That will only make it worse."

"You could have another accident and never be able to leave."

"Gabe, please, enough!"

He shuts up, and she passes out of South Woodstock, and the blur of scattered, bright leaves in the valley signals that hunting season starts in a few days when Cliff will tramp out into the mostly bare trees and desiccated leaves to kill a buck. She takes the right turn up the bumpy dirt road heading into the woods and Gabe's cottage.

He has been meditating ever since he stopped talking. She knows because she heard his soft controlled breath and sensed his calm gradually grow, but she thinks how calm can be deceptive, too, and now she senses his gaze on her, so she glances at him, his dark eyes shiny from some private inner sight.

She looks ahead, toward his tiny rented cape, yellow aluminum siding, sloping, paint-chipped front porch. She parks at the mouth of the gravel drive. Gabe doesn't get out, just sits and says, "I can't let you go back alone."

But then the front door flaps open and Carla steps out of the mustard yellow house. She's wearing black slacks, white shirt, and she stands, legs spread, arms crossed, a pose of female strength. Nikki says that she's going home alone and won't change her mind. So Gabe finally lifts his fat old duffle out of the back seat, climbs out of the rig and limps on up toward his wife. His limp seems more pronounced with Carla stolidly looming up on the porch over him, as if there is nothing that Gabe could say or do to convince The Advocate that she is wrong.

Carla's staring over his head at Nikki, and the sun hits down on Carla's yellow hair and makes it shine like some sort of brassy halo or bright yellow wig. As Gabe steps up on the porch next to her, she doesn't even look at him, just bustles down the steps, straight toward the rig, steps right up to the driver's window and taps on the glass. Nikki presses the window down, and Carla smiles a little smile that stretches her upper lip and reveals her tiny upper teeth, slightly crooked but bright white. Her skin is surprisingly smooth, while Nikki feels conscious of her own lined, sun-browned face, and Carla says, "Nikole, I feel bad for you."

Nikki smiles slightly, like the guilty do, but guilt for what? For loving horses as much as Gabe does? No way to say, Carla, we didn't do what you seem to believe we did. Meanwhile, Gabe waits for his unjust punishment on the sloping, paint-splotched porch.

"But I feel worse for Cliff," Carla says. "He's the repressed type who could do damage . . . maybe to himself."

Nikki forces herself not to react.

And Carla adds, "Cliff has been suffering lately, and he won't say over what."

"But you think you know, don't you?"

Carla's sharp eyes narrow and she nods, then turns and strides off, dead red-yellowed leaves swirling in her wake.

◆◆◆

When Nikki drives up the circular drive to Northlands, she tells herself that Carla is wrong, Cliff is not a threat to himself or anyone else. He does need her, although he won't admit it, when what she desires is for him to say, Nikki, I've got to have you, babe. You're my all and everything.

Like after her sister's funeral, Nikki wanted her father to say he loved her instead of sinking into his grief. She kept crawling up onto his lap, and he kept setting her down, but she kept hovering, until he finally blurted out, "It should have been you."

Cliff's black Rover is parked as always in the drive by the willow tree. She rushes into the house, senses its emptiness, yet calls his name. Gets nothing back. Then she remembers it's almost hunting season. He's probably practicing down in the pit like he does each year in late October to prepare for November first, when the woods turn into a war zone for a month, too dangerous to trail ride horses easily mistaken for deer.

She leads Beau out of the trailer into his stall, unwraps his shipping boots, tosses him a bale of hay. He's unsettled from the trip, so she leads old Druid out of his stall, crossties him, tacks him up, then goes back into the tack room to pull off her shoes and yank on a pair of old field boots, then heads out, mounts the old guy and starts off at an arthritic trot for the gravel pit up on the plateau past the high west field. Cliff took the ATV, and she visualizes meeting him with his rifle down inside the pit, both of them polite, her saying, "I'm so awfully glad to be back," and him saying, "Welcome home, though it took you long enough." All perfectly appropriate, she tells herself, as she jogs Druid past the fenced-in pastures and up the path that runs several acres long next to the wood line, then down the shadowy path leading through dense woods to the river. She guides Druid left along the river road, the leaf-laden water flowing slow and shallow on the right, and gets to the fork and heads left up the curling, leaf-strewn bluff path through groves of mostly scotch pine and bare birch. She passes on the left the shambles of the farmhouse foundation and the small, overgrown, lichen-infested family plot with its tilting, black iron fence and open gate where spirits sift out. Then she comes to the high yellow-brown west field where she had her fall, which she blocks out now, tries to think positive. And yet . . . it was over there, only fifty yards or so away, by that pine grove, that she could have died.

Veering off, she takes the wide path through the birches and soon hears dry, crisp cracks, gunshots muffled by the deep pit. She heads up a short incline to the yellowed scrub brush lining the top of the pit, sees the ATV by some sumac, dismounts, and ties old Druid's reins securely to the branch of a leafless oak. She starts skidding down the slippery gravel slope toward her husband at the far end of the played-out cavity, layers of yellow-gray sediment, the hole as wide as a football field, only longer.

Cliff's kneeling on a wide board at the far end, about a hundred yards back from a line of cans nailed onto weathered two by fours, his Persuader braced against his shoulder. A shot explodes, echoes, she covers her ears, a can pops up, twists, falls, even though it was nailed on, even though he must have seen her sliding, gravel spilling, down the steep, crumbly slope of the butt-ugly spent pit.

She scrambles, half slipping, and hits bottom, about forty yards across from the row of cans in the center of the pit. Cliff's got goggles on, probably earplugs in, yet he must have seen her. He does not look at her, only at the cans and shoots again, the roar hurts her ears, a nailed-down can pops, but holds its place. She's walking toward him now, keeping far to the left, hugging the wall of the pit. When she passes the warped two-by-fours, still about forty yards away, the shots stop. Cliff lowers the rifle tip. Good sportsmanship? Bullets cost a buck a piece for that Remington, single-shot, bolt action. He's having a shoot fest.

He still does not glance at her, not even as she walks closer, still off to his left. When she stops behind him, he lifts his rifle again, positions it, butt snuggly against his shoulder, cheek resting on the stock, sights through the scope, and very still, very calm, shoots again. A can dents, splits. Each shot ricochets through her nerves. Back erect, she stands still. Don't look down, she thinks, don't show your fear.

She looks up at the crumbly, ragged, high walls of the dirty yellow pit, at the blue circle of sky above. Then looks down again. He still doesn't look at her. She's invisible.

"Cliff, I'm back," she says, seeing his earplugs, knowing he can't hear.

Instead of laying down his Persuader, he slides back the bolt, reaches into his pocket, slides in five more bullets, slides the bolt forward, then at last he turns to face her and slowly hands her the rifle, butt first, barrel pointed down at the earth. She has practiced with him before. He said she should know how to defend herself. She knows you don't hand someone else a loaded gun. She should load it herself.

Is the safety on? She feels the heft of the long, heavy weapon in her small hands.

Then Cliff stalks off toward the cans, as if to replace the one can that fell, while the others still stand nailed in place to take further punishment. His broad back makes a wide target. She stands perfectly still, keeps the rifle pointed at the earth. He gets to the cans and lines up the wounded can with the others on the warped board, a neat, orderly line made by a neat orderly man.

Then he swivels to face her and calls, "Your turn."

He's directly in the line of fire yet waits.

But then he's walking slowly back, not to the left like she went, but smack center of where she'd shoot. Only about fifty yards away, then thirty, his chest toward her, his heart.

He stops in front of her, still about twenty yards back, and he stands. She holds the rifle barrel still pointed down. He waits.

Then he shakes his head as if she's failed some test, steps to her side and says, "Go ahead."

She can't answer, because he won't hear with his earplugs. He walks behind her, and she kneels on the board, lifts the rifle, butt against her shoulder, cheek on stock, and sights through the scope, braces, and shoots. The recoil rips into her shoulder muscles. Her ears ache. The battered cans simply sit, taunting her.

"Tough luck," Cliff says, loud enough for her to hear through the roar inside her head. She wants to ask for his earplugs but won't demean herself.

She cocks, pulls the trigger again, the roar, another miss, cocks again. This time, she holds her hands motionless, not the smallest flinch, and calmly pulls, a blast, a hit, a can twists in place.

After the last bullet is ejected, she sets the rifle down. She's still kneeling.

Out of the side of her eye, she sees him picking up his Persuader, loading it again. He's standing slightly behind with a loaded firearm. Her body tenses, and she feels that shaky high she sometimes gets when jumping a horse, teetering on the edge.

Then she turns to face him, the rifle slack at his hip, tip pointed down at the gravel as if he weren't even tempted when she knows he was. She knows because of one instant, when she had the Persuader, when he was in her sights.

"Earplugs!" she shouts, pointing at his ears.

He pulls out the plugs, toes ejected shells with his boot, emptied caps, worthless.

"Cliff, what do you want?"

He looks directly at her with his pale, hard gaze and says, "Let it go."

She looks down at the dust-laden gravel and doesn't answer.

He pivots, stalks across the pit to the rough path and starts to climb, and in moments, she follows, herd bound, can't help herself, jogging, then scrambling up the crumbling, shifting wall to the thicket-lined lip.

He climbs onto the ATV and drives off over the bumpy terrain. She quickly unties Druid, mounts and follows Cliff, the old gelding falling further behind the bouncing ATV, until up at the high west field, she calls, "Slow down!"

And feels a sense of déjà vu as the ATV lengthens the distance through the high grass, yellowed like last fall. This time, she doesn't follow but pulls Druid to a halt, dismounts, holds his reins, and he immediately lowers his head to graze. She sits down, legs crossed, in the desiccated weeds, near where she fell, and she tries to pray, to ask for guidance of whatever kind, but no guidance comes.

How has it come to this, Cliff daring her, when she is innocent, more or less, of what he suspects, and he is innocent too, probably, of her fall in these weeds? He was doing what his horse wanted, he said. She sits for a long while in the bleached, wilted grass, but feels no presence like she felt then.

◆◆◆

At dusk, when at last she comes down, Cliff's rifle is already fastened onto the Rover's gun rack. Tomorrow, before dawn, he'll come downstairs in camouflage gear, his blaze-orange vest hanging on a peg in the mudroom. She'll have risen in the dark to make a hunter's breakfast for him like she always has. Neither of them will mention that pit. That's how it is with them.

She goes inside, and he's not downstairs, so she treads silently halfway up the steps, far enough to see at the top, under the closed door of his office, a slice of light. Dusk falls thick and steady outside.

She goes back down into the kitchen and starts to make dinner. She used to love to cook from scratch, back when she had time, when her cooking was a gift. Now she thaws chicken breasts in the microwave, starts simmering a quick knockoff of her red wine sauce, sautés mushrooms in canned beef bouillon, not homemade stock, adds a cornstarch and water paste, not a flour butter roué, stirs. She tries to take refuge in old rituals even while her old friend, fear, whispers to go up after Cliff, to talk him out of being mad, so it all won't fester and grow worse yet. But she stays downstairs, feeling like a bad girl waiting for her spanking. That same sense of dread.

After a while, her cell phone rings. She checks the number on the small screen, Gabe's, so she doesn't pick up, doesn't know what Cliff can hear from above. Then the home phone rings twice and stops. Cliff must've answered the upstairs extension. She darts to kitchen extension, picks up and hears Gabe say, ". . . sure Nikki's all right."

"Gabe, I'm fine," she cuts in. "I'll call you back when I have time. Please hang up." She hears Gabe's click, then Cliff's, before she hangs up. She waits again.

Cliff still does not come downstairs. He must be freshly furious. Now she absolutely must go to him and make peace. Even knowing that the more he retreats, the more she goes after him, she takes the steps two at a time, knocks at his office door, says his name, no answer.

She opens the door and steps inside. He swivels his desk

chair around from the window where we was looking out over his acreage, faded yellow-green and dark rock gray, soft and hard like he is. His face perfectly blank, he says, "Your trainer seems concerned for your safety."

"Gabe has a lot invested in this."

"*Gabe* has a lot invested?"

She immediately regrets saying that.

Cliff swivels his chair back around, tilts back and looks out the window again. He says, "Some accidents happen for a reason."

Why's he saying that now? "Do you mean my fall?" She asks, in an accusatory tone, as if she blames him after all. Didn't she call after him to slow down, slow down, like she called today in the high west field, but both times he kept going.

"Are you saying it was God's will?" she asks.

He says nothing, just keeps peering steadily out as if he has never before seen the view.

If she pushes into him just a little more, surely she can get down in to where he's hiding. If she can draw him out, maybe she can forgive, and then he can. She takes a step toward him and says to his back, "Gabe and I have a professional relationship. That's all."

"So how was the B&B?"

"It was all on the up and up. We had to stop for the night. We were exhausted. Couldn't drive straight through."

"Yeah, all that action wears a body down." His back still to her.

She wants to swivel that chair right around, see his face, take straight on his double edge. But it would only drive him away. "Oh, Cliff, let's just be kind to each other like before!"

His back tightens like when he rode his horse ahead in the high west field, his back a wall. "No problem," he says. "Kindness, here we come."

She takes a few steps closer, close enough to touch. "I mean, Cliff, can't we be . . . tender again?" And her hand reaches out, lightly touches his shoulder blade.

He swivels round, his face thin-lipped. "Tender? You

want tender?" He shoves back his chair, and stands, his bulk imposing itself.

She steps back, a mistake, showing fear, so he steps toward her.

She takes one more step back. "It was for the horses' sake."

"Your godforsaken horses! I'll sell them to the killers!"

She quickly steps backwards out of his office and he's after her, and she's backing down the hall, her eyes on him, then his eyes shift to look over her shoulder, and his mouth opens as if to say something, and she glances behind. She's at the top of the long flight of stairs, at the edge, fear leaps and she looks back at him too close, facing her, and fear leaps again as his hands reach out as if to push.

She teeters, swivels, dashes down the steps two at a time, his boots clumping after her.

She races through the long living room, the kitchen, past the bathroom door still off its hinges. Why didn't she move out then? Through the mudroom, out the front door, toward the barn, the front door slams, he'll cut her off, she turns toward the paddock and hears his steps, his breath, right behind. She's trapped, her back against the fence, she turns and he's in her face, his breath hot. "If you touch me," she says, "I'll tell. You were going to shove me down the steps."

"My God!" he says, shaking his head, arms hanging at his sides. "You're going to ruin me."

"No. I wouldn't do that."

"Then keep the horses, give up the man."

Cliff, the deal-maker, still making deals.

"He's done nothing wrong," she says.

Cliff stalks past her to his Rover, climbs up in, and without looking at her, he starts the motor and backs the Rover up fast, flipping crushed granite, and he's off down the drive and heading north on Mountain View, going who knows where.

She rushes inside, heads upstairs to their bedroom, yanks open a few bureau drawers, wads clothes into a plastic shopping bag from the local tack store, and, before he comes back, she hustles downstairs and out to the barn into the tack room and tosses Beau's tack into a trunk—bridles, halters, grooming kit, medicine kit, blankets, lines and clips—clamps the metal trunk shut, drags it outside, shoves it up into the tack room of the rig, then goes back in, carries out boots, helmets, jackets, saddles and whips, and flings them onto the floor of the compartment. Then she goes into the paddock and captures Beau, hooks a line onto his halter, leads him out and into the barn, crossties him, straps on his shipping boots, then leads him outside to the trailer ramp. But Beau, who usually trots right on up, must sense her anxiety so he shies, and the longer she tries to load him, the more he dodges to either side of the ramp until she can't bear it and leads him to the trailer's left side, to the tack compartment door, holds his reins with one hand, and with the other hand opens the door, and grabs a dressage whip off the pile. She lets the door snap shut, leads him back to the ramp, and tap-taps his hind legs with the whip, but he keeps step stepping off away, so she lightly tap-taps, tap-taps his hocks, his hindquarters, until he can't bear the aggravation and trots up in. "I know just how you feel," she says.

Then she flings across the metal bar, and with all her strength heaves up the ramp, slides the bolt into place, steps round to the trailer's open narrow side door by his head, hooks his halter to an inside line, shuts the door, flips the latch, all the while moving double time and thinking she should take Gracie, too, but Gracie's almost impossible to load, and any minute Cliff could appear. For a moment she wonders what was he going to say at the top of the stairs just before she turned and saw herself at the edge? Was he going to warn her? Why did his hands reach out? To hold her back or shove her down? But then Beau gives the trailer a loud clanking kick, so she hops up into the cab, starts the rig, heads down the drive onto Mountain View Road, and turns south toward Meadowlark Stables. She'll rent Beau a stall and get her horse settled before she worries about where she'll go, but it won't be to Paradise.

GABE

HE'S BEEN LYING ON HIS bed for hours, unable to strategize with the drone of the TV from the living room, one of Carla's true crime shows with that deep male voiceover of authority that makes you think there's justice in the world. She must believe he'll come crawling out to her on his knees and repent for the fucking he didn't do. He lies stiffly and doesn't budge. He won't unlock that door, not after what Carla did. After Nikki dropped him off and drove away, he went inside, straight to the kitchen to get a beer, and on the door of the fridge, held up by a row of magnets, hung bright glossy photographs, big color blowups of strips of bare skin showing between a bent hole in the telltale slats of Venetian blinds. The goddamn missing slats in the blinds at the B&B, where Nikki had to go to the window and look out through. Photos like peep shows—bits of skin, a strip of white breast, a stripe of tanned, bare bicep, one shot of Nikki's pink mouth hanging open.

Carla must've hired some low-life detective. And then Carla came in from seeing Nikki off and stalked past him into the tiny living room and plopped onto the recliner, her arms crossed. He yelled, "Photos can lie. Did you show that pseudo porn to Cliff?" She said, calm and low-down, "This was *my* idea, not his," as if proud of it. Gabe thought, Goddamnit, this is the end of us. Humans, what good are they? If God exists, it's in horses, simple-minded beasts, not in humans with great big brains that only lead us deeper into shit.

Then in her recliner, his Advocate said, "There will be consequences." And he yelled, "I'm sick and tired of consequences. It's my time for rewards. Ribbons and trophies and gold plaques with my friggin name engraved on them." She just picked up the remote control and tapped on her TV show, blue light flickering on her face, the sound on mute, her eyes fastened on the tube, and she said, even lower down, "No more rewards for you. Nope. Not a one." His treble voice cut in, "I'll get rewards and more!" She said, "Sorry. Too bad." A stupid argument, once they'd have ended up laughing at themselves, but this time they kept going at it in an off-key duet, mute blue light flickering on her face. Ghoulish.

Gabe stalked past her, got to the bedroom door, before she said, "Do you really think that little two-timing bitch will leave her great big rich husband and her great big horse estate and her great big fancy horses to shack up with little old you in cheap motels? Watch out, or you'll end up living alone like before."

He slammed on into the bedroom and locked the door, and in the hours since, has tried not to feel shut in like he felt as a teenager, living alone in a cubicle of a room at the YMCA, and years after that, at low-level shows, living in the camper in the back of his pickup. He lies in bed and keeps trying to figure out what to do about the latest in a long line of fuckups. Carla knows some of them, but not the bitterness seething inside since his fall, for she'd loved him before, when he was a death-defying but disciplined athlete, who also had a devil-may-care good time. But now Carla wants him to do penance again. For what? To him, guilt is negative thinking, penance is a sin, mercy is a weakness, pity is the scourge of the weak, faith is the opiate of the oppressed, saints are self-righteous narcissists, martyrs are masochists. His philosophy in a nutshell.

He lies on the bed for quite a while, and she has turned

up the sound on the TV, the unrelenting drone of that know-it-all male voiceover. Her and her crime shows. He has committed no crime. But what if Carla showed Cliff those photographs, or worse, what if she described them in words, and Cliff visualized the rest?

Gabe takes his cell phone out of his jeans pocket, taps in Nikki's number yet again. She still doesn't pick up. He's left messages—emergency, better call, and so on. Doesn't want to record the details. Cliff could be tapping in. That's paranoia, which Gabe's against, although back when he was half paralyzed and horseless and in rehab, he figured out, if God exists, he's an amoral son of a bitch who lets his victims twist in the wind.

He hangs up and lies and listens to the muffled drone of justice, and he waits.

After a long while it seems, his cell phone rings, and it's Nikki. He quickly tells her about the photographs, but she interrupts to say Cliff didn't mention them, and she's safe, although she and Cliff had a bad fight, and she moved out and dropped Beau off at the Meadowlark, and she needs to be alone for a while. "So, Gabe, you should keep away for now." Then she hangs up.

He clicks her number. No answer. He leaves a message saying to call immediately. Waits. She doesn't call back. It's like she's teasing him. Stay away *for now*, she said. Hell, focus on the positive. She has left Cliff and chosen her true calling, so soon he and she and Beau will be together in paradise. It was all leading to this. It's no accident, Gabe thinks. He determined it. He climbs out of bed and imagines Nikki packing some of her things even as he tosses some of his stuff into his old back duffle, the two of them moving in unison, like when she rides. Then he unlocks the bedroom door and heads out. Carla's still filling up the recliner, eyes still fixed on her righteous show. But when he passes with his duffle, she says, "I've got things I could tell."

Threatening him now. Desperate. It makes him sad. He stops, and says, "Mama . . ." But she keeps staring at the screen. He limps past the kitchenette and glimpses again the big glossy photos stuck to the Frigidaire. That damned peep show—slices of skin through slats. She flickers through his mind, Nikki in that flimsy gown, almost see-through, but not quite. She asked him to get out of her room, so he did. They're fucking abstainers. He steps over, rips off the photos, stuffs them into his duffle, and slams on out of the place.

Once at his pickup, he glances back through the picture window, and to his surprise, Carla's still planted on the recliner, the blue light still flashing off the yellow walls, turning them green. She's not chasing after him again. Must have other plans. He takes one step back toward the house, stops, shakes that off, climbs into his pickup and tosses his duffle on the passenger seat. He's running off for more than Nikki, also for a selfless rush that makes daily life, like humdrum time with Carla, seem like an illusion. He's going to catch joy as it flies.

◆◆◆

A toilet flushes. Nature, hell. His assigned campsite is only five feet from tents on either side of his pickup, with its built-in camper, parked so close to the public toilets, he can hear each slow motion slurp from that cement block barracks.

He forgot to pack his checkbook, doesn't possess a credit card, so a campsite's all he could afford with cash on hand. On top of that, it's raining and the constant pinging against the aluminum roof of the camper kept him awake all night, and now in the morning its relentless pitter pat is driving him nuts.

He calls Nikki's cell yet again. She should have called by now. Maybe Cliff went after her. Cliff's not the sort to give in. "I've got to see you *now*. Are you all right?" Gabe says again, into her messages. A few feet from his site, two tarnished, rumpled men in out-of-season shorts pass by, a red rash speckled on a thick white calf.

A shower in the men's shower room, only thirty strides away, sputters to a stop. A toilet flushes yet again, a choking gurgle. Must be blocked. The spatter of rain. Water swallowing him up. Rain's his nemesis, sinks him back down into that foggy, dangerous underground. He's getting out of here, going where Nikki's sure to go.

He drives over to the Meadowlark, doesn't see her rig, but parks, gets out, goes inside the large tin-roofed barn, and Beau's there, pacing around a ten-by-ten box stall. He'll get ulcers closed in like that when he's used to all day turnout. Nikki won't leave him for long, jailed up to fester, possibly twist inside with colic. She'll have to come exercise him.

With the rain making it too slippery to jump much outdoors, Gabe goes to the indoor ring and into a glassed-in observatory deck, shut off from the rich, frothy smell of horsehair and sweat that he thrives on, and he sits in the shadows of the last row of seats and watches the ring, empty except for a row of jumps set up, and waits a few hours, until at last, Nikki leads Beau into the indoor arena. They're both beautiful, both muscled up, both stepping gracefully. Gabe forces himself to wait. She mounts, and after she warms up Beau, a walk, trot, canter around the ring for a while, she guides him toward the first jump, but her timing's off, knocks down a rail. She's already losing it. Cliff has taken away her faith in herself. Cliff's interfering again even when absent.

Gabe goes down the back steps, steps out into the ring, limps with alacrity across to them.

She abruptly halts Beau. "Gabe, I told you not—"

"You're timing's off," he says, takes the reins with his good hand, and holds them all three still. He hears her breath deep in and out, centering herself as he has trained her to, and he breathes along with her, both of them breathing in unison, even Beau quieted, the three of them a herd. After five minutes or so of silence, during which he's blaming fucking Cliff for her regressing even while he feels her body gradually relax, Gabe lets go of the reins and says, "Now do it right."

She trots Beau around and approaches the first jump,

his hindquarters rippling with the muscle that Gabe's fitness training regimen has built up, and Nikki takes the row of jumps almost perfectly in sync with her horse. And Gabe feels himself rising up with her out of the depths.

CLIFF

SO WHAT GOOD IS ALL of it? The valley's a pit. Beneath the rich topsoil, amidst all the rocks, lies a layer of either sand or clay. Before he and Nikki bought this place, they had the soil analyzed to determine if some was sand, so that water would flow through the sublayers and not turn the topsoil into a swamp, so that hooves wouldn't sink in too deep. That's why they built the riding ring on the south acreage up on a high sandy plateau because the low north acreage has clay beneath, so it turns into a wetlands in the spring, and even now in late fall, it's sludge.

It's so wet, got to keep the horses' hooves off of it for too long, or they'd get thrush. Nikki left Gracie behind, so she's in the near pasture with old Druid, the only horse who will tolerate her. Harley, the barnyard bully, stands alone in the center pasture, usually paired with his faithless buddy, Beau, who has deserted them.

Cliff slips on his mucking boots. It's the third day since Nikki left. The sun's just edging up over the tree line, a faint lavender strip. The hired help has already mucked and dumped the dung and shavings mix onto the pile in back. Ever more shit, Cliff thinks, from his doorstep, seeing a small part of the thirteen-foot-high manure pile that each day spreads higher and wider out from behind the barn. Last season, he didn't hire a local to spread the dung over the fields to fertilize the fallow pasture. The summer was too wet to grow healthy hay, so he had to have bales trucked in. No quaint, big hay rolls wrapped in white plastic decorate his fields. His last year's hay was all mold and rot. Would kill a horse to eat it.

He detours to the back of the barn to take a closer look at how much shit has piled up, and almost halfway up the mound, he spies a burrow, probably the work of the fat, sleek groundhog, king of the heap. Manure slips under Cliff's boots as he climbs several yards up the pile to stomp dung down into the hole, to stuff it shut. All season, out in the field, squads of groundhogs have drilled even more holes, so one of the horses was bound to step in a burrow hidden by high grass and break a leg. The horses are his responsibility now. Consequently, the day after Nikki left, he got out the John Deere tractor, hitched on the wagon, loaded in small red flags attached to sharp stakes, a bunch of rocks, and several six-packs of poisonous smoke bomb pellets with fuses like firecrackers. Then he drove out onto the pastures and marked each burrow by pounding a red-flagged stake into the ground, then drove back around again and into each marked hole stuffed a narrow smoke bomb, lit the fuse, then lay a rock over each hole. No exit for those glorified ground rats. He watched the holes awhile and imagined the action underneath, suffocating on poisonous fumes in the dark, a gradual easing into death.

But now today Cliss goes to his deck and shortly, to his wonderment, he sees the fat, sleek groundhog patriarch burst out of a fresh hole in the dung heap and scramble up. He stops halfway to his old perch near the pile's peak, stands on his haunches and peers about, then folds his tiny black hands, as if thanking God to have survived.

Can't bomb that rodent out of a crumbly heap in which a lit bomb would extinguish. Cliff stalks back into the house, upstairs to his closet, gets his Persuader and a pack of bullets, then goes back outside, sits on the deck in an Adirondack chair, and loads five bullets into the chamber. The groundhog has ducked down into dung again, so Cliff just silently sits with his Persuader cradled in his arms, and watches that dung heap and waits motionlessly for a clear shot.

The sky shifts from lavender to blue before the glossy shitpicker finally squirms out again, scampers up to the peak, sits up straight and preens, his little pointy face swiveling all around, surveying land that he clearly thinks belongs to him.

Cliff slowly lifts the rifle, gets the fat rodent in his sights, those little paws like hands, grooming his face. Cliff takes a long, steady aim, fires, and the groundhog flips, flops, and rolls halfway down the heap, a small mound of brown almost camouflaged by dung. The creature lies perfectly still. Death painless and quick. Lucky fucker. No more shit for him.

Cliff tells himself he did it for Nikki's sake. If one of her horses broke a leg in a burrow in the field, she'd blame him when she comes home, and she will come home. She won't leave him for long. Or his land, or Gracie, her hot show prospect. If only Gracie would stop being a bitch. Like Nikki was before she left, balanced at the top of the steps. She waited too long there, poised, as if daring him. Like the groundhog poised too long at the top of his manure heap.

It would've taken only a flick of the wrist to shove her down . . . yet he didn't. But Nikki ran and then stood still out by the paddock fence and said he'd threatened her and she'd tell, and then she left. Not long after that, Carla called to say Gabe had moved to an RV park south of South Woodstock, and she'd tracked Nikki to the Alpine Lodge in Woodstock, where she's supposedly living by herself. Then Carla mentioned again photographs from what she called, *the motel shoot*. Photographs that Cliff said again he wants no part of. He knows what he needs to know. First, Nikki moved out, then Gabe did. Can't be a coincidence. Separate places, so they can pretend they're not together.

Oddly, shooting the groundhog that plagued him only makes Cliff feel worse. Can't even eat its meat. Cliff once saw a coyote stalk a groundhog, nab the rodent in its jaws, shake it, get a taste, drop it, still alive, and the coyote trotted off. What a waste.

Like horses. Cliff's starting to resent them as much as his son Matt has ever since Nikki moved in. Matt is the only person he can talk to now, Cliff thinks, although Matt hardly ever calls, and Cliff hasn't since this all heated up. He ejects four bullets from his Persuader, gathers them up, sticks them in his pocket, then heads inside, sets the rifle in corner of the kitchen behind the living room door, and calls Matt in Seattle, gets an answering machine, and says, "Everything's going to hell, and I know where hell is, right here in that big manure heap, so hot inside that in the fall the dung ferments, steam drifting up, rodents burrowing down in, just shot one . . ."

Cliff shuts up. Wishes he had a delete button, hangs up.

He needs fresh air, goes outside again, but the fermenting, spoiled smell of dung wafts right at him. One spring, a neighbor's daughter had a wedding at his farm on the day after he'd spread manure on his fields, and the wind shifted, blew the sweetish, meaty stench back over the wedding party and all the guests. That's what can happen to a marriage, it can be full of shit.

Then he thinks of the groundhog, still splayed out on the heap, and wonders what Nikki will do when she gets back home and sees it. So he goes out to the barn, gets a shovel, heads over to the manure pile, climbs up the shifting, crumbling mass, dips the shovel down, and scoops up the heavy, fat slab of flesh, its once glossy coat matted with blood and dung. Then, holding the shovelhead as far in front of him as possible, he climbs down the pile, carries the carcass across the driveway and over to the ridge by the ravine leading down to the pond. But at the edge, as he shifts the shovel for leverage, the creature's head twists, and black shiny eyes stare at Cliff. A soulful glare. He heaves it on down into the ravine, where it plops on its back against a rock, its white underbelly facing up, little black hands limp. Cliff turns his back on it.

◆◆◆

At the Alpine Lodge, at ten p.m., Cliff raps on the door of room number eight. And waits. He knows she's inside, saw a light on, saw the cab of the rig in the parking lot of this cedar plank place built like a Swiss chalet and spa, a cheap knockoff of the Quechee Club, where he and Nikki used to belong. No sign of Gabe's pickup. But Gabe's probably inside, feeling smug, thinking he got what he wanted. He'll get smoked out. He'll get his nose rubbed in shit.

Cliff knocks again. The door opens, and he refuses to let one emotion cross his face. His Dad trained him well, deadpan, as he watches Nikki attempt a wavering smile. Even tremulous, her face is still lovely.

She waves him in with a tiny flip of her wrist. He still half expects to find Gabe inside, but the two-roomed suite is empty, only prefab oak laminate furniture, bright indoor-outdoor carpeting like a fake putting green, canned lights overhead. Nikki likes natural wood, table lamps.

He steps right on through the living room into the bedroom, can't help it. Expects to find the bed mussed up, but it's neatly made, bedspread goddamn iridescent gold, its polyester suffocating. He sleeps with pure cotton against his skin. Cotton breathes.

Cliff finds himself going to the closet, sliding open its door. Only a few hangers of her clothes. On a shallow shelf, neatly stacked riding britches, a few turtlenecks. On the narrow floor, three pairs of her riding boots stand in a straight, shiny row. No men's clothes.

Closets tell an awful lot. She's watching him. He didn't mean to open her closet door. It's as if it opened by itself.

He turns to face her, and it's as if somebody else is saying out loud, "You'd rather live *here* than with me?"

He can't believe he said what he felt. Might as well be naked. Might as well be belly up. He sits down on that ever-shiny, too-slick spread. To his surprise, she sits down next to him.

"Nikki, for Christ's sake."

"I live here alone."

"I see that."

They both sit in silence.

He thinks, Goddamn, she won't leave me and our farm for an itinerate dreamer burrowed in a dark narrow trailer in an RV camp. Smoke the fucker out!

Cliff sits stiffly and waits.

She stands up and glances at the cheap electric clock on the fake wood night table. Everything in this place is fake, Cliff thinks. No natural wood, no natural fabric, no natural, loving wife.

"I can't come back," she says.

"Not ever?"

"Not yet."

"You miss Northlands?"

"I miss you, Cliff. And I still love you, even though you're a hard man, as stubborn as they come."

"Never said I wasn't."

"And you're honest, but you don't say what you feel."

"Why bother? You know my weak spots."

"Am I one of them?"

He shrugs. He has given away enough.

She hesitates. She must know he's said all he's going to say. She says, "It's late."

Like she expects him to go. He says, "Yep, it is." But he still sits on the shiny bed.

"Cliff . . ."

"Yes?"

"Why don't you stay the night?"

"Stay the night?"

"We'll just be together. You know," she says, "as friends."

"Friends. Sure, hell."

She stands, turns to open the top drawer of the oak veneer bureau, and lifts out a red silk nightgown, not the kind a friend would wear, but not see-through either, and she goes into the bathroom to change. He can imagine inside the bathroom. A fake, gold-framed mirror eyeing her real naked, firm flesh.

She's no friend.

The door opens, she reappears, clad from neck to ankles in opaque red silk.

He goes into the bathroom next, fake oak commode, fake marble top, fake plastic-lined shower. A simple, small mirror reflects a creased, aging face that needs a shave. Desperation lights the pale eyes.

He takes a piss, strips down to his black boxers, goes back on out. She's already in the king-sized bed, covered up to her waist. He climbs in next to her, pulls the shiny spread over him, and imagines sweating through the night under it, suffocating in a polyester nest. He wonders if she can smell his panic it's so intense. He fears he has lost her, yet he cannot tell her that.

She slides closer to him, almost touching, so he slides closer to her, but as soon as their bodies touch, she curls onto her side, her warm, rounded backside curved toward him. He curls his big, rough body around her small silky one, spooning like they used to, and he feels this rush with his body cupped round hers. He feels overcome with unaccustomed tenderness in this fake prefab place under the shiny spread, and he tunnels in and smiles secretly at her small rounded back, feels his upper lip curl just a bit, and he keeps smiling offsides like that until they sleep.

CARLA

IT'S BEEN THREE WEEKS SINCE Gabe moved out. He called once, but she didn't pick up. He left a message saying he had to go down south, and he'd be in touch, but Carla has a plan to put a halt to his exodus. So she's waiting in the parking lot of the Alpine Lodge for her husband's lover to return to her rented room. Three hours of sitting in this little Honda, but Carla persists. She comes from a long line of determined folk who don't give up. One reason her parents fought so much. "If you don't like it here, Craig, move out!" her mother used to yell at her Dad. As a kid, Carla lost sleep thinking he'd vanish, but the next day he'd still be there, bruising for another round. Anything could set her mother off, a coat left on the couch, a tone of voice, an errand not done. Carla learned fast that the only way to win was not to budge. Once she and her mother had it out, fisticuffs, rolling around on the living room rug, her mother saying, "You're crazy!" Carla saying, "No, you are!" Even as a kid she knew she was sane, even when she lost her temper like her mother did, a temper she has not totally lost since Gabe's fall.

But she'd lost it before, and before Gabe. Drove some boyfriends away. Almost jumped out of a jerk's moving car once, and ran away from another guy who came on too strong, and spent the night in a nearby woods, everybody out searching for her. She didn't put up with any BS. So she didn't get many dates. And she wore figure-concealing clothes to hide her big boobs. The result of being brought up Baptist, with their either/or creed. You're either good or you're bad. Once she left home, she decided not to be a Baptist, but to be good. As much as she could. So she sits in this motel parking lot and waits, knowing she has good on her side.

Finally, her husband's corrupt lover drives into the lot and parks her fancy four-doored cab, crew seat in back, the trailer hitch empty. The extra-long gooseneck trailer, with its stalls and living quarters, must be over at the Meadowlark.

Nikole hops out of the cab and heads straight to the door of number eight. Her dark hair is smoothed back into a knot from riding. Usually, it tumbles down around her face, so it's like she peers out of blinkers, like if she can't see you, you can't see her. She's decked out in riding gear, black turtleneck, shiny black boots, and skin-tight beige britches, showing off a body that's way too thin. With that bird-boned frame, she'll probably get osteoporosis early and end up an invalid like Gabe. As the Bible says, she will be like the animals that perish and their form shall waste away.

Carla climbs out of her Honda and walks straight up to this imitation ski lodge even though the closest real slopes are over in Killington.

She knocks on the door, feels Nikole peering out through the peephole. Then the door opens, and from one quick glance inside, Carla recognizes the kind of motel room where she and Gabe have spent too many nights. She feels a rush of pleasure to see Nikole Swensen has sunk to this but refuses to set foot inside where Gabe must have been, and just says, "Let's take a walk."

Nikole nods, steps right out, doesn't lock her door, and they head along Main Street and take the first right onto Pine Street that leads up the hill, Carla noticing how steep the road is, though fortunately she has a good long stride, and Nikole quick-steps right along, strong from all the riding Gabe has made her do. It's Gabe's fault that Nikole is in such good shape.

"I came out of concern for all of us," Carla says, "but especially for Cliff. I called him the other day, and he spoke in a monotone. He seems depressed."

"Aren't we all?" Nikole asks.

Carla says, "It's hardest for the one who's been left."

Nikole breaks stride, slows, like she might balk, but then picks up the pace. And they're striding side by side, swinging their arms like those people who power walk to ward off death.

"I asked Cliff if there is some way I could help," Carla says. "He said the only person who could help him now was you."

Nikole, flitting alongside, says, "That doesn't sound like Cliff."

Actually, Cliff had said that no one could help. Carla says, "He's not himself. But I'm more myself than I've been in a while." During that same call with Cliff, Carla mentioned the photographs. He said, "Photographs can be doctored." Like Doubting Thomas. Like he's got to touch the wounds to believe.

She's still keeping pace with Nikole who's striding even faster now, as the white-framed houses are fewer and farther between the higher they climb. Carla's glad that she inherited good, strong farm genes, so she can keep up, although she's huffing a bit. She says, "Of course, Cliff doesn't say much."

"Yes, he usually doesn't," Nikole says, swinging arms, tromping straight uphill, almost to the top.

"So why not go back to him?" Carla asks.

Nikole stops midstride. "I can't go into that."

"And what about Gabe? He's one of the walking wounded, in every sense."

They're both standing now at the top of the hill, and below them the old picturesque town spreads out in a deep valley that's gaudy in late fall but soon will be frozen white and stiff.

"Carla, if Gabe's so bad, why do you want him back?"

"I've been through this before. He loses his sense of balance, no matter what pain it brings. And there are certain women, Nikole, who do that, too."

Nikole looks straight up at Carla. "Gabe's in it for the horses, not for me."

Carla's taken aback, thinking if there's truth to that, it would change all her plans, but then she pictures the photographs—the creamy negligee, Nikole's half-bare breasts—and she says, "Gabe's got a track record of being into the ladies who own horses, too."

At that, Nikole swivels and starts loping back downhill the way they came, passing small white houses, then more and bigger ones the lower they get. It's much easier going down, Carla thinks, striding along, keeping pace easily, yet now it seems as if Nikole's breath is also coming hard and fast. She's got a short stride and she only comes up to Carla's armpit, a little bit of a thing. Innocent-looking, deceptive. It occurs to Carla that she could lift up this little china doll and smash her down on the pavement and she'd shatter into little bits.

But Carla steps on briskly downhill, gravity her new friend, and says, "It all comes down to self-discipline and self-restraint."

"That sounds like something Gabe would say."

Now Nikole's the authority on what Gabe would say as well as Cliff? Nikole trades on her instincts, while Carla's got morals on her side. She takes longer strides, and they're back to Main Street and turn left. And on the corner by the displaced ski lodge, Nikole stops again to say, "I'm sorry for all this."

As if she actually expects instant forgiveness and no penance. Carla says, "Then make it right. Give up eventing. And my husband."

Nikole looks up at Carla and says, "We're innocent, at least of what you think."

Again, Carla wants to lift that little woman up, shake her till her thin bones rattle. But she says, "You haven't been innocent since the day you were born."

Oddly, Nikole nods at that.

NIKOLE

AFTER CARLA'S VISIT, NIKKI VISUALIZES going down south to be with her horse in paradise, where all is warm and sun-bleached, and the sea slides gently onto white sand, the footing soft on horses' hooves as she'll ride along the sun's path to find the animal's highest nature, the spirit within.

But, of course, she also wants to win, which means she must bring Gabe along. Yet she also still wants Cliff to come. Nikki resolves to meet with her husband and say it's all for the sport, for a pursuit of excellence. Didn't he once say he'd never again feel the joy he felt after a good bruising win on the football field?

She will go to Northlands to change his mind, and to pack. She wonders whether to call Gabe and let him know that she's visiting her home. Instead, she calls Cliff and says that she'll be stopping by, "to talk to you and to pick up a few things."

"What things?"

"Just what I'll need, you know . . ."

"To go down south."

"Yes, but . . ."

Cliff hangs up.

She knows if she calls back, he won't answer.

An hour later, as she pulls up into the circular drive, she stops to scan the beloved fields, where now in late fall, the browned and yellowed grasses wave, yet the horses still graze in the two fenced-in back fields. From afar, Gracie's a bright spot, golden mane and tail like tiny yellow stripes. In the spring, when Nikki comes back, they'll start training Gracie to compete Novice. Next to her, Druid grazes, a good old boy. And in a separate pasture, Harley, a big dark spot, ambles alone. Gracie and Harley both alpha horses, so they must be kept separate. Nikki misses all of them, and a nostalgia washes over her as Cliff must feel sometimes while he gazes out at his rich pastures, for Cliff has a romantic side he won't admit even to himself.

She parks the rig to the right of the Rover by the rhododendron bushes, as she always did, then trots up the front steps, across the deck. Through the picture window, she sees Cliff sitting inside at the head of the cherry Shaker table, where he so often sat, but now he presides over a family of empty chairs.

He seems bigger, a hulking shape, who now slides back his chair and lumbers toward the front door, for he saw her, of course, out of the sides of his eyes. It's his peripheral sight, like horses have, that makes her feel a spot of fear, but she breathes deeply and lifts her head. He opens the door and does not say a word, as she knew he wouldn't.

"May I come in?" she asks, although it's her house, too, isn't it?

"Feel free." He steps aside and waves her in, as if she's an honored guest.

She goes in and instinctively sits in her old place at the opposite end of the cherry table from his, so he sits down across from her, as usual. From here, she can see through the doorway into the living room, the black leather couch, hand-woven wall tapestry, blue Oriental rug, antique mission oak rocking chair, and in the bay window, all her cacti, still prickly and erect.

Cliff takes off his glasses, wipes them on the loose end of his denim shirt. Without glasses, his eyes are pale and small, watery and soft. She used to be able to touch his momentary, exposed tenderness, draw him out of his silences, keep making jokes, asking questions, flirting, and acting loving until he'd stick his head out of his shell and blink in the light, like he's blinking now . . . that flash of softness in his eyes, sometimes a quick delight, like goddamn, there's a whole other world out there, illuminated and radiant . . . before he'd retract and slide back into himself again . . . Yet those moments made it all seem worthwhile, and she thinks, *I don't have to stay at that lodge, and I don't have to go down south. I could just stay right here, right now, with a husband I still love, don't I?* Probably Cliff would say yes, and how much simpler that would be.

She sits perfectly still. And Cliff stays perfectly quiet. The silence carries the dead weight of familiarity. Then Cliff puts his glasses back on, his iced blue eyes again magnified, masked. Not like Gabe's dark eyes that see into the souls of animals and into hers, for we're all animals—instinctual, feral, loving.

"It's getting to be a bit much," Cliff says, gazing out at the pastures, at the horses, the only spots of color in the bleached fall.

"What is?"

"Taking care of three of them." He's bringing her down to earth again.

"I could have them all trailered off," she says.

"What's here is staying here."

Except for her, she thinks. "But they're all in good health?"

"As good as can be expected, considering."

"I see you're not putting Gracie and Harley together. That's good," she says. "They're both pasture bullies."

"I wouldn't put together what needs to be kept apart."

"You know what Gracie's like when she's in heat."

"I know all right. She won't let the poor guy alone."

He's parroting the right answers, like when she didn't get compliments from him, so she'd set them up, and ask, "How do I look?" Or, "Do you like this dress?" And he'd say, "Nyeah." New England speak again that could mean no or yes.

"Cliff, how have you been, really?"

"My feelings don't impact on you."

One of his dark jokes? She cocks her head, peers at him.

He keeps his expression perfectly straight, like her father's after he went bankrupt, and she remembers again after she first moved in, how Cliff often got monosyllabic for days at a time, the silence permeating the indoors. Once, early on, she convinced him to go with her to a couples' therapist, who asked Cliff why he felt down. When Cliff said he didn't know, the therapist said, "Then pretend you're not." And afterwards, Cliff seemed lighter, but gradually, he retreated back into himself.

"Cliff, really, are you really all right?"

"I'm really great, just great."

She stands slowly, puts both hands on the table, and leans toward him. "I have to go south and event. I still want you to come, at least to visit, will you please do that?"

He looks away, out at his rich, bright fields.

"You won't come?" she asks.

"You know I won't."

"Why not?"

He's gazing out at fields that are stationary and predictable, that belong to him.

"Cliff, I'll be loyal to you. Do you want me to be?"

She wants him to say, Yes, with my whole heart.

When he doesn't speak, she says, "If you don't come, in the spring, I'll come home, because I still love you."

She waits for him to say that he loves her too.

Again, not a word. Love is all or nothing for him, while for her it shifts from more, to less, to more again.

"Do you love me, Cliff?"

He smiles slightly and says, "As much as I'm able."

Quoting what she'd once said. He doesn't forget.

"Cliff, I'm going to go upstairs to get some of my things. Only the necessities."

Did he flinch? An eye twitch, a slight upward shift to his upper lip? "Go right ahead. Help yourself to whatever."

Odd that he's so accommodating when he's so dug in.

But Nikki goes through the living room and climbs the steep, soundless stairs. So well built, Cliff once said, that they don't creak. Now their silence seems painful. She heads toward their bedroom at the end of the hall. Over their bed, that framed print of a man and woman sitting in the prow of a small sailing ship on high seas, shaded in gray and black. Their hair blows about, the man's dark, billowing cloak surrounds both of them, their mouths set against a fierce wind.

How did she ever think she'd bring laughter into this house?

She slides a small, wheeled carry-on suitcase out from under the bed, nabs panties, bras, and nightgowns out of her top bureau drawer, stops, listens for his step. Only quiet.

She steps to the closets, hers on the right, with the full-length mirror on the back of her door, and sees a little woman with lips pressed so tight, she seems toothless.

She slides open her door.

The shock, it's almost empty. None of her clothes hang there anymore. In the far corner, on the only hanger, dangles Cliff's blaze-orange hunting vest, glowing faintly in the semi-dark. Propped next to it, butt on her closet floor, barrel pointing up, stands his Persuader.

His vest looks deflated, flat, grotesque without his bulk filling it. Hanging there where it shouldn't be. The rifle barrel shines dully in the dark corner. An ambush.

He knew she'd want to get her clothes. Simple black outfits, and her show jacket, jerseys, and britches. He's down there, waiting for this moment.

She's scared and angry both at once and expects to hear his step on the stairs, to be trapped up here, no exit.

Silence fills the space.

She must go down, get out, before Cliff senses her fear.

She tries to collect herself. Slowly, quietly, slides shut her closet door, then zips shut her half-empty case, and quickly goes lightly down the soundless, steep steps, through the living room into the kitchen.

Cliff still sits at the Shaker table in the exact same position as before, chin in hands, gazing out at the pasture.

She starts to pass, hesitates, can't help herself, turns back.

"Find what you were looking for?" he asks, turning slightly toward her. Was that a hint of curl to his upper lip, like Gabe's lip? But Gabe's half paralyzed.

"Yes."

"Good."

"I'll be going now."

"Knock them dead down south."

Part of her still wants to stay, another part wants to run right out.

He lifts his head to stare past her out the window at the horses again, if that's what he's staring at.

She heads on out, as he knows she must.

Yet even as she's climbing into the rig, her back tightens like in the gravel pit. She pictures Cliff quickly clomping upstairs, grabbing his Persuader out of her emptied closet, flinging open the double-hung window that overlooks the drive, and aiming the rifle—a crack shot. She waits for a bullet to pierce her head as she starts the rig, and braces, glances back through the window. Cliff still sits, his shadowy bulk still slumped at the head of the table, the former place of power, his head bowed, chin in hands.

As she drives off, up Mountain View Road, she wonders if that rifle is a threat, not to her, but to Cliff, and almost turns around and heads back. Almost.

GABE

HE'S LATE FOR THEIR WORKOUT and caught in traffic over the connector bridge. A construction jam, even in Florida, so Gabe's stuck staring at palm trees, their fronds swishing by a white-sand beach, as picturesque as he had wished, waves washing in and out, tracking symmetrical ripples on the sand, the sea lapping to a calm, predictable beat.

He'd be calm if his pickup wasn't stopped dead in a damned traffic backup so bad that even the sea birds seem arrested in flight. Egrets, herons, and pelicans perch on the shiny railing of the bridge arched over the canal where he's trapped. The big birds, wings folded, look deflated. Paradise is not living up to its reputation . . . not yet.

And Wellington, where they're training and practicing, is no picturesque, cozy little community, but groomed and gated estates, like the one in Ocala that hosted the first Florida event where they competed a few days ago, when Nikki placed a distant twentieth. She let Beau rush the fences in the ring, got a couple knockdowns. Instead of holding back, she rode all out, too wild. Self-destructive. And right after that show, when Gabe told her to follow the middle path, she laughed her soft laugh but with a new raw edge. Gabe feels frustrated. In paradise.

And ever since that show, he's had insomnia, lies awake

for hours. So last night, he got up in the wee hours, and, in his undershorts, started toward his balcony for fresh air, but through the glass sliders, glimpsed Nikki out on her balcony, adjoining his. She was hovering like a ghost in a billowy, long, white, shapeless gown that fluttered in moonlight, and he found himself wondering if the gown was transparent and then visualizing what was under it, visualizing bodily detail that he'd refused to picture at the B&B with her in her lingerie, but then that damned gap in the Venetian blinds. This time, he lingered in the shadows, unseen, until she retreated into her room. Then he went back to bed and lay awake and for the first time visualized the expression on her face if he had stepped out onto the balcony and she had seen his bare body, his atrophied left side. It made him sick to think his body could be repulsive. Years ago, women couldn't keep their hands off him . . . now he hasn't been touched in a half year or more. Self-pity, though, is for the weak. But so is pity. So finally, with the daylight, he fell asleep . . . then overslept.

By the time he got up, Nikki had already left for the barn to practice, a note thumbtacked onto her condo door. One-bedroom condos, not oceanfront, but on a tidal swamp, so when the tide is out, he and Nikki look out at muck like in Vermont in the spring. But she wanted a water view, in spite of it being farther away and costing more, in spite of Cliff cutting her off. She's got her own money, she said, enough to pay all expenses for the entire time, including paying him, and more. So, hell, go for it.

Yet he's not going anywhere now, caught in a traffic jam in his damned pickup that keeps stalling out, while he's trying to get to the barn for a vital practice session because their next competition is in two weeks. And Nikki's got to stop letting Beau rush each fence full blast, Nikki, who used to play it too safe and hold back. She's done a psychic flip. She's skilled at that.

And to make matters worse, Beau hates the big show barn, too many horses around from morning to night, so he's been on edge, and in the first few weeks went off his feed, then got an ulcer, so he couldn't compete. The vet prescribed Gastro-gard, two treatments at a thousand bucks. Since Beau recovered, they've got to give him bute tablets to keep him calm. All this illness while he's stabled at a grand southern horse estate. A horse doesn't know when he's got it good.

The traffic still stalled. Gabe tries to meditate his way out of his frustration and deep breathes for a little while but only thinks how much he hates traffic jams, then opens his eyes to see a pelican staring right at him, only a few yards away. A pelican with a big beak, like Carla's big mouth. He waves his hand, scares it off, and the pelican's sturdy body in flight has a force like Carla's with its forward thrust, compared with the blue heron still perched on the bridge. The heron a delicate, long-legged wader, stays close to shore, especially in marshes, but in flight it sticks out its long neck.

After that last event, Nikki said she couldn't focus, so Gabe asked why. She said she'd had another "Cliff dream" the night before cross-country, about how she and Gabe had rented the same motel room as Cliff and Carla and Lisa and Matt, and they were all six in bed together under the covers. "Ever since that dream," she said, "I've been wondering how Cliff can manage those three horses at Northlands by himself, and I wonder how long he sits each day all alone at the cherry table with his head bowed."

As if Gabe could answer that. Cliff's slithering into paradise. But now the traffic jam breaks up, and Gabe floors it.

◆◆◆

In a half hour, he turns his pickup onto the palm-lined drive to the stables, drives under the grand white arch, and flashes his pass to the guard in an air-conditioned booth. Gabe focuses and collects himself for the practice session ahead. If you're going to control a rider, got to first control yourself.

He pulls up into the lot and parks by Nikki's rig, gets out, and passes a few riders leading big Warmbloods. One of the women nods, gray-blond hair tied back in a tight knot.

He recognizes her, Missy Muldridge, from New York State, one of those who imports Warmbloods from Germany or Holland, top-trained horses that know more than she does. Maybe she has heard of his fall back then, and it finally slides back . . . the top-ranked stallion slowly buckled at the knees, slowly lay down on its side . . . the course vet with healthy, ruddy cheeks must have given it one shot of a sedative . . . then a second injection, then the stallion must have stiffened, lay still. Euthanized. So simply death can come. Gabe saw death, or hallucinated it, just before they carried him off on a stretcher into the ambulance, where he finally passed out.

The horse world is a small world, Gabe thinks now, especially on the higher levels. He feels like an imposter, and that makes him friggin' furious.

He limps on up to barn number eight and stops at the wide door to look down the aisle to where Nikki's got Beau cross-tied, his hind end toward Gabe. She's in jean shorts and is bent down from the waist, her hand stuck up inside Beau, under his belly, between his hind legs. She's cleaning his sheath. Got to do that with stallions and geldings. Beau standing head down, relaxed. Gelded or not, he's enjoying this, not modest like some, for as she pulls her hand out, Beau lets his long cock slowly slide down out of its sheath, exposed to view and to her touch.

She's got the tube of Excalibur in one hand, and with the other hand is slathering on the green gel to clean the cock of smegma so it won't get infected. Nikki's handwork brisk, skilled, a classic light touch.

"Got to have your hand on it, do you, Nikki?" he asks, stealing up behind her.

She jerks around like she's caught in the act, then has to laugh.

And he laughs, too, chortling like two kids, before their laughs slide to a stop, and he asks, "Ah, Nikki, why can't it be like this?" Meaning? He's not sure what.

She turns away, says she'll change in the women's room so they can practice.

Purposely ignoring what he said. She was right to do that.

Beau stands, head still down, seeming relaxed, cock still dangling limp, but shiny clean.

◆◆◆

Soon Gabe's standing in the center of an outdoor workout ring, a stopwatch cupped in one hand, as Nikki takes Beau over a triple, a combination, a couple oxers, her letting Beau rush the first oxer, so he veers off. Can't blame him. Nikki circles him back around, gets him over it, then canters at the triple, over it, then the Bounce. One stride between each rail, but they're going too fast, so she gets too deep, and Beau has no choice but to take down a rail, then he bucks on landing.

Gabe yells to focus, and he tries to focus himself but thinks, Goddamn, Nikki, your timing's off.

She speeds Beau up again, cantering too fast toward the second oxer, but the little guy instinctively adjusts his stride, clears the fence, gets her out of trouble yet again. And she's smiling, loving it, all high from going all out, slapping Beau's neck as if they've won something right when Gabe wants friggin' harmony, goddamn excellence, fucking perfection. "Goddamn it," he yells. "You're not trusting your horse, not seeing your distance. Give him a chance to do his job!" She can't let him down like this.

The smile slides off her face. She pulls Beau to a halt and just stares at Gabe like he's betrayed her when she's betrayed herself, while all around the outdoor ring, the fronds of the palm trees tremble in a murky, humid breeze, and plump droplets fall, warning of a tropical downpour.

◆◆◆

Two weeks later, before their next three-day, they'd trailered Beau inland to Ocala and rented two adjacent motel rooms with balconies facing a few scraggly palms, so Nikki said they'd have to visualize the water view. That night there's a welcoming party for all contestants, and Nikki wants to go.

Gabe says they should get a good night's rest, but she says she's riding better now, so she doesn't want any time to think.

And she is riding better, in a sense. Beau's more muscled up from workouts on the beach, his hooves sinking into white sand where he needs more power to move, like going uphill in Vermont. And Nikki has been building up her weak knee by jogging in the same white sand. And Gabe has been lifting weights at a local gym, so his body is even more obviously half built up, half not. Since he has been down here, day after day in the heat, he has grown more aware of his body—of the half of him that almost isn't there, the half that's a friggin' wasteland—and he's more aware of Nikki's body and how it almost reaches perfection, almost.

Also, he's more aware that Nikki has left Cliff. Although she claims she will return to him in the spring, Gabe does not believe she will reconcile with a prick who almost killed her. And, too, Gabe's free of Carla, more or less. Though she has called his cell a few times. It was brief and stiffly polite, neither mentioning those photographs, each asking how the other was. Once she asked how Nikole was, and he said, "It's the horses that count." He meant that, to a point. And then once, lying in bed, he called Carla because, against his will, he sometimes misses her deep gravelly voice, her big comforting presence, and he knows he owes her for this crack at paradise.

So Gabe goes to the party that night, and there's a live band in a big party room in an outbuilding, and there's way more women than men, as it used to be, back when Gabe savored that. But now when Nikki asks, he refuses to dance, in spite of getting high on champagne and the rock music stirring his blood. He knows he can only shake half of himself. He wishes he had never come, watching Nikki vibrate on the dance floor with a young stud who rides Olympic quality horses like Gabe once did, the guy ten years younger than Nikki, doing some serious hip action. Gabe's looking for detachment, can't find it. After that tune, Nikki swings back to him, saying, "Come on, all you have to do is stand in one place." He must be drunk because he heads on out onto the floor.

"Now don't get tricky on me," he says.

She smiles back her tricky smile that quickly slides off, and says, "Cliff didn't like to dance either."

Cliff again. Goddamn, Gabe's got everything riding on her, yet all she can do is talk of Cliff. Maybe because, Gabe thinks, only one half of him is dancing, one side isn't. It's hot and muggy inside, and he's waving his good arm, tapping his good leg, dancing a side shuffle step, pelvic action, Hey yeah, take a look at that, deformed, huh, is that what you think?

She's not watching him, her eyes doing their dancing drift. Before, women couldn't take their eyes off his body. Now Nikki's swaying again to the whamming beat, getting back into sync. He stands in one place and gyrates, her eyes drifting now below his waist like she eyed Beau's dick, dangling there, useless, which Gabe's isn't, far from it, very far, in fact, and he cranks it up, sways in place, tells himself to think positive, leans close to her and says, "Let's get the hell out of here."

◆ ◆ ◆

But by the time they get back to their rooms, he has convinced himself to go straight to bed, for the horses' sake. He says goodnight in the hall, and she hesitates, then goes into her room and shuts the door before he goes into his room, shuts his, and tells himself he must resist or else all his training these last two years will be worth shit.

He's wound up, paces for a while and limps over to his balcony sliders to look through glass not at low tide muck but at palms on a wedge of green abutting cement. But then he catches a glimpse of filmy white out on her balcony. This time, he shoves open his sliders and steps out onto his. He's three feet from her, separated by a low, four-foot-high concrete wall—how horses must feel in adjoining stalls, can see but can't touch.

"I just called Cliff again," she says. "He still didn't pick up."

Gabe tells himself Nikki is free of Cliff, she just doesn't know it yet . . . even as her eyes slide to gaze beyond him, at the palms, so his eyes shift. Only slack, limp fronds dangling, no tropical wind, none of the wild slapping inward drive that Gabe yearns for.

"What am I doing wrong?" she asks, over the half wall.

He has no idea what she's talking about.

Then she says, "I can't ride tomorrow. I've lost my feel for it."

He can't let her sleep with thoughts like that. "I'll be right over," he says.

She waves him on, one flip of one small hand.

In a few minutes, they're sitting together on her balcony, and they're sipping white wine. She sets the bottle on the little, white, iron table between their matching iron chairs.

Six floors down, it's solid cement, not soft snow like in Vermont. But it's late winter, and the heat's settled in, and this woman's sitting next to him in a white gown that would seem innocent if he couldn't see through it, just barely, only hints of skin, bits of her he has never seen, as she has never seen his built-up half compared with the atrophied side. He says, "I'll show you how to get it back."

"My seat?"

"Your feeling. Come on over here."

She peers at him in the dark.

"Here," he says and pats his lap. "I'll show you how to move."

She gazes down at the lot again, as if Cliff's out there, hidden behind the spiny trunks of palms with their limp fronds.

"It's all body position," Gabe says. "Got to find your center of gravity."

As if convinced, she gets up, takes the few steps to him and sits on his lap, straddling him, her face in his.

Gabe places his good hand on her center belly and his bad hand on her lower back and says, "Breathe in . . . hold it . . . there, like that . . . the center holds . . ."

They're breathing into each other's faces, and his good

hand slides lower, the thin gown slightly sheltering her, his bad hand lightly on her ass. He visualizes how her ass must feel, firm yet soft . . . And he says, "Now, bear down."

She's smiling slightly and presses her pelvis down on his good hand, for it's all about hipbones and contact, and yet . . .

"Press deep," he says.

And she presses harder against his fingers. "Like this?"

And he says yes.

And she shifts her pelvis, forward back against his good hand.

She must sense his hard-on because her hand starts to unbutton the cuffs of his long-sleeved shirt. He's a bitter, buttoned-down bastard, he thinks, and braces himself for her shock when she sees his bare withered side. She's busily unbuttoning left cuff, right cuff, center strip, tugging off left sleeve, right sleeve, no t-shirt. Damned the good muscled-up side, it only makes the bad seem worse. Her hand touches his bare bad arm. He sees her touch, imagines the free play of warm fingertips. After his fall, Carla massaged that arm, then slapped it with her open hand as if she'd force it to feel. Nikki just trails her fingertips along etched skin, stretched thin over thin muscle, thick bone. Goddamn, were horses worth this?

She's sighing deeply. Is it regret? If she pulls back now it's over with. But she leans forward, and he half feels the kiss, the half flutter of a tongue, and he feels through the thin white fabric the female body he has worked with, perfectly compact, an athlete's body, symmetrical, like his used to be, and she bends her neck and kisses down his shrunken arm and chest. As if to prove she can force herself? The hell with that. It's all body position . . . and he pictures pulling off her thin gown and her spreading her legs and him sliding inside where it's hot, and her riding him, posting, bearing down, moving in sync, timing perfect . . .

Except now she's looking up, and her eyes have drifted off again toward the dark, as if she expects Cliff to spy on them here like at the B&B. The absent husband always present with his damned magnetic silence, his sham calm. Gabe will expose that bad actor, strip him bare, bring him down. Then she says, "If we do this, we will lose."

"Lose the event?"

"Something we will never have again."

Gabe pulls back, sits straight, and because she's sitting on his lap with her hip bones tuned in to his, she instantly pulls back as well. Then she stands, so he does, and she's smoothing down her white gown, and he's yanking on his shirt, as if, of course, she is right.

Once dressed, he grabs the white wine bottle off the small white table, fills both glasses, hands her one, lifts his up, but says nothing, nothing at all.

Her eyes shift now to him, and she lifts her glass. They truly must put the horses first, they both know that, but he doesn't know what they'll both know after this.

She says, "To you, Gabe, and to what we have."

They click glasses and drink to that, even though he wants way more, especially now, but he lifts his glass again, flashes his twisted smile, and says, "And to paradise."

Nikki does not lift her glass. She again looks out at the parking lot, but in the night it seems to him like a wide empty expanse, like the brackish, algae-infested mud flats, like the quicksand in the bog where his childhood pony sank, got shot to death. And he senses without her saying it, that she's thinking yet again of Cliff.

NIKOLE

DRESSAGE—QUIET, REFINED, ELEGANT—IS USUALLY HER
most mediocre phase. But this morning, on day one of the
three-day at Ocala, Nikki rode in classic top hat, black tails,
and white britches, with her body in almost perfect align-
ment. She sat deep. She found her seat. Beau performed with
improved self-carriage, so they scored eighth. If she goes clear
in both jumping phases, and the top seven riders don't, she
could win.

Afterwards, she and Gabe rejoice in the soft, sticky, late
winter heat. Gabe, all lightness, lifts her up, and, one-armed,
swings her around in a victory whirl, sets her down and says,
"Now I know the kind of training you need."

Even in the midst of jubilation, she thinks that it wasn't
training last night, it was almost full-fledged adultery. And
she remembers after Gabe left, she slept alone and dreamt she
was back living with Cliff but had to move out because she
was having an affair and was going to pack her things and was
talking to Cliff in a room where she noticed that, instead of
carpet and hardwood, the floor was covered with sawdust and
wood chips. She thought, Why don't all people have floors
like this? And then Cliff was loading her things into a long,
dark, mahogany wood box. When she woke, she realized that
the wood shavings were like the bedding in her horses' stalls,

and the dark box was like a coffin, and she felt she must stay away from him.

Yet after dressage, she goes off by herself and calls her husband on her cell, to somehow make up for finally almost making his fears come true.

She figures she'll get his machine yet again, but this time, he picks up.

"I didn't expect to get you."

"Then why call?" he asks, the pragmatic Cliff.

She asks how he is, and when he says he's "great, just great," she tells him about her good dressage performance and says if Beau jumps like he usually does, she can place in the top five, and this could be her biggest event down here yet.

He says nothing to that.

"Beau was collected, like you are Cliff." And she visualizes the slow, graceful way Cliff moves, for a big man.

He says nothing to that either.

"So how's Gracie? I miss her."

"You miss your horse."

"And I miss you, too," she quickly adds.

"Gracie's been acting out. She's in heat."

"Sorry," she says, then wonders why she should apologize for a mare's sex instinct.

Cliff clears his throat and says, "I'm tired of you saying you're sorry for what you can't stop. I've had it!"

"You're not saying it's over?"

"Are you saying that?"

"That's not what I meant."

"Well then."

Again, they speak different languages. She says, "I wish, when I left, you had said you wanted me to stay."

"Oh yeah? Something going wrong down south in that decadent heat?"

"I only meant—"

"I know what you meant."

"No, you don't," she says, thinking yes, he does. And she remembers him saying to her once, "Nikki, to you the world is one big sexual arena." But the sex she wants most is with her husband, and the sex with Gabe, as far as it went, was still a sin.

"I just wish," she says, "that you'd come out and say if you want me back."

"Then you'd drop it all and fly right home."

"Is that what you want?"

"You ought to be able to figure that out."

"But if you want me back, surely you can wait a little longer."

"So that's that," he says.

And the line goes dead.

After that, all day, off and on, she feels as if Cliff is watching her, or somebody has been hired to watch again, and she hangs out with other riders to keep Gabe at a distance. Then at night, after a dinner for competitors, when she and Gabe finally go back to their rooms, in the hall, she tells him she must be alone.

He just gazes into her, the way he can, a glittery stare that keeps going down in.

"I have to focus on cross-country now, for the horse's sake," she says, using Gabe-speak.

"But after this event, Nikki, it'll be for our sakes."

She's on a crash course. Any way she looks at it, she'll take the fall.

◆ ◆ ◆

That night, she lies alone in bed and tries to sleep but can't, not with the thoughts furling in her head, the balcony doors open wide, faraway traffic churning faintly but nonstop, not at all the reverent hush like this morning during dressage. She tries to think of horses but thinks of Cliff asking about the decadent heat as if he knew she'd betrayed him, which she has, but only to an extent, because she vows not to make love with Gabe, at least not while she's still with Cliff.

Yet in the early morning, when she finally dozes off, she dreams she's with Gabe in a motel, and they have stayed there all night, and they have had sex, and she hears, through the thin motel wall, Cliff's voice rumbling, but she can't hear his words. Cliff has taken the room next to hers, and she wants to go to his room but soon hears a woman's voice at Cliff's door, and she wonders how she could have stayed away overnight and can think of no story to explain it and knows he will be furious, and she is afraid. She almost wakes but dozes again, and Cliff is saying he's going on a trip with this other woman, and Nikki says she wants to go with him and watches his blank face, but he does not say a word, and then she wakes.

It's as if she's on the coast again, and outside through the open sliders, waves are lapping in, lapping out, slowly shoving sandy mud so the marsh shifts. No solid footing in paradise.

Then she sees rattan furniture and brightly flowered cushions and a white rented room, and remembers she is inland. She must compete in cross-country today. Her dressage score was her personal best, so it's her best chance to place first. She gets up, tries to keep sin out of her mind, goes into the terracotta-tiled bathroom, starts to fill the tub, slips out of her white gown. But then her cell phone sings its tinny song from the other room, and she runs out nude. Too late, a message light. It must be Gabe this early, she checks the number . . . Cliff. Maybe he has relented at last and will say he loves her and wants her back. She clicks his message. "There has been an accident. Call home." That's all.

She instantly feels that old, familial fear, waiting for her father's punishment, punches in Cliff's number, and when, at last he picks up, she asks if he's all right.

"Sorry," he says, "but Harley broke Gracie's leg."

"What?"

"Gracie got loose in Harley's pasture last night, and she attacked him."

"What?"

"She kicked Harley, so he kicked back and broke her leg."

"What?"

"He kicked her only once. Gracie just stood there. Then she limped off."

"How can that be?"

"The vet came. Took x-rays. It's the splint bone, a vestigial bone, not a weight-bearing bone. But it's shattered, so they've got to operate to clean out the shards. She'll be trailered to the Burlington Clinic. They can't fit her into their schedule for two days."

The rush of bath water splashing over the tub. She runs back in, water sloshing onto the Spanish tiles. She turns off the faucet, and, cell phone in hand, sees a nude woman in the mirror. The woman looks sickly, emaciated, and she asks, "Will she be lame? Will she have to be put down?"

"They'll know after the operation."

"Who's trailering Gracie to Burlington?"

"I am."

"Who's nursing her afterwards?"

"I can handle it."

"Cliff, you've never nursed a horse in your life."

"If I can't, well then . . ."

Does he mean he'd send her to the killers? Surely, he wouldn't do that. "Cliff, I'm coming back."

"When?" He asks matter-of-factly, as if he knew she'd come.

She's suddenly suspicious. "How did Gracie get into Harley's pasture? You know they've never gotten along."

"You'll get the details when you get home."

She knows that's all he'll say for now, but his few words draw her in yet again. "Did she jump the fence? It's too high."

"When will you arrive?" he asks with a certitude that attracts while it repels.

"I'll try to be there for the operation. But first explain how—"

Cliff has hung up again.

Why did he seem so sure she'd come right back? It makes her want to stay in paradise.

She's standing in a spreading, shallow pool of water. She flips the lever in the over-filled tub, scoops up all the towels, throws them onto the floor to soak up the spill, and she wonders again how Gracie got into Harley's pen. Draft horses were bred to work all day, not just graze, so Harley's overcharged, aggressive, an alpha horse. And Gracie's too temperamental for her own good. She kicked first, Cliff said. Does he think she deserves what she got?

Nikki goes into the one other room, to the small closet, slips on jeans and a t-shirt, then heads out across the hall and bangs on Gabe's door. If she heads home, she must forfeit. Give up something they might never have again.

He opens up, and she says she got a call from Cliff, that it's bad news, and they need to talk.

Gabe turns his back, heads out onto his balcony and stares down at the barren lot.

She knows if she tells him that she's going to scratch, his dreams will be shattered like his body has been. She goes in and steps out onto the balcony after him into the soft summer heat.

◆◆◆

She has been driving for eleven hours, stopping only twice at truck stops to walk Beau, so he doesn't colic—lie down and thrash about until his intestines twist—the kind of pain in the gut she has had ever since she left paradise.

She couldn't leave Beau down there, so she had to drive the rig with him in the trailer, moving slowly through the night. Gabe insisted on following in his pickup. During her rest stops, Gabe kept parking and getting out and ranting again about how this was no accident. Look at Cliff's timing, right during their time in Florida, it was premeditated, Cliff put the two horses together on purpose, Cliff's an angry, controlling prick, who maimed an animal to destroy their dreams. And Gracie's a bitch, but she jumps like a winged angel, and Cliff knew that, so he had to break her leg.

Gabe has been trashing Cliff ever since Nikki scratched until finally she won't answer her cell. She told Gabe she must go back for the mare's sake. She doesn't mention that she didn't believe Cliff would intentionally hurt an animal because she's not sure of anything since her life has become so accident prone. She deserves this punishment but Gracie doesn't, she thinks, driving through Kentucky, horses, as if omnipresent, dotting blue grass.

She's got to travel straight through with no overnight stops in order to make it in time for the operation, but after driving into early morning darkness, she's punchy, weaving over the centerline, when Gabe, still trailing, calls her cell yet again. This time she's tired enough to pick up. "Pull over and rest," he says. "You're endangering Beau, not to mention yourself."

She taps Gabe off and drives on, only an occasional vehicle whizzing past. If she pulls to the side of the road, he'll get out and keep up his attack, but soon her rig's weaving again. She tries again to call the vet clinic in Burlington, but she's in a dead zone, and the rig wavers more, so the trailer sways heavily, off balance. She twists the wheel, tries to steer with the trailer's heavy sway, Beau trapped inside. If they topple, he's done for. She swerves off onto the shoulder, jams on the brakes, the rig jolting, the trailer slamming up against the hitch so it almost tips, but comes to rest.

She feels the familiar flapping of adrenaline, wings beating inside her belly, and she climbs out, hurries back to the trailer, flips open the side door. Beau's staring back, ears pricked, stomping, safely packed in shipping boots and blanket. He's in fine shape. She's the wreck.

Suddenly Gabe's next to her, his pickup parked behind, and he checks out Beau, then he tells her she's goddamned lucky, and now she must absolutely pull over at the next rest stop "because Cliff doesn't give a shit about your safety, but I do." She stalks to the cab, hops up in. Beau, anxious to be off, kicks against the trailer wall, loud metallic whacks. He could break a leg and end up in the Burlington clinic with Gracie. She starts the motor, but then Gabe's at the door and opens it and asks, "Do you want another accident?"

"If I stop to rest, I'll miss the operation."

"Look, I know why you want to be there. I do, too, but she'll be in a coma. So who're you really doing this for?"

For herself, Nikki wonders, or for Cliff? Why give up all she was working toward? But she says, "If I stop, do you promise not to follow me to Northlands?"

"Forget Northlands. After Gracie's operation, we'll pick her up at the clinic and trailer her right down to Florida, let her rehab down south."

"Gabe, if you follow me home, I'll fire you myself."

"You *wouldn't* do that!" He says, his good hand swinging up between them, palm toward her face, signaling halt.

She looks at him straight on. "Yes, I would." Gabe knows her well enough to know she means it. He breathes deeply, slowly, with long inhales and exhales. She knows him, too. He's trying to collect himself. To focus. To win.

Then he says, "If I don't follow you there, do you swear to leave Cliff again?"

Like reverse wedding vows, she thinks. I do solemnly swear to leave my husband.

She sits behind the wheel, bows her head, her hands already folded in her lap as if praying, for what? She lost God somewhere in paradise, so how can God get her out of this?

"If Cliff hurt Gracie on purpose," she says, "I'll leave him."

Gabe nods. "We've got a deal."

He's that sure Cliff's at fault. She says that she'll stop at the next truck stop, but she needs to rest alone.

Gabe nods, as if he knew she'd say that. He always has to feel like he's thinking ahead of her or her horse. Usually, she respects him for that, not now. For a moment, she wonders where he'll go when he gets back. To Carla? No, she'd devour him.

He says, "Cliff set you up. Like he did your fall. He's got a mean streak that you don't see because you don't have one. You forgive everybody but yourself."

She guns the motor, and he shuts the door, and she slowly drives off. But she thinks he's right, at least about her forgiving Cliff. For the Cliff she has loved is not cruel. He's a moral man. Strict, yes, and repressed, but devoted to those he loves. To purposely destroy her prize mare, he'd have to be a violent man, like the one who let his horse's reins slide through his hands, who kicked in the bathroom door, who almost shoved her down the steps, who hid his Persuader in her closet. That Cliff.

CLIFF

HE SITS SEALED IN THE glass observatory deck. About forty
feet below, in the operation amphitheater, Gracie's golden
bulk lies splayed out on a broad, stainless steel table, a hoist
underneath to jack it up to operating level. A vet thrusts a
hacksaw back and forth into her leg as if it's firewood. "The
splint bone lies right beneath the skin," one vet said earlier. So
they don't have to cut in too deep. But it sure as hell looks like
destruction to Cliff. If Gracie ends up lame, will he have to
sell her to the killers—prime ground dog meat? That depends
on Nikki.

Down below, the vets in white lab coats, speckled with
red, dig into the exposed red flesh with pincers, plucking out
what must be chunks of bone. Cliff can't see the small bits of
bone against the stark white walls that make the blood seem
too red, as if it's fake. Real blood runs darker, like the blood
of deer, or of men, like Gabe's blood will run if he sets foot
on Cliff's property again. Cliff's old football instincts perco-
late through his veins, the thrill of impact, go for the jugular, don't hold back, the bliss of bone-on-bone collision. Yet
not like these vets with their hacksaws and pincers, who chat
while they saw into the bone of a helpless animal.

It gets to Cliff, this butchery, after almost three hours of
watching it. And it gets to him, this limbo, after three days of

white-knuckling it, wondering if this mare's death could destroy any last chance for him with Nikki. He blames this mare like he blamed her for the other accident in the west field. It was Gracie's fault for being in heat last week, for bolting up and down her side of the fence that abuts Harley's, for leading him on, nickering, lifting her tail, waving her hindquarters, Harley a gelding, what could he do? His indifference made Gracie even more frenzied, her passion not reciprocated, so she galloped faster up and back, up and back, until Cliff thought she'd leap the fence, maybe break a leg. What a laugh.

That palpitating, mewing, bucking bitch in heat brought it on herself. Cliff had nothing, next to nothing, to do with it. Never blame yourself, his father said. Guilt sucks.

After a long while, one of the vets comes into the observation room, his white smock dribbled and spattered with red, like that abstract painter who squirted paint onto his canvases, goddamn pop art. The vet, holding in one hand a glass jar with whitish chunks in liquid, says that Gracie has pulled through and has a fifty-fifty chance of being sound, depending on the care she gets. Stall rest, twice-daily syringes of oral antibiotics, twice-daily changing the poultice for six weeks. The vet—too young, too blond, too healthy—says, "Infection is the main worry now. We can't predict if she'll be lame. From here on, it's up to you." Then he reaches out the glass jar to Cliff and adds, "Her bone fragments in formaldehyde."

The yellowish bits bounce, then whirl, then slowly settle on the bottom. Cliff takes the jar. A gift, he thinks, for his estranged wife.

The vet leaves and Cliff is left with the jar, and every time he moves, the shards bounce and shift as if alive. He almost vomits his lunch right there in the crisp, stark observatory deck, but he swallows it down, the half-digested dregs of a chicken salad sandwich he still tastes. With both hands, he carefully carries the jar down the steps and out to the Range Rover, but when he gets in and sets the sealed jar on the front seat, the shards whirl in a crazy dance. He has set the jar where his wife would sit if she hadn't run off with her damned trainer. If Nikki hadn't run off, then Gracie wouldn't be lying in a coma on a slab, and Cliff wouldn't be sitting here with chunks of her mangled bone in a cheap Mason jar. If Nikki hadn't run off with that curly-lipped, lopsided adulterer, then Cliff wouldn't have to nurse back to health a bitch that doesn't deserve it, not after teasing Harley and leading him on until something had to give.

◆ ◆ ◆

It takes Cliff a couple hours to drive home. He ordered a local transport service to trailer Gracie to Northlands because Nikki has the rig. But when he pulls up into his circular drive, he sees the rig parked by the rhododendrons where it always used to park. Hasn't seen it in four months. He feels this mix of relief and dread. Then the anger kicks in. Is her trainer along? Where's Cliff's hacksaw?

He lifts the jar off the seat, his clenched hands cradling the shifting mass, and he climbs on out, goes on over to the rig, sees it's empty, then looks out across his fields and spots Beau simply grazing by himself in the fallow middle pasture, his long, sleek neck bent, his body elegant, muscled-up, as relaxed as if he'd never left. The indefatigable Beau still doesn't comprehend how much life sucks.

Cliff steps up onto the deck and through the picture window sees Nikki sitting alone at her old place at the Shaker table, like he sat alone in his place when she came to get her things, which she didn't get. You never know what's hid in your closet.

Her trainer's not here. Cliff senses that. He's almost disappointed. And she's smaller, almost childlike, small-boned, sitting slightly slumped, eyes glancing sideways at him.

He goes on in, the jar clutched in both his hands.

He side-eyes her back, and she seems lovelier than before, more delicate, even though she's not delicate, far from it. She's as indomitable as Beau, except she's suffering.

He looks down at his hands with the jar and says, "Just left the Clinic. The prognosis is good. If Gracie gets proper care."

"Thank God!" Her tense face softening just a bit, not much, as if now she'll hide even her joy from him. And her sorrows, too. She who always used to vent. Well, he's a pro at keeping feelings hid. He's got her beat.

She's looking down at the jar in his tight hands.

He reaches it out to her and says, "A souvenir."

She stares at the floating bits, jiggling as he shoves the jar closer, and she takes it in her small hands. Only then does he say, "Bone shards. From Gracie's fractured leg."

Nikki sets the jar down so quick and hard on the tabletop that the bone bits leap and leap again. The yellowish shards gradually settle at the bottom and quiver in a heap as if alive, until they rest.

"Got to nurse Gracie twice a day," he says, "give her oral antibiotics, change the dressing on the leg, for maybe up to six weeks."

She just eyes the jar.

"I'll help," Cliff says, thinking, *This is my penance. But, for what?*

Now she looks up. "How did Harley break my mare's leg?"

He knew she'd get around to that. He falls silent. He hasn't played it all back in his own mind, let alone put it into words.

"How exactly?" she asks.

So he tells her about Gracie doing her mating dance, prancing up and down the fence line, Harley, not knowing why, half lured in, trying to nuzzle her over the rail, Gracie getting even more crazed, whinnying wildly, rubbing her hind end against the fence. "She was full of lust, but Harley was the wrong target," he says, thinking, *That slut.*

And she's asking, "Then what?"

Now it's come down to what he has blocked out. "I thought one of them would hurt themselves, so I got her lead line and went into her paddock and clipped the line onto her halter and led her into Harley's pasture. I let her go where she wanted to go . . . She trotted right toward Harley. He seemed calm enough, but when she got to within about three feet, she suddenly swerved and kicked him in the chest, blindsided him with both hooves. A wallop so hard I heard it from the gate."

He stops, as if that's the end of it.

"And then?"

"So then, of course, Harley let her have it, kicked, and got her in the hind leg. She squealed once, then limped off. In seconds she was undone, that quick. I barely saw it. An accident. Not Harley's fault. He gave back what he got."

Nikki peers at him. "Cliff, why did you put them in together? You knew they were both alpha horses."

"I thought they wanted each other . . . I thought, separated like that, they could hurt themselves. But it was worse together."

Nikki keeps peering at him like she's the judge when she's the one who should beg his forgiveness for running off. If Gracie hadn't been such a whore, then none of this would've happened. She drove him to what he did.

But he hears himself say, "If she's lame, I'll be sick at heart." A tremor in his voice. Where's that coming from? He's done nothing wrong. "And if she dies, I don't know what . . ."

Nikki peers at him for a few silent minutes, and Cliff feels it's all floating in the air between them, all that's been, and he thinks again, life sucks. And he says, "I can't handle this alone."

Now Nikki's jiggling the jar a bit, the bone bits doing a jig, floating up to the surface as if to take a breath, swimming round, and she says, "I'll stay and help . . . until Gracie's cured."

Again Cliff feels this rush of relief and dread. Would Nikki take off again?

He cannot allow her to do that.

◆◆◆

A month passes, and deep into March, the mare has had no relapse, although it's still not clear if beneath the long thin scab, an infection ferments. Meanwhile, Nikki still sleeps downstairs in her little den on the recycled hospital cot, and Cliff sleeps upstairs in their bedroom, where the bed feels like a priest's hard pallet. Often before he sleeps, Cliff senses her breathing down below and wonders if she's also lying awake, but refuses to go down and find out, as she refuses to come up. Only lately has he realized what he has been waiting for, what he has blocked out ever since she came back. Until she confesses and repents, he cannot begin to forgive. Forgiveness isn't religious, it's a contract. She has to admit that she's a miserable bitch for fucking her damned trainer before he'll even consider signing on the dotted again. Maybe Christ forgave the adulteress, but Christ wasn't married to her.

Yet during the whole long, below-zero month—the farm consistently ten degrees colder than surrounding towns—in this frost pocket of a valley, neither one of them mentions Gabe, except for once, just after she came home from Florida, when Cliff told her that guy was not allowed on this land. She didn't ask why, just asked when they would discuss it. Cliff just said, "After the mare is healed." Nikki agreed to that. Both of them postponing it. Cliff's still not absolutely sure if she fucked the guy or not. Though the last time he talked to Carla, she said Gabe was living at a campground in his camper just like when she'd first met him, and she'd warned him he'd end up like that if he betrayed her again. Cliff hung up on her. She hasn't called back. So all month, each day, all that has not been said festers beneath the surface.

And each morning and each night, Nikki and Cliff give Gracie her oral syringes of antibiotic. Nikki mashes eight big, white, round tablets of antibiotic with a mortar and pestle, then mixes that mash with applesauce to disguise the bitter taste, then spoons it into a sterile, see-through plastic syringe. Then they both go out to the barn, for it takes two of them. Gracie predictably tries to bite the hand that heals, so it takes Cliff's strength to hold her back. Nikki stands at the mare's head, sticks the syringe into the gap between the back teeth, pushes the plunger on the syringe, and squirts the medicinal slop into Gracie's mouth, the mare tossing her head, chomping, swirling her tongue, struggling to spit out the foul taste. At times, Cliff actually feels a sympathy for the bitch, suffering and fighting, both at once.

But then, just as they seemed to have made progress, Gracie seems depressed, hangs her head, doesn't bite or kick, instead lets them do what they want with her. She'd seem obedient if she didn't seem sick. Nikki unwraps the bandage from the leg, pats the hind leg down. No heat from an inner infection near the scar, Nikki says, then she pats Gracie down all over, while the mare stands, head bowed, and submits. It's almost a shame to see her bitchiness vanish, Cliff thinks. And then Nikki pats the mare's jowls under her neck, jerks her hand back and says, "Her jowls are swollen as big as oranges."

Again, they must call in the local horse vet, Dr. Buck, who trucks on over in his big black van, and examines the mare and diagnoses Strangles, a highly contagious disease of the glands, which she probably contracted weeks ago from germs in the local trailer Cliff had rented to truck her from the hospital in Burlington to Northlands. Once again, he feels at fault for something that he didn't intend. It's like all these last weeks he has done penance for a momentary lapse, a mistake, and now he'll have to do more penance, all to make up to a wife who must be an adulteress. If only he absolutely knew for sure. But neither one of them has mentioned it.

And to make matters worse, because Strangles is contagious, the vet places the entire farm under quarantine. The virus is so virulent, that before Cliff or Nikki can even enter another horse barn, they'll have to disinfect their hands, their clothes, even the soles of their boots. And Gracie must stay quarantined in her stall. Yet because Beau was in Florida, and the other horses have stayed all winter out in the field with the run-in shed, it is highly possible, the vet said, that they will not catch the virus.

Now twice a day, not only must Cliff and Nikki fill one syringe with crushed pellets and applesauce as before, they also must use an empty, sterile syringe to drain pus from the abscesses in Gracie's jowls. The mare, although calmer because she's half dead, acts up at this new assault, twists and stomps. So again, Cliff has to hold her head while Nikki inserts the tip of a new syringe into the drain hole that the vet sliced into the abscess. Nikki slowly pulls the plunger and a yellow-red mix gradually seeps into the syringe from the large, hard lumps under the mare's jowls, which each day keep secreting more noxious fluid, a seemingly endless fountain of pus.

Yet even with one syringe squirting medicine in, and another syringe drawing poison out, Gracie suffers in silence, as horses do. And over the weeks, Cliff finds himself feeling an affinity with this stoic mare. Maybe suffering can change a creature for the better. Maybe Gracie needed this plague, in order to be gentled. It took two simultaneous illnesses to calm her down. Misfortunes come in threes, Cliff's mother used to say. And one day in the barn, with him holding Gracie's head, while Nikki's draining yellowish pus into the clear plastic syringe, slowly pulling the small plunger back, she suddenly says, "Damn, it's jammed!"

"What?"

"The plunger."

He's holding Gracie's tossing head, but trying to help, says, "Show me!"

Nikki turns toward him and says, "See!"

She twists and depresses the plunger, but it doesn't jam, a squirt of puss spurts out, splats onto his face, into his eyes. He shoves the mare away, shouts, "My God!"

"I didn't mean to shoot you! I didn't!"

He wipes warm, slippery slop from his eyes, eyelids, cheeks, lips. Nikki's suddenly got this little lopsided half smile, like it's funny seeing him pus-faced. He pivots and runs full blast out of the barn up the hill in the dusk toward the house, waving his smeared hands overhead, yelling, "Why me? Why me?"

Pus stinging his eyes, still dribbling warm and slick onto his lips, he wipes his mouth again and hears her wild laughter from the barn, a hysterical girl's giggling, even while she cries, "It was an accident!"

Accident, my ass, he thinks, banging into the house, stomping into the downstairs bathroom. He grabs a towel and a washcloth, wipes the yellow, viscous fluid off his face, turns on the shower full blast, strips off barn jacket, sweatshirt, jeans, boxers, socks, all contaminated. He steps into the fucking hot shower, steam clouding the air, water jets stinging his skin. He snatches the bar of soap off the shelf and, standing in the sizzling downpour, rubs his skin raw with the cloth in the steamy heat, and keeps saying, "Fuck that bitch, fuck her!" Not suffering in silence like that fucking infected horse, hell no, not him. But after a while, he doesn't know how long, he notices that the hot water stings his flesh and steps out of the spray, and only then does he remember Nikki calling, "It was an accident!"

Like he said when Gracie got kicked, and before that when Nikki almost got killed in the high west field. "An unfortunate accident," he said. It was Gracie's fault. He had nothing to do with it. But now when Nikki called this assault an accident, he didn't believe her any more than she believed him.

He turns off the spigot, stands dripping in the tub. Maybe Nikki still blames him. Maybe, as soon as the mare is healed, Nikki will take off again, with Gracie and a clean conscience. His conscience isn't clean, even though his body is sterilized, friggin' purified.

He steps out of the tub, the pus-stained towel curled at his feet. He nabs a fresh towel off the rack, buffs his bare body, and thinks that's why Nikki left. All that blame. Maybe it was partly his fault. Maybe he should have listened more to what she said about keeping the horses apart. Maybe some accidents are under our control. Maybe others aren't.

His skin rubbed red and still stinging, and with the fresh towel wrapped around his waist, he opens the reconstructed bathroom door—intact, pure white—and he quickly trots upstairs to their bedroom, slides open his closet door for fresh clothes, sees his Persuader there behind his blaze-orange vest. Before she left for Florida, he emptied out her closet, boxed up her clothes, taped shut the boxes, propped the rifle in her closet, slid shut her door, and then caught a glimpse in her full-length mirror of an aged linebacker, half crouched as at the line of scrimmage. After she ran off down south, he took his rifle out of her closet and stood it back in his. Now her closet is bare inside, waiting to be filled in the patient way empty closets wait.

But now he's not patient. Now he knows what he's got to do.

He throws on fresh boxers, jeans, and a denim shirt, then heads back downstairs, grabs a parka off a hook in the mud-room, and hurries out to the barn, where she has been alone, dealing with that mare. Nikki has clamped Gracie's line onto a hook and refilled the syringe by herself—a pro at drawing out pus—and now Gracie's side-eyeing Cliff, and so is Nikki, filled syringe in hand, though not aiming it at him. He has to smile a little now himself, so Nikki smiles faintly back, and they both stand smiling a bit, and he says, "It was an accident."

Then she's smiling more and, syringe still in hand, she steps over to him and wraps her arms around his waist, her small, familiar body pressed against his, the syringe held out of sight behind his back. They're clinging tightly to each other in front of Gracie, who's still eyeing them. Never do bad when the horses can watch, Nikki once said. But this isn't bad. This is goddamned good, Cliff tells himself, so seize the moment . . . before the blame seeps back.

NIKOLE

SOON IT WILL THAW, NIKKI thinks, and mud season will
come, but during this in-between time in mid-March, she
can ride Beau outside, for although the snow has melted in
spots, the earth, still partly frozen, holds firm. She loves how
horses make you feel the earth, its texture shifting as the sea
sons shift. Down in paradise, it was the water that shifted
shape. In Vermont, it's the dirt.

And as the earth gradually thaws, so do she and Cliff. Ever
since the syringe incident, it's gotten warmer inside and out,
although she still sleeps in her study on the hospital cot, while
Cliff still sleeps upstairs.

It's still like living in limbo, she thinks. These last six weeks
she has felt her night thoughts drifting between Cliff sleeping
overhead and Gabe sleeping in his pickup at the campground
south of South Woodstock. He sends her repeated e-mails,
calls on her cell, leaves messages asking if she is safe and warns
her to get out. So at last, she picked up and said it's all under
control, and she has promised Cliff, although the Strangles
has healed, that she'd wait until the vet determined if Gracie
is sound.

She did not tell Gabe then that the longer she stays with
Cliff, the more she feels she never left, and that the longer Cliff
nurses her sick mare, the more she feels horses are part of both

of them. Like yesterday, when she went out to the barn to find
Cliff on his knees by Gracie's injured leg that he had unban-
daged and was stroking with hands large and strong enough
to snap a bone on a whim, but they kept gently massaging the
hind leg, a long, loving caress. And he kept at it, on his knees
like that, almost reverent, until he must've sensed Nikki's presence, when without looking up, he said, "Still doing my penance." Another one of his dark jokes perhaps, for Nikki gradually has come to believe that it really was an accident, that Cliff
believed if he put the two horses together, they'd be happier.
Cliff had Gracie's best interests at heart, Nikki tells herself.

Like he has hers, except when it comes to Gabe, for although Cliff hasn't mentioned Gabe, it has been brewing, all
that hasn't been said, and Nikki dreads the upcoming confron-
tation, because she knows that to stay with Cliff, she must fire
Gabe, even though the word will spread in the horse world,
and Gabe will be down and out all over again. How many
times can someone resurrect? What will become of him who
says to ride into the dark, the only trainer who got to her core?

Meanwhile though, for the horse's sake, she has started
working out Beau by herself, light interval training in the ring,
followed by hacking on the hilly trails, Beau sometimes bucking and bolting with the sheer energy built up from a few
months' rest. Just high spirits, not resistance, although with
each ride, his hijinks escalate. Sometimes she almost comes
out of the saddle at his sudden shifts and twists. She tries
to strategize, to foresee what he'll do next, but Beau, quick-
witted for a horse, often stays ahead of her, even though he
doesn't go over the limit like Gracie does. His bones are bigger, yet her stride is longer. He's the talented comedian, she's
the bitchy acrobat. Yet his acting up makes Nikki miss Gabe's
expertise again, for Gabe's light spirit lifted her up, his laughter light and crisp, not like Cliff's that booms from deep in
his chest like drumbeats, as if even Cliff's laughter is serious.
Gabe was more than her trainer, he was her muse.

◆◆◆

One day, in the midst of an early-morning ground fog drifting up as the land exhales the cold night, she gallops Beau alongside the stretch of jumps at the edge of woods on the path that Cliff bushwhacked through thick, high, bleached grass where groundhog holes were before Cliff stuffed them shut. Her blood up from racing, she feels fearless even though Beau spooks and shies each time they pass the grove of birch by the rough path leading up the rocky ridge. Finally, she pulls him to a halt at the mouth of the path and peers up into the foothills, tall birch and pine shrouded in mist, yet she sees, not too far up, a flash of something pale and blue shifting in the gray trees and rocks. An upright, two-legged beast limping. Or was it?

Some creature's up there making her feel as if she'll bust out of her skin. She can't resist and trots Beau up the rocky, root-ridden path. And on the first ledge, Gabe waits, leaning against a speckled boulder, his body dappled in shadows from outcropping rocks overhead. He knows she often practices in this upper field. She swings off and holds Beau's reins, as Gabe limps toward them, ignoring her, saying, "Beau, my good old boy." And he's patting, slapping the gelding's neck, Beau nuzzling Gabe's jeans pocket for sugar. And Gabe says, still looking at Beau, not at her, "Got to get in shape for the season. You must've missed me something fierce. How'd you ever hold up without your master, huh? I know your tricks. And your mistress is tricky too, right? Cutting me out of your herd. How do you feel about that?" He strokes Beau between the ears, which Beau loves, so he lowers his head, Gabe seducing the beast.

"You shouldn't be here," she says.

"So, Beau, I heard the vet's coming for Gracie this week. I've been waiting for that day. It's been a feat of self-discipline to wait, but we'll be together again soon, you and me, and the two females."

Of course, he'd spy on her. She is all he has. And her horses, but she says, "Gabe, I've got to talk to you, about your job."

Still looking at Beau, he goes on, "Only thing wrong,

I saw your mistress and Cliff going into that barn together each morning and night, ministering to a mare's leg that he as good as broke himself."

"Cliff didn't do it."

Gabe turns to her at last. "Nikki, there's one question I've got for you. Have you been fucking that good old boy?"

Taken off guard, she says, "I'm sleeping downstairs. Cliff's sleeping up."

"But that's not all, is it?"

"My marriage is private."

"Not since paradise it's not. You're all I think of."

"You think of Beau and of Gracie, too."

"Hell yes. Our future's riding on that mare."

Our future. And she senses how deep it is between them, deeper than before, for Gabe. But for her, it's deeper with Cliff. "If the mare is sound," she says, "I'll be training her myself."

"The hell you will. You can't handle her. Like you can't handle Cliff."

"You don't know that."

"You think you're done with me, but deep down in your dark, conflicted soul, you know you're not."

"Even if I know that, I'm still done."

He shakes his head. "You and your doublespeak."

She sticks her foot in the stirrup, swings up into the saddle.

"Nikki, you're a fine athlete, a real horsewoman. It's what fires you up. Admit it!"

She yanks on the inside rein, presses with her thighs, and Beau takes off cantering down the root-ridden trail, where he could trip, but he safely gets to the flat field and gallops back on the bushwhacked path along the tree line. She turns her head to look back up that trail into the hills, but Gabe is hidden by earthbound clouds, and as she searches for his shadow, Beau feels her lack of focus and immediately bolts down the long slope, the bit in his teeth, running now for the pure joy of it, flying past the fenced pastures, then past the paddock toward the barn. She fears he'll hit the barn wall at a dead run, but at the last moment, he swerves and charges through the wide open door, gallops down the wide aisle to his stall, where he slams to a halt, quickly lowers his head, and she slides down his long neck to land in the soft, deep pile of clean wood shavings. He stands still, eyerolls her and nods. He knew just where to safely dump her. The joke's on her yet again.

She's up and dusting herself off, only her breath knocked out, but she almost hears Gabe saying, Nikki, you let him get ahead of you again.

Like she let Gabe get ahead. She has been living in quarantine.

◆◆◆

After tending to Beau, she goes inside and sits at the Shaker table and knows it's coming to a showdown soon with Cliff. And she thinks how even their grown kids were shaken up by her moving out, even Lisa, although as a girl, she'd worked hard to split them up. When Nikki called from the Alpine Lodge to say she'd moved out of Northlands for a while—she didn't tell Lisa of any threats—and Lisa said, "Cliff's not so bad." Nikki said, "It's only temporary." Lisa asked, "It's because of the horses, isn't it?" Nikki said, "The horses aren't to blame." Then Lisa said, "You and Cliff better work it out. I don't want my life disrupted." A typical undergrad worried only about her own life, Nikki thought, but then Lisa added, "And, Mother, I don't want your life messed up either. Cliff's uptight and moody and has a temper, but he's been there for us." So Nikki said, "I've asked him to come with me, and I'll go back home in the spring, but I've got to compete all winter to make up for my fall." Then Lisa, being the shrewd child she was, asked, "Are you going alone?" Nikki hesitated, like the guilty would, then said, "I'm going with my trainer." Lisa asked, "You're leaving Cliff for that little runt?" Nikki said, "I need Gabe there to win. That's all there is to it." Then Lisa said in her most parental tone, "You get in your rig right now, and you get right back home to Cliff as fast as you can."

Even Cliff's son got upset. Just after Gracie's accident, a few days after Nikki came home, the phone rang, and it was Matt. As usual, he just asked if his dad was there. She said Cliff was out, and then, instead of Matt's getting right off as usual, he said, "So you're back." She realized that Cliff must have told his son, although Cliff never confided in anyone. Matt asked, "Staying around a while?" She said, "Yes, so why don't you come visit soon?" He said, "A family reunion for old times' sake?" She only said, "Your dad would like that." Matt said, "And you're the expert on what my dad likes." Using the same deadpan, tongue-in-cheek ironic tone that his dad has mastered. She didn't answer and Matt said, "Don't bring him down. Suck it up." And he hung up on her, as his father so often did.

Now Nikki sits at the Shaker table and wonders what it will be like to ride without the man who made her into the equestrian she is. Gabe worked on her body and her spirit. Though her body got her spirit into trouble, so she bows her head and prays for forgiveness, but hears only silence. She feels no presence like she felt whirling in the high field when she fell, no spirit hovering.

◆◆◆

On the day of the vet exam, Nikki is a wreck, wondering what might still lurk inside the seemingly healed mare.

Dr. Buck drives up in his big black van like a shiny, unmarked hearse. Not a good omen, Nikki thinks. He climbs out with his new border collie that starts bounding in circles, trying to herd the humans. Dr Buck's last border collie dashed behind his hearse as Dr. Buck was backing up, so he flattened his own pet. Not good publicity for a vet, yet he's one of the best. A short, hefty man, he's got thighs as thick as Cliff's, but a cheerier disposition, and he heads straight into Gracie's stall, lays his broad hands on her jowls, probes a bit, and reports that the last blood test was negative, and he finds no swelling, so he pronounces the Strangles cured.

The poison, Nikki thinks, has at last ebbed out of the mare, standing quietly for Cliff, who holds her lead line, as if this magnificent horse, over seventeen hands, formerly a bitch, trusts Cliff now. As if even this murderous creature can care.

Then the vet unwinds the bandage on her hind leg, runs his hands down the stifle and fetlock, and says that the scar has healed fine and he finds no heat, but first they must x-ray the leg, then trot her out. Nikki tries to visualize the positive, but she feels sick. With horses, seemingly so strong, so much can go invisibly wrong.

Dr. Buck takes x-rays with a portable, high-tech, black box and develops the plates right there. He says the x-rays show no floating shards. He'll send another set to the Burlington Clinic for the final answer, yet so far so good, he says, but now they must do the stress test and trot Gracie up and back and in circles on hard ground to see if she's off. He instructs Nikki to hold Gracie's halter while he flexes the leg under stress, then they'll run her out, the true test immediately after the stress. Nikki takes the mare's lead line, but Gracie shakes her head, baring her teeth, the bitch resurrected.

So Cliff takes back the line, and almost immediately, the mare stands quietly. The vet picks up the left hind leg, bends it back at the fetlock, holds it for a quick count, sets it down, and tells Cliff to trot her right out.

It's all come down to this, as Cliff trots the fine-boned golden mare on the line out of the barn into the outdoors. After months of stall rest, Gracie's blinking in the sudden light, shaking her elegant head, high stepping, whinnying to the horses in the far field, eyerolling at the grass, delighted to be alive.

But being alive isn't enough. She must be sound. As Cliff trots her out, Nikki and the vet eyeball the left hind. Gracie sets it down squarely, doesn't favor it. And then, as if she knows she might pass the test, she's prancing, ears pricked, a golden girl, a high-stepping debutante, gliding smoothly with her floating gaits, naturally under herself, even when she's out of shape. Cliff runs alongside, cantering her up and back, the

vet and Nikki still watching for the slightest hint if the hind is
offbeat . . . but it's a ballet, all loveliness, and Nikki's laughing,
and the vet calls to Cliff to halt and says, "Congratulations,"
and Nikki goes to Cliff and slaps the mare's neck, and Cliff's
stroking it, and Nikki's feeling as if yes, they've won.

And they're smiling as the vet says, "You've been through
a heck of a lot, now for God's sake, take pleasure in it." As if
he knows pleasure has been foreign to them.

They're still smiling as Dr. Buck drives off in his hearse,
which seems like a limo now, and Nikki says, "Cliff, you
saved her."

Cliff says, "No, we did."

And Nikki says, "So let's celebrate!" Feeling higher than
when she jumps, and they turn Gracie out by herself into a
paddock and watch her perform her floating trot all around,
naturally under herself, a natural slope to her hindquarters, a
natural confirmation for jumping, and she's shiny, chestnut
gold, healthy, and whole again, and they applaud.

It's hard to believe, Nikki thinks, that this burnished,
graceful mare almost killed her.

Then she and Cliff go inside, and he heads down into the
basement to his wine cellar and comes back up with a special
California Cabernet reserve. He uncorks it, and without waiting to let it breathe, pours them each a glass, lifts his, and says,
"Here's to healing."

She clicks her glass to his and drinks to healing. Then she
says, "And here's to you, Cliff."

So they click and drink to him. Then he lifts his glass and
says, "And, Nikki, here's to you."

So she drinks to herself. It feels good to have them both
drinking to each other. It feels right, for Cliff couldn't be this
joyful if he had planned that accident, she thinks.

Then they sit for a while and talk about Gracie's recovery, Cliff talking horse talk, which he hardly ever does, saying
that the mare is totally sound and lovely to watch with her
long gaits, and she has a spirit that doesn't quit, and, "She's
restored to grace." So then they both drink to grace. Before

long, they've drunk the whole bottle, swirling dark, rich red wine in their mouths, savoring every taste, taking pleasure together at long last. Afterwards, Nikki sits, still feeling high, her blood still up, and Cliff's blood's up too. She can tell by the way he sits up so straight now at the edge of his seat, poised for action, although he doesn't say it.

Instead, at one point, he simply shoves back his chair, stands, and waits. She wordlessly stands, too, reaches out and takes his hand, and it seems simple then, hand in hand, to walk to the silent steps and go up together. She won't fall, she thinks, not with his wide warm hand in hers.

They go into their bedroom, and it's her bedroom, too, even though she hasn't been in it since she found his Persuader in her private space. But now he slides a disk into the CD player, and Willie Nelson blurts out country soul in his achy breaky tenor, and although she prefers jazz, Cliff fast forwards to Willie crooning their old song . . . *"Even though I don't tell you . . . you're always on my mind . . ."* Cliff often used to play this song and he'd say, "That's what I think, even though I don't say it." Now he still doesn't say a word, just takes her in his thick arms and gently holds her. And as Willie wails, they sway a bit, and she leans her head against Cliff's hard chest, and they're turning slowly, step, step, and sway, slow motion dancing in front of her mirrored sliding closet door. She wonders if inside, his Persuader is still propped on its butt, if his blaze-orange vest still hangs deflated, but she will not slide back that door to look. She just visualizes her closet empty and nestles in his arms, and then, as they slowly step-step-circle-turn and sway to the beat in perfect sync, with her cheek pressed against his breast, she catches in her closet mirror a glimpse of Cliff's face. She has never seen it as tender, as exposed, as suffused with happiness, as it is now, when he thinks that she can't see.

Why won't he show her this secret tender face?

But he step-turns, leads her around, so she sees in the mirror only her own face, small and loving but perplexed, and when she looks directly up into his face, it's again a stillborn mask.

Yet she still feels deeply touched by her quick glimpse of his exposed, loving self, and soon they lie in bed beneath the poster of the purple and red couple hunched under a cloak buffeted by wind, and her body softens and gives with his soft touch, and before long, he gently rolls her over onto her stomach, his favorite position, familiar and erotic both at once, except now she can't see Cliff's face, and she wonders if, unseen, it is again suffused with love.

◆ ◆ ◆

The next morning, they eat omelets at the table across from each other, and he's burly handsome in a blue denim shirt, the sleeves rolled up to the elbow. She gets up, goes to him, circles her arms around his neck and strokes the pale, thick hairs on his forearms and smoothes the hairs down. An old gesture resurrected from their first years together, when she couldn't keep her hands off any part of him for long, until he nicknamed her "The Clinging Vine." Then she backed off, for he's a man of distances. But this morning she doesn't feel put off when he doesn't stroke her back because she couldn't stop loving him, even though she wanted to. So now, for a change, she doesn't feel restless with his silence as they sit.

But then Cliff asks, "Are you going to train her to compete?"

"I don't know yet."

"You don't have to give it all up."

"I knew when I came back and stayed that I'd have to fire him."

"I know what you need," Cliff says.

She looks up.

He's smiling that faint dry smile, and he says, "A new trainer."

She stares at him. She can't tell if his grin is loving or ironic, if this is a gift, or a taking back.

She shakes her head. "Trainers can't save you."

"Never said they could."

"Cliff, from now on you and I will tell each other everything, won't we? And we'll trust each other again."

He shoves his chair back, him and his distances, but he says, "Why not?"

She stands up, goes to him, wraps her arms around his neck again, and says, "Since I came back from Florida, I felt I'd have to choose between you and . . . the sport. But even if I'm sometimes bereft, I still want to be with you . . . nevertheless."

"Big of you," he says.

"And we'll be more open than we've ever been, and it will all be worth it then."

"It's not worth it now?"

She kisses his cheek and whispers in his ear, "Yes, it is."

Cliff sighs, then nods, then shoves back his chair, breaks the circle of her embrace, and says he has to check on the mare before he heads to the office.

He walks on out, but Nikki stays in her place. Through the wide picture window, she gazes out at the fields, blurred again by ground fog billowing, the grasses dimly lit, iridescent, as if this land is blessed, as if her marriage is. She feels an unaccustomed peace, and she sits a while and feels mellow until her cell phone rings.

She tenses, knows who it is, but clicks on, and Gabe says, "So Gracie's sound."

He was spying again, or else he checked with the vet.

"So, Nikki, now you can trailer her and Beau over to the Meadowlark. We'll set up interval training, develop a strategy."

"Gabe, we have to settle this. But not here."

"Sure. How about this afternoon at McCracken's at three?"

The only sports bar in Quechee, where she and Cliff used to go. She told Gabe that once. But she says yes, taps off, and heads straight out to the barn to Cliff. No secrets now that's it's new and pristine between them.

He's up in the loft with a pitchfork, forking bales down through the open trap door onto the wide-planked floor, dust puffing up. The long tines on the pitchfork above shine in the dim barn, which still must seem to Gracie, below in her stall, like a murky prison. Nikki calls up, "We've got to talk about my trainer." And immediately wishes she hadn't said *my*.

Cliff jabs the tines into another hay bale, forks it over the edge. It lands with a splat, not too close, but Nikki steps back. "Can you come down?"

The only sound is the rustling of the mare's constant, turning, turning, in her stall, then Cliff's clomping down the side steps. He kneels and breaks the bale twine with his bare hands, peels off a couple flakes of hay, then rises, passes Nikki, flops open Gracie's stall door, and bursts in, moving too fast. Gracie, startled, swings her hindquarters around, knocks him off balance, and he says, "You damn bitch!"

Nikki knows who he's really talking to. But she goes into the stall after him.

"Cliff, I've got to meet with him. I can't fire him over the phone."

Cliff stuffs the flakes into the iron hay rack, shreds of hay falling to mix with the pale wood shavings covering the rubber stall mat. Then he swings open the half door, steps out, closes it, and slides the latch.

"We're not going to let him stop us, are we, Cliff?"

He walks off without looking back.

She starts out after him to say that she will not leave him ever again. Then he won't harbor a grudge, or a hurt, or whatever it is he keeps inside. But in her head, she hears Gabe's voice, *Don't move the way fear makes you move.*

She's not afraid for herself, but for Cliff. Yet she stops in the stall, and the mare lowers her head and nudges Nikki's breast, and nudges it again, not hard, only enough to commiserate.

◆◆◆

At McCracken's, it's musty, windowless, dark. Nikki was last here a few years ago in the fall with Cliff, watching football on the big screen, clashing bodies magnified, Cliff cheering on the Patriots in his booming baritone, never more unleashed, less repressed than during a Pats game.

Now the bar's almost empty, the flat-screen TV is dead.

She paces over to a corner booth where Gabe sits with a

beer. He tips his good hand in a salute, while his other hand stays hidden beneath the table. His hiding his hand from her makes her awfully sad, and he looks sad, dressed all in black, black jeans, black long-sleeved shirt, cuffs buttoned—as if she doesn't know what he's like underneath. His dark eyes glow, opaque.

She sits across from him, leans back, folds her arms tightly across her breasts.

"So Gracie's made a comeback," he says.

"Yes. And she's not a bitch anymore."

"Once a bitch always a bitch."

"Like me?"

"You're no bitch. Not my Nikki," he says, flashing his off-kilter grin, one half- up, the other down, each side canceling the other out.

"I'm not your Nikki."

"Once my Nikki always my Nikki."

She shakes her head. "You can't train me anymore."

"Nikki, it's your conscious mind that messes you up. Got to trust your instincts, so I've got a whole new interval schedule written up for you." His good hand reaches under the table, pulls up a yellow tablet of paper. "I've got every day planned for the entire next month. And I filled in registration forms for the summer season, and set up Beau's Coggins test with the vet." He's opening the tablet, flipping through charts of sketched-in jumps with his little meticulous arrows pointing from one bar to the next. "See, I'm more on top of it than I've ever been."

"Cliff won't hire you back."

"You said you'd move out when the mare got better."

"I said if Cliff was to blame. But it was an accident. So we've reconciled."

Gabe shakes his head. "No such thing as an accident. We create them. I know. They don't happen on their own. Nikki, face the facts. First, Cliff almost killed you, and then your mare."

"He nursed her every day these last months. He saved her life."

At this, Gabe looks down, tap-tapping his fingers on the marred tabletop, taking it all in, probably plotting his strategy again, how to stay ahead of her, and Cliff.

After some moments, he looks up and says, "Carla visited me at the RV camp. She wants me back. Said I'd go under if I didn't come home."

"You still love her?"

"You're jealous, is that it?"

She's shaking her head no, though she once might have been.

He says, "You're back with Cliff, and you don't love him. Hell, these last weeks, all I had to do was lie around in my camper and think, and it became clear—my love for you that I'd felt all along, but I'd denied it for the horses' sake. Like you denied your love for me."

He's visualizing her love for him, to make it real. She says, "I'm going to show Beau by myself."

"Oh yeah? When?"

"At the Millbrook trial in June."

"The competition's stiff. You won't place."

"I will!"

"You'll rush, and he'll run off."

"I'll win."

"You'll lose."

"I'll place."

"Only if I'm there to help."

"Gabe, don't go to Millbrook and don't come to North-lands again. I don't know what Cliff would do."

"I know."

She's finally sick of Gabe knowing things, of him telling her what to do and not to do. He's reaching across the table for her with that one living hand, the dead one still hidden below. She quickly stands. "We'll talk again after you calm down."

He still sits. "You love me. You don't know how much."

She turns and walks out, but hears his voice, higher-pitched, "It's gone too far. You won't win, not without me. You can't."

Won't, and not, and can't, she thinks, and everything is negative.

CARLA

CARLA HEARS HIS PIECE OF junk on wheels come rattling up their gravel drive. She knew Gabe would be back after she heard from Cliff that he and Nikki had reconciled. No rich bitch would leave her high-class horsey life for long to shack up with a penniless, broken-down dreamer, so now Gabe must be desperate. Desperation has a look and smell all its own. Like when Carla went down to that campground to visit him after he first got back from Florida, he kept limping around his little site and couldn't sit still. The desperate keep moving like that, and all around that piney, outdoorsy smell, too sticky-sweet like air fresheners disguise what stinks. And he claimed innocence. He said he had abstained more than "anybody could imagine." Him pacing and piney-smelling like that. Did he really expect her to believe him again? Been there, done that.

Yet in spite of all of it, as she hears that too-familiar motor cough into her drive, she shoves herself up off the faded couch and flips off the TV. Discovery Channel. Lately, she likes to watch those wild animals fight to survive. Desperate, too, godless, like all animals, especially horses, and like rich horsepeople, especially Nikole Swensen. Although Gabe once said Nikole had seen some sort of apparition after one of her falls, like she believes in ghosts. But not in God, surely she can't. If you believe in God, you've got to be good. Carla steps to the little window and, through the gauze curtains, watches her husband step-limp up their front walk, his eyes gazing up like he's imagining her taking him back.

She runs one hand through her stiff hair, fluffs it up, sticks out her chest, and flings opens the front door. Gabe looks up at her—three inches taller and proud of it—and he says, "Mama, I'm back." Like the prodigal son, spoiled, deluded.

"No Mama lives here," she says.

"I'm sorry to hear that. She was a big woman with a big heart, bigger than most. She's gone, you say? I guess that means I'll have to mourn her loss." He's got that aborted crooked grin.

"Mourn your little heart out," she says.

Gabe flinches as if he hadn't expected this new, harsh, deeper voice, as if she's channeling for a baritone. And she feels as strong as a man, and she's bigger than him, and she's all righteously ruffled, furious.

"Mama, I can't say I'm sorry for my dedication to a sport. I can only say I'm back. You can let me in or kick me out."

She'd expected more groveling, not him standing there, spine erect, probably all that's erect, mother and son, pat, pat, kiss, kiss, be home by curfew time. But here he is, half muscled beach boy, half invalid, all of him on her doorstep.

She can't help it. She steps back, and he's inside. In moments he's on the faded couch. She brings him a beer from the fridge as if he's a guest. And she tries to forgive, just a little bit, to chip away at the mound of resentment that wants him to move back in, so she can make him pay in countless little ways until he expiates his guilt.

She hands him the Heineken and sits down next to him. He takes a swig and says, "I didn't expect to be here." And he's looking furtively around like there's something wrong with her immaculate house after that smelly, overcrowded campground.

Maybe it's her knickknacks that he hates but that she inherited—little porcelain creatures like the three monkeys, one with hands over ears, one with hands over mouth, one with hands over eyes. Hear, speak, and see no evil.

He sucks his beer, his uneven shoulders slumped, ponytail dangling to the left, lopsided face unshaved, mismatched eyes bloodshot from sleepless nights.

She says, "I figured you'd get lonely during those long nights in your trailer all alone."

"I'm used to long nights. I'm nocturnal."

"But it must be especially lonely since Nikole and Cliff hooked up again. He called and told me you met with her one last time."

Gabe sits, doesn't react, which makes her nervous, like she's on first date, a preteen again, taller than most boys, always trying to make up for her size by being extra nice. A Mama even back then, Nurse Carla. It was Gabe's vulnerability that first attracted her, and his striving for a perfection he'd never reach. She knew before his fall, he'd end up broken.

He's staring now at the blank TV, just sits and sips his beer, not spouting words for once.

She picks up the controls, taps the TV on, changes the channel, some commercial, a typical black, shiny SUV, sort of like Cliff's, zipping along the typical deserted mountain highway. She presses mute.

Gabe leans forward, staring at the SUV as if Cliff's in it, Gabe's body coiled tight, his lips pressed tight, as if he's going to crack.

"So tell me, Gabe, what's going on inside you?"

He still stares at the screen, some reality show, now a lush beachfront house, six gorgeous, sexed-up men and women, mouths moving fast. Somebody's going to get voted off.

He says, "I feel indebted to you for all you've done for me."

"Gabe, I don't blame you for trying to make it big again. Too bad you didn't. But it's your own fault, and, of course, it's hers."

He sinks down into the sofa, shuts his eyes, and suddenly with his trim body slouched and his dark gaze shuttered, he looks smaller, younger, reminding her of one of her boys in third grade, a little brat who only seems sweet when he gets sick, and then she sends him to the nurse and visits him while he lies on that sterile cot and tells him he'll be just fine, as she'd tell her own child if she hadn't had that hysterectomy—her uterus ripped out, all that blood. And now Gabe seems sick, and she pities him like when he was broken after his fall. In the hospital, he was too proud to ask for help, so she acted as his fierce advocate, kept those doctors and nurses hopping. Carla, the scourge of intensive care. But once they got home, as Gabe gradually revived, he started calling her "too merciful," or "too self-sacrificing," or, "too ever-present."

But now, he's still slumped way down on her faded couch, and his head's still tilted back, eyes still shut, almost as if he's in a coma, as if she's in control again.

She's on his right, his good side, and her left arm slowly slinks forward and lightly touches his pony tail. She waits a bit, to see if he'll open his eyes, but he doesn't shift, so her left hand drifts across his chest and rests on his numb left arm. For quite a while, her hand just lightly strokes his numb left side as he simply sits slumped with his eyes still shut. Then her fingertips slip down and lightly stroke his left wrist, his hand, the hardened flesh like cardboard with a little give to it, but she keeps stroking the side that can't feel, until she feels a flicker of forgiveness, a few moments of tenderness for her delinquent perfectionist, arch enemy, beloved child.

GABE

One month later, on a hot June morning at Millbrook—
only three hours away, a day trip, so no need to mention it
to Carla—Gabe sits under the porch roof of barn number
fifteen, next to the outdoor warm-up ring. And he looks up
the slope at the big white owners' tent with plastic windows,
like a wedding tent, dented by a light wind, six bright flags
flipping—United States, Canada, Britain, Ireland, New Zea-
land, Australia. If it weren't for Cliff Swensen, Gabe would be
a legitimate participant instead of a trespasser on his own turf.

He tilts back on the folding chair, keeps his eye out for
Nikki, who won't permanently shut him out, not for fucking
Cliff Swensen, who doesn't know who Nikki truly is, while
Gabe knows she and he are fellow fanatics. He sits in the
shadows and waits and watches the trim competitors stroll
past with their grooms, students, and stable hands, while at
the concession tents, workers hawk their wares—tack, riding
togs, horsey art, beer and wine, grilled food—and at the far
end, some vendors sell trailers and vans. Next to them, the
Porta Potties stand in neat rows, waiting.

From his perch, he can also see Nikki's shiny silver rig in
the private parking lot for competitors, about a hundred trailers lined up. Two days ago, on another day trip, he watched
with binoculars as her rig pulled in. She seemed too small be-

hind the wheel. He caught a glimpse of a swatch of her dark, shiny hair, then next to her in the passenger seat, the bulked-up, ape-like shoulders of her estranged husband. For Cliff and Nikki are still estranged, in spite of her saying they're not. The easiest person to deceive is yourself. Although Gabe doesn't. Through meditation, he has learned his own inner dark, a shifting force like the tide. Yeah, sure, Nikki and Cliff did look like a couple when they arrived, climbing simultaneously out of the cab, marching in lockstep back to the trailer, her sliding back the bolt, Cliff flipping down the iron ramp, making it look light with his damn thick arms. Cliff, a perverse, repressed alpha male masquerading as a calm, self-reliant businessman. Cliff, the instigator of accidents. Accidents happen for a reason, like Gabe's, riding flat out in rain and muck, killing a noble horse instead of his sorry self, and he visualizes again the stallion, hobbling in place, his fetlock at an odd angle, hoof flopping. Gabe's fault, so he's got to make up for it.

It's humans who are dark, and it was the darkness in Cliff that enticed him to get Nikki and Gracie out on the trail, and later to turn Gracie loose with Harley. Cliff's not man enough to own up to his own violence, so his wife believes he's a damned healer. Expose the hypocrite. Even though, when Nikki and Cliff first arrived, Gabe had to watch from afar as she led Beau out of the rig down the ramp, the gelding backing smoothly out, prancing a bit, as if that prankster's perfectly happy without his trainer. Even the horse deceiving itself.

Nikki led Beau into Barn fifteen, where Gabe knows they've been assigned to stall thirty-nine. When he first got here, he did what he always did when he was gainfully employed as trainer, went into the office, to the competitors' table, and picked up a sheet with stall assignments, warm-up and starting times. He knows exactly where she'll be and when. Yesterday, day one, he watched from a small barn on the periphery of ring three while she rode dressage. She placed middle of the pack, too stiff, Beau's transitions off. Gabe didn't spot Cliff. Probably skipped dressage as usual.

Now Gabe will watch her warm up for cross-country, so he'll be able to predict if she can go clear. He can still think ahead of her. She can't fire him and think he'll stop riding along with her. Too late for that. He tilts back in the aluminum lawn chair and looks like he belongs. Nobody thinks to check if he's got a competitor's pass.

He pulls out a red thermos. He stole Carla's recipe for horse show daiquiris. She doesn't know he's here. She wouldn't approve, not with her and him sharing a bed but acting like he's back in rehab. Carla's still waiting for him to repent, which he in all honesty cannot, although sometimes he wants to press his face into her great big tits, her warm hands patting his back, her deep voice saying, "There there, everything will be all right." Like she used to now and then, before he left for paradise. Carla is The Saint of Perpetual Comfort, when she isn't pissed, and when she is, she's the Advocate of Perpetual Suffering.

He unscrews the thermos lid, takes a good long sip, closes his eyes, takes a few deep, cleansing breaths, but he feels himself gradually slide down into that darkness like after his accident. Fuck positive thinking. As the Buddha said, we are all of the nature to suffer. Now it's Cliff's turn. Gabe's had his share. Cliff thinks possessions are permanent, while Gabe knows everything's in flux. Cliff thinks he's got a separate self while Gabe knows that self is unreal. And horses sense that, herd animals, one merging into the next.

Then, promptly at eight a.m., Nikki's assigned warm-up time, she rides Beau into the workout ring. Gabe has shifted deeper under the overhang of the nearby shed. Still no sighting of Cliff. He could have stayed a few miles away at the Horseman's Motor Inn, where they checked in two days before. Gabe knows because after dressage yesterday, he followed Nikki there. In the front yard, a giant, fifteen-foot, wooden white horse stood prancing too stiff, like that giant wooden horse in Troy.

Gabe's half-hidden in the shadows under the shed roof while he watches Nikki and Beau warm up—walk, trot, canter, intervals—she's uptight, so Beau is. She's strong but not totally focused, holding back slightly on the reins, on herself.

"You're behind," Gabe wants to call, but he'd give away his hiding place. He'll wait.

Now she circles Beau toward a simple cross rail, but as Beau lifts off, she tugs on his mouth, so Beau shortens his approach, lifts off, pops the rail.

Gabe can tell her now to give Beau his head, or else he can shut up, let her lose the event. If she loses, maybe she'll blame Cliff for firing her trainer.

Nikki's got self-carriage and balance as she circles Beau back toward the cross rail, but this time she slightly overcorrects, takes off from too far back, still doesn't let Beau choose his spot, so he barely clears the fence, gives a little flip of a buck to show her she's not in sync.

Gabe starts to call out, stifles it. She turns her head, glances toward the shed, stares. She must sense him there.

She turns away, circles Beau again, heads toward a vertical, takes off from a bit too far back yet again, so he ticks. At last, for the horse's sake, Gabe steps out into the light.

Nikki halts Beau and stares at Gabe so hard it seems she's turned hard inside, but that can't be.

He limps over and says, "Hey, Beau, old boy, you need me. You know that, even if nobody else does."

Beau tosses his mane and gazes up over Gabe's head at a dark mare gliding past in the nearby lane. She's led by some young stable hand, who has no clue what's at stake.

"I'm doing this alone," Nikki says.

"You're not alone when every word I ever said is in your body and in your mind."

"I'll place," she says, as if she's a top rider who can train herself. She's got years and miles to go before she reaches that pinnacle, if ever. Gabe almost reached that height. The air is thin up in that empty space. It's hard to breathe.

He's still got the choice to let her lose after cutting him

out. But he can't stop wanting to win. "You're holding Beau back. Trust his courage, his agility. Give him independence. Take the jumps again."

For thanks, she swivels Beau around and trots him away, out of the ring, his hooves kicking dust onto Gabe's boots and jeans. She doesn't look back. Let her lose. Then she'll come crawling back.

A few buildings away, she dismounts by the competitors' barn and leads Beau on inside. Only trainers, riders, owners, or grooms allowed in. A privileged place, where Gabe no longer has a pass.

◆◆◆

In a half hour, he waits on course by a corner jump that's in a glen of oaks, so the rails are half in the shade, half in the sun, a nasty, dappled spot with two rails at right angles. She's got to go double clear to win after her dressage score. He can see from where he is about fifty yards across to the Loons, a water hole with big, flat, black wooden loons nailed onto both side posts. He's sitting on a hillock in a blasting sun, and through the earth, in his right buttock, he can feel the vibrations of hoof beats, his left buttock senseless.

Does he really want Beau to clear those jumps? The announcer squawks that number thirty-five, Nikole Swensen, has cleared Montgomery's Labyrinth and is heading for the Loons. Soon number thirty-four, a big, chestnut Warmblood rocks at a slow gallop down and easily skims over the Loons, several long strides, two easy lifts, takes the corner jump, lumbers on. In a few seconds under two minutes, according to Gabe's stopwatch, Beau flies up over the slope, Nikki not holding back anymore but overcorrecting again, riding at the edge of control. The sportsman in Gabe hopes she'll make it. The lover hopes she won't.

At the Loons, she lifts off too close, but Beau rises up, splashes over the rail, gallops sloppily up the bank. Then, right by where Gabe sits, instead of sitting up to help balance at the corner jump, she puts her weight too far forward. Beau senses the shift, questions, abruptly halts at the fence, Nikki flies sideways off, lands face-first in gravely dirt. Beau stands, reins dangling, shaking his head, frothing at the bit.

Somebody says to get an ambulance, and Gabe's limping over to her, flat on her belly. He touches her back, saying, "Nikki, just lie there." But she slowly sits, blood trickling out of her nose, tiny pebbles embedded in her cheek. She says she only had her wind knocked out. Gabe turns to catch Beau's reins, but he canters off, reins swinging, and the announcer's calling, "Loose horse on course, loose horse on course." Beau coasts smoothly along, no trace of a limp. Gabe turns back to Nikki, who stands on her own, although shakily. She doesn't even glance at him, and the small cluster of spectators silently watches as she walks slowly off, no limp, spine straight, after her runaway horse. "She brought him in too fast," a woman behind Gabe says. Then the spectators turn to watch for the next contestant, and the jump judge says, "We'll have a bigger crowd at this jump after this." Some fans hoping for another fall, more dramatic, with broken bones and blood, like his.

The field ambulance bumps over the hill and pulls up, too late, and the loudspeaker announces that number thirty-five, Nikole Swensen, left her tack, but horse and rider are fine.

Now that it's over, Gabe is seriously pissed. How dare she undercut all his training? Her fall is her own fault.

He lurches top speed down the long slope after her, figuring Cliff will be waiting by the finish. Hell, have it out at last.

He stalks at a tilt past the finish, still no sign of Cliff, catches up to Nikki at Barn number fifteen, comes up behind her, and says, "You were ahead of him."

She keeps her back turned, so he can't see her face. "Cliff will be here soon. He was watching by the Splash."

"So what? Now he'll know you need me to win."

She waves one hand, batting off his words, and steps into the barn. Doesn't she see that to betray him is to betray herself?

He follows her in, where, as Gabe guessed, Beau waits, unrepentantly tugging strands of hay out of a rack in his open stall. Nikki hurries into the stall, slides off Beau's tack, hangs it on pegs by the half door, pats down the length of all four legs. Gabe says, still to her back, "We need to go back to the basics again. We need discipline."

At the word discipline, she sighs and finally turns, and Gabe sees her face, a few tiny pebbles still stuck into her left cheek. She sees him staring and picks them out. They leave miniature red marks that will heal, not scar. Then she wipes trickles of blood from her nose onto the back of her hand. He should have asked if she was all right.

Down the hall, a woman passes, someone he knows by sight from other shows, one of the owners in a polo shirt, khaki slacks. She nods at Nikki, ignores Gabe.

Nikki shuts Beau in his stall and quickly heads back toward the mouth of the long barn, Gabe hobbling after her and saying, "At least your damage isn't permanent."

She shakes her head, walks faster, like it makes no difference, when he knows if pain passes, you can get over it. But if it's permanent, it festers in your gut. He follows her and only says, "We'll still place this season, if we work together."

She stops, her eyes on the open barn door. "Gabe, you *must* leave me alone."

She's only saying that because she's shaken up. He says, "Look, I haven't ever felt a love like this." Though now this love weighs him down. He's not light, aloft, sailing up. He won't say that.

She heads out of the dim tunnel into daylight, and she's jogging now with her short gait, not looking back. He senses not to go after her. He'll wait until she calms down. He stands in the barn doorway and watches her disappear around the corner and vanish. She's heading in the direction of the finish, where Cliff must be by now. Cliff, the finisher.

Gabe goes back in, and into Beau's stall. Beau's still chomping on hay, a middle-aged gelding who runs on grit. Gabe inhales the seductive scent of hay, saddle soap, sweat, dung, and horseflesh and tells himself he'll never give up the horse world. He runs his good hand across Beau's high withers, his slick, straight back, his sloped, firm hindquarters, and savors the bond of human and beast. If there's reincarnation, he wants to come back as a Thoroughbred, high strung as all hell, scopey, furiously fast.

But then he hears the one-two beat of human steps, ducks out of the stall, bolts the half door, and turns to see a bulky man's shape darkening the barn's entryway. The guy marching closer, down the center of the long aisle, but no, not Cliff. A shorter, pot-bellied man, dressed in a security guard uniform. He steps up and asks, "Sir, you got a pass?"

Did Nikki tip this guy off? No, she'd never turn Gabe in, no matter what he did.

"No pass, then you gotta go," the old guard says.

Hell, grab the lunge whip from that hook, wrap the long leather line around the guy's fat neck, yank it tight. But no, Gabe thinks, he'd be ousted for good. He deep breathes, tells himself, Don't move the way rage makes you move.

He shoots the guard a cracked, twisted smile, limps right past and out of the cool, dim barn into the sweltering, blinding sunlight and heads straight past the row of show barns toward the public parking lot and his roasting claptrap of a rusted truck. He glances back, the piss-ass guard watching, arms folded, and then, as Gabe passes a few hundred yards east of the finish, he looks over toward the competitors' parking and sees Cliff, his hulking back to Gabe. Cliff's facing Nikki, her little arms batting at air, telling him off.

If Cliff takes one step toward her, Gabe will go take the asshole out, but Cliff stalks off across the main walkway toward their rig, Nikki following, arms fluttering like wings, like she's saying, "Cliff, it's all your fault I lost, so I have to leave again because Gabe and I took a vow that I must keep because I believe in discipline." Cliff gets to the rig first, hops up the step, goes into the living compartment, and shuts the door. She's too late so starts rapping on the door that Cliff must've locked. Before long, she turns away. Gabe's sure now she'll look toward the visitors' parking lot where he has stopped in full daylight and is waving his right arm overhead, but she turns in the opposite direction, toward the course, and wanders off, past the finish line and up the winding dirt road along the slope, back toward the jumps, as if she's only a spectator.

Gabe's dying to go have it out with Cliff right now, this entitled owner who thinks he's God and can cast Gabe out like the old fart of a guard, who's still watching, for Christ's sake. But no. Collect, collect. Think ahead. If he goes after Cliff here with no strategy, Cliff, twice as big and not crippled, could win. Best thing is to get out, for now.

In moments, Gabe's in his pickup, revving the motor, and thinking if Nikki doesn't contact him, he'll have to pay a visit to Northlands. Maybe he'll even bring Carla along. Cliff couldn't turn Gabe away with Carla in tow. Not Big Mama, Cliff's confidant, loyal to the bitter end.

Gabe used to think the four of them were so different, but what they've got in common is they're all four stubborn as hell. Even tricky Nikki, the contradictory one, is digging in. But somebody has to lose. *And it sure as hell won't be me*, he tells himself. Thinking fucking positive.

CLIFF AND NIKOLE

CLIFF'S CLATTERING DOWNHILL, HIS SOLES sliding on stones and pebbles that roll, then stop. Rocks have a consistency, a solidity, yet a beauty, too, a patina from the elements, glittery spots and stripes, sun-kissed in the late afternoon glare. He collected stones as a kid, labeled them—shale, granite, limestone, mica, quartz—stored them in his bureau drawers and made them his own. Now he stops on a ledge in the foothills, in the shadow of the narrow bluff with the cave on top, Dekorah's peak, where Indians used to hide to scout, and he gazes for a little while down at his fields, where each spring after the frost, his rocks sprout like living things.

From high up, his valley is a jigsaw of fitted together bits of grass, pond, water lilies, earth, and beneath it all, more rocks. And down there, in the center of the fields, is the white box of a farmhouse, where Nikki waits. He wants to go back down to her, yet he feels a tension, too, as he has ever since she came home, his adrenaline pumping whenever she's around, maybe a Pavlovian response, his body trained by her to expect pleasure and pain. She keeps him on edge, where he's at his best.

She still loves him, she said again just the other day. So why doesn't he feel blessed? Maybe because blessings come from up in the sky somewhere, while he believes in the earth, in rocks underfoot. He starts down again and almost slips on loose shale as he passes granite boulders sparkling as he hurries past. He stayed too long doing target practice in the gravel pit, even though shooting at stationary tin cans doesn't give him the kick it used to. Better to have a moving target. His Persuader's tucked under one arm, safety on. He refuses to glance around for intruders, like his wife's trainer.

But Carla's trying to retrain the horse trainer. She called Cliff's office to give him an update after Gabe first came home to her. She said at first he'd acted absent, sitting around watching video replays of the Rolex and the Olympics, but lately he goes out in his old truck, disappears for half a day, or all day and won't say where. "It must have something to do with horses because now he's not as depressed. He's got this heat inside, a flicker in his eyes, like when he's fired up before an event, but no event is coming, right?" Cliff thought of Nikki still taking Beau out on long morning hacks, trotting him up and down hills to keep him in shape, for what?

He scrambles down the ridge path, sweat running down his face, like in Iraq, where all he did was sweat, soaked in his own animal stench, like a hot, lathery horse after an event. Events Nikki said she was giving up, right after her fall at Millbrook. She followed him to the rig, waving her hands around, and saying how eventing was supposed to be fun, "but with no trainer, it's deadly serious." Yet she sounded bereft, as if it was the ultimate sacrifice. So Cliff asked again, "Why not hire a new trainer?" She said, "Because then the old one would never let me alone." Cliff stalked to the rig and shut himself in. Once her knocking stopped, he looked out of the skinny window and scanned all around before he spotted Gabe over by the visitors' lot, right out in the open and waving one arm around. It took all Cliff's strength not to bust out, but Nikki walked away and disappeared up the hill, so Cliff let that little twisted dick stand there in broad daylight, looking scrawny and shrunken, even sort of lost. But ever since, Cliff has no idea what that insidious intruder, who takes her no as a yes, will do next.

Now step-sliding further downhill, spattering pebbles and slices of shale, Cliff passes a stand of birch, a good hiding place, and finds his eyes sliding that way. He feels watched, and his hunting instincts kick in, senses on high alert as he passes scotch pines mixed with blue spruce and treads quietly on soft, shallow beds of needles hiding the stones he keeps slipping on, his eyes flicking up over granite boulders above, a fortress, no way to flush out somebody who might not be there. Wait until your opponent reveals his strategies.

Cliff hits bottom and emerges from the rough, twisted path into his sloping valley fields and makes his way through high grass, past the white PVC fencing, only the best. Then past the barn with its prominent cupola, a bit of whimsy, but he still savors it, as he savors the deep lily pond down in the ravine, and the tended perennial gardens and the wild asparagus plot, although there's a spattering of kudzu by the deck. Have to get the backhoe to dig out the root balls. At last, he comes to the rambling, white farmhouse that Nikki chose, her dream house. So why doesn't he feel relieved to be home?

He looks back and scans the foothills, rough and dense, but he wants to be with his wife and heads on inside, his Persuader barrel pointed down, safety on. She's hovering in the kitchen by the stove. She likes to cook alone, as if cooking, too, is a secret act. They're skilled at secrets here. But now they'll be more open, or so she said not too long ago.

He's going to carry his rifle upstairs to its place in his closet, but she half turns and says that dinner is ready, then turns back. So he steps to the far corner of the kitchen and quietly sets the rifle behind the open door to the living room. Not a bad hiding place. Maybe he'll keep it downstairs for a while. Without turning around, she asks why he took his rifle along on his hike.

"Target practice."

"In July?"

"Wouldn't want to lose my edge."

He sits down at the Shaker table and waits for the quail

she has stuffed with apples, almonds, and fresh dill. Quail he shot during bird season and gutted himself. They will be moist and tender, and he's salivating now for what she makes, and for her, and for normal family meals like this, and for a normal married life, such as it is.

She carries in his plump, browned, small bird nested in a bed of pasta and white onions on a white plate, then she goes back and brings in her own smaller bird on a matching white plate. She's wearing a white blouse that's cut low, which he likes. She sits at her place at the opposite end of the table. He digs right in, swallows a bite of her soft, perfectly cooked offering and then, too quickly, starts to swallow the next, but it catches in his throat. He coughs it up, puts his napkin over his mouth, spits the small, soft mass into it, balls the napkin up in his fist, and hears himself say, "That fucker's out there someplace."

She nods, as if she knew.

He says, "If we wait him out, maybe he'll give it up." Like waiting in a blind for a quail to flit up, the whir of wings, the shot, the twist midair, the fast, silent fall.

She shakes her head no. With her mouth turned down and her small hands clasped, she looks if she's mourning that asshole's absence, as if Cliff's happiness with her, such as it is, still depends on that little prick who's got more power over her than Cliff thought. He thought that he and Nikki had reconciled. He thought that her twisted trainer was in the past. Cliff wants to gut the guy.

"Good quail," he says, and manages to swallow the next bite and keep it down.

◆ ◆ ◆

The next morning, he and Nikki sit again at the Shaker table for breakfast, and he's carefully swallowing bites of one of her lightly browned Brie omelets. She's not saying much, but that's all right. He steals a look across at her, sitting in the direct sunlight, and is struck with how tight and unlined her

skin still is, her fine-featured face still lovely to him. No cause
to tell her that. She knows how he feels.

She's looking out the window again. Her gaze seems to drift
lately to something beyond. Maybe she's searching for her trainer, secreted somewhere among rocks. Or maybe she's meditating,
or silently praying to some amorphous God floating in air.

Still, Cliff feels like telling her she's lovely, sitting all seemingly dreamy, peering out at the early morning sun kissing the
glowing, sloped lawn and high fields beyond.

But it's then that he hears the familiar rattle of the battered pickup chug up the drive. He checks his watch. It's
seven o'clock. Just when the bastard used to report for work.

"You stay in here," Cliff says coldly, staring at her harder
now, wondering again if she knew.

"I can't," she says, staring out the big plate window straight
at the truck, shaking her head, twisting her little hands.

"It'll be worse if you don't."

Then as Cliff stands up, that old yearning for impact
sweeps over him in a rush, a brimming for contact, the weaker of two forces yields. Collide, and a burst, the crunch of
your opponent's bones, the grunt of breath. You don't feel it
for you've hit the sweet spot. Bliss. Absolute bliss.

He tells Nikki to stay in the house no matter what. Then
he strides out onto the deck, the beaten-down, bankrupt Ford
pickup just pulling to a halt in the shadow of the oak, where
it always parked. Cliff stands, boots planted, legs spread, arms
held out from his body, his body a weapon.

Gabe slides out from the driver's side of his wreck, and
then the passenger's door clanks open, and surprisingly, Carla
steps on down with a burst of bright yellow dress like she's going to a wedding, for Christ's sake. Cliff didn't see her at first
in the shade. What the hell is she doing here? Why didn't she
call and let him know?

Gabe's step-limping toward the house and side-eying
Cliff on the deck, Cliff perched high up over the little guy,
who's carrying a scuffed, black duffle bag. What the hell, is he
moving in? Cliff stares down at it.

Gabe lifts it high up in his right hand and says, "Some tack of Nikki's that I'm returning."

Cliff's thinking, Collide and destroy.

Gabe says, mouth twisted into his customary half smile, "I'm here to settle things all friendly. Get the business over with."

And Carla's nodding yes.

Gabe's looking behind Cliff, and Cliff turns his head. Nikki's at the open door. Shit. She steps out next to him. Gabe's bad hand is stuck into his jean jacket like a little Napoleon. Still acting cocky even after he's been fired, his reputation ruined. A loser.

"What's left to settle?" Cliff asks.

"You two owe me," Gabe says.

"For what?"

"Severance pay."

Gabe's standing seemingly loose-jointed, his screwed-up body looking relaxed, right hand still holding his cheap black duffle. Keep your eyes on his right side, Cliff thinks.

"How much?" Cliff asks, thinking he'll pay whatever it takes, surprised the guy will take a bribe.

"As you can see," Gabe says, his tenor voice smooth as a singer's, "I came back here with Carla."

Carla looks past Cliff at Nikki, who has stepped nearer now.

Gabe says, "And like Carla said, we can settle this like adults."

"You said that?" Cliff asks Carla, looking directly at her now for the first time.

And Carla nods.

"Yep, in these last weeks," Gabe says, "we patched it up."

Carla nods again, standing soldier stiff.

"So we decided, Carla and I," Gabe says, "to settle it once and for all. Didn't we, Carla?"

"It's the only way to move on," she says.

"So why don't you invite us on in, so we can sit and negotiate?" Gabe asks. "You're quite the negotiator, aren't you, Cliff?"

Cliff's body still pulses with the craving for impact, but Carla's in on it, so he steps back from the open door and he waves them in.

They come up the steps, Gabe limping across the deck, with Carla on his dead side. Her sunny yellow dress hurts Cliff's eyes.

Nikki says, "We can settle it right here."

But Gabe heads on inside with Carla after him, then Cliff, with Nikki last, single file through the mudroom into the kitchen, to the Shaker table. Cliff sits in his place at the head, his back to the living room, and Gabe sits opposite, in Nikki's place, his back to the mudroom. Carla sits facing out the picture window, between the two men. Nikki just stands and says she'll get her checkbook to settle accounts, and she hurries into her little study and hurries right out with her fat, black purse. She's in a rush to get it over with. She goes around the table and sits facing in, across from Carla, opens her purse, and takes out her checkbook. Paying the fucker off out of her own funds.

Gabe tilts back in his chair, making himself right at home, and says, "Yeah, Carla and I are going to try again."

"Good for you," Cliff says.

"We're giving it a second chance."

"More power to you," Cliff says.

"And I hear you and Nikki are having another go at it, too."

"We are at that."

"So, Cliff, you're a dreamer, like me. We're one of a kind."

Nothing Gabe has ever said gets at Cliff more than that. Again, his body craves impact.

But Nikki interjects, "Gabe, what do I owe you for your severance?"

Cliff stifles a smirk. She's buying Gabe off. She rummages in her black hole of a purse, pulls out a silver pen, folds back the cover of her red checkbook, signs a blank, blue check. Then, pen poised, she eyes Gabe.

Gabe eyes her back, that sideways half smile wiped off his face.

"Six months' severance plus a bonus for placing in a three-day in Florida," Gabe says. "I never got it . . . what with that—"

"Oh, yes, a bonus," she cuts in. "Much deserved."

"*Much deserved*," Gabe says, mocking her official tone. "And add an extra bonus, for overtime . . . in paradise."

Overtime in paradise. Cliff's tanked up to leap across the table, flip it over, full force take the little fucker out.

But Nikki asks, "How much extra time would you like added on?" Keeping her voice extra calm as if talking to a horse.

"For every minute down there," Gabe says, leaning closer, in her face, giving her that distorted grin. "I was working extra hard around the clock."

She sets down the pen with a little click.

Cliff's had it with this loser's lip, reaches across, grabs the checkbook, the pen, writes out a check for six months' wages, writes Gabe's name in the *Pay To* blank, and on the *Memo* line below, writes Unemployment, then slides it across to Gabe, who takes the slip of paper and folds it in the middle without even glancing at it or at Cliff.

It kills Cliff, the way the fucking hypocrite won't even look at the check. As if he hasn't been bought off.

Gabe sticks the folded check into the pocket of his long-sleeved, white shirt. A white shirt, Cliff suddenly thinks, when Gabe usually wears denim blue or black. The prick has dressed up for this.

Then, Gabe leans even closer to Nikki, inches from her face, and says, "Come on. Confess. You know you love me more than Cliff."

Immediately Carla's shaking her head no.

Nikki leans back and quickly says, "Gabe, it's over with."

"Tell Cliff. Tell him who you love more," Gabe says.

"Stop it now!" Carla says.

Cliff knows, he knows who Nikki loves, his blood pulsing hard and hot to get the guy he's been laying for all season long.

But then Nikki says, "I love Cliff."

"See, Cliff," Gabe says. "She can't say she loves you more. Hear that! It's what she didn't say."

"Gabe, you said we'd settle this like adults," Carla says, her big hand clamped on his withered arm, where it does no good.

"Nikki," Gabe says, "Cliff doesn't see into your sweet, dark heart."

Cliff shoves back in his chair, but doesn't get up, doesn't spring, not just yet.

Gabe says, "Nikki, you know you got to leave him again."

"Take your check and get out!" Cliff says.

"Gabe, come on, let's get out of here!" Carla's standing up, her bulk shadowing them.

"But, Mama," Gabe says, not looking up at her, "you wanted to come."

"It's not Cliff you should be after."

Strange, Cliff thinks, for Carla to say that. With his last self-restraint, he says, "Gabe, you got what you came for, now go."

"You don't tell me when to go!" And Gabe reaches down under the table with his good hand and swings the faded black duffle up onto the table top, something inside clunks, and one-handed, he yanks down the zipper.

"You're outta here," Cliff says, springing to his feet, crouched to start around the table, the line of scrimmage, but Gabe's hand quickly dips into the duffle, lifts out a handgun. He sets the gun on the tabletop, an old .45, its barrel pointing toward Nikki, his right hand on the grip.

Cliff stops, judges the distance, Gabe directly across, about five feet, the table between, a flick of a finger, and Gabe could shoot her. Too much distance for Cliff to make impact. Use strategy. It doesn't make sense. Why shoot Nikki when she's what Gabe wants?

Then Nikki spreads her arms and says, "Go ahead, Gabe, go ahead!" As if daring him.

"Nikki, don't you see?" Gabe asks, his good hand sliding slightly off the gun's grip. Cliff glances toward the half open living room door, his Persuader concealed behind it, a five-yard dash, a quick cut left. Too far, but Gabe probably won't shoot him in the back. Then Gabe says, "Nikki, we're not separate. We're one." Cliff kicks back his chair, crouches low and charges, ducking and weaving toward the threshold, he's almost to the door, only three strides to go, when he hears Nikki scream, "No!" And Carla's deep wail, like a man's, and a sharp, dry, crisp crack, and he feels a hot stab of pain between his shoulder blades.

Keep charging, he's a bull, a linebacker, can take that and more, can take it all, give it to me, go ahead, charging full force, swinging the door open, his Persuader glows, another sharp sting cutting deeper in. Keep on charging, seems slower now, maybe only one more step, nobody can stop him, the perfect tackle, but he hears this wail and another crisp crack like bones breaking in a perfect impact, that force even as he's falling. He slips and slides onto his back, lies flat and looks over, can see his opponent's feet under the cherry Shaker table by the tapered table legs, tan Timberland lace-up boots, scuffed and stained. He looks away and sees so close the upright rifle stock, gleaming dark mahogany, untouched, and sees beneath him on the blue Persian rug, soaking into the intricate arabesques, a dark pool spreading, red and blue make purple, and he remembers red on Nikki's helmet when she almost died. Your fall in the field was my fault, he wants to confess, and Gracie's getting kicked, my blind fault, but hears Carla saying, "No, no, don't touch him." He looks up and sees Nikki's delicate face over his, sees the fine pores, the small ovals of her nostrils, the gleam of moisture on her open red lips, and he smiles wide, gives it all he's got. Wipe that grin off your face, his father said, Your bubble will burst . . . Cliff wants to warn Nikki, your bubble will burst, but he's bursting inside, yet he feels her warm breath, her warm lips on his, her warm breath filling his aching chest, warming his cold heart, finding his sweet spot . . . absolute bliss.

❖❖❖

Nikki tilts his head to the left, breathes into his mouth, turns her lips away to take the in-breath, and breathes out between his lips, and prays, Lord have mercy. She tries to collect herself, to keep breathing into his mouth, to press her lips to his, to breathe out, Lord have mercy, to turn away for the in-breath, to turn back, visualizing it's a kiss, a long, deep kiss, until she hears Carla's low voice saying something to her, or to Cliff, or is Gabe still there? But Nikki exhales warm breath again into Cliff's cooling, open lips, keeps kissing long and deep, even hearing Carla's voice, must be on a phone, saying something about a shooting, giving Northland's address. Why is she doing that?

Carla saying Cliff Swensen has been shot.

No, he has not.

Carla saying he is dead.

No, he is not.

Nikki tunes out, keeps breathing into him, so he's breathing. And she's kneeling over him, warm slippery red on her hands, and she visualizes him kissing her back and feels his lips grow firm again, so now it's not her lips pressing hard on his, it's his pressing hard on hers. But she feels a warm liquid seeping into her white blouse. And then she feels heavy hands on her shoulders, big, strong hands tugging her off, and a deep woman's voice says, "Can't you see he's gone!"

Nikki opens her eyes, for they've been shut. She looks down and sees her husband's eyes, pale, transparent, staring at nothing in particular, surely not at her, and that deep voice says, "In the name of Jesus, get off of him!"

Jesus? What has Jesus got to do with this? Nikki's on her knees, bent over him, her face in his, but his eyes are cast off, watching something else. And now strong arms are yanking her up. Don't look down, she thinks, but she does. He's lying spread eagle on his back on the blue Oriental rug, and that dark red pool is blood, his denim shirt and her white blouse soaked with it. She's breathing hard, light-headed from breathing so much, and the woman's pulling her away and leading her out onto the deck, where Nikki sinks down to her knees again, and wants to pray, but Carla's barking orders, "Don't you go back in!"

It's all rising up, and Nikki vomits onto the dark boards, vomits red and yellow onto the other woman's black, shiny shoes and thick, white ankles, and the deep, take-charge voice says, "I'll be right back."

Nikki tries to stand but feels light-headed and lies down on the cool boards like she lay in the high field after her fall. No high weeds wave now, though from the distance, she hears a high-pitched whinny, a squealing like a mare in heat, but no, a faint siren, growing louder. How long has it been before Carla comes out with a white towel, reaches down, and lays it on Nikki's brow? The cloth feels cool and damp and soft. Why is Carla being kind? Now Carla's face looms above, and looking down, her cheeks sag into two sacks of flesh as she says, "This was your fault," in a tone of bitter belief. And, with the siren whining louder, the deep, clear voice says, "So remember, it was self-defense."

Then Carla has gone, and Cliff has gone, although Nikki breathed into his mouth. And she's breathing hard again, sitting up, light-headed, when a light, wiry shape suddenly appears, like a tilted sprite, on the deck. She looks up into his face, awfully pale for a face always tanned. Gabe kneels next to her and looks her in the eyes with his intense, shiny gaze and says, "This is what you wanted."

She shakes her head, no, no.

He's kneeling close enough to feel his warm breath. "Nikki, I did it for your sake."

Then his lips on her lips are warm, not cold.

She jerks her head to one side, vomits again, bits of yellow egg mixed with bits of red.

Sirens shriek louder, and Gabe has vanished. Blue stripes swing over her, swing round again, blue stripes sliding round mixed with red, and she sees it, the trooper's car, brown and white, pulling up in the drive by Gabe's rusted, blue pickup. What's his old heap doing here? She fired him. She's sitting up, dizzy, lights whirling blue, like the high field whirled all yellow when Gracie almost killed her, and maybe Cliff was only almost killed.

Maybe Cliff is inside, waiting. She stands, convinced that he's inside, and weaves to the window, presses her face to the glass. Her breath spreads in a white fog, so through it she sees only dim shapes. It's as if one of the shapes is Cliff's. He's side-eyeing her through the window, as he so often has. He's hovering just on the other side of that glass wall, only a thin pane separating them. He'll protect his property. He's sitting in his seat at the head of the Shaker table, his spine erect, thick arms crossed over his barrel chest, telling off those troopers in his abrupt way, saying, "This is my land. Get off of it. It's over with. You're fired!" She rubs the fog off the glass with her hand. Inside at the table sits only Gabe, hunched in her seat. He's staring straight ahead, not seeing her, and she thinks, God, if one of us had to die, why not me?

CARLA AND GABE

CARLA HAD TO PRY OPEN the fingers of Gabe's right hand, still clenched on the grip of the gun. Didn't touch it herself, fingerprints. "Gabe, you let go!" she said. He just kept staring down at Cliff, where she refused to look. She had to bend each of Gabe's fingers way back before the gun dropped onto the tabletop. At that moment, he got up, went out onto the deck, said something to Nikki, and then the sirens shrieked, and he came back in. Now he just sits staring down again at Cliff. Why didn't Gabe hide that weapon? She wouldn't conceal evidence herself.

Troopers stomping now up onto the deck, yet he just sits. "Gabe, don't you freeze on me," like he's in a coma again. She takes a napkin and shoves the gun across the tabletop out of his reach, while a second car pulls up, more blue sirens, more men in brown with round brown hats. One's bending down, gray gun drawn, to say something to Nikole who, through the window, seems to lounge in her Adirondack chair. Interrogate Nikole, that's right.

Carla pats down her hair, smoothes her dress, got to look respectable for the four men in big, round-brimmed brown hats, two bending over Nikole, two hustling up to the deck. In one white hand, a gun, bigger than the one on the tabletop.

Carla pulls herself up to her full height. The bigger the

crisis, the stronger she gets. "Gabe, do you hear me? You say it was Nikole's fault." He still just sits. "Gabe, you say she drove you to it."

Was that a shift of half his lips? He sits, and across from him on the floor, Cliff's cherry chair lays still overturned, its legs all stiff. She wants to set that stark chair upright. Hates it lying only eight feet or so from where Cliff's lying in a red pond over by the open door, where his rifle stands, untouched. Cliff must've slipped and flipped onto his back. She wants to take his flung-out, long arms and cross them over his thick chest. She won't look at him. Everything's a mess. Her fingers itch to tidy up. "Gabe, do you hear me? Do you hear me, huh?" What a time for him to fall silent. "Gabe, say you shot once, a warning shot, then you waited. You gave him a chance, but he kept going, remember that." Gabe's still stares down at Cliff, as if any minute now Cliff will sit up.

Forgive me, Cliff, I never wanted this, she thinks. But she says, "Gabe, remember, it's self-defense." Gabe still sits, both hands downturned in his lap, his young, fleshy hand next to the wrinkled old man's. It's the young hand that shot the gun, but now it looks as limp as the useless one. It's up to me, she tells herself.

Two troopers hustle on in, guns not pointed at her because she was the one who called and said her husband shot Cliff. A blond, curly-haired one goes to Gabe, and the baby-faced one heads toward Cliff, crouches down, and takes his pulse. As if that cop can't tell from that pool of blood that he's gone, like Nikole who had to keep sucking at his lips and stole his last breath. Now the baby-faced one shakes his head, and the curly-haired trooper tells Carla to stand back, so she takes one step. And she glances again out through the big picture window, where Nikole reclines in the Adirondack chair like a lady of leisure basking in the sun. Entitled? Not anymore. Two troopers bend over her.

Inside, the curly-haired trooper lifts the gun with a cloth. And the baby-faced one is pointing behind the half-open door, at what Cliff was running towards. Carla didn't see the rifle until after Cliff fell, sat with her back to it, facing out, her eyes on her husband. She says, "See. It was self-defense." Or, she wonders, was it Cliff who acted in self-defense?

The baby-faced one steps to the propped up rifle, that's close but too far from Cliff, and shakes his head.

Carla says, "You must've known it was there, right, Gabe?"

He only sits with that same inward-turning gaze, like when he meditates. What does he see inside?

Then the baby-faced one orders her into the living room to split her and Gabe up, and she follows the cop but somehow does not look down at Cliff, only a few feet to her right. She keeps her head up, even when she calls, "Gabe, you feared for your life."

The cop tells her to shut up.

And soon she sits on the cold leather couch in the living room, while the trooper's on the rocker, and he's questioning about who and where and when and how. She keeps smoothing her yellow dress over her knees, her sweaty palms leaving unsightly damp streaks. She tells how Gabe said he was going to Northlands to finish business and told her to come along. And how Cliff met them on the deck and invited them in, and they went in and sat at the table and seemed cordial, just doing business, until Gabe said something that got Cliff all upset and . . . But now she hears from the kitchen Gabe's treble voice, saying something about taking out his gun . . . he's mumbling, ". . . so then I shot." He should add something about protecting himself, but he shuts up. She can't have that. She calls out, "Gabe, you remember what I said."

Her trooper threatens to charge her with interfering with an investigation and starts asking her ominous questions like if she knew Gabe had planned this and what state of mind was Gabe in. And suddenly he asks, "Did you know your husband carried a concealed weapon when you left your house for Northlands?"

As if she's an accomplice. That's it! She's on her feet, striding back across the room toward Gabe, calling, "Gabe, you demand a lawyer!"

Her trooper's right after her, and at the threshold, she forgets, looks down, and Cliff's still sprawled on his back, right where he was on the blue Oriental rug. He's drowning in a deeper slough than before, blood seeping into the rug and into the cracks between floorboards. They must have red on their soles. Should get a mop and clean it up. What an unholy mess! She glances down at Cliff's face, and his pale eyes are open, peering up her dress. She presses it down with both hands, keeps pressing it, and suddenly knows she's losing it. The dead can't see. Cliff would've gotten a kick out of that. She lifts one hand and shapes a quick, faint cross over him, who didn't believe.

Then she steps around the red pool, hustles through the open door, and glances back. In the corner, the rifle still stands, oiled and polished for the kill. Did that first shot come before or after Cliff flung open the door? Why did her back have to be turned?

Cliff, forgive me, she thinks again, as she steps into the kitchen and says, "Gabe, you saw that rifle there. That's why you did what you did."

Again, her trooper says she'll be arrested, too.

She says, "We demand a lawyer."

Gabe's trooper says Gabe has waived his right to an attorney.

She steps right up to Gabe and clamps him on his right shoulder as hard as she can. Knock some sense into the guy. He just sits. She squeezes hard and says, "Can't you see he's in shock? We demand a lawyer, don't we, Gabe?"

He must feel her grasp because he says, "Yes."

Forgive me, Cliff, she thinks a third time and says, "Cliff swung open the door, Gabe, and you saw that rifle hidden there. That's why you did what you did."

Her trooper says to her, "You're under arrest."

No sense in both her and Gabe being locked up. So she says, "My husband was driven to what he did by Cliff's wife."

Both troopers are immediately all over that, asking what did Cliff's wife do and where and why?

Carla says, "It's bound to come out, so I'll say the truth. She had an affair with my husband."

Both troopers look out at Nikole through the glass, and one asks if Carla has any proof.

"Gabe said in this very room that Nikole loved him most. That's when Cliff leapt up to go for his rifle over there."

She never thought Gabe would say that. Not to Cliff.

Now her trooper's leading Carla straight out onto the deck where Nikole's still slumped in the white Adirondack chair, her eyes flitting toward them, as if waking from a dream to see the nightmare she's in.

The troopers stand over her as Carla's trooper starts asking her questions, and soon asks if she had "relations" with Carla's husband.

But then an ambulance screeches in, red light clashing with the blue still flickering round, and Carla shouts over the siren, "Nikole, none of this would have happened if you hadn't done what you did."

Nikole looks up and says, "Oh . . . yes." As if confessing.

The troopers stare down now with outright suspicion at the little bitch. Maybe they're thinking she hired Gabe . . . It's usually the mate who's behind it, and Gabe's got a check signed in Nikole's handwriting in his white pocket. Surely they'll find it. Before they left this morning, Carla asked, "Gabe, why wear your white dress shirt?" He said it was "a dressy occasion." An outdoorsman like him. It made her suspicious. Don't tell those troopers that.

The baby-faced trooper leads Gabe, handcuffed, out onto the deck. From the ambulance, men in white come running up, lugging a stretcher, oxygen tank, and other useless paraphernalia, to rescue somebody who is dead, though those eyes still seem to see.

In the commotion, Carla steps next to Gabe and says under her breath, "You say it was an accident."

But half his upper lip twists up.

Another siren's droning, more blue fireworks striping the air, the lawn. And one trooper says her husband must go.

So she takes Gabe's good hand, now in handcuffs—must be as numb as his bad one—and she squeezes that cold, calloused hand and says, "I'll help you get what you deserve." Even as the terrible thought rises up, *He has this coming.*

Then his trooper leads Gabe, like he's a horse on a lead line, toward a brown car, as Carla's trooper says that she and Nikole must go in for questioning.

It's Nikole they should interrogate. She's the one responsible for her husband's death.

Meanwhile, Nikole still reclines in that Adirondack chair, and she peers at the troopers, as if they're ghosts.

Another siren flares, and yet another troopers' car roars in. Two more hop out, and six put their heads in a brown huddle by the deck, kudzu poking up, maybe three feet high. But beyond it, the fields stretch all aglow in morning sun, acres of grasses shiny and glossy, as if blessed.

Carla stands on the doorstep and waves to Gabe inside the car as if she's the mistress of this horse estate, and he's about to go off to one of his big deal championship events. But there will be no more events for Gabe, not ever again, not Novice, Preliminary, Intermediate, or Advanced, not dressage, cross-country, or stadium. When he got crippled, she thought he'd quit. But no . . . it took a killing.

He must be handcuffed to the door handle, for he doesn't wave back. Doesn't even seem to be looking at her, but at Nikole, curled on the Adirondack chair. Then the first troopers' car pulls out with Gabe, slouched down, like a lost juvenile delinquent in the back seat.

While the other troopers tromp toward the deck, Carla takes her chance and quickly leans over her husband's whore, close enough to smell her vomitous breath and sweet-sour sweat, and looks directly into that little, broken, china doll face and says, "You say it was an accident."

At the word accident, Nikole flashes almost the same, exact, cracked grin that Gabe did.

◆◆◆

From the rear seat of the troopers' car, reeking of fake ever-green from a miniature cardboard pine tree dangling from the rear view mirror, Gabe takes a last look back at Nikki on the deck chair. Carla's leaning over her, as if giving comfort. Why would she do that? But Big Mama will believe in him, and Nikki will, too, for she knows he wouldn't have done what he did if she hadn't craved freedom in her dear, dark heart. And Nikki knows if she'd tried to leave Cliff again, he would have arranged another so-called accident. Gabe still feels the force of the big man, testosterone and sweat, thick body stiff, tensing to spring, so Gabe, as nimbly as he's dodged hooves, yanked out his old .45. Animal instinct, but . . . he can't re-member what happened next, Cliff's broad back turned, go-rilla shoulders, that extra-long reach in his thick, curled arms, but hell, an easy target, and Gabe remembers hearing one shot, only one. Isn't that what Carla said before the troopers came, Nikki out on the deck? Didn't Carla say that Nikki put him up to it? Carla's mouth sucked in, tiny wrinkles lining her lips. Now the siren's screeching like a million mares in heat, and he tries to remember what he said to the troopers in the house, so at the station when they question him, he has no inconsistencies, what cops call lying, when life's made up of inconsistencies. Inconsistencies are all you've fucking got. Except for death.

At the station, they'll ask him for details that he doesn't remember, although he remembers Cliff, the bull-headed landowner, treating him like shit. Yet all Gabe did was set his dad's old .45 on the table top, and it angled toward Nikki as if by itself, and then he only talked of love, for Christ's sake, what's wrong with that? Cliff couldn't face up to real love, his blind spot, Gabe knew that, and before long Cliff lost it and lunged toward the living room door, half shut. And Nikki screamed no. A warning, Gabe thought, for him, not for her Cliff as he bucked and weaved. Next, a shot, Gabe remembers one, but Cliff kept marching. A warning shot, it must've been, Cliff lumbering on as if the shot had missed. All Cliff had to do was freeze, but no, he flung the door open, and behind it, that rifle shone, so it was self-defense, like Carla said. The rifle so near, but too far. Cliff set up a goddamned ambush.

Now, siren shrieking, Gabe's got to collect himself, like he did before the cops busted in. He sat at that table and stared down at Cliff, his denim shirt turning red, and Gabe breathed in death and breathed it out, and it calmed him down. In meditation you don't judge, just focus, but he can't focus now with that damned blue light swishing and the siren shrieking. All he really wants is Nikki here on the back seat, right next to him, for he trained her to sense what another creature feels, so she'll feel what he lacks. He visualizes her now on his good side, her scent of fresh air, lemon, and magnolia, stronger than the sweetish evergreen. She fills the space, senses his emptiness, slowly strokes his neck, and says, 'I know you did it to save me. I'll stand by you even through death.' And he feels understood. He feels collected. He feels a preternatural Buddha calm.

The car's slowing, pulling up in back of the squat, yellow-brick station near Woodstock. He won't get to see her soon, since he'll be locked in a cell smaller than Beau's stall, two strides across, two strides back. Carla will defend him though. His Advocate. Yet she could have called Cliff and warned him they were on their way to Northlands. She could have refused to go along. Cliff took in death like he took in everything, that surface calm, just sinking slowly down, silent even as he sank, blood spotting the back of his denim shirt. Got to give Cliff this, he met his death with dignity. He lay on his back and never said a word, and then his wife draped her body over his, as if she'd flung herself on his funeral pyre. Gabe hadn't expected that. But he had expected Cliff to attack. Got to think ahead of the horse, or man.

Gabe feels collected now. Trained himself to keep cool under pressure. Deep breathe. Get it straight. One shot that seemed to miss. So why did one trooper say four holes in the back? That doesn't sound like something Gabe would do. Who shot those other three shots? An inconsistency. Still, self-defense.

They park in back of the station, not too far from the Green Mountain Horse Association, with its rocky terrain, where Nikki evented their first time together . . . jumped like she had angel's wings, except for when she lost focus . . . Then later down in paradise, the soft heat sliding in, she stood out on her balcony in a faint breeze, her white gown flickering like see-through angel's wings . . . and he's Gabriel, an angel's namesake . . . a perfect match.

A trooper's opening the back car door, unlocking the cuffs from the door handle, letting Gabe climb out, relocking the cuffs behind Gabe's back. He can't feel the steel clamp around his hands. The trooper peers strangely at Gabe and asks if he's all right. The trooper's got sick breath, like spoiled beef, must have vomited. A young kid. Probably his first corpse. This kid can't understand the kind of training it takes to keep collected at times like this. Gabe will eventually be set free because he only brought a gun along for protection in case Cliff finally cracked and tried to kill the man his wife really loved. Nikki will believe his story. So will Carla, and the judge, and the jury, if it comes to that.

Now they've got him inside this stale station, a small-town jail with a sort of Betty Crocker look to it, stuffy, cozy, closed in. In the rear, though, behind that iron door are the cells, no bigger than stalls. In this mustard-yellow interrogation room that they're leading him into, chained like some animal, he'll say it was self-defense, another in a long line of tragic accidents.

PART 3

CARLA

SHE WAS AN INNOCENT WITNESS, so why when she took
the witness stand, did the prosecutor have to ask if she knew
Gabe had a gun in that duffle before they left their home
that day? Carla said, "I don't know what I thought." He said
to answer no or yes. No. Then he asked if she saw Gabe put
the duffle in the truck? Yes. Did she question why they were
going to Northlands? Yes, Gabe said it was to settle business,
to end it.

Now she sits on the long bench in the high hall of the
courthouse and awaits the verdict, along with strangers, and
horsepeople, and also Lisa and Matt, both pacing up and
back on the black-and-white marble floor. Nikole didn't even
bother to show up. Of course, in the last year, Nikole has become a hermit, no, a pariah. Serves her right. The adulteress
was the prosecutor's star witness.

Carla's testimony didn't help Gabe much. She said she sat
with her back toward Cliff and her eyes on Gabe, so when
Cliff stood to make a run for it, she saw only her husband's
good hand quickly nab the gun and shoot. She did not testify
to Gabe's eyes when he shot, his good eye narrowed to a slit,
as if aiming through a sight.

Yet she seemed a reliable witness because she's a respected
schoolteacher, an honest, conservative citizen with a Baptist

upbringing, and now with good secular values. That prosecutor couldn't dislodge her.

Nikole's testimony was the most damaging. She testified she had an unobstructed view, and that she saw Gabe pull out his gun and taunt Cliff until he made a break for it, and then Gabe shot Cliff in the back, and Cliff was not within reach of his Persuader when Gabe first shot.

If Gabe gets first degree, not manslaughter, it is because of Nikole Swensen.

In spite of that, Gabe testified that Nikole had not conspired with him, that he had acted on his own. So now Nikole sits up in her horse estate, which she inherited. True justice has yet to be served. Carla will set that right.

She still can't believe Gabe denied his affair on the witness stand. Said he'd only "slipped once." Made everybody not believe one word he said. As if one lie makes the rest untrue, when sometimes you have to lie, but Gabe lies to himself.

Now she sits and waits on this pew in this high, hushed hall with muted light sifting down through dusty windows, a kind of anxiety-ridden reverence pervading the air, until finally a guard appears from a side door and announces the verdict has been reached. Right away, they all file inside the old courtroom, its dark-wood witness stand like a pulpit. Carla's thinking Gabe actually might get manslaughter because he testified to imminent danger, said he'd brought a gun to defend himself against a stronger man, said he'd had no intent.

She would have believed him, if it weren't for what happened that day, just before she and Gabe left their place to go to Cliff's, what the prosecutor had hammered her on, but what she would not confess because she does not know what she knew or not. Will not confess it, even to herself.

Now she sits in a pew, folds her hands, and thinks whether first degree or manslaughter, Gabe will be sent away, and he deserves his punishment.

◆◆◆

Two weeks later, sitting in her tiny living room, she thinks Gabe moves in another realm, like during her last visit with him. After the verdict, he was transferred to a state penitentiary, so she had to put up with going into The Trap, a gray steel door that opened, then shut her into a steel room with another shut steel door. It was only her and a couple of guards who patted her down and made her put all her personal stuff, even her coins and belt, into a gray locker and lock it. A guard took her locker key, and she felt stripped, like a prisoner herself. The line is thinner than she'd thought between her and them, although she has done nothing to deserve that fate, nothing that she knows of. She only went along to Northlands that day as Gabe's chaperone, her role in life.

Then a guard opened the second door and led her down a hall with that awful ammonia stench, which doesn't disguise the desperate, and into a visitor's room filled with other women, kids, and guards. She took a seat by the see-through wall, and another guard led Gabe into the gray room, gray floor, walls, ceiling. The orange jumpsuit made him look like a clown. And since his arrest, he'd been working out with prison weights too much. His body more lopsided than before, so is his mind perhaps, for he acted like he was in a trance, tuning her out, or maybe meditating again, his old escape hatch.

She had so hoped for manslaughter, but the jury sided with the prosecution and with Nikole because her unarmed husband was shot in the back. A mandatory sentence of life with no parole. Carla, naturally, thought Gabe would be totally depressed. She thought he'd be broken again.

But he sat behind that see-through Plexiglas wall and looked calm, even serene. She figured maybe he'd repent in that transparent confessional, or tell her he was sorry for leaving her alone and in debt, but he started in talking about his appeal and saying he could still prove imminent danger, which would mean manslaughter, but he had to get through to Nikki to help, and she would not return his calls. "Help how?" Carla asked. Gabe started in about how Nikki knew he had no escape, so it was an accident. He said, "She forgave Cliff his accident, so she'll forgive me mine, and she'll change her testimony."

"You still believe in that little bitch?" Carla asked, her temper heating up.

Gabe said, "Mama, do this one last thing for me." As if he were on death row, when there's no death penalty in Vermont, and when, truthfully, his being shut up has its advantages. The whole last year in prison before and during the trial, he's been a captive audience. Like one of her elementary school kids, he has to be reliable, be punctual. No more running off truant to Florida.

But in prison he said, "Would you go talk to Nikki and explain how I had to bring that gun along to protect myself? You know I had to better than anyone."

Carla didn't appreciate his implication, and said, "I don't know anything of the kind."

He pressed his face up to the Plexiglas. "Mama, I don't know what I'd do without you, I really don't. You're a woman who believes she knows what's best." He seemed to actually mean that. And, since she wasn't done with Nikole herself, she said yes, she'd go, for his sake. Gabe sighed and said, "You're the best." So relieved, so pleased that she instantly regretted saving yes, and almost said, 'Gabe, you dug your own grave, now you lie in it.' He's buried alive. He just doesn't know it yet. Even after the guilty verdict, he's still thinking positive. It makes her sick.

◆◆◆

Three days later, she drives up the hill to Northlands, where from the crest, the extravagant valley farm splays out below, white rectangles of farmhouse and barn, white squares of fences. Man-made rectangles and squares taking over the countryside. Excess. And Nikole has inherited it. When Carla turns up the drive, the only signs of life are the tiny horses in the distance, the nearby paddocks stained with trails of dark manure, no longer scooped up into the fermenting pile behind the barn. The whole farm festers with a meaty stench.

Nikole is finding out what true loneliness is, a hollow space that nothing fills, not even God. For horses are false idols. Worship them, and you get condemned, like Gabe, who way back after his fall, freshly nerve-damaged, said, "The only reality is death." Yes, there were signs he'd do what he did.

Carla parks by the gleaming gooseneck rig, more excess, absurd now, all that craving for what? She heads toward the red front door. Red for prostitutes. Carla wears her somber, navy blue trial dress with a white collar and cuffs. By the weathered deck, kudzu thrives, over six feet, burrowing from buried root balls as big and hard as coconuts, to choke the gardens. Where's God's design in that?

The last time she set foot on this deck, Nikole sat in the Adirondack chair while her husband lay dead inside.

Carla knuckle raps on the red door and doesn't stop rapping until at last Nikole opens up. She's in a long, white terry robe, although it's the middle of the afternoon, and she has dark shadows under her eyes, dark hair wisping around her prisoner-pale face, no more farmer's tan. Gone the collected, well-groomed, porcelain horsewoman.

Nikole simply waves Carla in, as if she'd expected this visit, and she wraps her white robe around her emaciated body, no hint of her former pretty posture. She leads Carla through the kitchen, Carla sidestepping where Cliff once lay, the blue Persian rug long gone, Exhibit F. They pass they puckered, limp cacti in the bay window, and Carla sits on the leather couch and Nikole on the rocking chair in front of that hunk of rug hanging on the wall instead of where a rug should be, on the floor.

Carla says, "Nikole, your eyes are little, like you need some sleep. And you're so thin, there's nothing to you."

Nikole only asks Carla if she'd care for a coffee, tea, or wine.

Acting like the well-bred hostess, even now. Two can play that game, and Carla says tea.

Nikole walks out, long, white robe flowing like an ascetic desert nomad.

Carla collects herself, has her questions rehearsed. Nikole will finally get the cross examination she deserves.

When Nikole returns, she's carrying a tray with two porcelain teacups and saucers, a sugar and creamer, and a sunny yellow teapot. She sits, pours tea, and politely asks, "Sugar or cream?"

Carla says that she'll take both although her strict Baptist mother said to take her tea black and "Don't ask for extras."

Nikole heaps several teaspoons in, pours in a stream of cream, and hands the tea over. It's almost white, but Carla sips it, sickly sweet. Nikole sips her own tea, which is black, and that black tea irritates Carla more than anything since she arrived. She sets down her cup and cuts to the chase. "I'm here because Gabe asked me to come. He wants you to testify at his appeal that there was an imminent threat."

"To change my testimony?"

"He says he had no escape."

"Do you believe that, Carla?"

"As you know, Nikole, my back was turned for the first shots." Carla feels like she's defending herself, so attacks. "Didn't you know that rifle was behind the door? You could have warned Gabe and stopped it."

"Carla, I had no idea Gabe would do what he did." Nikole sets down her cup and saucer, leans forward, elbows on knees, and asks, "Did you?"

"Of course not."

"But didn't you know the gun was in his duffle before you left your place? You know him better than anyone."

Carla falls silent at that. Suddenly, she's back at her house that day, Gabe sitting down next to her on the faded couch, carefully setting the duffle by his boots, and saying, "Carla, we've got to go to the Swensens, to end it." She asked, "What's in the bag?" He said, "A bridle of Nikki's that I've got to return." Why would he return old tack at time like this, she wondered. And she reached down and picked up the duffle, too heavy for a bridle. He snatched it from her hands and headed out the front door and said she better come "to keep the peace." She thought it was too late for that, but she grabbed her purse and headed out after him. He tossed the bag into the truck bed, and she heard a heavy clank. Did she know it wasn't tack then? She has forgotten what she knew and what she did not. She remembers she was in his pickup, and he was driving like a maniac over potholes and ruts, and she asked, "Why bring me along?" He said, "Cliff trusts you, so he'll let us in." She wanted to leap out of the truck, but he'd never stop.

Nikole's waiting, leaning so far forward that her white robe drapes on the floor.

And Carla says, "I never meant for it to be Cliff."

Nikole nods. "You wanted it to be me."

"You bet I did!" Carla blurts out. "You deserved it!"

Nikole stands and says, "Yes, I did." She pivots and strides through the living room into the kitchen toward the front door.

She's kicking Carla out, demeaning, yet Carla gets up and follows her.

At the front door, Nikole stops, and with one hand on the doorknob, says, "We were both part of it."

Carla feels a smile stretch her upper lip and bare her teeth, as she says, "And now neither of us has a man."

The door opens and she's outside. She takes a deep breath, how good it feels, how liberating, to have told the truth at last.

NIKOLE

DURING THE YEAR AND A half since Cliff's death, Nikki has mostly stayed shut in at Northlands, under quarantine again. She refused to let anyone inside, except for Lisa, who brought food and newspapers, and also local gossip that was almost all bad, rumors of Nikki conspiring in Cliff's murder in order to inherit his land.

She went out only to give depositions or attend hearings and finally the trial, and she didn't ride or go out into the fields, except to feed the horses. No stable hands would come to this cursed place to feed or muck, so all winter long the horses have been turned out with just run-in sheds for shelter, their dung slowly sinking into snow and slush. They run barefoot in the fields, no shoes so no farrier. Their once-sleek coats have grown into shaggy winter pelts. Her horses have transformed into primitive beasts, roaming wild.

Gone the ShowSheen, Excaliber, hoof conditioners, vitamin supplements, the currying, brushing, mane braiding, and hose bathing. Gone, too, the endless practice rounds in enclosed rings, the synchronized lifting over jumps, a search for perfection. A human desire.

The horses sense that loss, and they keep their distance, except when she feeds them. Horses are more loyal to their herd than to humans. Their resistance draws her in. Yet some days she cannot bear to look into their soft, dark eyes.

For since Cliff's death, she has sunk into a blurred space, where shadows shift like the ground fog that often smolders in the valley and foothills. Like on the gray day of her husband's memorial service, a few days before the trial, a service Lisa planned because Matt had flown in to hear the testimony. Matt had refused to speak to Nikki since his father's death, and he didn't speak even at Northlands when Nikki gave him an urn with a third of his father's ashes that Nikki had measured out. Ashes that reminded her of the bone shards from Gracie's broken leg that still floated in formaldehyde in the Mason jar on the glass kitchen shelf. The three of them carried the three urns up into the foothills where Cliff so often hiked and stood on the ledge under Dekorah's Peak. They tossed bits of pulverized Cliff into a stiff breeze, bowed their heads, said a silent prayer, and Nikki asked for forgiveness . . . didn't feel it . . . So she opened her eyes and looked up at the narrow peak with its small cave, two small holes on either end. A lookout for Indians, Cliff once said, who believed that spirits linger on earth for a time after death. But Nikki didn't feel his presence.

Except in court, as soon as she took the stand, the air thickened around her as if someone were right next to her, hovering, And later she sensed a prickling down her back when the black-suited prosecutor finally asked exactly when her husband was shot in the back. She knew the timing could do Gabe in, but said, "Gabe shot *before* my husband got to the living room door, *before* Gabe saw the Persuader."

Before the trial, at the small service, on the way downhill, his son said to her, "You set my father up for a fall." A fall? She almost laughed at the irony of that, but kept silent. Her silence must have meant guilt to Matt because then he said, "If Gabe gets manslaughter, I'll sue you for everything you inherited." Even though he'd inherited the trust funds, and she had only the farm, but it wasn't Northlands he was after. Then he headed on alone down the path, a lean and lithe young man skittering over rocks and roots, a kick to his step, a fast, forward thrust, his gray sports coat blending with gray rocks and mist until he simply, quietly, disappeared.

Yet Lisa rejoiced at the verdict and came back to Northlands straight from court, where Nikki couldn't bring herself to go, and ran upstairs to where Nikki lay in bed, burst in, and said, "We won!" Nikki wondering, What does winning have to do with it? Lisa said the verdict was first degree, life with no parole. Nikki felt nothing, lay perfectly still, and thought, If I hadn't gone to paradise, none of this would have happened.

Lisa said, "May Gabe suffer in hell for what he did." Nikki still said nothing. Lisa peered down and said, "Mother, don't tell me you *forgive!*"

Nikki said, "Gabe told me he did it for my sake." And Lisa said, "When they convicted him, they acquitted you. So, Mother, you're absolved." But Nikki still felt that she had, in a way, conspired in it, both she and Gabe craving the thrill of flight, riding for a fall, daring death. Then Lisa said, "You've got to get away from all this. Sell Northlands."

Nikki said, "Cliff wouldn't want that."

Lisa, being Lisa, said, "Cliff won't know." But Nikki visualized him there right then listening in, the three of them in a ghostly, dysfunctional, familial communion.

"At least sell the horses," Lisa said. "Start out new. Horses are the root of this evil."

But Nikki replied, "It's not the horses."

Yet even after the verdict, Nikki still couldn't believe, without a doubt, that Gabe planned the killing. She remembered how Lisa also said that when the verdict was read, Gabe seemed perfectly calm and sat totally straight, elbows pinned to his sides. As if, Nikki thought, he was visualizing himself riding again.

◆◆◆

The afternoon after Carla's visit, Nikki lies under white sheets and stares across at Cliff's empty closet. Lisa packed all his clothes and sent them to Goodwill. To the right, Nikki's closet door is shut, and in its full-length mirror, she visualizes Cliff and her during their slow dance after she'd returned from paradise, their graceful step-turn-sway, his creased, sharp face reflected, softened by his secret smile.

An early dusk sifts in, the time of day she has come to detest, when she can see, yet cannot. Out the bedroom window, the horses blend with the grass that merges into trees that fade into mountains that blend with the sky. It's at dusk when the dead live on. Nikki tries to pray, but gets only silence again.

The bedroom is the worst place, for she dreams of Cliff. That night, Nikki dreams that Cliff went out on a date with a young woman and left Nikki at home with her dream mother, who had smooth, lovely young skin. And the mother said, "You can use all those words, but all you have in the end is memories."

In the morning, Nikki goes outside and is struck momentarily blind in the sudden daylight, like Gracie must have been when she emerged after her long stall rest. It's hunting season, when the birds and wild creatures hide in the woods and underbrush, and when Cliff hid to shoot them. Their eviscerated carcasses still fill the deep freeze down cellar. It was a deep freeze outside all the last long winter, thirty degrees below some days in Cliff's deep valley. Cliff stalked out to meet the cold, while it drove her in.

She sits in the lotus position under the willow on the low hill, and the long, thin branches close her in, their pale tendrils swaying in the small breeze, warm air stealing into the midst of fall. She gazes over at the weed-ridden, dead gardens by the deck, kudzu, yellowed now, still as tall as young trees. Go kudzu. Take over the place. Gardening is a pastime for masochists who repeat the same punishment each season, like eventers do.

She can't focus for long before bits of the trial float up again like debris, and she wonders yet again if Carla was right, if there was an imminent threat, if Gabe felt Cliff had a rifle close by, and that's why he shot, for Gabe has a sixth sense to see ahead. She should know by now if there was intent, Nikki thinks. Her testimony convicted him. Yet she still has doubts.

So she goes into the house and at last calls the prison to

set up a visit. The officer says she must wait to see if she is on Gabe's list of officially approved visitors. She bets her name is at the top.

◆◆◆

A week later, she sits on a straight-back chair in the long, thin prison visiting room, cement walls like the walls of her balcony in paradise, and a gray guard leads Gabe in. He's wearing an orange jumpsuit, and he limps over and sits behind a thick glass wall. Gabe looks distorted, tilting more to one side, his muscles more built up on his right. Prison accentuating the difference between his good and bad sides. For he has a good side. She knows it intimately.

And when she looks into his soft, dark eyes, they seem filled with warmth and love, and it's almost impossible to believe that he planned Cliff's death, that it wasn't a crime of the moment, of passion.

Gabe picks up his telephone, so she picks up hers. "Nikki, I knew you'd come."

She didn't know that. "Gabe, how have you been?"

"Collected. Focused."

"How can you be?"

He leans toward her and speaks into his receiver, although only a few guards linger, far enough away not to hear. "I do walking meditation, three strides up, three strides back, and I shut my eyes and see those faint floating shapes, you know, that you see when your eyes are shut, and I focus on them, and it calms me down. I've given up all restlessness, all craving. We have to give up all bitterness and live one breath at a time. For everyone is but a mere breath."

Is he talking of forgiveness? He leans closer to the glass, his eyes glimmering with some new, fresh insight, like she used to believe he had. She wonders if he's had a sort of prison conversion experience. And he softly says, "I've let it all go. It was an illusion. The only thing real is the moment, and we are all of the nature to suffer, to die. It was of Cliff's nature, too."

Gabe waits. Does he mean that Cliff's death was in the nature of things? That Gabe feels free of it, of killing?

"It's all transitory," he goes on. "It's about awareness and watching the breath, and going inwards, and so, Nikki, let's you and I sit together like we used to." And he shuts his eyes and tells her to shut hers. But she cannot. And then he's saying, "Breathe in and out and ride the breath."

Without his knowing it, she watches the right half of his face, tensed, the lines drawn tight. Only the dead side is calm, the left side has almost no active nerves to register craving, or anger, or fear. It's all some terrible accident that they ever met.

"Gabe—"

"Go where everything is transitory, give up all ego, and prepare yourself to visualize the truth . . ."

He must think that her eyes are shut, the right half of his face tensing more, wrinkles pulling taut, as he says, "I couldn't run away that day, there was no escape. I had to stay and defend myself . . . so now you visualize the appeal . . . you're sitting up on the stand and reading through the transcript . . . and you say that you made a mistake, that I had to do what I did. You say I didn't shoot Cliff before I saw the rifle, it was after, because it all comes down to that. To what was before and to what was after."

He stops and waits, eyes still shut, still imagining it himself. Both eyelids have deep folds in them, the left lid puffed and crepey, the right lid drawn tight. She has always only looked to his right, focused on the good eye, not on the left, smaller and still, focused inward on its own world. The left eye shows more who he is.

He goes on, his voice like a chant, "I didn't plan it. No intent."

She watches closely the partially atrophied, paralyzed side of him, and his left eye just sits as if made of glass. There's a terrible truth in how his left side does not feel his words. That's his calm, she thinks. Detached, let go.

She says, "You shot Cliff in the back before he got close to that door. Before you even knew that rifle was there."

At last, he opens his eyes, the left eye only a slit, yet it can see, and she stares into his suffering. We are all born to suffer, to die.

"Nikki, if it's manslaughter, I'll get out early on parole."

She looks into his half-dead eye. "And what would you do when you get out?"

"You know. We'll train Gracie to be the best, and then when my parole's over with, we'll take her down to paradise."

"Which we never should have left?"

"You got it."

"And what would we do in paradise this time?"

"Visualize that, too . . . you sell Northlands and we buy a farm down south, a gated saltwater horse estate, rows of fat, shiny palm trees on each side of the long, white gravel drive, an indoor ring with the best new synthetic footing and soft lights overhead, where you'll ride with only the soft swoosh of hooves, your breath mixed with the horse's breath, and outside, it's only a hundred yards to the beach where you'll ride on sun-kissed white sand, where the waves never stop, and where your horse senses the expanse and opens up, and you let it go, you transcend yourself and all that's been, you perform beyond yourself, and so does the horse, you go beyond ribbons, you jump into the dark, beyond attachments and craving, into sheer presence."

He stops and waits again. He talks of presence when he believes in absence, in death. She asks, "You visualize all that?

"All that and more. Ever since we met."

"It's what you planned, Gabe, isn't it?"

His right eye leers at her sharply, while the other eye just sits content in itself, unperturbed by all that's been. From that calm, nerveless eye, she knows at last what he has done.

She says, "You came to taunt Cliff, to goad him into losing control so you could shoot him dead and plead self-defense, then get me to let it all go and transcend the past."

"So we can have a goddamned national reputation for excellence . . . for perfection."

"Gabe, perfection doesn't exist."

"So what? It's all illusion."

"So is your saltwater horse estate. You won't get out of here."

"I will if you do what I tell you to."

"Like I used to. You were a step ahead of me."

"Nikki, you know you got to think ahead of the animal."

"You had intent."

"My intentions were for all for the best. Better than the best."

"It was premeditated."

"If it was, and I'm not saying it was, then it was for your sake."

"And for the horses'?"

"So we can transcend. Perfection. It doesn't get any better than that."

◆◆◆

Dusk creeps slowly in. Again, she sits outside in the lotus position under the willow, its stringy branches switching in the breeze, and she smells sour manure and sweet hay, the air perfumed with decay. Again, she can't meditate. Even after Gabe has confessed, more or less, she's still in the shadowland where she has been since Cliff's death. And again she's alone, Lisa back at college, and as she left she said, "Mother, get over it. Move on." Much as Gabe had said.

Nikki opens her eyes and sees off in the two back fields, horses' hindquarters and horses' heads poking out of the two run-in sheds. They're standing front to rear, swishing tails, batting flies off each other's faces, protecting each other from the late Indian summer heat, not killing each other. They deserve better than to be kept outdoors untended, not groomed, not exercised, muscles turning slack, even Beau, her once-buff little competitor, looks like a backyard horse, whiskered, muddy, dull. She has broken the basic contract—if a horse serves you, you take good care of it. You are its steward for as long as it's yours.

Gradually, an early evening mist envelops the animals. The ground fog thickens until they disappear. She goes silently into the barn, then carries buckets of grain out to the fence of one pasture, then the other, and the two pairs of dust-encrusted creatures canter up to their two separate gates. She pours measured cups of grain into the shallow pans on the ground, and while they slobber up pellets, she hoses water into their buckets. The horses don't turn their soft eyes directly onto her, yet their eyes see almost all around, peripheral vision like Gabe thought he had. He thought he could see ahead of horse or human, as if he had the gift of prophesy. And now she must do what Cliff wanted her to do when he was alive. Prove to Gabe that he must let go at last.

◆◆◆

A few weeks later, two strange horse trailers sit in the drive. One, a fancy eight-stall rig from Massachusetts, the farm's name inscribed on the sides in large red script, two hired guys waiting inside the crew cab for their turn. The other trailer is a battered two-horse Kingston, into which Harley and Druid have already been loaded to go to their new home at a local farm. They'll be used during the summers as school horses, so they'll get regular exercise and daily turn-out. A good life for older horses, Druid twenty-eight years old, Harley twenty-three. Harley's a Dungeons and Dragons horse, a 1,500-pound warrior, stomping around inside the small trailer now. He's still got heft and force like Cliff. The old, rusted trailer rocks. Druid stands quietly in the adjoining stall. Arthritic, he has calmed down enough to simply accept what comes. She has owned Druid for almost two decades, almost half her life, but she stands, hands on hips, head up, and, although bereft, refuses to weep.

Old man Carbonneau, a lean wraith of man with a tensile strength, starts up the motor of his rusted red pickup, drives the trailer very slowly off down the drive. She watches them go. She has also sold her fancy horse rig and most of her tack. Although, for some reason, she kept one pair of Vogel boots, one Stubben jumping saddle and bridle, one Rambo winter blanket and one summer sheet, a first aid kit, and a solitary bag of grain. Souvenirs?

As soon as that trailer disappears over the hill, the two young dudes in jeans and t-shirts hop out of the cab of the fancy trailer. A horsewoman from Dover bought Beau and Gracie. This lady will show Beau in Preliminary three-day events, and she will have Gracie trained by a professional. Beau and Gracie will live on an estate with a post-and-beam white barn and a white PVC fence. They should feel right at home. They won't miss me, Nikki tells herself. Horses are more attached to their herd than to humans. She can see why.

She straps on Beau's shipping boots, runs her hands down his big-boned, clean legs, and tries not to visualize what Gabe would do if he knew Beau was leaving. Beau's no Olympic athlete, but he performed on heart. Full of impulsion, at any point, he could have bucked her off since she was often a little behind. Better to be in front than behind, Gabe often said. But sometimes she and Beau worked as one—those fleeting, delicious moments of transcendence. Can't will them to come, they come on their own.

She wraps her arms around Beau's neck. He swings his head around, nibbles at her sleeve. Still fooling around.

The two young guys wait at the barn door and stare at her as if they're sizing her up, checking her hindquarters, her legs, as if she's also on the sale block, this adulteress widow at this cursed place.

One of them grins at her, as if enjoying it.

The other one stares off at the farmhouse and fidgets in place, anxious to escape.

She'll load Beau first, for Gracie has not been trailered since her operation.

Nikki leads Beau up to the trailer ramp, and he just walks right on up after her. She ducks out the narrow side door, flops it shut, reaches through the open window, clamps the chain of the lead line onto the side hook, and steps back. He's already tugging strands of hay out of the hay bag. No false sentiment for that jokester.

The trouble with light spirits is they move on like sprites, with no conscience to speak of. Gabe once seemed to be light-hearted, but he was obsessed, craving what he didn't have, but so was she, clinging, insatiable, dying to win. Ride into death, he said. She'd thought if anybody died, it would be her.

She goes into the barn and leads out a prancing Gracie, shaking her head, all long-legged and fine-boned, not a Warmblood's big bones, but the color of burnished gold, with sloping hindquarters and fetlocks, built to jump. Nikki's got a leather lead line attached to her halter. The young dude with the sly smirk steps up. He's got a lead line with a chain attached to wrap round her nose and yank tight for more control. Nikki shakes her head, no, and leads Gracie on a simple leather line to the trailer, but Gracie's already all worked up, the only horse who senses this is a major event, and she side steps back. Nikki leads her up to the ramp again and again, each time Gracie not setting one hoof on it, but prancing, bucking on the line, at last rearing. When both young guys get behind to shove the big mare up the ramp, she kicks out, kicks again, swinging her sweaty, muscular hindquarters from side to side until they back off.

For the next half hour, no rattling of oats in a can, no whip tapping makes the smallest impression on this bitch who keeps rearing, getting more fired up, until finally, in her frenzy, she rears higher and throws herself over backwards, lands on her back, but instantly scrambles up onto all four legs, starts to trot off. Nikki grabs the dangling lead line so Gracie won't trip on it, then with both arms, yanks the mare to a halt, Gracie dancing in place, not hurt, delicate and strong at once.

Nikki leads Gracie away from the ramp, halts her and softly says, "Babe, it's all right, we'll do what you want, you win a blue ribbon for being yourself." Then Nikki looks straight back at the two guys and says, "I'm keeping her."

The one dude, the smirk wiped off his face, asks, "What's this?"

"No contract has been signed. I'm keeping the mare."

"Fine by me," says the anxious one.

The rude one shakes his head. "Mrs. Anderson will be pissed."

"Let her be," Nikki says, not caring anymore what anyone wants.

Gracie snorting and pawing one hoof at the dirt. She and Gracie belong together, Nikki thinks. Two bitches.

She's keeping a green, erratic mare while she lets the balanced, kind show horse go. Beau, who ran for the joy of it, footloose and light-hearted, is still inside the trailer, still tugging hay from the net bag.

The two guys hop up into the cab, and in moments, the glitzy Massachusetts rig rumbles down the drive. Nikki stands and watches it go. "Beau, you double crosser," she says aloud, but doesn't mean it. A horse has no conscience, feels no guilt. Horses are pragmatists. Let me be reincarnated as a horse, she prays.

And she could get her wish soon, for she is left with this roll-eyed, killer mare. Nikki leads the prancing horse back into the barn, and soon Gracie's turning, whirling in her stall. The old two-horse Kingston trailer with Harley and Druid is long gone, and the fancy rig transporting Beau heads up over the hill. Gracie's herd has vanished, and she senses now her abandonment and whinnies wildly after them, kicks her stall walls, whirls and whinnies high-pitched like she's in heat, while Nikki, still in the stall, dodges to get out of the mare's reach but doesn't leave. She stays and listens as the mare wails, her off-key, falsetto rising, shrieking a high-pitched dirge.

◆◆◆

For however many weeks, during the waning show season, Nikki finds herself training the horse that drove Gabe to what he did. Though it wasn't the horse's fault.

She does groundwork with Gracie, lunges her in the ring, then mounts and does basic walk-trot-canter intervals, trots her over ground poles, then takes her over low rails. Gracie lifting consistently over jumps, clearing the low rails by several feet, yet afterwards she still often bucks, bolts, or runs out. But it's just this unpredictability that draws Nikki to the mare. These sporadic outbursts are a lure, for Nikki craves risk more than before, so soon ring riding isn't risky enough. She must ride the mare over cross-country fences on her land, even though Gracie's too green to jump safely in the open. But this dark edge is what Nikki wants.

The morning of her solitary cross-country event, she wakes before sunrise from a dream of which she remembers only the end, when a disembodied voice said, "Follow the spirit." Follow which spirit where? Yet as she lies awake in the dim, early dawn, she can still hear the dream voice, neither male nor female, but completely clear. She has not followed any spirit since Cliff's death, and now, lying in bed, she visualizes his spirit, hard, yet vulnerable, like when he nursed the mare's broken leg and Nikki accidentally squirted him in the face with pus, and he ran away yelling, Why me? Like he might have thought when he died, when she bent over him and pressed her lips to his, and he couldn't ask, Why not you?

Now the dawn light sifts weakly in, and she quickly slides out of bed, pulls on black practice britches and a black turtleneck. It's November, hunting season, so she should wear a blaze-orange vest, affix blaze-orange tape onto her helmet, but no time for that. She looks at her closet, once empty except for Cliff's blaze-orange vest and his Persuader, propped on its butt, barrel pointed up. Before hunting season, he had that Persuader down in the gravel pit, a yellow, crumbling ugliness, the roar of shots deafening, Cliff's back a broad target like it was for Gabe that last day.

Now she's in a hurry to get it over with.

She trots downstairs and out to the barn, gives Gracie her morning grain, waits, then lets the mare go into the near paddock, gets the small John Deere tractor, hitches the small wagon onto it, loads in some jumping rails and blocks. She'll set up her own cross-country course in the far back field up along the woods, where they used to practice, the jumps taken down after Cliff's death. She will finally let go and ride all out, no holds barred, like she rode as a girl, fearless, into death.

She drives the John Deere slowly, the wagon bouncing over ruts, out into billowing, early morning ground fog, clumps of clouds filling in the ravine, blanketing the pond with its radiant fall lilies, mist filling in the river valley, the trees shifting . . . gray, amorphous shapes.

She heads past the paddocks, up the slope, and at the tree line, stops the tractor, steps down into damp leaves, her Wellies slip sliding, tracking a smeared path in the high, yellowed grass. She lugs out the rails and blocks and drags them to set up two verticals, two cross poles, two roll tops, each jump only three feet. She doesn't know how high Gracie will fly in the open.

Before long, she has the grid of jumps set up along the overgrown path that used to be beaten down by hooves from all the intervals she practiced here, Gabe calling out, "Elbows in," or "Look up," or "Trust your horse," or "Do it again" . . . his patience infinite, with horses . . . now only the faint whoosh of wind. She turns to go, but can't help gazing up the rough, root-ridden path into the foothills, where once Gabe spied on her from up on the ledge, and where after the trial, she, Lisa, and Matt each carried a portion of ashes in alabaster urns up to the ledge beneath Dekorah's Peak and tossed bits of Cliff into air. And in this moment, she wonders if she sees a flicker up there, a human shape. A stray hunter perhaps who drifted in the fog onto her posted land at the beginning of hunting season? Cliff never lost his way in nature. He lost it with his family instead. They all lost their way, in spite of their love.

She drives the tractor back down the slope and through the far field past the west paddock and the ravine to the barn. She gets off and nabs Gracie's lunge line off the gatepost and heads into the paddock after her. It takes a half hour of arm waving to herd the skittish mare toward the gate, where Gracie finally stands still and allows Nikki to snap the lead onto the halter, lead the mare into the barn, crosstie her, and tack her up. Gracie drags out her taunting, not like Beau, who played quick pranks. Gracie's resistance is persistent, resolute, her spirit still unbroken.

But that is what Nikki wants. Now it will be only her and this mare, who could take those jumps, or buck her off, or kill her.

Before she mounts, Nikki tightens the girth and dares, "Go ahead, do what you do, act out!"

But Gracie stands aloof, perversely not stomping or kicking as she usually does when she's tacked up. "Good ground manners," one horseman said, "can mean bad under saddle."

Nikki mounts. "Gracie, be a bitch, go ahead, bolt, buck, give it all you've got."

For Nikki's going to have it out at last. Get it over with.

But the mare resolutely stands as quiet as a nag.

Nikki presses the leggy chestnut to walk out of the ring. Facing the wide open fields, Gracie's fine-boned head lifts up, eye white-rimmed, but Nikki trots her off, Gracie skimming fast with her big, floating gait through high dying grass, past the pasture and up the hill to the edge of the woods, where Cliff once filled in groundhog holes with poisonous smoke pellets. Only now, when Nikki thinks of those creatures dying so her horses could live, does she remember the hunter she maybe saw and thinks she should have worn a blaze-orange vest.

But again, she doesn't go back for it. She canters Gracie in circles for a while to warm up, and Gracie tosses a couple little side-winding bucks, nothing serious. So Nikki heads her toward the first jump, a simple cross bar, Nikki keeping a light rein, and the mare gathers herself and leaps too long with her long stride, but easily coasts over the fence, Nikki looking up toward the next rail, Gracie galloping in a quick burst, too fast, but clears it, lands, tosses another couple bucks, but Nikki instinctively sits them. And so it goes over the vertical, the roll up, Nikki keeping the mare straight, although the next time after they clear the line of jumps, Gracie lets loose bigger, twisting bucks, upping the ante. Yet Nikki savors the high, finally fearless, saying, "Go for it, let go at last." Circling the mare to fly over the grid again, when suddenly up in the woods, sharp dry cracks. Rifle shots.

Instantly, Gracie bolts, gallops full blast along the tree line, flying through high grass to the overgrown path down toward the river road, Nikki out of control, breathing hard, riding the breath, only her and the horse down the rocky trail until they swoop onto the flat road where the mare veers left, running flat out now for the sheer hell of it, on the gravel road past the clear river, Nikki keeping a light seat, light hands, barely in contact. Let go, ride the breath, detach, drop who you are. As the road forks, and Gracie, heated up, swerves left, charges up the narrow path through thick trees toward the high west field, branches scratching Nikki's face as she rides into shadows, an accident perched on the back of a giant. Detach, focus, drop body and soul. Past the ruined farmhouse, the fenced-in, overgrown family plot where spirits lurk, and up toward the high west field where she was thrown so high before that she had time to twist midair, that stark impact, smacking hard ground, knowing she was broken, not knowing how much.

She looks down, and the mare stumbles over twisted roots but rights herself, surges up to the opening into the field, and they burst into the open free space, tall yellow grass and goldenrod, Gracie pulling against the bit. Here's to you, Cliff. And Nikki lets go. Her fingers open, the reins slide through her hands, and she gives Gracie her head, the mare springing into the expanse of high yellow, past swaths of pine and birch, Nikki pressing with her legs, urging her mount on, faster yes. Detach, drop body and soul, ride into the dark, to the spot where she fell, sensing the mare will buck there, visualizing it. And she looks down, but they streak past the spot, toward the wall of birch further ahead, a white blur, but at the very tree line, Gracie abruptly swerves left, lets loose a few quick little bucks. And Nikki lets go, casts herself off into air, does not twist but falls headlong, and finally falling, thinks, What took me so long?

She lands on hands and knees in a scratchy thicket and waits for her body to break, to collapse, but it's crouched like a four-legged creature in thick underbrush, burrs, and fallen leaves that must have cushioned her fall. She waits for her sight to fail, to pass out like before, but the copse of bushes stays clear and defined. Small, speckled yellow leaves cling to thin, mottled branches.

She peers about. Gracie's standing not even ten feet away, reins dangling, not running off like before. The mare surely can't care if Nikki rises or not, yet Gracie has halted, and waits, sides heaving, eyerolling Nikki, as if to see how she is.

On all fours, she crawls out through the thick brush and tells herself to detach, to see herself as if from the mare's eyes . . . a predator crouched and crawling through bright leafless prickly bushes and yellow grass that parts in her wake. Why doesn't the mare bolt? Nikki wonders, feeling oddly detached and calm. And it's all yellow, burnt orange, and dying around her, yet the mare's a burnished gold, and Nikki inhales musty, yellow air.

She sits back on her haunches as the mare simply grazes close by in grass up to her withers. She yanks up dried, yellowed shoots by the roots, munching away as if Nikki doesn't exist, yet Gracie waits. The only sound the mare chomping, the occasional faint click of teeth. Nikki kneels, deep breathes for a while, shuts her eyes, and soon she sees faint shapes shifting. Nothing's still, the air fluctuates, and she feels a faint breeze as warm as breath on her cheeks and lips, like Cliff's breath when she lay in this field before, when he asked, "Nikki, are you all right?" And she sees his face, reflected in her shut eyes. No glasses, his pale eyes exposed, watery, translucent, and his soft smile suffused with love, as it was reflected when they slow danced. She feels again his embrace, his thick arms gently wrapped round her, and she asks for his forgiveness, but he doesn't say a word, yet she feels a peace, only for moments, before she lets him go. She opens her eyes, and the waxy, wavy field seems like a mirage. What was real was what she saw with her eyes shut.

But wait, there's Gracie—golden chestnut, slightly lit by a half-clouded sun—shaking her thick mane and chomping bleached grass, tearing off clumps of yellow at the roots.

Nikki stands, takes a few two-legged steps, and feels no pain. She is here in this field. She urged the mare on. The mare knows that. But now Gracie stands, neck bent, and grazes on blanched, tasteless weeds. This high-spirited mare is killing time, covering up that she's waiting, showing mercy.

Nikki walks over the few feet, takes the dangling reins, and remounts the oddly calm animal. Have to get back on after you've been thrown, or you'll never ride again.

She sits astride the horse, both motionless. Nikki sits and then, even though she might never again event, she gathers the reins, shifts her seat bones, sits deep, eases the mare into an extended walk. Soft hands, soft legs, she balances and slowly canters the newly tamed, but not broken, horse back across the field and shifts her seat, so Gracie slows, then walks down the winding, root-ridden path, the mare quiet, perfectly in sync, no, not perfectly, but as good as it gets, almost perfect. Then at the river road, Nikki's legs nudge Gracie to turn right and to trot, and the mare shifts gracefully into her floating, collected trot, so lovely and light that Nikki's bending forward and slapping Gracie's neck, slapping her arched neck, saying, "Good girl, good girl. You're the best. You've got what it takes." As if they've won, and the fall trees glimmer with faint oranges and reds, dying, yes, but Nikki's softly slapping Gracie's sleek neck, forgiving as she was forgiven, saying, "We're one. Feel that." And riding the breath and letting go, she's at one with her horse simply cantering lightly now on the gravel road alongside the narrow river, shallow and leaf-strewn in the fall, tiny waves rippling, the water clear enough to see the bright, many-colored river stones shining beneath. "Good girl, good girl," and stroking Gracie's silky neck, hooves scattering dried fallen leaves while Nikole and her bitch fly easily over the hard-packed earth.

Acknowledgments

With deep thanks to Philip Spitzer, my literary agent, for believing in my fiction; to William Betcher, for his avid editing, critique, and encouragement; to Richard Hoffman, mentor and esteemed reader; to Roland Merullo and Betsy Sholl, for their invaluable comments on drafts; to my son, Theo Dolan, for his astute, honest insights; to Joyce Johnson, a mentor who believed in one of the first versions of this novel; also sincere appreciation to Gretchen Butts, equestrian and judge, for her expert editing of the eventing details; to Diane Arenberg, dedicated horsewoman, for her insights; to Katie Grose for meditative friendship; to Richard Letham, painter, for his passionate cover art; also, unending gratitude to Alan Davis, New Rivers Press editor-in-chief extraordinaire; and to Suzanne Kelley and Nathan Rundquist of New Rivers Press for their professional editorial assistance, as well as to their student team.

About the Author

Lee Hope is editor-in-chief of *Solstice: A Magazine of Diverse Voices.* Her fiction has received a Theodore Goodman Award, a Pennsylvania Council on the Arts Fellowship, and a Maine Arts Commission Fellowship. She has published stories in numerous literary journals, such as: *Witness, The New Virginia Review, The North American Review, Epiphany,* and *Sou'wester.* Her short story "What to Take in Case of Fire" received an honorable mention in *American Fiction,* Vol. 13, (New Rivers Press), winner of the 2015 Midwest Book Awards for an anthology. Lee founded and directed a low-residency MFA program in Maine and played a role in founding Pine Manor College's MFA program. She has taught creative writing and literature at various universities. She is currently president of the Solstice Institute for Creative Writing, a nonprofit. And she teaches for Changing Lives Through Literature, which brings literature to people on probation.

About New Rivers Press

New Rivers Press emerged from a drafty Massachusetts barn in winter 1968. Intent on publishing work by new and emerging poets, founder C. W. "Bill" Truesdale labored for weeks over an old Chandler & Price letterpress to publish three hundred fifty copies of Margaret Randall's collection, *So Many Rooms Has a House But One Roof.*

Nearly four hundred titles later, New Rivers, a non-profit and now teaching press based since 2001 at Minnesota State University Moorhead, has remained true to Bill's goal of publishing the best new literature—poetry and prose—from new, emerging, and established writers.

New Rivers Press authors range in age from twenty to eighty-nine. They include a silversmith, a carpenter, a geneticist, a monk, a tree-trimmer, and a rock musician. They hail from cities such as Christchurch, Honolulu, New Orleans, New York City, Northfield (Minnesota), and Prague.

Charles Baxter, one of the first authors with New Rivers, calls the press "the hidden backbone of the American literary tradition." Continuing this tradition, in 1981 New Rivers began to sponsor the Minnesota Voices Project (now called Many Voices Project) competition. It is one of the oldest literary competitions in the United States, bringing recognition and attention to emerging writers. Other New Rivers publications include the American Fiction Series, the American Poetry Series, New Rivers Abroad, and the Electronic Book Series.

Please visit our website newriverspress.com for more information.